AIDS

The Medical Mystery

Frederick P. Siegal, MD *and* Marta Siegal

D0533259

GROVE PRESS, INC./NEW YORK

57994

RC
607
A26
S54
1983
C.2

#98346̄79̄

First Hardcover Edition 1983
First Printing 1983
ISBN: 0-394-53505-7
Library of Congress Catalog Card Number: 83-48298

First Evergreen Edition 1983
First Printing 1983
ISBN: 0-394-62496-3
Library of Congress Catalog Card Number: 83-48298

Library of Congress Cataloging in Publication Data

Siegal, Frederick P.
  AIDS

  1. Acquired immune deficiency syndrome.
I. Siegal, Marta. II. Title. III. Title: A.I.D.S.,
our nation's number one health threat.
RC607.A26S54   1983   616.97   83-48298
ISBN: 0-394-53505-7
ISBN: 0-394-62496-3 (1st Evergreen ed. : pbk.)

Manufactured in the United States of America

GROVE PRESS, INC., 196 West Houston Street,
New York, N.Y. 10014

5   4   3

AIDS: The Medical Mystery

This book is dedicated to the men, women, and children who have struggled fiercely against a ruthless, invisible enemy within.

Acknowledgments

We are extremely grateful to Drs. James Curran, director of AIDS Activity of the Centers for Disease Control; Lewis Thomas, chancellor of Memorial Sloan-Kettering Cancer Center; Kanti Rai, chief of Hematology at Long Island Jewish Hospital; and James Oleske, director of Pediatric Allergy, Immunology and Infectious Diseases at the New Jersey Medical School for taking time out of their incredibly busy lives to review our manuscript and make invaluable suggestions.

Much of the clinical information in this book is based on shared experiences with such dedicated physicians as Joseph Hassett, Charles Zaroulis and Michael Greenberg at The Mount Sinai Medical Center, and Sheldon Landesman and his colleagues at Downstate Medical Center. Our experimental collaboration with Carlos Lopez and Patricia Fitzgerald at Sloan-Kettering has been highly rewarding; and our laboratory could not have functioned without the devoted, conscientious technical assistance of Kokila Shah and Domenica Imperato.

Essential to our work are the monthly meetings on AIDS, organized by Commissioner David J. Sencer, at the New York City Health Department, where physicians and other health professionals exchange timely facts and observations about the epidemic as it unfolds. The statements of Mel Rosen, executive director of the Gay Men's Health Crisis, Michael Callen, an AIDS patient, and of Dr. Marcus A. Conant, reprinted in the Appendix, are only a selection of eloquent pleas to legislators that were instrumental in stimulating public funding for AIDS research.

Our editor, John Thaxton, provided a remarkable blend of encouragement, astute critical skill, and intense interest in the subject, which made for a constructive and enjoyable working relationship. We are also indebted to Dr. Robert A. Good, whose pioneering work and inspired teaching contributed greatly to our understanding of the immune system and particularly of immune deficiency diseases. Most of all, we thank the hundreds of patients who through the years have taught us all the rest.

Frederick P. Siegal
Marta Siegal
October 1, 1983

Contents

Foreword

This is a readable, illuminating and authoritative book for anyone interested in knowing about AIDS or about the impressive power of the scientific forces being brought to bear to solve the mystery of a disease that impairs the mechanism of immunity itself. Just as the polio viruses destroy nerve cells and cripple or kill the victim, or the hepatitis virus destroys liver cells, so it seems that an as-yet-undetermined agent may be the cause of the destruction of cells of the immune system necessary for defending us against microbes in our environment or those that sometimes harmlessly exist in our bodies.

This timely volume describes what is being done to identify the causative and contributing factors leading to AIDS, so as to reveal how they may be avoided and how ultimately a means for prevention may be found. There will be a sequel to this book when the mystery and the problem have been solved. However, as an up-to-date, balanced and responsible account of the saga of AIDS, this book will valuably inform both the lay and the professional reader alike.

Jonas Salk, M.D.
La Jolla, California

Chapter 1

Nature's Deadly Experiment:

A Prologue

Despite its benign-sounding acronym, Acquired Immune Deficiency Syndrome has quickly emerged as the newest/ and possibly most unique of all plagues. Unlike previous epidemic diseases, which have usually slipped through the intricate network of the immune system, AIDS destroys the fiber of the system itself. Other scourges—cholera, poliomyelitis, influenza, even the Black Plague—have been the work of single microorganisms, identifiable if uncontrollable agents of disease, that have infected a body unprepared to protect itself with specific defenses. AIDS has introduced a new dimension: instead of merely eluding, it directly attacks the sophisticated structure of immunity that evolution and individual experience have built, leaving its victim vulnerable to myriad organisms with which he had previously learned to live in relative harmony. In a grim way, AIDS is a remarkable experiment of nature that has been simultaneously baffling us with its frustrating mysteries and providing us with new insights into the complexities of the immune system.

The recognition of AIDS as a new phenomenon was somewhat like the process of the blind men describing the elephant. To those doctors who first observed an extraordinarily rare form of skin malignancy, Kaposi's sarcoma, occurring in a cluster of young homosexual men, it appeared that a new "gay cancer" had surfaced in the United States. To those who began reporting unprecedented collections of pneumonia cases caused by the unusual organism Pneumocystis carinii, and to those who were witnessing, also in a homosexual population, inordinately severe oral and anal ulcers resulting from the ubiquitous Herpes simplex virus, it seemed they were encountering what the media would come to call a "gay plague." However, when reports began coming in of cases with similar manifestations occurring in groups as diverse as intravenous drug addicts of both sexes, heterosexual Haitian immigrants, hemophiliac recipients of blood clotting factors, infants of affected mothers, and odd cases that could not be lumped into any logical group, it became clear that AIDS was anything but an exclusively homosexual epidemic.

When, in the fall of 1980, a young man called Joey appeared for a consultation at the clinical immunology service of our medical center, he had already become the despair of several New York internists. They had tried treating him for a series of infections that cropped up as quickly as the doctors could think of drugs to manage them. At 23, Joey was exhibiting the symptoms of a full-blown immune deficiency disease that he had no business having. He had no history of chronic infections; he hadn't had any cancers, or any treatment with drugs that suppress the immune system, either by design or as an unavoidable side effect. It was not apparent to us then that within a distressingly short period Joey would embody many of the terrible physical manifestations, social dilemmas and medical challenges that would soon be recognized as the legacy of AIDS.

Obviously sick for a long time, emaciated, his face grey, Joey looked terrible. A black scab that obstructed his nostrils covered the tip of his nose and obscured his upper lip. He was reluctant to talk and we couldn't be sure at the moment whether his reticence stemmed from pain or depression. His mother said he had been running a fever for weeks, or perhaps months. She said he hadn't been eating enough, that he needed his nourishment. She figured he'd lost at least thirty pounds. The whole family was visibly concerned: several relatives accompanied him to the consultation.

In the examining room, away from his hovering family, we were able to elicit the information we needed. Joey had used drugs, quite an assortment of them, in fact, though never, he insisted, by "shooting them up." Mostly, he liked inhalants, the ones called "poppers," which he sniffed when he went dancing. Occasionally, he took "uppers" or "downers." When asked to provide his sexual history, he reluctantly admitted he was gay, that from about the age of 16 he had had many sexual partners, most of them met casually in the nightspots he frequented.

The membranes of his mouth were spotted with a white coating recognizable as thrush. His lymph nodes were swollen, abnormal sounds in his chest suggested chronic infection, and his spleen was enlarged. He also had a shallow but painful ulcer, the size of a hand, surrounding his anus. It wasn't difficult to imagine how uncomfortable it must have been for him to sit, walk, talk, eat, even breathe. Obviously, he would have to be admitted to the hospital. The workup would need to include, in addition to the routine blood tests and chest x-rays, extensive cultures for bacteria and viruses, a search for parasites and a battery of immunological tests to assess the ability of his cells to cope with infection.

Although Joey wasn't aware of it, we had seen within the previous few months, in the same medical center, four other young men with a similar story: horrendous infections with no apparently predisposing history of congenital immune problems or deliberate immunosuppression. Their only common denominator was homosexual activity. Already all too familiar with the uncontrollably downhill course of these men, we realized Joey's prospects looked dismal unless some aggressive new treatments were attempted. No one was surprised when the results of the various laboratory tests we performed bore witness to an immune system under siege. From virtually every lab to which his samples had been sent came reports that something ominous was growing. His body had become a veritable culture medium for the exuberant multiplication of germs.

Our immediate task was to deal with the infections that could be identified. After more conventional drugs had proved unsuccessful, drugs unavailable a few years ago, some of them not yet used at our institution, were brought out of the research laboratories and tried on Joey. When mycostatin failed to control the Candida albicans that coated his mouth and esophagus, making it painful for him to speak or swallow, and the much more toxic amphotericin B had worked only slowly, we tried a new anti-fungal agent, ketoconazole, which cleared the infection in a few days. The Food and Drug Administration had only recently approved this drug. We suspected, after two entirely discouraging experiences, that the gigantic ulcer on his buttocks would not respond to the standard anti-herpes medication, adenosyl arabinoside.

Fortunately, the experimental drug acyclovir could be obtained for "compassionate use" under FDA rules. To use such an agent, a doctor had to provide a written rationale to the company that had developed it; the FDA had to approve it; and the physician had to be acceptable to the company, Burroughs Wellcome, as an "investigator." In our written request we described Joey and three other patients we had observed over the preceding six months, all of whom had developed similar ulcers. Because the four men were homosexuals, we planned, in time, to describe the group as representing a new syndrome. Events, however, speeded our report along much faster than we anticipated. The pharmaceutical company was impressed not only by Joey's need for acyclovir, but also with the group of patients we had written to them about. The company contacted the Centers for Disease Control in Atlanta and alerted them to our problem in New York. Shortly before this the CDC had been notified by physicians in Los Angeles of occurrences there of an unusual form of pneumonia among homosexual men.

An official of the CDC called us before the acyclovir arrived on the evening's flight from North Carolina. Would we be willing to include our cases in a report of immunodeficiency among homosexual men that the CDC planned to publish in their weekly national health report, the

MMWR? Already affecting far more than four gay men from New York City, this was clearly not just a local problem. For us, the epidemic that was to be called AIDS had suddenly taken shape, and we found ourselves inextricably involved right from the start.

The drug acyclovir was little short of a miracle. What adenosyl arabinoside had failed to accomplish was swiftly achieved by this new agent. Joey's seemingly incurable wounds began to heal, and the pain he had felt during the preceding four months rapidly disappeared. The scab over his upper lip, under which herpes viruses had been multiplying, disappeared as the skin under it recovered. His nose began to take its shape again. The massive ulcer around his anus also cleared up, while his fever, until then not really explained, regressed. Joey seemed a new person, and, armed with a brown plastic bottle of ketoconazole, was ready to go home.

We suspected his discharge would be only temporary, and, indeed, he was back within a few weeks with recurring small ulcers where his old ones had been. Now it was relatively simple to obtain more acyclovir and to retreat the herpes. Unfortunately, his return indicated how forlorn our hope was that the earlier successes with acyclovir might also have corrected the immune defect. It was becoming apparent that the "magic bullet" for herpes would not also serve as a cure for the underlying disease.

By that time, the summer of 1981, the CDC had alerted the world to AIDS. Physicians at several medical centers had recognized many of the syndrome's opportunistic infections and had described one of the neoplasms, Kaposi's sarcoma, that frequently takes advantage of these immunologically compromised victims. Joey, sadly, wasn't to be spared much. During the course of his retreatment for herpes infections, he noticed a black-and-blue mark, the size of a quarter and slightly raised, on his back. It didn't hurt, but it was definitely new and seemed to be getting bigger. We ordered a biopsy of the lesion, and when the pathologist confirmed our suspicions of its being Kaposi's sarcoma, a different, more aggressive overall therapeutic approach seemed necessary.

The skin tumor described in the late 19th century by the Hungarian physician Kaposi had been rare in the Western world until now, occurring only in elderly men and having little significant effect on their health. Although sometimes troublesome, it rarely metastasized and hardly ever by itself caused death. The exception until now was the exotic occurrence of this disease among children in equatorial Africa, where it exhibits a more virulent, often lethal behavior. That Kaposi's sarcoma developed in patients whose immunity had been depressed by the drugs used in kidney transplantation was known to doctors by the late 1970's, as was the intriguing fact that in almost half such patients one could make the tumors regress by allowing the immune system to recover. In kidney transplant cases reversing the immune deficiency was relatively simple: the intentionally suppressive drugs used to keep the patient from rejecting the kidney could be stopped.

In one respect Joey seemed lucky. The tumor didn't appear to progress rapidly, and the herpes responded again to the acyclovir. This gave us time to consider what to do next. In the earlier cases we had seen, the progression of various infections had been so rapid, their responses to treatment so poor, that attempts to improve the immune system couldn't practically be carried out. But as we saw or heard about more and more of these patients, it became increasingly clear that Joey would die unless we could somehow reverse his immune deficiency. Sooner or later he would encounter an infection we wouldn't know how to treat or his tumor would become aggressive and kill him.

The urgent problem facing us was how to reconstitute Joey's terribly compromised defense system. Where should we begin? Which precedent should we follow? Then, as now, the precise nature of the immune defect wasn't understood. We had no specific target to shoot at, no special rationale for therapy. We were aware of a number of drugs thought to augment, in certain clinical situations, the immune system. We were also painfully aware of their shortcomings: most were either weak or efficacious only in very restricted settings. Since we did know that Joey had a deficiency of one hormone associated with thymic function, it seemed reasonable to treat him with a crude preparation of thymic extract. We decided to try thymosin fraction V, submitting again the requisite plea for compassionate use to the drug company that manufactures it and to the FDA. The company gave us the thymosin; Joey's immune function tests were expectantly tracked. Nothing positive happened. On the contrary, Joey continued to run an unexplained fever and several new lesions of Kaposi's tumor appeared on his skin. A few phone conversations with colleagues ascertained that others on our checklist of possible drugs had been tried, without benefit, in cases similar to Joey's. Only one, rather drastic alternative treatment hadn't been explored: a bone marrow transplant.

Immunologists today know that most of the cells comprising the immune system come from the bone marrow. An extensive research effort in the 1960's made it clear that one could replace a damaged immune system in an experimental mouse by transplanting bone marrow cells taken from another, closely related mouse. Late in that decade a few courageous pediatricians had attempted marrow transplantation on children born without immune cells, children whose siblings had died because of the same congenital immune defect and who would certainly themselves have succumbed to infection had they been left to their own immunological devices. Happily, many such children are alive today because of that willingness to experiment in the face of seemingly overwhelming odds.

Our precedent for bone marrow transplantation lay in those pioneering efforts performed in congenitally defective children. All the tests had shown Joey to be severely immunodeficient and to resemble such children in many respects. We would follow the lead of the pediatricians, but could we expect success? There were plenty of reasons to suspect that we might not. For one thing, Joey was very ill with ongoing infections, some of which could inhibit the acceptance of a grafted bone marrow. For another, Joey's defect was acquired, not congenital or genetically determined. Whatever caused the defect might still be lurking in him, capable of causing disease again in any new cells we gave him. For yet another, we might expect rejection of the graft by Joey's remaining immune system, or an attack on Joey by the newly transplantated cells. In the latter case we knew that if the grafted cells were inappropriately stimulated, they might well survive in Joey's body and generate yet another disease by inciting a graft-versus-host reaction. Such a new disease would only compound his troubles: if severe, graft-versus-host disease can itself be fatal. Marrow transplantation held its dangers for Joey. In addition, there would be some risk for the marrow donor since general anesthesia would be necessary for the marrow aspiration procedure. But the approach, with all its hazards, now seemed both essential and ethically justifiable. We had seen enough of AIDS to know the direction in which Joey's life would go if no risks were undertaken.

Having come to grips with that decision for ourselves, we then needed to obtain approval from the chairman of the Department of Medicine, to discuss the plan openly with Joey and his family, and, ultimately, to put it into writing as a new "protocol" for the scrutiny of the hospital's committee on human experimentation. This group of medical and lay persons would have to be persuaded that our plan was acceptable on ethical grounds, that the potential benefits to the patient outweighed the possible risks. To do all this would take time, time we weren't sure we had.

Joey's will to live swayed a strongly supportive family to agree to our proposal, after discussing it among themselves and with various other doctors. Together with our associates in the blood bank and other members of the hospital staff who would be involved in the transplant, we set about writing our protocol. The resident in clinical immunology, a dedicated young physician who carried out many of the procedures and day-to-day care of the patient, spent days preparing the document. For background he cited the extensive literature on marrow transplantation and the prior experience of those of our team who had done marrow transplants before in leukemia, severe forms of anemia, and congenital immune deficiency patients. When the protocol was submitted to the committee on human experimentation, the group acted with unusual speed because of the urgency of the situation and approved the transplant. Our next challenge was to find a suitable donor.

As potential donors, Joey had, in addition to his parents, three sisters and one brother. Selection of a marrow donor depends primarily on obtaining an ideal match from among several closely related people. The best possible is an identical twin, and had Joey had one, he would certainly have been selected. Next best is usually a sibling compatible for certain tissue types known to be important factors in determining whether a graft is accepted or rejected by the recipient. Even marrow donors identical to the recipient in tissue type usually differ from him in some measurable way, some "marker." The presence of this marker permits the transplant physician to know if the graft has been accepted, when and if cells carrying the marker appear in the recipient. The chance that any one sibling will be precisely matched by tissue typing—that is, HLA-identical—is one in four. Armed with the knowledge that our chances of finding a donor were excellent, we assembled the family for HLA typing. It turned out that Joey had one HLA-identical sister, who would certainly have been selected but for an unforeseen and insuperable problem: she had an impairment of her own that precluded our obtaining proper informed consent.

Joey's brother, whose whereabouts were uncertain, hadn't been typed. When it appeared that the absent brother might be the next best match, we were faced with the problem of locating him. A social worker was enlisted to help in our search, and after innumerable phone calls and detective work involving the participation of family and staff, we contacted the brother who was in a distant state. As luck would have it, he was willing, but had no money for transportation to New York. We worked out complex arrangements for him to travel by bus to the nearest large medical center with the capacity to perform HLA typing, and we waited anxiously to learn whether he would indeed be a better match than the remaining sisters. News finally came that he was no more compatible than other, accessible family members. We then decided that the father would be the most suitable donor under the circumstances.

Joey was, in theory, an almost ideal recipient, because one of the tissue types, the crucial HLA-DR, was represented twice in his chromosomes. This homozygosity —reflecting inheritance of the same gene from both parents—permitted us to use as a donor any immediate family member who had at least one gene identical to Joey's. Another important reason for his being a potentially good candidate for a successful "take" lay in the immune deficit itself, the very inability of his cells to mount a rejection response. His total white cell count had drastically diminished, so much so that he had almost negligible numbers of those lymphocytes thought to be responsible for graft rejection. In culture, these lymphocytes, the cells of his immune system, had failed to respond to a number of standard stimuli that test their capacity to multiply. When his white cells were mixed in the laboratory with those of other people, they failed to react significantly. We regarded Joey's lack of "natural killer" cells, which had contributed to his susceptibility to Herpes simplex virus, as being in his favor when it came time for transplantation, because these virus-resisting cells also appear to be involved in graft rejection and the triggering of graft-versus-host disease.

Joey's father, a heavyset but healthy man in his mid-50's, had a matter-of-fact approach to his son's dilemma. It was never clear how much he knew, or surmised, about the genesis of Joey's illness. We were rather hesitant to inform him that he had been selected as the best donor available, but he agreed without reluctance, as though he had already prepared himself emotionally for this event. Taking time off from his job, he came for admission to the hospital on the day before the transplant and underwent routine tests designed to ensure his fitness. His physician, not a member of our transplant group, knew that he could stop the process at any time before the marrow donation began, if he felt the donor was at significant risk. Surrounded by the entire family and a number of close friends, Joey and his father signed the necessary consent forms. In addition, Joey's social worker, several residents, and the floor nurses were present. Perhaps because we shared a sense of expectancy and hope, this gathering had about it an air of ceremony.

The bone marrow transplantation procedure was carried off without any complications for either donor or recipient. The father awoke in the recovery room only two hours after we had started, having donated about ten-thousand-million white blood cells. Destined for a vein in his son's arm, these were hanging in two small plastic bags. He left the hospital next morning without a complaint.

For Joey, as for most other such recipients, bone marrow transplantation was an essentially innocuous and passive act. The marrow cells are given, simply, like a blood transfusion, with the expectation that they will find their way to the right place and begin reproducing. For the physicians, the process involves watching and waiting for evidence of improved immunologic function, or for evidence that the donor cells have gained a foothold. We knew that Joey's father's cells, unlike his son's, could react strongly to certain stimuli and that their response could be readily demonstrated by a simple skin test. Joey's immune system was so depressed before the transplant that his cells couldn't muster themselves to make such a response. We reasoned that if the marrow were to become engrafted and his immune functions restored, Joey's skin test would become positive. But our hopes were not realized: his skin test never became positive; his immune function never improved.

Five days passed quietly. Joey's room was darkened, and in the wake of the excitement of the previous days, we were all subdued and anxious. Then, a ray of hope appeared in what under any other circumstances would have been a completely trivial symptom: a faint but definite rash erupted on his chest and arms. Was this a graft-versus-host reaction? Did this mean we had a successful "take"? Would immunologic reconstitution or a severe graft-versus-host disease follow? A piece of skin the size of a nail head would tell the tale. The pathologists considered the biopsy of his rash "compatible with graft-versus-host reaction, grade 1." But that fleeting eruption was, sadly, all we would see of the millions of cells we had given him. They had disappeared into Joey's body, leaving behind them only this reddening of the skin for a few hours.

Joey's spirits plunged sharply; his depression seemed appropriate considering the new lesions of Kaposi's sarcoma that had appeared and his continual loss of weight despite full intravenous feedings. There were other worrisome signs. The neurologists confirmed our fears that some ill-defined brain disease had taken hold of him. He continued to decline despite our efforts to explain and control this final assault. Joey died in the spring of 1982, a little more than two months after the transplantation attempt, only a year after we had met him. He was 24.

The family wouldn't accept the idea of an autopsy. Joey had suffered enough, as had they. Theirs was an understandable and common enough response, but to those of us involved in the struggle with his disease, the family's decision only heightened the tragedy. It deprived us of potentially important knowledge, information that could help other patients in the fight against a new disease. AIDS had taken one of its first victims, in a manner that was to become typical of its course. There were soon to be a great many more deaths, and many other frustrated efforts in various medical centers to halt the onslaught of the disease. Ours had been only a skirmish at the beginning of a deadly war.

CHAPTER 2

What is AIDS,

and What Isn't?

AIDS has evoked more fear than perhaps any other disease in recent history. Because it appeared mysteriously, spread rapidly, and has caused much suffering and death, the syndrome has generated enormous anxiety among possible victims, health workers and the general public. Doctors, clinics and hot-lines across the United States and, now, those in many other countries are being besieged by calls from worried people who wonder if they have the disease or may be susceptible to it. It is unlikely that these anxieties will abate until the major questions are answered: what is the cause, or causes of AIDS? who is vulnerable? how long is the incubation period? how is it transmitted? how can it be prevented? Although the solutions to these questions must, unfortunately, await a period of research that may seem intolerably long, it is likely that once the presumed causative microbe is identified there will be rapid progress, facilitated by the high level of current medical technology. While we shouldn't underestimate how much is still unknown about AIDS, we do already have a substantial amount of accumulated information, particularly about the syndrome's manifestations and patterns of occurrence.

The most familiar fact about AIDS is that it affects certain groups preferentially. These risk groups are suspected of sharing an infectious agent—most probably a virus—that is transmitted by intimate contact, usually sexual or blood-borne. Homosexual men, in whom the syndrome was first identified, continue to comprise the vast majority of victims (at least 70%). The next group, male or female intravenous drug abusers, constitute a smaller proportion of patients; their exact numbers are difficult to assess because their generally poor access to medical care no doubt results in an under-reporting of cases. This group is followed in frequency by Haitian immigrants and hemophiliacs who receive clotting factor infusions. Both of these latter groups have been considered to be predominantly heterosexual. Infants of mothers who either have AIDS or fall into one of the high risk groups and recipients of blood transfusions from affected blood donors make up a small percentage of the cases to date. In addition to these, there are scattered cases that don't fit conveniently into any of the above categories, but, in these, a sexual or blood connection can't absolutely be ruled out since it is often difficult to obtain a completely accurate personal history of contacts or exposures.

Although the risk groups cannot be linked to each other in any direct pattern of communicability, the cases themselves show a remarkable degree of similarity. The symptoms of AIDS, while protean in any individual patient, are surprisingly uniform among the various risk groups. Once the disease establishes itself, a stereotypical clinical picture —whether the patient is a homosexual man, a female drug addict, or a hemophiliac youth—emerges. Laboratory tests on the cells of patients from the various risk groups display similar functional deficits.

Non-specific Symptoms

The main problem physicians confront in diagnosing AIDS lies in distinguishing, among a vast array of non-specific symptoms and findings, those that could easily suggest diseases other than AIDS from those that signal the early development of the syndrome. It is often difficult to determine where other, perhaps less ominous diseases end and AIDS begins. The "working" definition provided by the AIDS task force at the Centers for Disease Control does not, unfortunately, help in solving this diagnostic dilemma. Originally intended as a guide to reporting cases to public health officers and identifying groups at risk, the CDC working definition appears, in retrospect, to have been an excellent delineation of the fullblown syndrome.

Reportable cases of AIDS are defined by the presence of at least one of a group of bizarre "opportunistic" infections (infections a healthy immune system would easily destroy) or of Kaposi's sarcoma, which, in the words of the CDC, are "predictive of a defect in cell-mediated immunity." These features indicate AIDS only if they exist in a person who has had neither previous treatment with certain drugs (whose side effect or main action results in a suppression of the immune system) nor a history of underlying illnesses known to create a susceptibility to frequent, severe infections. Obvious examples of definitive cases would be a gay man of 25 whose skin is covered with lesions of Kaposi's sarcoma, or a female drug addict who develops Pneumocystis carinii pneumonia.

Other, relatively uncommon disorders of the lymphoid system, such as Hodgkin's disease, lymphomas and leukemias, and congenital immunodeficiencies, are associated with some of the infections seen in AIDS. Treatment for disorders such as systemic lupus erythematosus, rheumatoid arthritis and other so-called "autoimmune" processes also predispose patients to many of these secondary infections, as do the drug therapies used to prevent rejection, via suppressing the immune system, of transplanted kidneys and other organs. When a patient has such preexisting problems, AIDS cannot be definitively diagnosed. Similarly, since Kaposi's sarcoma has been known to develop, though infrequently, in elderly men, patients with this skin tumor who are older than 60 cannot be classifed as having AIDS according to the current working definition. In general, AIDS affects a younger age group than do most adult lymphoid diseases or cancers. The average age for all the risk groups combined is 35.

Before describing the details of the typical features of AIDS, it's perhaps best to tackle the problematical grey area of equivocal symptoms, which may or may not represent the beginning phase of the disease. Many of the early symptoms of AIDS are nonspecific; they are also characteristic of the numerous ailments that commonly affect the same risk groups. Chief among these is hepatitis, which is prevalent in homosexuals, drug addicts and hemophiliacs. Fever, malaise, fatigue and nausea are just some of the non-exclusive symptoms of both hepatitis and AIDS. Tuberculosis, especially frequent in Haitians, also exhibits features that overlap with those of AIDS (including fever, weight loss and lymph node enlargement). In younger persons, whether male or female, common viral illnesses—infectious mononucleosis, recurrent sore throats and transient fevers —are not unusual. Among gay men, any number of other sexually transmitted diseases—gonorrhea, syphilis, and the complex of infections and infestations comprising the "gay bowel syndrome"—can produce manifestations that may be confused with AIDS. These include localized lymph node enlargement in the groin, fever, skin eruptions, diarrhea and abdominal or anal pain.

Diagnosing AIDS in children presents many special problems. A family history here is crucial, since a number of hereditary defects can produce severe infections. Prior to the identification of AIDS in infants of mothers known to be drug addicts, partners of AIDS patients or AIDS victims themselves, pediatricians knew of such immune deficiency diseases as the DiGeorge and Wiskott-Aldrich syndromes and severe combined immunodeficiency, all of which were characterized by life-threatening infections. Non-specific symptoms of infection may also be caused by malnutrition.

Among the features differentiating AIDS from the common cold, influenza and other ordinary afflictions is that the symptoms of AIDS tend to be chronic and progressive. Almost every person has experienced fatigue, fever, chilliness, some sweating at night, lymph node enlargement, coughing and diarrhea for at least a brief period. When these problems persist, or are unusually severe or progressive, in a person from one of the high-risk groups, they can't be considered normal. But it must be emphasized that even in these respects many other chronic and debilitating diseases can mimic AIDS. Before our awareness of AIDS, a medical textbook worth of other illnesses could be summoned to explain these complaints.

Hierarchy of Symptoms

It's possible to construct a hierarchy of AIDS symptoms, starting with those just listed and ending with manifestations that definitely signal a profound defect in cellular immunity. Loss of weight is a non-specific symptom, which can be either trivial or serious. When it is limited to a few pounds and associated with transient diarrhea, it is not a cause for concern. But when the process persists, and the loss continues unabated, an explanation must be sought, whether the weight loss is accounted for by diarrhea or only by a lack of appetite. Shortness of breath is another non-specific but highly worrisome development. If someone from the high risk groups has difficulty in breathing, the complaint needs to be investigated vigorously, via chest x-rays, pulmonary function tests or bronchoscopy. Visual disturbances, mental confusion and, in some cases, even headache, depression or sleepiness are high on the ladder of symptoms that should prompt aggressive diagnostic efforts when they appear in persons at risk, especially in the presence of other concrete findings.

In general, enlargement of the lymph glands is a normal response of the immune system to an attack by foreign substances. Lymphoid tissue is the major site of the body's immunological filter system, and swelling of the lymph nodes usually confirms that the system is doing its proper job. When any infection occurs, the body responds by mobilizing the cells of the immune system, lymphocytes and monocytes, which travel to the site of infection and swell the lymph nodes and other lymphoid tissues. These are the places in which the cells interact with each other in learning to cope with harmful organisms. Anyone who has had tonsillitis, infectious mononucleosis, or even a boil on his skin is familiar with this normal physiologic process.

Danger Signs

Common, though not invariably present, in patients who eventually develop AIDS, is a generalized enlargement of lymph nodes, "lymphadenopathy." Those most frequently affected are groups of nodes in the groin, armpits and neck. Sometimes other lymphoid tissues also swell, including the tonsils, the spleen and the nodes at the elbows and even those within the chest and abdomen. In some homosexual men, lymphadenopathy precedes the development of AIDS and is therefore considered by some physicians to be a "prodrome," or first sign of AIDS. Interestingly enough, it has been reported that a number of homosexual men have had enlargement of nodes for as long as a decade. It's not clear, therefore, whether lymphadenopathy is actually an early stage of AIDS or whether, simply, it coincides as an independent phenomenon in the same community. Doctors know that for many years before AIDS was identified, lymphadenopathy was also widely prevalent among intravenous drug abusers.

Lymph node enlargement is normally transitory; if it persists it's a danger sign. When a local group of nodes is enlarged without an obvious accompanying infection, or multiple groups of nodes are affected, it is reasonable to perform a biopsy. Through microscopic examination of specially stained slides of the lymphoid tissue a pathologist can determine whether particular infections are present, or rule out malignancies originating in the lymphoid system or elsewhere. In the lymphadenopathy syndrome of gay men, nodes on biopsy most often appear to be immunologically stimulated without any immediately obvious cause and, therefore, don't yield any specific diagnosis.

To better understand this association between AIDS and

persistent, generalized lymphadenopathy, groups of homosexual men with enlarged lymph nodes are being studied in several medical centers. After only two years of observation, as many as 10-20% of patients with this non-specific finding have come to fit the CDC's case definition for AIDS. Unfortunately, it seems likely that these figures will continue to rise at an unpredictable rate. While not all cases of nodal enlargement foreshadow the development of AIDS, such manifestations must be carefully followed. A number of physicians working with the syndrome believe that effective intervention in the course of the disease will be possible, if at all, only at this early stage of its development. For this reason, patients with lymphadenopathy only are being favored in some drug trial protocols.

Minor Infections

A group of relatively minor infections have also been observed among gay men in apparently increasing frequency during the AIDS epidemic. These infections are considered to be related to a temporary depression of immunity. As the true incidence of these complaints is not known, it is possible that the recent interest in AIDS has only raised our consciousness of these problems. The painful herpes zoster eruption commonly known as "shingles" is the result of the varicella-zoster virus, "VZV." Almost everyone is exposed to varicella-zoster, usually in childhood epidemics, and virtually all people except those with congenital immune deficiency experience a relatively mild illness familiar as chicken pox. Like other herpesviruses, VZV can go underground (it can hide for many years in nerve tissue in a latent, symptomless state), only to be reactivated long after the original attack. Reactivation, which sometimes results from discernable immune alteration but more often goes unexplained, leads to the development of painful, itchy, weeping skin lesions that generally confine themselves to the pathway of a major nerve. Shingles primarily occurs in seemingly healthy, often elderly people who have no serious underlying illnesses. In such persons the skin lesions are resolved within two to three weeks. When herpes zoster reactivation occurs in persons with severe immunological compromise, the virus can escape from the nerve pathway and spread widely on the skin. This generalized type of reaction is unusual even in fully developed AIDS.

Other viral diseases of the skin—common warts and molluscum contagiosum—sometimes are unusually extensive or troublesome when the individual has an immune defect. These diseases are so widespread in our population that in an isolated case they cannot be regarded as indicative of AIDS. However, an intractable problem with either of these conditions should at least alert physicians.

Thrush (candidiasis) is another common infection that may or may not be suggestive of an immune defect. Familiar to most of us because of its frequent occurrence in young children, thrush is typifed by the accumulations of cheesy white material on the mucous membranes of the mouth or the vagina. It often follows the use of broad-spectrum antibiotics, usually tetracyclines. The appearance of this fungus infection illustrates the breakdown of the intricate equilibrium that exists between our immune systems and certain microorganisms as well as a system of checks and balances among the microbes themselves.

A Delicate Balance

Candida albicans, the organism that causes thrush, is part of the normal "flora" of the body's microbial garden. It is one of the countless germs that live on or in us, causing no disease but rather contributing in various ways to our well-being by helping to digest our food and providing us with vitamins. These bacteria, fungi and the viruses that in turn inhabit them keep each other in line by producing substances that inhibit one another. When we use an antibiotic, we take advantage of such substances. For example, tetracycline, which comes from soil organisms, slows or stops the metabolism of some, but by no means all, of the microbes in our bodies. Since candida happens to be resistant to tetracycline, thrush develops fairly often in persons taking the drug, as other inhibitory microbes are killed off.

Like several of the organisms that accompany AIDS, Candida albicans is an opportunist—it takes advantage of a void by moving in. The fungus is held in check not only by other microorganisms but also by our immune systems. Young children, who have relatively undeveloped immune systems, are more prone to thrush when exposed to antibiotics than are normal adults with mature immune systems. People with severe forms of immune deficiency can develop thrush spontaneously, even if they haven't altered the balance of their normal bodily flora by taking antibiotics. The appearance of thrush without prior medication in a person from one of the AIDS risk groups is a troubling sign indicating a significant degree of immune dysfunction. We have been following a number of homosexual men with candidiasis who do not as yet have overt AIDS. If the thrush becomes severe and extensive, and involves more than just the mouth or vaginal lining, it is sufficient, according to the CDC's criteria, to classify the patient as having AIDS.

Paradoxically, there are some ailments that actually reassure us that a person's immune system is intact. Also characterized by latent infection, Herpes simplex virus, like its cousin varicella-zoster virus, has evolved an intimate and successful host-parasite relationship with mankind. The recurrent cold sore is its most familiar manifestation, but Herpes simplex also causes genital infections. After the initial exposure, which is frequently unnoticed, skin lesions may reappear in the same general areas of the body through which the virus originally entered. These reactivations seem to occur in response to stress or illness, but in people with normal immune systems they last for only 5 to 14 days. The individual whose recurrent Herpes simplex infections continue to follow this benign course has passed a significant test of immune function and probably doesn't need to worry that he has AIDS.

On the other hand, the failure of the immune system to control certain types of infection signifies that something fundamental has gone wrong. In 1980, doctors knew that

Pneumocystis carinii infection virtually never occurs in people uncompromised by drug treatment and that Herpes simplex virus infections are self-limited. They knew that Kaposi's sarcoma wasn't a problem for young people in the western world—dermatologists considered the disease an extreme rarity even in the elderly. The appearance of Pneumocystis pneumonia and Kaposi's tumor in previously healthy young men was so out of the ordinary, such an obvious violation of basic medical rules, that alert physicians immediately perceived the need to investigate the phenomenon. In these extraordinary cases began the recognition of AIDS.

The definition of a full-fledged case of AIDS grew almost directly from the perception that these infections (Pneumocystis carinii pneumonia and chronic ulcerative Herpes simplex) were indicative of an immune deficiency disease. They couldn't exist in the face of normal defense mechanisms. But as the number of cases grew and our experience with the process widened, other infections joined those that suggested an underlying difficulty. The more familiar ones, tuberculosis, candidiasis, and toxoplasmosis, were not in themselves so unusual. What was extraordinary was their aggressive pattern of behavior, their persistence in the face of previously effective antimicrobial agents. Then, we were suddenly confronted by afflictions most doctors had never heard of in humans—cryptosporidiosis and isosporiasis—or perhaps only as obscure case reports glossed over in medical journals. And most peculiar of all was that aberrant tumor Kaposi's sarcoma: how did that fit in?

Opportunistic Infections

Parasites

Pneumocystis carinii, the organism causing the most obvious and common infection in AIDS, was first described as a disease-producing agent in the 1940s. It was recognized as the cause of fatal outbreaks of pneumonias in malnourished, sickly refugee and newborn children at the end of World War II. Not a bacterial or viral form but a protozoan, pneumocystis came to be an important problem only with the advent of effective cancer chemotherapy, whose unfortunate side effect was the profound depression of immunity. The disease it causes when given the opportunity is frequently slow to manifest itself and subtle at its outset. Its hallmark is a consciousness of effort in breathing, or dyspnea, at first almost imperceptible but later obvious and rapidly progressive if nothing is done to remedy the situation. The symptom is accentuated by exertion, such as climbing stairs or a hill. Fever is not invariably present, and in the early stages of the infection there may be nothing significant detected with the stethoscope or even x-rays. Tests of pulmonary function, especially of the ability to transfer oxygen and other gases across the normally permeable membranes of the lung into the bloodstream, usually confirm the suspicion that an unseen infection is brewing in the lung. Only late in the development of pneumocystis do the chest films become abnormal and the lungs sound congested.

Like many of the other microorganisms that cause trouble in AIDS, pneumocystis is part of almost everybody's personal entourage, one of those bugs that travel with us from childhood. Evidence for this comes from the prevalence in adults of antibodies against pneumocystis, which indicates that most people eventually acquire and coexist with the organism without knowing it. In some cancer hospitals, small epidemics of Pneumocystis carinii pneumonia have been reported. This suggests that person-to-person spread among susceptible individuals is capable of leading directly to disease. But, for the most part, it is believed that this protozoan becomes, simply, more active in the absence of an intact protective immune system in its human host.

The usual method of diagnosing pneumocystis involves the insertion of a flexible tube, the fiberoptic bronchoscope, into the airways of the lungs. The doctor can then observe and obtain infected tissues. These are processed by a pathologist or a microbiologist, who uses special dyes that render the parasites visible. Essentially the same approach can identify certain other opportunistic organisms that cause lung disease in AIDS—cytomegaloviruses, mycobacteria, fungi. Fiberoptic bronchoscopy is the diagnostic procedure most widely employed in this situation. Through the microscope, the process that causes breathing problems can be easily understood—the organisms can be seen in the air sacs of the lung, where they seem to stimulate the production of foamy material that obstructs the flow of air. This same foam is responsible for the noises the physician hears through the stethoscope as congestion and for the x-ray changes that ultimately appear.

In the halcyon days before AIDS, treating pneumocystis was relatively straightforward once it was recognized. Physicians could obtain from the CDC a highly active but experimental drug, pentamidine, which usually had the capacity to control the infection. Possibly because in many patients the pneumocystis pneumonia was the result of a transitory, though severe, immune defect that followed cancer chemotherapy, responses to the medication were frequently good: a recovering immune system could clean up after drugs that inhibited but didn't kill the microbes. In AIDS, we are finding treatment for pneumocystis less reliable, even though an important new drug combination, trimethoprim-sulfamethoxazole (Bactrim, or Septra), has been added recently to the physician's bag. Some patients with AIDS simply do not seem to respond to either drug. Some respond slowly, only to develop serious side effects; some get better but continue to harbor the organism, as evidenced on repeated bronchoscopy. In spite of this, lung function can improve sufficiently to permit apparent clinical cure, sometimes for periods as long as a year, without continuation of the medications. Once established, however, pneumocystis pneumonia in AIDS patients tends to recur, since the immune deficit does not remit. Interestingly, some AIDS victims seem to escape this infection, which suggests that these individuals never encountered the organism.

Protozoan infestations are a worldwide problem. Malaria and amebiasis, among others, are major causes of morbidity in the developing nations. In the United States or

Europe, neither has been a special problem in AIDS. Besides pneumocystis carinii, two other protozoans have emerged as important pathogens for AIDS patients: toxoplasmosis and cryptosporidiosis. Toxoplasma are carried in domestic animals, most often cats, and can cause a self-limited disease that resembles infectious mononucleosis as well as symptomless infection. Transmission to humans seems to take place via contact with cat feces or by eating contaminated, inadequately cooked red meat. AIDS is associated with severe disseminated toxoplasmosis involving primarily the lymph nodes, the brain and the eyes. When it affects the brain, abscess formation can lead to confusion and various other neurological manifestations; in the eyes it can result in blindness. Fortunately, if it is identified promptly by the ophthalmologist or through a CAT scan of the brain, toxoplasmosis can be effectively suppressed with available drugs. Treatment, usually with a sulfa drug combined with an antimalarial, should probably be continued for the duration of the patient's life, since the disease tends to recur when the medication is stopped.

One of the most remarkable infections that has come to light during the AIDS epidemic is cryptosporidiosis. Its causative agent, cryptosporidium, wasn't associated with human disease until about 1975, when it was observed to induce severe and persistent diarrhea in a few patients with congenital immune deficiency. Harbored, like toxoplasma, by a variety of domestic and farm animals (such as puppies, kittens, calves, and turkeys), cryptosporidia can be transmitted easily from animals to man and vice versa. The diagnosis of cryptosporidiosis in an AIDS patient is extremely grave, since there is no satisfactory drug regimen available for controlling the severe diarrhea that leads to emaciation. It becomes difficult, sometimes impossible, to maintain adequate nutrition and fluid balance, even with intravenous feeding. A more benign and brief diarrheal syndrome occurs in veterinarians and other persons who come in close contact with domestic animals. Recent reports indicate that in addition to their more familiar manifestations, both toxoplasma and cryptosporidia can cause pneumonia in AIDS patients.

Viruses

Following the bizarre protozoan pneumocystis carinii, the most frequent agents causing serious infections in patients with AIDS are common viruses. When Herpes simplex is out of control, becoming persistent and progressive, it is a sign of underlying immune deficiency disease. Typical signs are the cold sore or the genital blister that fail to heal in due time, with the skin around the lesion continuing to break down in ever widening circles as viruses move from cell to cell, forming a shallow, red ulcer.

Ulcerative herpes was so unusual when it first appeared that most doctors seeing the early cases of AIDS didn't appreciate the nature of the process. The patients were thought to have some strange form of venereal disease, or non-specific bowel ailment, somehow eroding its way onto the skin around the anus. All sorts of medications were triedwithoutsuccess. Even the skin biopsies showing cell forms typical of infection with herpes viruses weren't initially taken at face value. The question was seriously raised whether the virus wasn't some sort of secondary infection. When the immune deficiency of these men was finally recognized, a search of the medical literature confirmed the rarity of such manifestations. Even most specialists in infectious or immunodeficiency diseases were not familiar with them. What eventually convinced us of the central role of herpes viruses in the skin ulcers was their dramatic response, after months of treatment failures, to the new drug acyclovir (Zovirax), which is known to be selectively effective against Herpes simplex virus, both types 1 and 2.

Genital herpes has been proclaimed a plague in its own right. Although accurate statistics are unavailable because herpes is not a reportable affliction, estimates by the popular press of 20 million cases in the United States are not out of line. The genital form of herpes infection, usually caused by type 2 virus, is most often transmitted sexually. Its spread from person to person, like that of AIDS, is accelerated by promiscuity, although its significance for the victim is by no means as serious. And, even though its initial symptoms can now be palliated with acyclovir, genital herpes is recurring and incurable. Antiviral drugs can effectively stop virus production in certain herpes infections, but in the long run, Herpes simplex, even if well treated with antivirals, will return simply because the drugs do not limit the latent virus's ability to reactivate.

Although latency is a major problem in controlling herpes, it is not the only one. The defense against Herpes simplex is only partial even in healthy people, as witnessed by the ability of the virus to reappear in the face of serum antibody and cellular defenses that would stop another pathogen in its tracks. The secret of its success lies in the location of the latent infection itself. Herpes viruses, once within the nerve cells of the host, are relatively sheltered from the immune system. They do not emerge into the blood stream, where they would be vulnerable to neutralization by antibodies, nor do they apparently alter the nerve cell sufficiently to make it recognizable to the destructive sentinels of the cellular immune system. Instead, the virus presumably travels down the nerve to skin cells. In contrast to nerves, infected skin cells express antigens, the molecular targets that are recognized as foreign by other, active immune cells. Normally, the virus-infected cells are killed by the inflammatory cells, eventually limiting the local process of destruction embodied in the cold sore. In AIDS, some of these elements are lacking and the relentless process of skin erosion results in gaping ulcers.

Another problematic feature of herpes viruses is their tremendous variability. The number of possible permutations and combinations in viral DNA, the molecules of genetic material that determine different strains, is almost infinite. There are potentially so many types that for each person there might be a separate viral strain. This great variability confers an important survival advantage on the herpes simplex virus. Unlike most infectious agents, the Herpesviruses are able to circumvent the partial immunity of people, reinfecting a person who is already infected with a strain that is only slightly different. Sexually active men and women may acquire new herpes infections even when they already harbor another. Furthermore, having herpes doesn't guarantee that you won't get more of the same. Indeed, it is possible to reinfect oneself by scratching one part of the body and then transferring the virus by scratching the skin elsewhere. It can actually be shown by DNA fingerprinting techniques that the virus in the new site is identical to that in the original sore. The phenomenon of herpes again illustrates how well balanced the relationship between host and parasite usually is. The virus can survive forever; it can spread from person to person, from cell to cell, or even across an expanse of skin in an individual. It can cause discomfort and pain, but it doesn't kill its host.

Even in the AIDS patient, Herpes simplex virus doesn't usually kill its host. It primarily invades locally, at sites surrounding body openings—the genitals, the anus, the buttocks or thighs, and around the mouth and nose. On the face it is more likely to be type l, whereas in the other areas it is usually represented by type 2. The skin ulcers can lead to the development of rather grotesque scabs, which despite their bad appearance may heal dramatically for a time with effective administration of acyclovir. Unfortunately, when the drug is stopped, the viruses recur in the same sites.

Herpes can also invade the brain. Since symptoms may not appear until very late in the disease, doctors may not be able to forestall permanent brain damage. For this reason, treating local herpetic skin ulcers with only topical antiviral ointments in immune deficient patients is probably unwise. Instead, oral or intravenous therapy should be employed to prevent spread to the central nervous system. Another problem encountered in ulcerative herpes infections is that the sores permit access to the body by other organisms that can cause acute disease. For example, perianal ulcers may provide an easy route of entry for fecal organisms, which can cause fever and deep-seated infections in these already sick individuals. Herpes, and perhaps other viruses, may be involved in some of the skin and anal cancers that are seen in gay men.

Cytomegalovirus (CMV) is another agent that causes serious problems in patients with AIDS. A member of the herpes group, CMV is also capable of latency, but it chooses to reside during its inactive phase in the kidneys and urogenital tract rather than in nerve cells. The virus is concentrated in urine, semen and sperm. It travels via the circulation mostly within white cells and has a propensity to infect the endothelial cells lining blood vessels. This may have special significance for the development of Kaposi's sarcoma, which involves cells of such endothelial origin. CMV can be passed from person to person by intimate contact, blood transfusion, or congenital infection across the placenta. Children born with CMV infections may resemble infants with AIDS. Though usually present without symptoms in the adult, CMV can elicit manifestations resembling infectious mononucleosis: fever, lymph node enlargement, fatigue. In the past, cytomegaloviral infections have been a major problem in organ or bone marrow transplant recipients. But, in transplantation as in AIDS, it has been difficult to sort out whether CMV was a major cause or only the result of immune suppression.

Like many viruses, CMV is capable of turning off certain aspects of the host's immune system. This immune suppression is also caused by hepatitis, measles, and Epstein-Barr viruses, and probably even by common live virus vaccines. Whether such repression of the immune system is ultimately more beneficial to the host or to the parasite is unclear. If unchecked, the immune system can go overboard in responding to a perceived threat from infection. The reaction can cause extensive tissue damage. The question is, which is preferable: tissue destruction or runaway infection?

Because of the immunosuppressive potential of cytomegaloviruses, they are thought to be an important factor in the development of AIDS. Some investigators consider CMV a leading candidate for the primary cause of AIDS, and others regard this viral group to be among several contributory factors. Like Herpes simplex viruses, cytomegaloviruses are extremely variable in their genetic makeup, their DNA. Myriad strains of the virus may occur, each with a slightly different antigenic specificity. Because one mode of transmission is through intimate sexual contact via semen, these viruses are spread widely by promiscuity. They are highly prevalent in urban homosexual communities. Studies on the exposure rate among patients seen at VD clinics in the 1960's and 1970's showed that about twice as many homosexual as heterosexual men had evidence of infections with these viruses. This difference is attributable to different patterns of promiscuity in the two groups. In the person who has frequent exposure to a great multiplicity of viruses, it is suspected that repeated infection, each time with a slightly different strain, may occur. For those homosexual men who are highly promiscuous, this represents an essentially constant bombardment with immunosuppressive viruses that could set the stage for, if not actually precipitate, the development of AIDS.

Unlike HSV, which does not seem to become widespread in the body, clinical CMV disease in AIDS patients is manifested by disseminated infection. Pneumonia that resembles and frequently coexists with Pneumocystis carinii is the most easily recognized aspect of active CMV infection in the immunocompromised person. When it affects the lining of the intestine, CMV can be associated with ulceration and severe diarrhea. It can cause progressive infection of the retina, leading to blindness, and it can affect tissues throughout the body in ways not yet fully enumerated.

Epstein-Barr virus is yet another of the herpes group. This type is most familiar as the cause of infectious mononucleosis, an illness common among adolescents, although it can affect people of almost any age who haven't encountered the virus before. Like the other herpesviruses, EBV also doesn't often cause symptoms, and it too has a latent phase. This virus has a predilection for B lymphocytes, cells of the immune system involved in the production of antibodies (the antitoxins and other gamma globulins that normally help fight infections). When EBV enters the body it infects the B cells, greatly stimulating their normal tendency to multiply and make antibodies. Without appropriate controls, these proliferating B cells would quickly form tumors or leukemias.

Human beings have evolved a specialized but efficient control mechanism within their immune system to deal with this virus infection. Other cells, the T lymphocytes, have the capacity to recognize and stop the EBV-induced proliferation of the B cells. In a counterattack, they also multiply and suppress the B cells that are infected with the virus. The symptoms of infectious mononucleosis represent the external manifestations of this internal war between components of the immune system. Eventually, a standoff is reached in which EBV-infected B cells persist in the body in a latent phase but do not proliferate or make antibodies, while the T-cell defenses to the EBV are greatly reinforced. The reaction by T lymphocytes to a threat presented by EBV infections typifies one form of immune response, about which more discussion will follow in the next chapter.

By the age of 40, most people in the United States have acquired the Epstein-Barr virus. Some EBV-infected B cells persist for the lifespan of the individual, usually without causing disease after the initial symptoms. In some other areas of the world, such as equatorial Africa, the population is probably exposed at an earlier age because of climate and sanitary conditions that accelerate disease transmission. Malignant tumors of B lymphocytes, especially Burkitt's lymphoma, usually associated with EBV that they harbor, develop with disturbing frequency in these regions of Africa. Nasopharyngeal carcinoma in China is another EBV-related tumor. These cancers are believed to be uncontrolled outgrowths of cells stimulated by EBV but no longer effectively resisted by T cells and other mechanisms that normally keep the lid on.

Patients with AIDS often behave as if they had a reactivation of EBV. Levels of antibody proteins (gamma globulins) in the blood rise, sometimes dramatically, because B cells in blood and tissues are activated prematurely to produce them. Biopsies of lymph nodes, mentioned earlier, usually reveal a pattern that pathologists associate with chronic stimulation possibly secondary to EBV. This "immunoblastic lymphadenopathy," along with transition to an apparently malignant process called "immunoblastic sarcoma," is seen also in patients with a hereditary disease in which the body selectively fails to cope with EBV-infected cells. In AIDS, the immune defect mimics this serious familial disease. In addition, some homosexual men have now been found to have tumors of B cells that bear EBV and closely resemble African Burkitt's lymphoma. These tumors differ from immunoblastic lymphadenopathy in their morphology and course but they probably reflect a similar lack of T-cell control over EBV-infected cells. Such tumors remain outside of the formal case definition of AIDS, which excludes patients with all lymphomas except those primary to the brain. But, because they occur in a population at risk for AIDS, they are suspected of being related. Their development may be a close parallel to that of Kaposi's sarcoma.

Certain viruses that are not a part of the herpes group also have been opportunistic agents in AIDS. These too are usually benign fellow travelers of mankind, not causing trouble until defenses are down. Adenoviruses are widely distributed in nature and incite acute respiratory infections in many individuals exposed to them. But they rarely lead to serious disease in adults. Outbreaks of respiratory illness among army recruits living in close quarters have been an important public health problem, but death of an adult from adenoviral infections is sufficiently rare to warrant a report to a journal. Patients with AIDS develop chronic and sometimes widespread infections with adenoviruses, though even in AIDS they are not usually lethal. About 35 different types of human adenoviruses exist, and several of these have been recovered from urines or tissues of patients with AIDS. Despite their differences by conventional typing methods, the AIDS-related adenoviruses are very similar in their DNA makeup. They are closely related in their structure to those adenovirus types that have been isolated, in recent studies, in tissue samples from patients who had been immunosuppressed for renal transplantation. Because of the common features of these adenoviruses, they have also been proposed as the possible infecting agent of AIDS.

AIDS patients, like kidney- and bone-marrow-transplant

recipients, have their share of pneumonias for which no specific cause can be identified. Inflammatory processes are seen when biopsy specimens are examined, but no organism is present. These situations generally don't lend themselves to treatment, and are presumed to be viral in origin.

The category to which wart-causing virus belongs, the papovavirus group, is also highly varied. Some related viruses have been implicated in the development of a brain disease in immunosuppresed individuals: progressive multifocal leukoencephalopathy (PML) is chiefly a disorder of the white matter of the central nervous system, characterized by a gradually worsening disturbance of coordination, movement and consciousness. Insidious in onset, the disease is not accompanied by fever or a stiff neck as are many central nervous system infections. PML accounts for only a few of the increasingly frequent organic brain syndromes being associated with AIDS. A larger group of patients has a syndrome of progressive somnolence, depression and brain dysfunction, which to the clinician looks like some form of encephalitis but which in CAT scans, biopsies and even autopsies shows no specific characteristics or viral forms. Some AIDS patients who either avoid or survive more common severe infections eventually succumb to this hitherto unfamiliar brain disorder.

Bacteria

Among the bacteria that cause disease in AIDS patients, avian tuberculosis, the form normally associated with birds, is the leader. Named Mycobacterium avium-intracellulare after its propensity to grow inside cells, this microbe has been detected in a very large proportion of AIDS patients. The inordinate prevalence of this organism among AIDS patients probably indicates that it is far more intimately associated with mankind than we suspected before the AIDS epidemic. Medical information previously available seemed to show that exposure to avian tuberculosis primarily affected people living in the southeastern US. AIDS cases in California and New York, however, have been extensively afflicted by M. avium. Curiously enough, it seems to be less of a problem among Haitians with AIDS than the standard agent of human tuberculosis, Mycobacterium tuberculosis hominis. These differences among the risk groups with respect to opportunistic infections are probably related to their previous exposures. Haitians, for instance, come from a part of the world where active human tuberculosis is much more common than in the United States. Consequently, any Haitian's chance of having been previously infected with Mycobacterium tuberculosis is substantially greater than any American's.

Most people exposed to either the human or avian tubercle bacilli control these bacteria at the time of primary infection. But centers of infection are presumed to remain undetected in but alive within the host. Positive responses to skin tests variously known to health workers as tuberculin, tine, or Mantoux reactions probably reflect the continued viability of these bacterial clusters. Apparently, maintenance of active immunity against tubercle bacilli is essential for the continued inhibition of these organisms. In situations of abnormal immune suppression, such as steroid therapy for control of certain diseases or the profound immune impairment characteristic of AIDS, these foci of infection can become reactivated and the bacteria within them can cause widespread disease.

Mycobacterial infections tend to be chronic and debilitating. They are characterized by profound weight loss, fever and drenching night sweats. The mycobacteria can invade the bone marrow and make their way to almost any organ of the body. Sometimes they cause major swelling of lymphoid tissue, as evidenced on biopsy. Lymph node enlargement in a single area rather than as a generalized reaction often reflects the presence of mycobacteria. This seemingly localized form of tuberculosis has been observed in patients who later develop AIDS, but it can also occur as a truly limited disease amenable to standard drug therapy. When the avian form of tuberculosis affects humans with AIDS, the disease is usually generalized. Occasionally, other types of mycobacteria arise in AIDS and, for the most part, tend to be unresponsive to treatment.

One of the main features of mycobacterial infection in AIDS is the decrease, or lack, of normal inflammatory cell responses to these organisms. Whereas patients with active tuberculosis who do not have AIDS produce a typical cellular infiltrate that a pathologist can recognize as a "granuloma," AIDS patients often fail to do so. Granuloma formation is dependent on the intactness of those components of the cellular immune system that control mycobacterial infection; in their absence, the normally orderly inflammatory response to these infections is lacking, and only non-specific, disorganized reactions take place. This leaves an incredible concentration of bacteria growing unimpeded in the tissues. The microscopic appearance of the tissues in such infections is in some respects similar to that of a form of leprosy in which the immune system is overwhelmed. (Lepromatous leprosy is also characterized by the presence in tissues of mycobacteria without granuloma formation, whereas in the more common, tuberculoid form of the disease, the granulomatous inflammatory process is relatively more effective and fewer bacteria are present.) One of the pitfalls of this atypical manifestation on biopsy in AIDS patients is that the pathologist, observing no granulomas, does not suspect mycobacterial infection and thus fails to do the special stains required to detect the organism. This can lead to a missed diagnosis.

Treatment of the various forms of tuberculosis seen in AIDS is extremely difficult. Despite the availability of drugs that actively inhibit the growth of these microbes in the test tube, the clinical response is slow, even with Mycobacterium tuberculosis hominis. Still more troublesome is the avian form, against which standard antituberculous drugs are less active even in the laboratory. Two recently developed drugs inhibit the Mycobacterium avium-intracellulare and some other atypical (formerly non-human) bacteria now being discovered in AIDS patients. As with most such drugs, they slow the growth of the organisms, thereby permitting effective development of the natural system of defenses —which, of course, is by definition lacking if such organisms could gain a foothold in the first place. The net result is that mycobacterial infections tend to be chronic and progressive despite maximal treatment. This situation illustrates the circular dilemma of AIDS therapy.

In 1976, the outbreak of a deadly pneumonia at an American Legion convention in Philadelphia provoked an intensive effort by investigators at the CDC that led eventually to the identification of a new group of organisms, Legionella pneumophila, named after their victims. These bacteria grow especially well within cells, as do mycobacteria. They too have been found to take advantage of immunocompromised persons, including patients with AIDS. The pneumonia caused by this group of organisms can resemble that caused by Pneumocystis carinii and some of the other opportunistic agents. Unlike those others, though, Legionella probably does not have a longstanding relationship with its victims. It isn't normally present in the environment but is probably picked up from contaminated water or water vapor during a lag in immune defenses. By now at least two different Legionella species have been recognized to cause disease in AIDS patients. Effective, rapid diagnosis depends to some extent on the availability of species-specific antibodies that can detect these organisms in biopsy specimens.

Listeria monocytogenes is another bacterium that likes to live inside monocytes and macrophages (hence its name). Somewhat surprisingly, relatively few patients with the immune defect of AIDS have been affected by listeria species, but it does occur and should be considered to be part of the spectrum of infectious agents causing bloodstream invasion, meningitis and other complications of the disease.

Very few common bacteria seem to cause serious trouble for AIDS patients. One that does is salmonella, which is endemic in animals and is ingested by people through uncooked or tainted foods. Most domestic animals, including pet fish and even turtles, can harbor strains that can infect humans. Salmonellosis usually causes a diarrheal disease, sometimes accompanied by fever and overwhelming fatigue. In one form of salmonellosis, typhoid, the main symptoms are high fever, chills and a rash. Some people infected with salmonella can eventually develop a symptomless coexistence with these organisms. These unsuspecting carriers can pass the infection to others. The susceptibility of homosexual men to diarrheal disorders included under the "gay bowel syndrome" can partially be explained by their exposure to salmonella in feces through oral-anal contacts.

Salmonella share with most other bacteria dangerous to immune deficient patients the propensity to grow inside cells. In addition to causing diarrhea, they can invade the bloodstream. Like all of the bacterial diseases, with the possible exception of severe Mycobacterium avium-intracellulare infection, salmonellosis does not by itself define an AIDS case. The reason for this is that non-immunosuppressed people can also develop infections from these organisms. Salmonellosis seems to be especially prevalent among children who fit the clinical picture of AIDS.

AIDS patients are not safe from bacteria, including pneumococci and staphylococci, that sporadically trouble ordinary persons. They can produce pneumonia, bronchitis and abscesses in almost any part of the body, and are usually more severe than in the person with a basically healthy immune system.

Fungi

Infections with molds, or fungi, are seen in AIDS patients as they are in many others with depressed immunity. Candida albicans, discussed before, is the most frequent fungus to become active in this situation, but it is probably not the most dangerous since it can usually be controlled with antifungal drugs. Such is not the case with Cryptococcus neoformans, which in its form but not its behavior resembles Candida and other yeasts. Cryptococcus is a nasty germ. Although it rarely produces disease, when it does strike it can cause a form of meningitis and encephalitis, an inflammation of the brain and spinal cord. Half of the cases occur in previously healthy people, who apparently catch the infection by breathing it in from the environment. Even though cryptococcosis can be cured with long courses of therapy with toxic drugs, in a majority of cases there is permanent brain damage. In AIDS patients, limited experience with cryptococcosis indicates that the prognosis is far worse than for the average victim without AIDS. The disease is likely to spread outside the nervous system and involve the liver, heart and kidneys. So far, cryptococcal meningitis in severely immunodeficient patients has not responded to any available drugs.

Among other intractable fungal infections in AIDS patients, identified usually at autopsy, are aspergillosis, nocardiosis, and mucor mycosis. One reason that infections with some of these fungi are so devastating for such people is that such invaders are normally countered by the cellular branch of the immune system, the very part that is undermined by perhaps the nastiest of all the germs yet discussed, the elusive agent of AIDS. Others of the fungal infections probably relate more to late immunological or host defense complications of the disease, as it involves phagocytic cells.

Kaposi's Sarcoma

The skin tumor described by Kaposi in 1864 was an indolent, relatively mild process that most often appeared in the elderly. Affecting chiefly Jewish and Italian men in Europe and America, the classical form of the disease has usually involved the skin of the feet and ankles, sometimes the wrists and hands, gradually migrating towards the trunk. In these patients it has been associated with the development of other malignancies, particularly of the lymphoid system. Kaposi's sarcoma is a multicentric disease (one in which individual tumors arise independently at several sites). The lesions are bluish or pink patches, slightly raised above the surface of the skin, generally neither itchy nor painful. In elderly men they eventually coalesce into larger masses, which are more psychologically than medically threatening.

Under the microscope, after appropriate staining of biopsy material, the Kaposi's tumors exhibit a mixture of cell types. Most of the tissue mass is composed of spindle-shaped cells and endothelial cells; these two types seem to be related to normal cells lining blood vessels. Typical of the Kaposi's lesion also are collections of red blood cells throughout the spindle cells, as well as macrophages, large scavenger cells that have ingested breakdown products of red blood cells.

In areas of equatorial Africa, Kaposi's sarcoma is quite common and far more dangerous than it was in Europe and in the United States before the 1980's. The African version has tended to affect young boys and girls and to involve lymph nodes and deeper tissues, such as the lungs and intestine. It progresses much more rapidly in Africa and frequently becomes lethal unless treated. The disease that was recognized in homosexual men in 1979 more closely resembles the African variety than the relatively indolent form known in the West. But, even in the recent version there is a broad clinical spectrum: some patients have an extremely aggressive disease, while others a less troublesome form.

Since the AIDS epidemic, Kaposi's sarcoma has been chiefly a problem of male homosexuals. Relatively few intravenous drug abusers and Haitian entrants, and only rare women with AIDS, have had this manifestation. Hemophiliacs with Kaposi's have not yet been reported. We can probably view this distribution in much the same way we interpret the incidence of Mycobacterium tuberculosis hominis in the Haitians—it is probably based on differing degrees of background exposure to the cytomegalovirus (CMV). Kaposi's sarcoma, like its ostensible parent, AIDS, behaves in some ways like an infectious disease. It is closely associated with CMV and the evidence so far points to a causal relationship.

The work of Italian medical investigators in Africa and the West showed that most patients with Kaposi's sarcoma had evidence of exposure to CMV. This was not so with other viruses studied. Antibodies to CMV were present, but to EBV, Herpes simplex and others (in Europe and the U.S.) they were far less prevalent. The same investigators found that the virus itself would grow out of cultured tumor tissue, and that parts of the CMV genes became incorporated in the genes of Kaposi's sarcoma cells. The implication is that the virus can become latent and later reappear during culture. Thus it might play a role in the development of the skin lesions. As has been mentioned above, CMV has an affinity for endothelial cells that compose a large portion of the Kaposi's tumor. Cancer researchers consider this integration of the CMV genes into the tumor cells highly suggestive of a process that can transform normal cells into malignant ones. Since many homosexual men have a frequent and heavy exposure to CMV as compared to the other groups with AIDS, they would be expected to be particularly prone to the development of Kaposi's sarcoma, provided other predisposing factors, many of them still unknown, were present. The genesis of Kaposi's sarcoma is analogous to the process envisioned in EBV-associated malignancies. The immune defect of AIDS leads to a situation in which the KS agent, normally suppressed even in the individual exposed to CMV, is allowed to flourish.

One way of looking at the relationship between Kaposi's sarcoma and the characteristic infections of AIDS is to regard the tumor as also opportunistic, arising only when the victim is immunologically compromised. Since classic KS occurs with unusual frequency in two ethnic groups, Jews and Italians, the strong suggestion is that genetic factors are involved in the genesis of this peculiar tumor. Indeed, some of these factors have been defined. There are certain structures on the surfaces of cells, known as "histocompatibility," "transplantation" or "HLA" antigens, which determine many immune functions, such as acceptance or rejection of a tissue graft from one individual to another. One of these antigens, HLA-DR 5, was reported to be present in a disproportionately high percentage of Jewish and Italian patients with Kaposi's sarcoma. The relationship of DR 5 and other histocompatibility antigens to susceptibility to KS, or even to AIDS in general, is a controversial area of active research. In gay men who harbor CMV, a major defect of immunity combined with the appropriate histocompatibility antigen seems to constitute a scenario for the development of Kaposi's sarcoma.

There have been a few homosexual men who have developed Kaposi's sarcoma without opportunistic infections. Some of these have fared quite well; they have responded to chemotherapy or other treatments, such as interferon. It's not clear yet how their immune status relates to their favorable prognosis. Most patients with KS, however, have had opportunistic infections by the time the Kaposi's is diagnosed, or have developed them afterwards. These patients have a worse prognosis than those with KS alone.

The skin lesions of Kaposi's sarcoma are so distinctive that they can often be tentatively diagnosed by an experienced physician or dermatologist. However, a biopsy is essential to discriminate Kaposi's from other, somewhat similar skin conditions. When the biopsy is positive, the doctor should determine the extent of the KS. The areas to which KS is known to spread are usually investigated by chest x-rays, lymph node biopsy and fiberoptic endoscopy (in which a special flexible tube is inserted to visualize the internal surface of the intestine, stomach, and esophagus).

Because the current case definition of AIDS includes patients who have KS alone, the prognosis for the disease is variable. Indeed, some men are alive after treatment for Kaposi's that was diagnosed at the beginning of the epidemic. Unfortunately, once the opportunistic infections have gained a foothold, the process seems progressively severe and irreversible: almost all such patients have died within two to three years. About those individuals who have only non-specific symptoms that do not meet the CDC's criteria for AIDS, not even tentative predictions can be made, since some have improved or gone into remission and others have declined. Lack of a definitive test for AIDS makes predictions in any borderline cases impossible. The patient and the doctor must then watch, wait, and hope, for only time will reveal the outcome.

CHAPTER **3**

The Immune System

as Target

Looking back almost four years, it is now possible to put AIDS in some sort of perspective. We have come to realize that for all their apparent variety, the manifestations of the syndrome represent a very limited group of infections and an extremely narrow spectrum of malignancies. A key observation is that almost all the infections seen in AIDS involve microbes which thrive best inside cells rather than in the "outside" world of the serum, the liquid part of the blood. This fact has provided a clue to those investigating the disease process.

For some time, immunologists have known that the body's defense against intracellular parasites—viruses, fungi, mycobacteria or protozoans—is almost entirely controlled by a fairly discrete set of mechanisms called the "cellular" immune system. By attacking this part and, relatively, sparing other aspects of the system, AIDS has left behind a lead for the medical detective, who must search for the defect within an area that has already been narrowed down. Like a scalpel excising a part of this system, AIDS has posed the challenging question: can we identify this missing section of the whole, find the lesion that opens the door for all the resulting afflictions? If so, we can perhaps unlock the door or learn how to close it. In any case, we will understand a little better how the body's defense against these diseases works. Under admittedly trying circumstances, we will have learned the message of nature's deadly experiment.

There are special reasons why AIDS patients have particular problems with intracellular organisms. Antimicrobial drugs are of little value against such infections because they do not effectively get to the parasites. Of the scores of currently available antibiotics, very few can penetrate cells, and their activity is largely limited to attacking the microorganisms after they have destroyed the infected cell and escaped into the tissue fluids, ready to infect another cell. In addition, most antibiotics are only capable of inhibiting the proliferation of microbes, not of killing them outright. Even when certain bacteria or fungi are sensitive to a particular antimicrobial, the drug only slows down the organisms, leaving the immune system to do the actual job of killing and disposing of the bug. It is easy to see why the immunodeficient person, especially one who has a defect in the very branch of the system devoted to this task, should have such difficulties.

A Little History

AIDS is a paradigm of the havoc that results when the delicate balance evolved over millions of years between man and his microbial environment breaks down. This epidemic has reaffirmed just how crucial that balance is to our survival. Nature has provided all animals having a backbone with a survival kit, with a complex of cells and molecules that comprise the immune system. As one ascends the evolutionary ladder from the simplest organisms to the vertebrates, the means of resisting invisible invaders become increasingly sophisticated. In man, the immune system is second only to the brain in power and intricacy.

The capacity of the body to learn to recognize foreign organisms and to mount an effective counterattack the second time around was surmised in ancient times. A remarkable account of the plagues in Athens, written by Thucydides some 24 centuries ago, testifies to what was apparently even then common knowledge. During the epidemics, possibly of typhus or bubonic plague, there were survivors who nursed the sick without being afraid, for, having had the disease before, they knew they would not become ill again once they had recovered. The term "immune" itself derives from a Latin word for a person exempt from public service or taxes, and by extension, someone not susceptible to disease.

Attempts to take advantage of the body's ability to learn from exposure, to induce immunity from a variety of diseases, were made in Europe from the Middle Ages onward. Deliberate inoculation of scrapings from smallpox sores into infants was introduced into England in the early 18th century by Lady Wortley Montague. The wife of the ambassador to Constantinople, Lady Montague had learned of this desperate but sometimes effective means of preventing that dread disease from the Turks, who, in turn, had imported the practice from China. Over the protestations of her advisors, she had apparently protected her own child in this way from smallpox, which killed (according to Voltaire) roughly one third of its victims and devastated the population of Europe.

These immunizing procedures, popularized in the English court of George I, led half a century later to the far less hazardous use of inoculation with cowpox. Edward Jenner, a county doctor, performed a brilliant series of experiments in which he actually adapted an insight gained from English milkmaids. This was the observation that such women frequently contracted a mild disease from cows, cowpox, but were spared the disfiguring or deadly smallpox. Without knowing why the milder disease should confer immunity to the more severe one, Jenner set about proving that protection from smallpox could be provided by inserting pus from a cowpox sore under the skin of a healthy child.

Resisted at first, the practice of vaccination (named after the French word for cow) eventually became widespread. Jenner's procedure for deliberate immunization ultimately led to the eradication of smallpox from the earth in 1980, just about two centuries after its introduction. The English farm girls and Jenner had taken advantage of two important features of immunity: first, that it could be induced by a related but less dangerous disease process; and second, that it had a memory. Jennerian vaccination was a strictly empirical method, based only on observation of epidemiologic patterns. The germ theory of disease was not developed for another hundred years; nor did major advances in immunology occur until a century later.

Although the invention of the microscope had long permitted the observation of a previously invisible world of living organisms, the concept that such germs actually caused disease was by no means easily accepted. It remained for the genius and daring of Louis Pasteur, a French chemist, to demonstrate unequivocally that such was the case. Pasteur, who first proved that the fermentation of wine did not happen without microbes, proceeded to show that numerous diseases of domestic animals and humans were caused by specific organisms. His primary interest was to find a way of preventing these disorders.

Pasteur's greatest discovery, largely due to dogged perseverance in the face of concerted resistance by the medical establishment of his time, was also sparked by serendipity. During a vacation period, one of his associates accidentally left a virulent culture of chicken cholera out on the laboratory bench. After some weeks the forgotten brew was employed in experiments designed to show that the bacteria in the culture given to chickens would cause them to become ill and die. But, to Pasteur's frustration, the material failed to kill the birds as it had before. A fresh batch was tried, but also failed, though it induced fatal disease in animals that had not received the aged material. Pasteur realized that the old culture had been somehow weakened, "attenuated," during its long period of neglect on the bench, retaining the ability to immunize but losing its capacity to kill. His laboratory began to deliberately weaken microorganisms for use as vaccines. These efforts led to the control of anthrax, which had plagued cattle, and culminated in a vaccine against rabies, a uniformly fatal disease in humans.

Pasteur's treatment for rabies was developed before viruses could be seen or cultured. It was based strictly upon evidence, which some would consider circumstantial, that an unseen infectious agent was present in the diseased rabbit spinal cords he dried in order to attenuate the virus. How similar it seems to Jenner's problem with smallpox, or even to ours today, when circumstantial, epidemiologic evidence indicates the presence of an agent of AIDS, but none has yet been isolated. Pasteur's spectacular work eventually led to most modern vaccines, including those against yellow fever, polio and the common infections of childhood. The development of a vaccine, of course, is one ultimate hope of current AIDS research.

Other investigators soon showed that even killed microbes, or their toxic products, toxins, could be used to immunize and prevent disease. But the process was poorly understood at first. A major advance came in the discovery in the 1890s that immunity to the toxins of the organisms causing tetanus and diphtheria lay in serum proteins that could be readily transferred from animal to animal. These neutralizing factors, called antitoxins or antibodies, were believed for a time to constitute the immune system. However, even before the end of the 19th century, great biologists —including Metchnikoff, who discovered phagocytosis, and Koch, who recognized that cellular reactions protected against tuberculosis—indicated that immunity was not just confined to the serum, that cells of various descriptions play a central role in the process.

Non-specific Immunity

The simplest, most primitive form of immunity is nonspecific—that is, not requiring prior exposure to a foreign organism in order to fight it. Even invertebrates possess this type of self-defense. Besides their chief protective organ, the skin, humans are armed with antimicrobial factors in the body fluids, including saliva, tears and semen. Within the blood serum, there exists a series of enzymes known collectively as the complement system. The complement molecules can coat the surfaces of microbes in such a way that they can be swallowed by phagocytes, particle-eating cells. Most of the time, this process is also facilitated by antibodies.

Phagocytes, whose odyssey takes them to every corner of the body, have the ability to ingest and kill microbes. They represent a very old and basic component of the host defense. Reminiscent of amebas, these cells are distributed in various forms in essentially all multicellular animals. Macrophages, as Metchnikoff called them (when he discovered their protective function in starfish), are rather large cells whose outer membrane is constantly being internalized. This allows them to ingest particles that stick to their surface. Before foreign particles, such as bacteria and fungi, can be eaten by the macrophage they must be made palatable by factors known as "opsonins"; in man, these consist primarily of antibodies and complement.

Related to the macrophages, but smaller and more mobile, are other white cells called "granulocytes." These are equipped with a variety of toxic substances stored in tiny sacs, which appear as bright granules in stained microscope preparations. The contents of these granules, mostly enzymes, can digest and eliminate a variety of germs. When they release their contents, the granulocytes self-destruct; but no matter, they are quickly replaceable, produced in great abundance by the bone marrow, where all the cells of the immune system originate.

Phagocytic cells set up shop in various tissues, where they go by different names. The nomad of the blood is the monocyte, which, like most of the other white cells, performs a variety of mopping up functions. When cells die for one reason or another, such as infection or trauma, the monocytes or macrophages engulf the dead cells and other debris. If it encounters offending organisms, the monocyte can often eat them or slow them down by deploying a multitude of enzymes and other substances stored within its granules. Most of the time the monocyte-macrophage can ingest free particles reasonably well by itself, provided that conditions are right. In the normal human body, other components of the vastly complex immune system make certain that conditions for phagocytosis are favorable most of the time. However, the monocyte sometimes encounters microbes that are not easily killed or inhibited. These are the intracellular pathogens that cause so much trouble in AIDS, which for reasons of their own actually flourish in the seemingly inhospitable environment within the phagocyte's body.

Under normal circumstances, phagocytes don't battle against the microbial world alone: they get help from other white blood cells, the lymphocytes, which contribute the "brains" of the immunologic defense.

Lymphocytes

Lymphocytes are a relatively late development in evolution and constitute one of its highlights. In general, vertebrates have such cells, but the lower animals don't. Through a microscope, they are unprepossessing cells with little body. Unlike the monocytes, which have a substantial cytoplasm, lymphocytes are usually not much more than a nucleus. They generally lack granules and can't ingest particles. But they are packed with genetically programmed information and incredibly specialized skills. Almost every lymphocyte is capable of seeking out and recognizing a foreign molecule that has entered the host's body. The substances recognized by lymphocytes as foreign are called "antigens" because they cause the lymphocytes to make "antibodies" in response. And, since it is thought that there is a specific lymphocyte for each separate antigen, the number of potentially different lymphocytes defies the imagination. The job of the lymphocyte is to circulate through the body, looking for "its" antigen, essentially feeling its way by means of receptors, molecules on the cell surface that can catch hold of any antigen around. If it never finds its particular antigen, a lymphocyte can recirculate in the body fluids for years, perhaps for the life of the person it serves.

If, on the other hand, it meets its proper mate, the antigen it was made for, a remarkable series of events takes place. The cell swells up and begins to divide. Its daughter cells and their progeny all have the same receptors, all remain committed to the original antigen. The process gives rise to clones of identical cells that now have multiplied the capability of their precursor many fold. The daughters form an army of cells that can respond vigorously if that antigen ever again enters the body. The immunologic memory that Jenner unknowingly capitalized upon when he immunized farmers with cowpox was retained in invisible armies of cowpox-recognizing memory cells, lymphocytes ready to do battle against a second onslaught of cowpox. Despite their sophistication, lymphocytes can be fooled. Smallpox virus is sufficiently similar to cowpox virus that some of the same lymphocytes recognize antigens on both viruses. So, immunizing in order to expand the clones of cells reacting to cowpox can cleverly induce protection against the more deadly disease.

In swelling and proliferating, lymphocytes release factors that allow them to communicate with other cells. This process is what makes their response an effective one, and it is the source of most of the help the monocytes and macrophages need to kill the bugs they have swallowed. These factors signal the macrophages to become more active, to intensify their mechanisms for overcoming organisms that otherwise would not be killed. Indeed, much of the control of microbes adapted to living in cells rests with this collaboration between the macrophage and the lymphocytes that have receptors for those microbes.

In certain immune deficiency diseases, including AIDS, this process of intracellular communication and cellular response breaks down, with disastrous results. For example, children born with defective lymphocytes, or with an inability to respond to some of the communication molecules, fail to control these organisms. Theoretically, the same sorts of problems could arise if the monocytes, rather than the lymphocytes, were deranged. It is not yet clear whether macrophage function is in itself defective in AIDS; we are currently conducting experiments to explore this question.

Until only about 15 years ago, antibody production and

macrophage activation were the only well studied aspects of the defense against the kinds of infections afflicting AIDS patients. We now know, partly because of AIDS, that resistance to these microbes is an even more complex process than it was thought to be. Our current view of the immune system is built on enormous amounts of effort expended by literally thousands of scientists working with human patients, monkeys, rats, mice, and rabbits, producing mountains of scientific literature. Some of the most important work has depended on the development of technology that has facilitated stepwise advances. Methods such as chromatography, electrophoresis and electron microscopy made possible basic chemical and morphologic observations. The science of immunology itself provided some of the most important tools —the use of antibodies to localize molecules in cells, to isolate agents, and to characterize cells by type.

Antibodies labelled with visible dyes have enabled immunologists to distinguish cells of different groups on the basis of their surface characteristics, or "markers." The labelled antibodies attach only to those cells having a particular surface marker. It was in this way that lymphocytes were initially confirmed as belonging to two broad groups: B and T cells, corresponding to their distinct functions within the lymphoid system. At first, B lymphocytes were identified by the presence on their surface of molecules which represent the antigen receptors. Subsequently, artificial (hybridoma) antibodies were invented which could similarly identify T lymphocytes and even their various subgroups. These identification markers were not just interesting for academic reasons but because they reflected functional categories of cells. T-cell subset markers have played an important role in detecting abnormalities in the blood cells of AIDS patients.

Division of Labor Among Lymphocytes

Although they resemble each other closely, even under the most modern microscopes, various kinds of lymphocytes perform many diverse tasks. Only certain lymphocytes have the capacity to make antibodies; others are specialized to kill cells infected with viruses; and still others to regulate the entire arrangement. Ultimately stemming from a common primitive cell in the yolk sac of the embryo, lymphocytes in man are produced throughout life in the bone marrow. Before they become functional, however, lymphocytes are further processed in primary lymphoid organs. There, under the influence of maturing factors, they become equipped for their preassigned jobs. Those that find their way to the thymus in early life and are persuaded (by factors unknown) to stay there for modification become T (thymus-dependent) lymphocytes.

The cells that are destined to produce antibodies are, in humans, processed in the bone marrow, rather than in the thymus, and travel through the circulation to lymph nodes, tonsils and other lymphoid tissue. It is in the lymph nodes that these different cell types eventually get together for communication. The nodes are the village green where lymphocytes exchange information. Here B lymphocytes receive the message that a foreign substance has intruded, and they set to work by transforming themselves into plasma cells. These are in essence tiny antibody-producing factories, releasing their immunoglobulin products into the serum.

In the 1960's, several creative scientists independently demonstrated that removing the thymus and other central lymphoid organs from animals impaired their ability to carry out specific immune functions. Their work followed up on the discovery that removal of a special organ (called the bursa of Fabricius) from young chickens took away their ability to make antibodies. Since that time, many workers have shown that defects in any of the lymphoid organs or cell groups can produce a variety of specific clinical problems. Patients with inborn or acquired immunodeficiencies can display any number of selective impairments, resulting from insults to lymphoid organs or cells caused by defective genes or by agents that are usually unidentified.

B Cells: Humoral Immunity

The ultimate metamorphosis of the B lymphocyte is the antibody producing plasma cell. The products of such cells are remarkable proteins, immunoglobulins. These molecules are as varied as the cells that generate them, since they are one means by which the immune system specifically recognizes antigens. Immunoglobulins have been found to fall into several classes, each of them having a somewhat different set of responsibilities. The most prevalent form in the serum are those of the G class, IgG. They neutralize toxins and act as opsonins for phagocytic cells (as previously described). This is the only class of immunoglobulins that can cross the human placenta and protect the newborn against dangerous infections.

A more complex type of immunoglobulin molecule is IgM, which protects the bloodstream from incursions by especially threatening bacteria that normally inhabit the intestine or sometimes cause urinary tract infections. For example, such organisms as salmonella are effectively coated by IgM, which in its turn activates the enzymes of the complement system. This reaction attracts phagocytes to the area of infection and enables them to eat the bacteria. IgM is also known to be the B-cell's receptor molecule for binding antigen. It is possible to detect IgM on the surface of B lymphocytes; in fact, this is the chief marker by which B cells are identified when a person's lymphocytes are analyzed, not only for immune deficiency diseases but leukemias and lymphomas as well.

The type of antibody that primarily protects the mucous membranes of the nose, throat, lungs and intestine is IgA. It prevents the billions of microorganisms present in the gut from entering vulnerable interior parts of the body. Amounts of these three major types of antibody in the serum reflect the individual's state of exposure.

In people with normal immune systems, common infections, especially chronic ones, lead to rises in serum immunoglobulin levels. By contrast, certain patients have many severe or chronic infections but immunoglobulin levels fail to rise, and remain low or undetectable; or there is a selective decrease in one of the immunoglobulin classes. Such patients may have one of several immunodeficiency syndromes. A condition known as hypogammaglobulinemia results from an impairment of antibody-forming cells. Its manifestations include frequent or chronic sinus, ear and lung infections. An absence of significant antibody, called agammaglobulinemia, is rare and serious. It can result from a hereditary x-linked birth defect, or, later in life, from a tumor of the thymus gland. Patients with this condition have problems coping with infections of the respiratory tract and sometimes of the bloodstream. Injections of large amounts of gamma globulin, derived from pooled normal serum, usually help to provide such patients with protection.

The discovery that B lymphocytes can respond to a number of stimulants in culture has been extremely helpful in assessing antibody production, since the behavior of B cells in the test tube probably reflects the reaction of lymphocytes to antigens in the lymph nodes, bone marrow and tissues. Patients with B-cell defects fail to effectively generate plasma cells in culture or in life. Interestingly, studies with cultured cells have shown that the fault does not always lie in the B lymphocyte. Plasma cell production, it turns out, is a highly cooperative venture. It is dependent on interactions among various cell types within a culture and presumably also in the individual responding to infection. The maturation of B lymphocytes into fully productive plasma cells is regulated by a complex interplay of "helper" and "suppressor" T lymphocytes, as well as other accessory cells, such as monocytes.

T Cells and Cellular Immunity

One of the troublemakers in AIDS is tuberculosis. It was through study of this disease in the 1890's that the great German microbiologist Robert Koch recognized the importance of cellular reactions in the defense against bacteria. He found that when he experimentally infected guinea pigs, they developed a state of "hypersensitivity" to the tubercle bacillus, M. tuberculosis. He could demonstrate the sensitivity by injecting killed bacilli into the skin of the infected animal. An intense reaction would appear after about two days—a relatively long time compared to the few minutes to hours it took to elicit a skin test involving antibodies. Koch recognized from the delay and from the microscopic appearance of the lesions he caused that they were distinct from other types of immune reactions. With the staining methods he had developed, Koch could see under the microscope that the swelling and redness involved collections of small and large cells having round nuclei. These cells —lymphocytes, monocytes and macrophages, as they were later named—were evidently responsible for the development of the immune reaction, which he called "delayed hypersensitivity." Koch appreciated that the reaction had to do with the animals' ability to resist tuberculosis.

In the 80 years or so since Koch's description of this cellular response, we have developed a better picture of how it protects us from infections like tuberculosis. The skin test, which is widely used by doctors to detect significant exposure to TB, is actually a model of the way immune cells cope with certain kinds of microbes. The physician injects an extract of the germs, containing their antigens, into the skin of the patient, usually on the forearm or back. The material is collected by macrophage-like cells in the skin and held on their surfaces. The ever-wandering lymphocytes filter past until one, carrying the appropriate receptor, finds "its" antigen, and begins to swell with interest. People with normal immunity who have had contact with tubercle bacilli have already developed multitudes of such cells, since they have been "sensitized" by the germs, expanding clones of cells to meet the infection. People who haven't been exposed have only a few cells that will stop and pay attention. The more cells that collect, the greater the reaction that will eventually appear.

The cells first arriving at the site begin to send out messages that excite the interest of many others in the general vicinity. Like sharks attracted to the smell of blood, they swarm towards the antigen. These later cells come in many varieties—monocytes, other lymphocytes, granulocytes, other white cells—and in such quantity that a bump on the skin forms. Sometimes the reaction is so intense that some of the skin cells are actually killed in the process. In contrast, if the person tested hasn't been exposed, the few cells that do appear fail to call in many others, and no reaction can be seen with the naked eye, so the test is considered "negative."

Negative delayed-type hypersensitivity tests can mean either that the person wasn't ever exposed to tuberculosis, or that something is wrong with the antigen-recognition system. AIDS patients frequently have defects in this reaction, even when it is tested with antigens from germs that they are known to have experienced in the past, like mumps virus, tetanus toxoid or Candida albicans. By skin-testing in this way, physicians can assess the integrity of an important component of the host defense.

Role of the Thymus

When immunologists began to study the influence of the thymus on immunity by removing it, they found that delayed skin reactions failed to develop normally. If they excised the thymus from newborn animals, the animals were unable to respond, but if they took the thymus from an adult animal, the skin reactions could develop. From such experiments, they concluded that thymus-dependent cells were involved in the skin reactions. Because the outcome of thymus-removal (thymectomy) depended on when the operation was performed, they understood that cells must go through a process of education in the gland, after which they can perform their duties independently and for a long time.

While adult thymectomy seemed to exert little hardship on animals because the crucial cells had already been programmed, the same operation early in life led to severe illness. Newborn mice deprived of the organ failed to grow as fast as their unoperated siblings; they wasted away and died. Yet if the same animals were reared in an environment free of germs, they could thrive normally. The runted animals suffered from infections, sometimes ones that couldn't be defined, and the thymectomized mice, even if grown in protective custody, had other abnormalities. They would not reject transplanted skin that had been taken from unrelated animals, whereas normal mice would slough off foreign skin within days or at most weeks. Even tumors from other animals would grow in ones whose thymus had been removed early enough. The thymus-dependent lymphocytes ("T cells") obviously had capabilities essential for the integrity of the body in its resistance to infection and to foreign cells. Functioning T lymphocytes are necessary for survival in mice and in men.

As we have gone beyond these early experiments it has been possible to dissect in considerable detail the processes leading to the development of thymus-dependent immunity. The life of a T cell begins in the bone marrow; these early cells are carried into the blood and find their way to the thymus gland, lodged behind the breastbone in front of the heart. Here they become enveloped in the bosom of the large nurturing cells of the gland itself. The factors made by the thymic tissue cells incite changes in the lymphocytes. These hormone-like molecules signal the lymphocytes to undergo a stepwise transformation into mature T cells. The process is a rite of passage during which the T cells learn to discriminate "self" from "non-self." Somehow they learn to tolerate cells properly belonging to the body they protect, while becoming antagonistic to cells that are foreign, including microbes and some cancers.

Suppressors, Helpers and Killers

During this process of maturation into immunological competence, two major types of T cells emerge. Each type has surface proteins that are slightly different from those coating the other. These differences are used as markers by scientists studying the cells, who employ sophisticated reagents (hybridoma antibodies) to discriminate among them. Depending on the laboratory in which they are manufactured, the reagents go by different names, but in general they are regarded as distinguishing two functional groups: the "suppressor-cytotoxic" and the "helper-inducer" subsets. (The suppressors are labelled by the antibodies known as Leu-2 or OKT-8; and the helpers, by Leu-3 or OKT-4). As their names imply, some of the T cells in these two categories exert an influence on other cells to produce a desired effect. The helper cell promotes antibody production by B cells and enhances various other functions; the suppressor cell, in general, dampens these activities, preventing overstimulation. As a whole, the system is an intricate network, in which the two groups hold each other in check. If one or the other gets out of hand, the system goes haywire. Too much suppressor activity can lead to a number of immunosuppressed states. Some aspects of AIDS may reflect such imbalances.

As has been prominently publicized, there is an observed imbalance in the ratio of the T cell subsets defined by monoclonal antibodies, the "helper to suppressor ratio" (OKT-4/8 or Leu-3/2 ratio) in AIDS. Normally, helper cells outnumber suppressor cells by about two to one. In virtually all AIDS patients, this ratio is reversed, so that there is usually a marked predominance of "suppressor-cytotoxic" cells in the blood. Many physicians believe that the immunosuppression in such patients is caused by this abnormal distribution of T cells. However, there are several reasons why we should not jump to that conclusion. Chief among them is that similar changes in T cell subsets can occur transiently or even persist for several months in many other infectious diseases, as for example in CMV infections or in infectious mononucleosis (caused by EBV). Transient shifts in T lymphocyte subsets occur so commonly in apparently normal people with infectious diseases of various types that they are almost certainly a generally occurring physiologic response.

The inversion of the T cell subset ratio that has been found in more than 80% of homosexual men in urban areas probably indicates that they have been exposed to infectious agents such as CMV and EBV. It does not necessarily tell us that they are all harboring AIDS. Whether these changes are reversible after a time if the person alters his lifestyle, reducing his exposure to viral agents or other factors, is not yet known. One reason we do not have the answer to this seemingly obvious question is that the methods for detecting T cell subsets by monoclonal antibodies have only been introduced within the last five years, and were not employed in the study of people now known to be at risk for AIDS until the epidemic began. We know that these changes may last for months, from the relatively few patients who have been followed with these tests since the start of the AIDS epidemic. These homosexual men might be considered to have "early" AIDS, as they have several of the syndrome's immune disturbances, but they do not seem to get worse—indeed some have exhibited improvement in these parameters. They could perhaps have a milder form of the disease, or their cellular imbalance could reflect only exposure to a multitude of other peoples' germs.

Within the suppressor-cytotoxic T cell category are lymphocytes that have the subspecialty of killing other cells. How do they know which cells to target? When viruses penetrate cells, they subvert them to their own purposes. In order to multiply, viruses must borrow the cell's protein-manufacturing equipment and energy supply, which they themselves lack. This need to parasitize cells in order to reproduce characterizes all viruses. Because the virus preempts the cell's metabolism, the cell begins to synthesize proteins that have the earmarks of the virus. Such viral protein molecules show up on the surface of the infected cell. The immune system now notices these new proteins as foreign antigens and begins to mount a response to something it perceives as "non-self." Among the cells called in as hired killers are cytotoxic T lymphocytes with the capability of seeking out and attacking virus-infected targets. They do this by approaching their mark very closely and shooting toxic factors into the vulnerable cell.

Natural Killer Cells

Nature hasn't relied solely on T lymphocytes, which are,

after all, a highly advanced adaptive mechanism, to provide the entire defense against viral infections. Antibodies, for example, can directly neutralize certain viruses, such as polio, when they try to reach the nervous system through the bloodstream. But once viruses reach the relative safety of the infected cell, they are not vulnerable to attack by these mechanisms. In most animals there is a form of natural resistance that does not need prior exposure to a microbe before being spurred to action, but is ready and waiting at all times. Unlike T cells, which depend for their effectiveness on previous experience with particular organisms, and are slow to start their work, natural killer (NK) cells don't require sensitization. They destroy their targets in much the same way that T lymphocytes do, but they aren't as finely tuned and can apparently attack a wide variety of damaged cells. Much of what is now known about natural killer cells has come from recent observations of their activity against herpes viruses, which play such a large role in AIDS. NK cells are frequently impaired in patients with AIDS, particulaly in those who have Herpes simplex virus infections.

The importance of natural killer cells is supported by the fact that their absence in newborn infants coincides with extraordinary susceptibility to overwhelming HSV infection, and that as NK cells begin to appear in the infant, so does the ability to fend off HSV. This is why an active HSV infection in the mother around the time of delivery is so hazardous to the infant. Babies infected with herpes during passage through the birth canal can develop fatal or severely crippling disease since they lack the natural killer cells against the virus. It is crucial for a pregnant woman with HSV to be carefully followed by her obstetrician in order to avoid this disaster, possibly by delivery of the child through Caesarian section. Women who have chronic herpes because they also have AIDS risk transmitting both illnesses to their babies.

Once past the first week or two of human life, natural killer cells against HSV appear in the circulation of all normal children, and the subsequent risk of fatal HSV infection becomes virtually nil. The association between low NK activity and extreme sensitivity to HSV in newborns is a major piece of evidence that these lymphocytes are crucial factors in the cellular bulwark against infectious diseases in people. Children develop this function without exposure to HSV but, significantly, do so only after they have safely left the womb.

Why, though, should these crucial cells not arise earlier? One reasonable speculation is that they might interfere with the immunologic balance that permits mother and fetus to coexist during pregnancy. The fetus is, after all, a bundle of cells that are in part foreign to the woman's body, since half of the baby's genes derive from the father. Therefore, a lowered state of immunity, a kind of immunological truce, must exist between mother and fetus, so that the pregnancy is tolerated and allowed to continue. Perhaps the presence of NK cells in the fetus would threaten this truce. If so, evolution has provided elegantly for the existence of two mutually antagonistic biological functions, both essential for survival of the human species: pregnancy and host defense. The defensive function can develop only after the reproductive job has been completed.

There are several forms of NK cells aside from those involved with controlling HSV. Their activities depend so much on ways in which they are measured in research laboratories that the question has been raised whether they might not be merely a test tube phenomenon rather than an important protective function. The growing knowledge of these cells gained directly from work on blood from AIDS patients will undoubtedly help clarify their role in a short time. Much interest has centered on their possible involvement in the surveillance against malignant cells. It would be particularly valuable to know whether defective NK cell activity is responsible for the development of Kaposi's sarcoma.

Constituting only a small proportion of the white cells in the blood, NK cells are present among lymphocytes that seem to be neither T cells nor B cells. They are found in experimental animals missing a thymus and T cells, and in boys with congenital agammaglobulinemia, who lack B cells.

NK cells differ also in appearance from T or B cells, being somewhat larger and having granules in their cytoplasm. They also lack the surface markers associated with B or T lymphocytes. Consequently, NK cells are generally included among a category known as large granular lymphocytes, LGL. The LGL comprise a fascinating group whose various functions—and existence as an independent type of blood cell—have only been appreciated in the last ten years. They are an important source of the molecules that carry messages among the cells of the immune system. The principal message-bearing factor they seem to make is alpha interferon.

Interferons

Interferons are a class of natural antiviral substances apparently produced by all cells. They have been subclassified into three main types, depending on their source. Interferon "alpha" derives from LGL; "gamma," from activated T lymphocytes; and "beta" from most other cells. These molecules serve a dual function. They were initially recognized as stimulating an "antiviral state" in cells they contact, preventing further viral reproduction and infection of new cells. More recently, we have learned that interferons function, along with a number of other polypeptides, to enable cells of the immune system to communicate with one another. Alpha interferon, for example, can activate NK cells, augment the killing of intracellular pathogens by macrophages, and intensify the action of cytotoxic T cells. All these immune effector cells would probably work less efficiently if some of the large granular lymphocytes failed to make interferon.

In a large series of AIDS patients we studied (in collaboration with Dr. Carlos Lopez and his group at Memorial Sloan-Kettering Cancer Center), we found that blood cells from AIDS patients with opportunistic infections produced very low levels of alpha interferon, as compared to cells of normal individuals. However, in patients having only Kaposi's sarcoma, without severe infections, the production of this type of interferon was normal. It seems that a breakdown in the ability of LGL to generate alpha interferon is a specific deficiency in the natural defense system that is closely associated with predisposition to infections but not, apparently, necessary for the development of Kaposi's sarcoma. An interesting related finding was a longer survival among patients with just KS (whose cells usually manufacture interferon) than among patients with both KS and opportunistic infections (whose cells generally fail to make interferon alpha). The complex relationship between susceptibility to the opportunistic infections of AIDS and cellular immunity may well rest on these abnormalities of alpha interferon production, which further efforts are needed to clarify this issue.

Other workers have described high levels of circulating interferons that resemble alpha in patients with AIDS, as well as in some unrelated diseases. Of special interest is the finding that relatively well gay and hemophiliac patients who had especially elevated levels of interferon in their blood later developed either Kaposi's sarcoma or opportunistic infections. (Many others had moderately increased amounts of interferons but didn't seem to get ill). Extremely high serum levels may prove to be an important early warning of serious trouble ahead. This phenomenon is being actively investigated as a possible test to distinguish, among those with "prodromal" symptoms, patients who will eventually develop fullblown AIDS. The curiously discrepant abnormalities of low production (by cells in the test tube) and high serum levels in the same patients present a paradox that is so far not understood. Unlike alpha interferons, gamma interferons are produced fairly normally by AIDS patients' cells. Among the questions that still need much exploration is whether the different interferons have different functions in the containment of disease.

Interpreting the Immune
Deficiency in AIDS

Analysis of the immune system in patients with severe infections was done in several medical centers early in the AIDS epidemic. In such very ill people, almost every facet of immunity seemed to be impaired or altered. Perhaps this should not come as a surprise, considering how intertwined the various immune cells and their functions are. The web of immunity is so complex that disturbances of one cell type must certainly affect others, so that, for example, failure of LGLs to produce alpha interferon would be expected to seriously affect the body's ability to mount a T killer cell response to viral infection. Sorting out these changes to find the one that is really at the root of the problem has become a fulltime occupation for some immunologists.

Because there is currently no specific test for AIDS, clinicians trying to establish a diagnosis before infections or tumors arise must try to define the function of the immune system as well as possible. A number of laboratory tests are in use on a tentative basis that seem helpful, but they must be interpreted carefully in the context of the whole patient. Some, like the skin tests for delayed hypersensitivity, the T cell subset ("helper to suppressor") ratio, and interferon alpha production, have already been discussed. Others, based on abnormalities found in the relatively limited number of cases fitting the CDC's definition, are being studied as well.

A general shortage of lymphocytes of all types (lymphopenia) is common among AIDS patients, especially those in advanced stages of the disease. It is not yet clear why this occurs. One of our own conjectures is that the unidentified AIDS agent, presumably a virus, attacks a lymphoid stem cell in the bone marrow, damaging its capacity to proliferate. We do know that the ability of lymphocytes to multiply when stimulated with standard activators, known as mitogens, is often severely diminished in AIDS patients. In general, as their infections progress, their lymphocyte proliferation in response to these stimulators declines. For this reason, a panel of mitogens (usually including phytohemagglutinin, concanavalin A and pokeweed mitogen), each capable of stimulating a slightly different group of cells, is used to test a patient's lymphocyte function.

Together with B and T cell markers, mitogen stimulations comprise an essential part of the laboratory workup to determine whether a person has AIDS. However, about 10% of AIDS patients who have opportunistic infections and a sizable proportion of those with Kaposi's sarcoma have normal mitogen responses and even more have normal lymphocyte numbers when the diagnosis can first be made. Unfortunately, the normal values almost always deteriorate once opportunistic infections become fully established.

For many years, clinicians have used delayed hypersensitivity skin tests as a measure of cell-mediated immunity. The patient who could make a delayed hypersensitivity reaction had the necessary cells to complete the entire arc of immunity from antigen recognition to the generation of an inflammatory reaction. To our surprise, as with the mitogen responses and lymphocyte counts, some very ill patients with AIDS have been able to make satisfactory skin responses. So, none of these tests has been invariably useful as an index of AIDS.

Other functions of T cells have been studied to a more limited extent and most, such as the development of cytotoxic cells, their ability to help in antibody formation, and to proliferate when confronted by other people's cells, have been impaired in AIDS. Interestingly enough, despite the relative or absolute predominance of cells having markers of "suppressor-cytotoxic" T cells, they do not appear to act as especially strong suppressors of normal T cell activities. The exact functions of the few T cells remaining in the blood of patients with AIDS aren't known.

Explanations for the progressive T cell depletion seen in AIDS are not easy to come by. Some patients have antibodies in their blood that react against and could destroy lymphocytes, but they are not universally detectable and are of uncertain significance. It has been reported that T cells and monocytes from some AIDS victims work together to release a factor that inhibits helper T lymphocyte functions. Morphologic abnormalities of the thymus have been noted, and some workers have suggested that a thymic defect could lead to severe immunodeficiency. This last idea flies in the face of a fair amount of experience in other diseases, such as myasthenia gravis, in which deliberate adult thymectomy has been done for years without incurring the sort of severe immune deficiency seen in AIDS. It seems therefore unlikely that an acquired thymic defect would lead to AIDS if thymectomy doesn't do so.

Actually, conflicting data have emerged concerning changes in thymic factors in AIDS. The hormones that play so important a part in the maturation of lymphocytes in the thymus can be detected in the blood under normal conditions. Several specific proteins have been isolated from the thymus gland which are capable of inducing subtle changes in immature thymic lymphocytes paralleling normal maturation. Apparently the gland is active in producing these hormones in considerable amounts until around the age of thirty, when a gradual decline begins.

In some cases of AIDS and of its prodrome, some of the hormones, especially that known as thymosin alpha-1, are unusually elevated in the blood, while others, notably "facteur thymique serique" (serum thymic factor), are depressed. What these disparate results signify needs clarification. It was initially hoped that measurement of the thymic hormones could eventually become a useful index of disease, perhaps even a relatively specific test for AIDS, since assays for them are fairly simple to perform. Unfortunately, follow-up analysis seems to indicate far too many normal values in patients having AIDS, and too many abnormal ones in patients who don't have the disease. In addition, lysozyme, a product of active macrophages, and beta-2 microglobulin, a substance released by the destruction of cell membranes, are often increased in patient urine or in blood. However, as with the thymic hormone tests, measurements of these are not specific for AIDS alone, nor are they abnormal in all AIDS cases.

B cells of AIDS patients continue to make immunoglobulins in large amounts, and the clinical syndrome of anti-body deficiency that occurs in agammaglobulinemia is not often seen in adult patients with AIDS. Nevertheless, challenge of the immune mechanisms by an antigen never before encountered seems to result in either minimal or absent antibody responses, perhaps because helper T cells, not sufficiently available, are especially needed when new antigens are presented. It seems likely that Epstein-Barr virus is partially responsible for the massive overproduction of immunoglobulins sometimes accompanying the disease. Extraordinarily high levels of antibodies to EBV itself are detected sometimes in AIDS.

The effects of EBV may account for other immunological changes seen in AIDS. B cell proliferation induced by the virus may inhibit normal B cell responses to antigens and participate in the depression of specific antibody formation. In addition, uncontrolled B cell proliferation may be the original stimulus that leads to the tumors of B lymphocytes occurring in homosexual men and thought to be related to AIDS, such as Burkitt's lymphoma and immunoblastic sarcoma.

The seemingly uncontrolled antibody production in the disease is associated with the circulation of "immune complexes," aggregates of immunoglobulins that are assumed to be binding some antigen. These complexes can interact with cell surfaces, as can some antibodies, known as "autoantibodies." Directed, ironically, against antigens that are usually part of the "self," autoantibodies can be damaging to the person whose own plasma cells produced them. Autoantibodies and immune complexes that attach to red cells, lymphocytes, platelets (small cells involved in blood clotting) and granulocytes all participate in the destruction of these blood components and thus complicate the lives of patients by making them anemic, still more susceptible to infection, or likely to bleed into the skin and other sites. In this way, B cell abnormalities can have important clinical implications in AIDS.

The prolonged incubation period for the disease is often greeted with astonishment, and has led to speculation about the possible role of "slow viruses" in its genesis. An understanding of the nature of immune cells, however, suggests that the human defense system itself is the prime source of the delay. Lymphocytes have a very long life in the body. T cells, at least, and probably the others as well may survive for the life of the individual. If irreversible damage to the bone marrow, thymus, or some stem cell occurred at a particular time, its effects would not show up as susceptibility to infection until the supplies of mature lymphocytes already in the blood at the time of damage were nearly exhausted. This might take months or years, depending on the rate of obsolescence of these long-lived cells. Our experience with periodic observation of homosexual men who have made the transition from prodrome to overt AIDS seems to support the concept that the disease does indeed involve a gradual loss of immunocompetent cells. An intense effort has begun in several research laboratories to understand this depletion. Solving the mystery of the insidious disappearance of cells would constitute a major step towards reversing the disease.

CHAPTER 4

Epidemic: Who, What, When, Where, How?

Since its mysterious debut in our society about four years ago, AIDS has claimed about 2,500 victims; more than a thousand are dead already. Its rampage continues at a relentless pace as the number of cases doubles every six months, with no letup in sight. Tragically, the overall mortality rate has been around 45%, and no patient with opportunistic infections has survived beyond three years. Although seemingly discriminatory in that it selects primarily gay men, AIDS is not an intrinsically homosexual disease. It has affected men, women and even children by the accident of its epidemiology. And it has not been racially exclusive, attacking whites and blacks and a variety of ethnic groups.

Although the vast majority of the cases have occurred in New York and California, most of the other states in the U.S. have reported instances of the syndrome. In 44 states, AIDS is now a notifiable disease. Doctors and hospitals are required by law to report all new cases to the state health authorities, who, in turn, pass on the information to the Centers for Disease Control in Atlanta. Cities in more than 20 countries of Europe, Puerto Rico, South America and elsewhere in the world have also had patients with AIDS. A formal European group for AIDS surveillance is also being organized, with the aim of developing a uniform system of recording data from diverse countries. All these new mech-

AIDS CASES BY QUARTER YEAR SYMPTOM ONSET

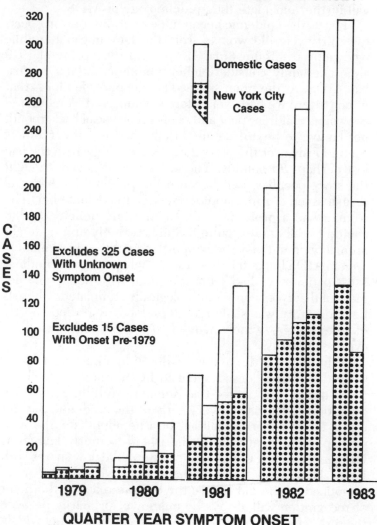

Domestic Cases

New York City Cases

Excludes 325 Cases With Unknown Symptom Onset

Excludes 15 Cases With Onset Pre-1979

CASES

1979   1980   1981   1982   1983

QUARTER YEAR SYMPTOM ONSET

09.14.83

anisms should help to generate more accurate statistics that will further elucidate the epidemiology of AIDS.

For us the epidemic began imperceptibly. In retrospect, the thirty-year-old woman from the Dominican Republic who came to Mount Sinai Hospital in the Spring of 1979 almost certainly, considering her symptoms and her origins, had AIDS. At the time, she had an inexplicable illness that fit no pattern we had ever before encountered. A mother of two young children, poor and of uncertain social background, not known to be a drug addict, she had had fever almost continuously over the preceding year, during which she had lost perhaps 30 pounds. The attending physician thought the story peculiar, and because the patient also had oral thrush asked our immunology service to evaluate her. The woman had a profound cellular immune deficiency that couldn't really be explained. She had the lymph node abnormality, immunoblastic lymphadenopathy, now commonly seen in AIDS but at the time a seemingly paradoxical finding. Most patients we had seen until then with nodal enlargement of that type were immunologically stimulated, whereas her immunity was strikingly depressed. She died shortly of pneumonia, which proved to have been caused by cytomegalovirus.

Why begin a discussion of the epidemiology of AIDS with a case that doesn't seem to fit the mold? Chiefly to point out at the outset that someone fulfilling the case definition and surfacing very early in the epidemic was not gay, a drug abuser, a Haitian, or a hemophiliac. She was, perhaps significantly, from the island formerly known as Hispaniola, which the Dominican Republic now shares with Haiti. How many patients there were who slipped away unnoticed as she did before the disease reached the point of recognition will always be unknown, primarily because the sort of immunologic workup she received was not widely available to people of her background of poverty. At the time, most doctors wouldn't even have thought to inquire about the state of her immunity. "Probably some rare tropical fever" would have been the usual extent of the speculation. But the lessons of this case are instructive when considering the epidemiology of AIDS.

Epidemiology encompasses the who? what? when? where? why? and how? of disease. It is the study of the spread of diseases, and of how particular agents cause specific illnesses. Traditionally, epidemiology dealt with communicable or infectious diseases like plague, cholera, measles, malaria and yellow fever. The practitioners of this medical specialty were the detectives who sought out the wells from which cholera spread in London, who recognized that rats and their fleas transmitted the Black Death, who discovered, sometimes through the ultimate personal sacrifice, that yellow fever was carried by *Aedes aegypti* mosquitos. In more recent times, especially as many of the questions surrounding clearly infectious diseases were adequately answered, the epidemiologists turned to other issues, such as investigating the risk factors involved in various cancers, the development of coronary artery disease, stroke, Hodgkin's disease, and other afflictions of humanity. The association of Kaposi's sarcoma with cytomegalovirus is really the result of such a perspective.

As with many other diseases before it, the first real understanding of how to prevent and control AIDS has come from the study of its epidemiology. Before the germ theory of disease, Lady Montague and Edward Jenner began the control of smallpox by immunization. Their efforts were based solely on epidemiologic considerations. In England, Dr. John Snow halted a cholera epidemic by capping the wells whose tainted waters carried the disease, long before anybody had heard of *Vibrio cholerae*, its causal agent. The message from history is that we don't necessarily have to know the exact cause of a disease in order to control it. It is sometimes enough to know its epidemiology.

What is an epidemic? Is AIDS really an epidemic disease? According to the classical definition, an epidemic exists if a large proportion of a group of people is affected by a particular disease. More recently accepted criteria for epidemic disorders, however, merely require that the incidence of a particular disease significantly exceed what has previously been experienced by the community. Epidemic diseases are, therefore, outbreaks occurring in a limited time and place, and among a limited group of people. Pandemics, like the influenza of 1918, are epidemics that can involve just about everybody all over the world.

In contrast, endemic diseases are those that persist in a geographic area or population group over long periods of time and involve essentially constant numbers of people. When circumstances change, endemic diseases can turn into epidemics: bubonic plague is endemic to particular areas of the world, such as India or the Southwestern United States, involving small numbers of individuals every year. If local conditions favor increases in the rodent (and flea) population, the number of human cases of plague may rise significantly, constituting an epidemic. Plague isn't seen in New York City, except for isolated cases brought in from other areas. Consequently, even a few cases of the disease developing in, say, the South Bronx, especially if they were considered to have resulted from transmission by rats, would constitute an epidemic.

Epidemic diseases don't have to be infectious or communicable. Coronary artery disease, lung and breast cancer have been regarded as epidemic in our society by many health authorities; lung disease caused by asbestos exposure has been epidemic among former shipyard workers. Legionnaires' disease, though caused by a bacterial infection, was apparently not spread from one person to another—it is infectious but not communicable. Unfortunately, current epidemiological evidence points to AIDS as being both infectious and communicable, although not highly contagious.

AIDS certainly meets the definitions of an epidemic disease. Like hepatitis B, its spread seems to be restricted largely to people who come into direct, close contact with one another. Hepatitis B, caused by a known virus, has been a national epidemic for some time. Like AIDS, it is not a disease that just anybody gets; it is limited to those who are directly exposed through intimate, usually sexual, activity or blood infusion. It isn't spread casually through the air or via food or water. There appears to be little danger to those who don't have intimate or blood contact with its carriers. The epidemiology of AIDS is in many respects similar to that of hepatitis B, and since that virus is now quite well understood, the similarity between the two diseases has provided a handle for epidemiologists and other scientists in searching for the AIDS agent.

If AIDS existed at all in the temperate zones before about 1978 or 1979, the syndrome must have been so subliminal as to be unrecognizable. A review of medical literature before then has yielded occasional cases that could fit the current definitions of the disease. In Europe in 1976 and 1977 a few persons who had lived in equatorial Africa developed illnesses that in retrospect were almost certainly AIDS. It's reasonable to believe that a few cases of AIDS were cropping up sporadically, unappreciated for what they represented, perhaps for years. But around 1978, something mysterious happened that altered the situation and led to the current outbreak. A puzzle for the epidemiologist is to discover what that event was. Most of us working in the field now believe that an infectious agent was introduced from endemic areas elsewhere into communities not exposed to it before, immunologically unprepared to cope with it, and capable of facilitating its rapid transmission from person to person in ways not previously common for that agent. This led to the conversion of a very low-frequency event into an epidemic.

The identification of AIDS as an entity, a disease one could describe and name, is the result of two factors: that it occurred within a readily recognizable group of people, and that doctors share with one another tales of their interesting cases. A dermatologist from New York and another from San Francisco realized, while discussing their patients, that they were both finding young gay men with Kaposi's sarcoma; an immunologist at one New York City medical center described his incredible case of ulcerative herpes to a colleague specializing in infectious diseases at another institution, who happened to have an almost identical case. In this way, a few peculiar cases became a syndrome.

Who Has Been Affected?

Homosexual Men

One of the few indisputable facts about AIDS is that it affects primarily young male homosexuals. Nearly 95% of all AIDS cases have been men between the ages of 20 and 49. Although the statistics vary somewhat with shifts in case reporting and changes in lifestyle in response to publicity about the disease, more than 70% of AIDS victims are gay or bisexual. Since homosexuality has been practiced thoughout recorded history, the obvious question about the AIDS epidemic is: why has it happened now? And since there are homosexuals in virtually all areas of the world, with sizable gay populations in many urban centers, why did the disease break out in the United States, initially in two communities a continent apart?

The Kinsey report bears testimony that homosexuality was a part of life in the United States well before the gay liberation movement of the 1960's and 1970's. There are historical references to homosexual activity in the colonial period. Currently, the number of practicing homosexuals in the U.S. is estimated at more than 10 million, but this figure can't be easily verified because of the social stigma that still limits disclosure of homosexual activity. Gay communities thrive in most major cities in the U.S., yet the disease appeared first in the coastal centers of gay life. Even now, about half of all AIDS cases occur in New York City, which has the world's largest gay population, followed by San Francisco and Los Angeles. A look at the time course during which the disease has appeared in the other urban centers indicates that AIDS seemed to have its center in these three cities, and to have spread thereafter to the other communities. It is the impression of some immunologists in Houston, Denver, Chicago, Dallas and other cities throughout America that, once alerted by reports of the disease, they started to see gay patients with just adenopathy and, only later, patients with the fullblown syndrome. These clinical observations suggest that the disease was at first introduced into the coastal cities and later spread from there to the heartland. European physicians began to see cases of AIDS as well; those first patients had all apparently had sexual contact with men from the U.S.

Before growing evidence forced us to concentrate on the infectious aspects of AIDS, efforts to figure out the reasons for the timing of the outbreak centered on identifying recent changes in sexual or social features of the gay lifestyle that put homosexuals at a special risk of acquiring opportunistic infections and Kaposi's sarcoma. The most important risk factor identified at first was promiscuity, often facilitated by the relatively recent commercial promotion of gay sex in the form of bathhouses and backroom bars. These settings permit open solicitation of sexual activity with multiple anonymous partners, which greatly enhances the likelihood of disease transmission.

Gay men statistically have a far greater number of sexual contacts than heterosexuals, and they are much more likely than straight men to have intimate relations with unfamiliar partners. Since lesbians have not been afflicted by AIDS in any significant numbers, homosexuality *per se*, as a psychological preference or a moral issue, doesn't seem relevant. Probably the most important factor discriminating between gay men and lesbian women is the lack of sexually transmitted diseases, in general, among the latter group, reflecting marked differences in patterns of exposure.

Moreover, the physical practices of gay men as distinguished from those of lesbians or of heterosexuals must be regarded as playing a role in acquiring and transmitting disease. Active or passive anal sex, including anilingus and fist fornication, were reported to be associated with increased risk. But it is also possible to contract AIDS by conventional intercourse between the sexes: a recent study reported a number of female partners of AIDS victims who themselves came down with the disease. In addition, one or two female prostitutes—surprisingly few so far—have been described as having AIDS. Most female prostitutes who have had AIDS have also been drug abusers. Because of the reporting system, they are classified as addicts. The coexistence of two potential risk factors makes positive identifiction of the more important one impossible at present.

At the beginning of the epidemic, when clues were eagerly sought about differences between the gay and straight life-styles that might indicate the key to the cause, it appeared that such "recreational" drugs as amyl and butyl nitrites might be the lead. These inhalants, popularly known as "poppers" or "rush," have commonly been used by gay men, as well as some heterosexuals, both to achieve a "high" and to relax the anal sphincter muscle so as to facilitate penetration during anal intercourse. Available legally in many forms, as liquid incense, room odorizers, or vapors for snorting, such volatile liquid nitrites are among the most popular substances used by homosexual men.

Little is known about the effects of volatile nitrites on the human immune system; in experimental animals, nitrite exposure was found by the CDC to have no detectable immunosuppressive activity. Limited studies conducted with homosexual volunteers who were regular users indicated they experienced some immunosuppression; these results, however, were not entirely confirmed by other investigators. And as experiences of physicians with AIDS patients widened, we began to encounter some homosexual victims of the disease who hadn't used such stimulants at all.

The Centers for Disease Control conducted a study to unravel the exposures that might predispose certain men to the development of AIDS. The concept of the study was to compare a group of homosexual AIDS patients with a randomly selected group of healthy gay men of similar age and socio-economic background. They found, through use of a questionnaire, which, among other issues, examined drug use, that AIDS patients did employ significantly more drugs than AIDS-free gay men. But the increased use of nitrites in the AIDS-affected men couldn't be separated statistically from their greater frequency of anonymous sexual partners.

In fact, the one most important difference that did emerge from the CDC "case-control" study was that AIDS victims were, on the whole, more promiscuous than the average gay male. Having sex with more than 60-100 different partners in a year was found to be closely associated with a higher risk of contracting AIDS. Promiscuity itself, however, could not be regarded as a sufficient explanation for the appearance of the disease. Physicians who specialize in caring for AIDS patients number among their cases some who were not particularly promiscuous. In fact, there are situations in which the AIDS victim was the monogamous member of a gay couple, while the other partner, not overtly diseased, had had sexual encounters outside the main relationship. By this means, the healthy but non-monogamous partner had carried the deadly strain to his mate.

Despite these exceptional cases, the association between multiplicity of sexual partners and AIDS does indicate that an individual's chances of contracting the disease are increased by exposures to more and more people, one of whom may be infected. Simply put, it's a matter of chance, combined with a susceptibility factor that is not yet understood. A person can be unlucky and pick up the disease from one infected partner, who may be only a carrier, or he might never come in contact with the pertinent infective agent. Obviously, with increasing numbers of different partners, one's chances are increased. Promiscuity does not cause AIDS, but it certainly promotes its spread. In that sense, it is like any sexually transmissible disease. The case-control study emphasizes this point, since the development of AIDS is correlated with other venereal diseases. It is clear, not only from gay patients but from the other risk groups as well, that the crucial element in transmission is exposure.

Intimate sexual contact appears to be the chief way of spreading AIDS among homosexuals. Whether anal intercourse is an especially important factor is currently under debate. The CDC's case-control study didn't reveal it to be a clearcut risk factor, but other investigations suggest it may be important. A number of AIDS victims are primarily the passive partners in anal intercourse, but the extent and importance of their contact with other bodily secretions and excretions is extremely difficult to evaluate. The mucous membranes of the rectum in gay men are frequently traumatized and inflamed. Some engage in "fisting," in which a partner's fist is pushed into the anus and the rectum. Many have a history of multiple, recurrent bacterial, protozoal and viral infections of the gastrointestinal tract, including shigellosis, amebiasis, giardiasis and salmonellosis. The genital and anal surfaces in homosexual males often show effects of many sexually transmitted diseases, including herpes, syphilis, gonorrhea, non-specific urethritis and venereal warts. The prior damage to these surfaces may actually facilitate entry of an agent of AIDS. How much oral contact among people through kissing, anilingus ("rimming") or fellatio is involved in passing on the disease is still basically unknown.

In searching for theories to explain the incidence of the disease among gay men, one early concept was that the immune system was overloaded by the constant barrage of foreign antigens represented by the various organisms introduced during gay sex. It was suggested that the mucous membranes of the rectum and gastrointestinal tract were not adapted by evolution to withstand the onslaught of myriad new microbes and other substances. This repeated exposure to foreign organisms, it was argued, produced the immune suppression which was recognized as AIDS.

Although the concept that immunological overload causes AIDS has not been absolutely disproven, its validity has been seriously undermined by the emergence of the syndrome among non-homosexuals, particularly among young children and recipients of blood transfusions. Mere promiscuity as the cause also couldn't explain, in a community in which it had been a way of life for years, the sudden appearance of this new disease, nor could it be squared with the gross differences in attack rates for AIDS in different cities that have active gay communities.

Other red herrings complicated the issue while AIDS was still considered a disease limited to homosexuals. It was hypothesized that sperm, possibly entering the circulation through small openings in the rectal mucous membranes during anal sex, has an adverse effect on the immune system. This notion is based in part on the finding of antibodies to sperm in the blood of some homosexual men, which also seemed to react with T lymphocytes. Anti-sperm antibodies might inadvertently attack a person's own T cells and lead to a T cell immune deficiency. But women who have similar antibodies, sometimes associated with fertility problems, don't get AIDS, and many AIDS victims, as it turns out, don't seem to have such antibodies at all.

Social patterns of homosexual men are a key to the transmission of AIDS. Needless to say, since sexual activity of gay men is largely limited to other gay men, the spread of AIDS has been fairly confined to that community. However, bisexual men with AIDS are potentially capable of spreading the disease to females. A number of wives or female partners of bisexual (or drug-abusing) AIDS patients have either contracted the disease or have exhibited immunological changes suggesting exposure. Gay men who travel widely have transmitted the disease not only to previously unaffected communities within the U.S. but also abroad to such countries as France, Switzerland, Denmark and even Australia. The fact that many countries, such as Japan, have numerous homosexuals but as yet no reported cases of AIDS, indicates that their intercourse, social and literal, with American gays has not been extensive enough to lead to AIDS. By contrast, the travel of homosexuals to Haiti, a popular vacation spot of gay men, now appears to be a crucial link in the epidemiology of the syndrome.

One of the most telling observations favoring AIDS as a communicable disease centers on clustering of cases. Several examples are now known in which groups of men who had identifiable contacts, rather than anonymous ones, could track the deadly march of the disease through their ranks. In one instance reported by CDC, possibly 18 or more cases of AIDS were traced to one peripatetic individual. Of a close-knit group of 19 men who shared houses in a gay beach resort over 5 years, at least four have developed the disease. These men generally restricted their sexual contacts to one other partner but, nevertheless, had intimate exposure to others in the group from time to time. The attack rate in this cluster, a remarkable one out of five, is far greater than that observed, for example, in the gay precincts of San

Francisco. The factors responsible for such a high incidence in some circumstances are not yet understood.

Intravenous Drug Abusers

Intravenous drug abusers, especially those who share needles, comprise about 15-20% of AIDS victims. Most of these are young men, and some, at least, are probably either homosexual or bisexual. A number of AIDS patients are prisoners and have the dual risk factors of homosexual activity and drug abuse. Most prisoners who have had the disease probably acquired it as heterosexual drug abusers before their incarceration, though developing symptoms once behind bars. Of the relatively few women who have had the disease so far (females comprise about 5% of all AIDS cases), more than half were IV drug users. The majority of drug abuse-related cases are also from New York City or New Jersey; significantly, until very recently, there were few, if any, victims of AIDS among drug addicts on the West Coast. This discrepancy isn't understood, but it may relate to the socio-economic status of heroin and other intravenous drug abusers, which is generally different from that of homosexual men who are not addicts. Their travels are certainly much more limited. Therefore, a drug addict from New York is not very likely to share a contaminated needle with one from San Francisco. Drug abusers in the West may not overlap as much with the gay community as they do in New York City.

Interestingly enough, a substantial proportion of drug-related AIDS cases have emerged not from the addict population so much as from those who intermittently use drugs for social or personal reasons. Many of these individuals obtain their illicit drugs through the more-or-less openly commercial ventures known as "shooting galleries." Often at storefront locations in run-down neighborhoods, shooting galleries offer their clients a variety of drugs as well as the necessary equipment for their injection. Heroin, cocaine and "speed" (amphetamines) are supplied in a prefilled syringe. After the needle is used it is usually returned to the dealer, who refills the apparatus for his next customer. The needle may see the inside of upwards of 50 different veins in the course of an evening, and bloodborne diseases can thus be spread to as many victims at the same time. For drug abusers, the shooting gallery can have the same effect as the bars and baths have for the gay community—the creation of a deadly chain letter. The patrons in these commercial drug parlors seem to run a greater risk of acquiring AIDS than true addicts, who may share their needles among fewer people.

The manifestations of the disease in both male and female IV drug abusers, including opportunistic infections and Kaposi's sarcoma, have been generally similar to those of the homosexuals, but they have occurred in slightly different patterns. Among drug users, Kaposi's sarcoma has been much less frequently a part of the AID syndrome than among gays. The epidemiologic significance of this requires explanation. It may be that some factor essential to the development of Kaposi's sarcoma is more prevalent in the gay community than it is among addicts. The known relationship between Kaposi's sarcoma and the cytomegalovirus provides an important clue. CMV exposure in the gay community is almost universal; evidence points to repeated infection, probably by multiple viral strains, each contributed by a different partner. This favors the possibility that gay men might acquire a Kaposi's sarcoma-producing strain of the virus, which perhaps happens less frequently among drug addicts. But the phenomenon isn't really understood.

Haitians

About the time AIDS was first recognized among gay men and drug addicts, physicians in the major city hospital in Miami, Florida began to see Haitian immigrants who had peculiar opportunistic infections. At first, the young Haitian refugees were thought to have severe tuberculosis, but alert pathologists realized that brain toxoplasmosis, an extremely rare disease in adults, had killed these patients. Strong similarities began showing up between the Haitians and the previously reported groups—the spectrum of opportunistic infections, as they became better appreciated, resembled that in homosexual men. Kaposi's sarcoma appeared in a few Haitians; and their basic immune defects were found to be indistinguishable from those of the other affected groups. However, the Haitians denied being drug addicts or homosexuals. By the time 29 cases had been seen in Miami, Brooklyn, N.Y., and a few other cities, it was appreciated that this group was indeed another focus for the new mysterious disease that had come to be called AIDS.

The epidemiologic puzzle at first was to understand the connection between the three risk groups, since there was no obvious link among them. Was it really one and the same disease in the three diverse populations?

The demographics of AIDS among the Haitians differs somewhat from that of the other groups. The disease was seen initially among recent refugees, the "boat people," mostly black, poor and male. Some had evidently brought it with them from Haiti, disembarking, already with fevers and sweats, from the small craft that deposited them on American shores. But others who turned up with identical problems had been in the United States for some time, as many as 8-10 years, and, unlike their compatriots, some were middle class members of the New York community. What did these people have in common, aside from their country of origin? Haitian-American community leaders, already concerned about adverse publicity associated with the "boat people," balked at the idea that Haitians were a risk group, asserting that the affected individuals really fit into other categories and that the Haitians had been singled out as scapegoats because of their unpopularity.

To be sure, epidemiologic analysis of this community has been exceedingly difficult, especially because of the marked suspicion with which official epidemiologists have been regarded by the victims. Investigators were sometimes thought to be agents of the U.S. Immigration and Naturalization Service, and treated accordingly; in other cases, denial of the facts because of severe taboos against homosexuality in Haiti may have played a role; and in a sizable proportion, unfortunately, the patients were either too ill, or the language barrier too formidable, to permit adequate questioning. Some died shortly after arrival. Consequently, far too little is known about the exact modes of transmission within the Haitian community at present. But the fact remains that people from the island of Hispaniola were arriving here bearing the marks of the illness, clearly mandating an investigation of the disease within Haiti itself.

Medical investigators from the CDC and from the University of Miami Medical School went to Haiti's capital, Port-au-Prince, while tropical medicine experts from Cornell University, already in the Haitian provinces studying diarrheal diseases, began to focus on the problem. Quite early in their search, these workers were able to find, in the capital city, a handful of cases of aggressive Kaposi's sarcoma, all in young men. They had been diagnosed by a French-trained Haitian dermatologist who had recently returned to his native country. These patients were apparently not so affected by opportunistic infections as were their countrymen who had moved to the United States (only two of the original eleven had toxoplasmosis). A preliminary review of local pathology specimens in Port-au-Prince seemed to indicate that the earliest cases of Kaposi's sarcoma in Haiti dated from around 1979—certainly not before. The Cornell group's reports suggested that the intractable diarrhea that is now a recognizable feature of AIDS among Haitians was first seen about the same time AIDS appeared in the U.S. They also noted that AIDS in Haiti seemed to be largely an urban disease, just as it is in the U.S. The Albert Schweitzer Hospital, situated in a rural area of Haiti, had not recognized any cases at all.

In the midst of these investigations, it was pointed out that Haiti has for some time been a popular vacation spot for American and European homosexuals. Immediately, speculation arose that Haiti might be the source of AIDS. A warm climate, a poor local economy and a powerful American dollar, have provided tourists with relative luxury and inexpensive sexual contacts with the local population. A Haitian physician, interviewed on a New York television program in July, 1983, indicated that only in the last 5 years have rural Haitian men and even young boys been leaving their extremely impoverished regions to become male prostitutes in resort areas frequented by foreign homosexuals. Such migration to urban areas might well provide the answer to the question: "why now?" It is conceivable that a disease which may have existed undiagnosed in the far reaches of the tropical countryside was thus brought to an urban area. Haitian men and boys offering their bodies for money frequently don't consider themselves gay, at least not openly. Information about homosexuality in Haiti is extremely difficult to elicit, not only because of secrecy surrounding the subject but because of communication problems with local dialects.

By July of 1983, more than 110 cases—about 5% of all patients with AIDS reported in the U.S.—occurred among persons of Haitian origin. Most of the cases have been seen in Miami, New York City and New Jersey. The Haitian patients are generally about 5 years younger than their non-Haitian counterparts; they have been in the U.S. for variable periods, some as long as 11 years. Most claim and are reported to be heterosexual and not intravenous drug users, although, as mentioned before, this information remains unproven. Women with AIDS account for about 10-15% of the Haitian patients. Their relative rarity has been attributed to the fact that, among recent immigrants, only about 20-30% have been women. But it is significant that several of the infants suspected of having the disease have Haitian mothers. Like AIDS patients from the other two risk groups, the Haitians often have antibodies to hepatitis A and B and cytomegalovirus, indicating that they too have been exposed to those agents. Most of the Haitian men, in one study, also had antibodies to syphilis, but the presence of related infectious diseases in Haiti may nullify the significance of this finding.

At a meeting of the Haitian Medical Society in Port-au-Prince in mid-1983, attended by several representatives of the American and French medical communities, it was stated that most AIDS cases in Haiti share risk factors—chiefly homosexuality—with cases in the U.S. and Europe. It is the contention of Haitian spokesmen in general that their people are no more prone to develop AIDS than any other group, except insofar as they too involve themselves with the gay life-style or in drug traffic. It seems appropriate for the present to consider this information in the light of the predictable reluctance of Haitian representatives to support the concept of Haiti as a hotbed of AIDS.

It is understandable that members of a particular national or ethnic group wish not to be stigmatized as potential carriers of any disease. Although we can all sympathize with the plight of Haitians, or, for that matter, anyone who suffers discrimination as a result of being considered capable of transmitting AIDS, it is impossible to deny that Haitians in this country have had a vastly greater incidence of AIDS than almost any other identifiable group. The attack rate, estimated conservatively to be 102 per million among Haitians in the U.S., is about tenfold that found in Americans, and is comparable to the 124 per million in American male homosexuals. Links between Haiti and AIDS are substantiated further by several compelling situations. A young Frenchman on his honeymoon, apparently a virgin before his marriage, contracted AIDS after receiving several units of blood in Haiti following an automobile accident. Two other recipients of Haitian blood, in Canada, have also developed AIDS. A nun, who had spent over 30 years in Haiti before returning to Canada in 1979, became ill and died in 1981 of a disease that her doctors retrospectively recognized as AIDS. She had had a single sexual contact during her years in Haiti. These incidents, as well as the migration of already ill Haitians to the U.S. and France, suggest that the disease is quite prevalent in Haiti; that it predated AIDS in the United States; and that it may be endemic there.

Many questions remain about the "Haitian connection," as it has been called. Was the disease always present in Haiti, or was it only recently introduced (as the facts so far appear to say)? How is it that some Haitian-Americans have lived in the U.S. as long as 11 years before becoming ill? And why, if AIDS was endemic in Haiti long ago, didn't we see cases that in retrospect we would call AIDS among Haitians in the U.S. before 1980? How is the disease maintained in Haiti now? Is homosexuality the chief means of transmission, or are insect vectors involved?

Haiti has perhaps the most serious malaria problem in the Western Hemisphere, attesting to the presence of Anopheles mosquitoes (able to carry malaria) that could be adapted to transmission of other diseases. Haitians are said to seek medical help, under some circumstances, from "injectionists," non-physician healers who treat them with shots of innocuous or folk medications, employing needles and syringes that have not been properly sterilized. The suggestion that some voodoo rites involve the sharing of blood through skin incisions has been vigorously denied by some Haitians, but hard facts on this issue are not available. Such practices, as well as transmission from mother to newborn, may be invoked to partially explain the relatively high incidence of hepatitis B among Haitians (or those from other developing countries) at home and in the U.S. Without some way of being transmitted, hepatitis B would not be widespread in a community such as theirs. AIDS, of course, seems to share many of the epidemiologic features of hepatitis B, and could be maintained in the population in much the same way.

Hemophiliacs

More than 18,000 American males suffer from hemophilia, "bleeder's disease." A protein, essential for a series of reactions that cause bleeding to stop after an injury, known as Factor VIII or antihemophilic globulin, is either missing from their blood or not functioning properly. Without this factor, severe hemophiliacs die at an early age from trauma or internal bleeding, or at best suffer from progressive deformities of the joints caused by the inevitable small injuries involved in day-to-day living. Since the development of Factor VIII concentrates and their widespread use, the lives of most hemophiliacs have been immeasurably improved and lengthened. However, the recognition that AIDS was occurring in hemophiliacs who were not, for the most part, homosexual was a great setback for clotting factor recipients. It also added a new dimension to the epidemiology of the immunodeficiency syndrome.

As recently as the 1960's, hemophilia could be treated only after bleeding had begun, by the infusion of multiple units of fresh or freshly frozen plasma (the liquid portion of the blood containing the needed factor), each unit taken from an individual healthy donor. However, prevention of bleeding through plasma infusion wasn't feasible because the huge volumes required would overload the circulatory systems of the patients to an intolerable degree. Blood bankers learned they could concentrate the Factor VIII, which was present only in small amounts, by chilling the plasma. The clotting factor was insoluble at low temperatures and could be separated out from the rest. This paved the way for the commercial preparation of factor concentrates, in which batches of plasma from many donors are pooled in large vats, chilled and further processed. The result is a highly efficient, economically feasible way of providing this life-saving factor to large numbers of patients, in a volume small enough for each patient to be treated in advance of bleeding episodes. The availability of this preventive treatment on a regular, often weekly basis, administered at home, revolutionized the medical management of severe hemophilia and gave the patients a new lease on life.

Unfortunately, because of the way in which it is manufactured, Factor VIII concentrate can't be made free of viruses. It hasn't been possible to sterilize the crucial clotting molecules because they would become inactivated during such a procedure and consequently rendered unable to perform their desired function in the recipient. In addition, as is theoretically the case with any pooled blood product, incorporation of plasma from even a single donor carrying an infectious agent contaminates the entire pool from which the concentrate is made. Plasma pools destined for the preparation of Factor VIII can contain contributions from 2500 to 22,000 different blood donors. The risk that some viral agent would be included, even though vastly diluted out, is therefore substantial.

A variety of infectious diseases can be transmitted from one person to another by the transfer of blood products —including malaria, syphilis, babesiosis, several forms of hepatitis (including hepatitis B), infectious mononucleosis (EBV) and cytomegalovirus (CMV). For this reason, blood banks routinely ask certain questions of potential donors, so as to exclude those persons likely to be unwitting carriers of these illnesses. A history of hepatitis, of serving in the military in a malarious area, or of having symptoms suggestive of these disorders have been standard reasons for donor exclusion in the recent past. Today the routine processing of blood from donors with acceptable medical histories includes testing for some of these diseases, and the subsequent elimination of those units having antibodies to syphilis and evidence of communicable hepatitis B. But only about two decades ago, before the discovery of the Australia antigen, hepatitis B was a major hazard for recipients of blood.

The way in which hepatitis B virus was identified is perhaps worth a digression, not only because it exemplifies the time frame from discovery of an agent to the manufacture of a vaccine against it but also because it emphasizes the role of serendipity in science—of a "prepared mind" being in the right place at the right time and capitalizing on it. A certain amount of good luck has often been an essential ingredient in the chain of events leading to significant advances in the study of disease. In the early 1960's, when "serum hepatitis" was a scourge among transfusion recipients, Baruch Blumberg was studying the genetics of serum proteins. He observed, in the blood of a particular Australian aborigine, a substance he hadn't known of before. On further study, he found the same protein, which he called "Australia antigen," in sera from patients with leukemia. He speculated that the substance might be a specific feature of that disease. To determine whether the antigen was associated with certain known proteins, he shared samples containing the material with another scientist. The sera contained proteins that the second physician recognized to be characteristic of patients with liver disease. The leukemic patients also had hepatitis; this clue helped focus Blumberg's attention on that disease, leading to his Nobel prize-winning discovery that Australia antigen was, in fact, a part of the virus that causes hepatitis B. Although a transmissible virus had long been suspected on epidemiologic grounds, this direct proof was needed. By 1969, it was possible to detect easily traces of the virus in blood, and some laboratories began doing so routinely to prevent the use of any such blood for transfusion to someone else. By 1972, such tests had been mandated for all blood banks. Subsequently, researchers learned how to detect other components of the virus, and how the body responds to infection with the agent.

Armed with this information, which took about 10 years to accumulate, the pharmaceutical industry was able to develop two products for the control of the problem. The first was hepatitis B immune globulin, rich in antibodies from exposed donors (frequently male homosexuals), which minimizes the severity of infection in the recipient. The second was a vaccine (also largely derived from donations by gay men), first used experimentally about five years ago and now commercially available. The vaccine has given us the means by which this frequently lethal disease can be almost completely prevented.

Before the exclusion of Australia antigen-containing plasmas from the blood pool, hemophiliacs had always been prone to the development of hepatitis B, and many had chronic forms of the disease as a result. Perhaps it should therefore have not been surprising when cases of AIDS appeared among them. But even so, a sense of anxiety spread among medical workers involved in the epidemic when the news reached them that AIDS affected this group, for the blood supply of this nation had seen enough problems already. Beginning in 1980, the first hemophiliacs became ill with a disease that, a year or two later, could be recognized and reported as AIDS. These men and boys (essentially all hemophiliacs are male because the disease is tied to the sex chromosomes) were, for the most part, heterosexual and not of the world of illicit drugs. The older patients, who had struggled with a chronic, debilitating, painful illness prior to factor concentrates, and were in the process of building a more stable existence, were faced with yet another catastrophe. They had contracted a deadly disease from the very source—other people's blood—that had just given them back their lives.

By the summer of 1983, 16 American hemophiliacs had been officially recognized by CDC as fitting the case definition, and several more await official tabulation. Other cases are known to exist in Canada and Europe, where Factor VIII concentrates manufactured in the U.S. are also administered.

The frequency of hemophiliac cases of AIDS—about 1 in 1250—is relatively low compared to those exposed. Perhaps 40% or more of the U.S. hemophiliacs require concentrate for maintenance, while the rest, with less severe forms of the disease, use cryoprecipitated (cold-separated) plasma in individual units only when bleeding begins, or at times of high risk, rather than regularly. The average severe hemophiliac goes through several different lots of Factor VIII annually, so that he is exposed to literally tens of thousands of blood donors each year. Portions of each lot of the concentrate are distributed to perhaps 100 different hemophiliacs. Thus a carrier of a disease who donates blood into a particular lot potentially exposes about one hundred hemophiliacs. The severe hemophiliacs, at special risk because of their use of factor, have an attack rate of about one case of AIDS for every 500 recipients.

One of the many peculiarities concerning AIDS in hemophilia is the fact that none of the first cases had derived their Factor VIII from the same lots. Unlike victims of food-poisoning epidemics, they hadn't shared a single, traceable shipment of contaminated material. For each patient with AIDS, there were around 100 others who had received the same lots yet hadn't become ill. Some of the considerable controversy over the significance of the hemophiliac cases bears on this point, so it is important to try to explain it.

Why haven't more people, all exposed to the same presumably contaminated material, come down with AIDS? Explanations have to be tentative at present, but certain reasonable hypotheses can be proposed. In 1978, 1979 and

1980 there were relatively few cases of AIDS in the U.S., and presumably few persons who carried the disease without having symptoms that would prevent their donating blood. Perhaps only one among 20,000 donors whose plasmas were combined to make a batch of concentrate was a carrier. This manifold dilution (20,000 to 1) would thin out the putative infectious agent to such a degree that it might affect only a few people. Additionally, the long incubation period of the disease might play a role in delaying other cases associated with particular lots of concentrate. Finally (and for this there is some evidence), the disease may be harbored in a minor form by many Factor VIII recipients, achieving its full expression in only a few.

Evidence supporting the existence of symptomless cases of AIDS is strongest for the hemophiliacs, although similar results have been obtained in gay men. A common feature of AIDS is a reversal of the ratio of the two principal types of T lymphocytes. Virtually all full-blown cases express this abnormality, as do most homosexuals with the lymphadenopathy syndrome. Surveys of recipients of Factor VIII in its various forms and at different dosage schedules have been done in a number of hemophilia clinics, in which T cell subsets have been analyzed. A substantial proportion of those hemophiliacs who are the most heavy users of commercial Factor VIII concentrates have striking T cell disturbances. In some studies, such disturbances are less prevalent, or totally absent, in hemophiliacs who receive only single unit (non-pooled) cryoprecipitate.

Thus, the T cell subset reversal seems to be associated mostly with exposure to the product from pooled plasma, reflecting its greater risk of contamination. As in gay men, the high frequency of T cell subset disturbances in hemophiliacs may be interpreted as indicating widespread exposure to an infectious agent (or agents) unknown, or as markers for the many exposures to infectious agents (hepatitis, CMV, EBV) known to afflict both groups. Of interest are T-cell subset deviations among hemophiliacs in Australia, where only single unit-derived cryoprecipitate from volunteers' plasma has been used. Very few cases of AIDS have surfaced in Australia, so it is unlikely that significant numbers of blood donors there can transmit the disease. This implies that molecules of Factor VIII—or one of its protein contaminants—may alone account for the observed changes.

AIDS in Blood Recipients

Shortly after the discovery of hemophiliacs with AIDS came another disturbing case: an infant who, ill at birth for reasons apparently unrelated to AIDS, had required massive transfusions of blood components. Seven months later, the child was admitted to a hospital because of severe infections, and by the age of 14 months, he had a series of illnesses that were considered typical of AIDS. Investigation of the 19 blood donors for this child turned up a 48-year-old male resident of San Francisco who had been well when he gave blood. However, 8 months later, the man became ill with typical AIDS and subsequently died. This baby wasn't the child of an AIDS victim nor did he have any known contact with AIDS patients. It was, even then, difficult to attribute the child's disease to factors other than the blood transfusion.

Some physicians didn't initially accept the diagnosis of pediatric AIDS. But as events have unfolded, that first transfusion case in a child was followed by others in people of any age, while other children with AIDS from other sources also surfaced. Sporadic transfusion-related cases began appearing in people who had neither evidence for nor any likelihood of being subject to the same social or physical risks as the previously described victims. Among these were elderly women who had received relatively large numbers of blood transfusions during cardiac surgery; they were clearly not homosexual, Haitian, drug addicts or hemophiliacs. Their only possible link to AIDS was through the vehicle of blood. Although tracing sources of blood units hasn't turned up donors having AIDS, as in the case of the California child, most cases involve at least one suspicious donor from a risk group. There is no longer much doubt that blood transfusion alone can account for a significant number of cases. In addition to those associated with multiple transfusions, a significant proportion of the 5-6% of AIDS patients with "no known risk factor" have had one or two units of blood as long as three to four years before the onset of symptoms. This transfusion history must be viewed as significant in the absence of other possible mechanisms of transmission.

The transfusion-associated cases of AIDS have been relatively rare. An estimated 12 million units of blood components—transfusions of red blood cells and plasma for severe anemia or bleeding during surgery or after trauma, of platelets or white blood cells for patients undergoing chemotherapy for cancer or leukemia—are administered annually in the U.S. These are given to perhaps 3 million recipients. Thus, the chances of developing AIDS from any single exposure to a blood transfusion are remote, at least judging from the recent past.

Indeed, it has been argued that the very few examples of transfusion-associated AIDS (only 25 had been officially tabulated by the CDC by August of 1983—19 in adults, 6 in children) might reflect coincidence rather than a contaminated blood supply. However, considering how recently the disease was introduced into this country there must have been very few carriers capable of transmitting the disease to others two or three years ago. Those few unknowingly infected blood donors, even if highly assiduous in their blood-giving, could still only have passed AIDS directly to a handful of people a year. Since the disease takes at least 6-7 months to manifest itself clinically, but may take as long as four years after the time of exposure, some of those 1980-81 recipients would not be expected to be ill even now. Add to that the very great probability that not all those exposed will ever develop AIDS—a good rule in any infectious disease—and the current rarity of transfusion-associated cases becomes at least understandable.

It would not be surprising, given this sort of analysis, if we saw a steady—perhaps even geometric—rise in cases attributable to blood products in general for at least the next two or three years, emerging from among those who did unfortuately receive blood products from carriers. Working from the cautious public-health perspective that

AIDS is transmitted by an infectious agent, blood banking officials began to restrict donor populations in the spring of 1983. As their efforts appear to be largely successful, we should expect a downturn of new transfusion-related cases of AIDS in about 1986.

Now that preventive efforts have been mounted, the odds of transmission by blood collected recently should be greatly diminished. Since blood transfusion is crucial for the survival of many patients who have had severe trauma, for those requiring major surgery and for others with blood diseases or cancers necessitating certain therapies, it is important to emphasize that the risks of contracting AIDS though blood transfusion have already been minimized. Questionnaires designed to eliminate potentially risky donors are now used in most major blood centers. Because of the raised level of consciousness and dissemination of information about AIDS, many individuals who consider themselves as falling into the hazardous donor categories have voluntarily stopped giving blood. For these reasons, anxiety over blood transfusion at present is largely unwarranted and could lead to unnecessary deaths.

It is perhaps worth noting that certain blood derivatives are far less likely to transmit AIDS or, for that matter, any disease, than are Factor VIII concentrates, plasma, whole blood or blood components (like platelets) containing cells. Even products of pooled serum, such as gamma globulin (used to prevent polio, hepatitis or measles), specialized gamma globulins like varicella-zoster immune globulin or hepatitis B immune globulin (the latter frequently made from serum of homosexual men who have lots of antibodies against hepatitis B) do not seem, for example, to be implicated in AIDS transmission. Their safeness, at least until now, can be ascribed to the processing and fractionation of the serum, which either removes or inactivates infectious agents.

Taken together, the presence of AIDS among drug abusers sharing unsterilized needles, recipients of blood products and possibly Haitians connected with injectionists strongly supports the spread of AIDS via inoculation through the skin. The fact that the recognized cases have multiplied in essentially geometric progression leads us to the conclusion that the cause of AIDS is itself a replicating organism—a microbial agent. A poisonous substance or factor of life-style wouldn't be expected to increase in this manner. Thus, despite the relative infrequency of known instances of blood-borne AIDS, their very existence has greatly enhanced our understanding of the epidemic.

AIDS among Contacts of AIDS Patients or of Carriers

Further supporting the infectious agent theory of AIDS, secondary cases of the disease have been recognized among contacts of the risk groups who are not themselves clearly homosexual, drug abusers or Haitians. Most of them have been sexual partners or children of AIDS cases or of people from the risk groups who must be assumed to be symptom-free carriers of the disease. We think that the carrier state for AIDS must exist, not only because of the California child whose platelet donor was well at the time he gave blood but also because of the several monogamous gay patients whose less restricted, overtly healthy partners apparently conveyed AIDS to them.

More than 25 children, most of them from New York City, Newark, New Jersey or Miami, Florida have been found to have a severe cellular immunodeficiency that in most respects resembles AIDS in adults. Perhaps as many as twenty different forms of congenital immunodeficiency were known to affect children before the description of AIDS. Several of these pediatric diseases resemble AIDS more closely than do the immunodeficiency disorders of adults, which usually involve severe deficits of B cell function and antibodies and are distinguishable from AIDS in other respects. The recognition of AIDS in children, without the availability of a specific test, now rests on circumstantial, epidemiologic evidence.

It's pretty well confirmed that AIDS does exist in children. Several pediatric cases that clinically fit the diagnosis have been subjected to the same immunologic analysis as adult cases and were found to have similar abnormalities: altered T cell subsets, depressed lymphocyte responses to mitogens, greatly reduced production of alpha interferon, and elevated antibody production (hypergammaglobulinemia). These features, as well as progressively worsening immunodeficiency, aren't typical of any of the previously known congenital immune deficiencies. Most similar to AIDS among the inborn disorders is Nezelof's syndrome, a poorly characterized illness thought to represent a variant of severe combined immunodeficiency of childhood (SCID). Whether Nezelof's original description was of a case of a true inborn error of metabolism affecting the immune system or of a sporadic case of AIDS in a child, cannot be determined in retrospect. But, even the Nezelof syndrome was extremely rare before the AIDS epidemic, whereas now, in a limited geographic area, so many unusual pediatric immunodeficiencies have been reported that they could, by themselves, be regarded as constituting an outbreak. Furthermore, most children suspected of having AIDS are offspring of Haitians or intravenous drug abusers who have indications of abnormal cellular immunity, and a few have mothers or fathers who actually have AIDS. It's doubtful that the increased frequency of this immune defect merely reflects greater awareness of the existence of AIDS in adults; the rise looks to be genuine.

In most of these cases, AIDS appears to have been transmitted to the child from the mother. No specific information permits conclusions regarding the relative importance of the transfer of disease across the placenta during pregnancy, exposure during the birth process (as occurs with Herpes simplex), or passage via breast-feeding. But we need only consider the intimate oral contacts that exist between mother and infant to understand the difficulty epidemiologists must have in trying to sort out the mechanism for passage of AIDS to the young. Since some children who eventually developed AIDS were placed in foster care shortly after they were born, the implication is that they contracted the disease before, during or immediately after birth. In one family reported, the immunodeficient mother, a drug-addict and prostitute, had four female children, all of different fathers. Only one of the children lived with her during infancy; the others were in separate foster homes, and all had immunodeficiency resembling AIDS. Three of the four children have died.

In at least one case, the mother of an affected child not only was well but had normal T cell studies, while the father, a drug addict, had the lymphadenopathy syndrome with wasting, and the live-in uncle, both homosexual and a drug abuser, had AIDS. While this instance has been argued as an example of the disease being transmitted by casual household contacts, several alternative conclusions seem possible from the pathological family history cited in the report. Details of homosexuality, child abuse or incest are often kept secret from public health officials, making exact determinations of epidemiology difficult or sometimes impossible. The contacts among family members living together in a household are far from casual, even in the absence of sexual exposure. There is a significant chance of inapparent inoculation through sharing of razors, accidental cuts and the like, as well as the sharing of non-sexual intimacies, such as kissing.

One factor possibly contributing to the development of AIDS in very young children is the immaturity of the newborn's immune system, which makes it extremely susceptible to other infectious diseases like herpes and hepatitis B. Having in effect a normal immune deficiency in the first days or weeks after birth may thus make infants especially vulnerable to an agent causing AIDS.

Intimate heterosexual contact has been documented as a probable mode of transmission of the disease. Several examples have been cited of women with AIDS who were apparently neither drug addicts nor of Caribbean extraction but whose only exposure was through sexual intercourse with an AIDS patient or intravenous drug abuser. In addition, perhaps twenty clinically well male or female heterosexual consorts of AIDS patients have been studied, most of whom have abnormalities of T cell subset distribution. In this

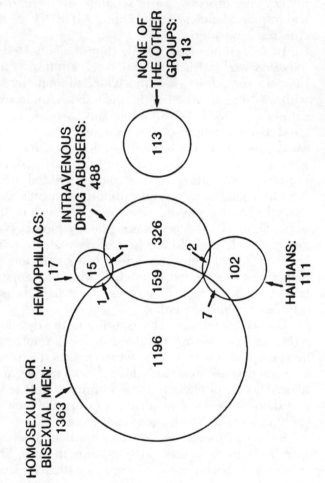

OVERLAP OF GROUPS AT INCREASED RISK FOR AIDS

UNITED STATES, JULY 26, 1983

N=1922

HEMOPHILIACS: 17

INTRAVENOUS DRUG ABUSERS: 488

NONE OF THE OTHER GROUPS: 113

113

15

1

326

2

159

102

1

7

1196

HOMOSEXUAL OR BISEXUAL MEN: 1363

HAITIANS: 111

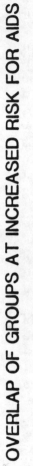

respect, they resemble about 80% of sexually active gay men in New York City and a large proportion of hemophiliacs, who express similar T cell abnormalities. Insufficient information is available to identify the specific sexual practices involved in creating these changes, which may reflect exposure to an AIDS agent. Gathering of data on anal intercourse, on oral-genital and oral-anal contacts in heterosexual couples, though a formidable project, would probably be helpful in formulating preventive measures for AIDS in both gay and straight communities.

AIDS in Europeans and Africans

Crucial clues to the transmission and origins of AIDS have come from Europe, which has had more than 150 cases of the disease in the last several years. The earliest cases recognized were in gay men who had had contact with American homosexuals. The very existence of these supported the infectious agent theory. As the epidemic has evolved, two other pieces of information have come via Europe that added insights about transmission. First was the appearance of cases in gay men who had had no contact with homosexuals in the U.S. but had travelled to Haiti. Second, and more important, was the appreciation that both black Africans and Europeans who had lived or travelled extensively in Africa were coming down with AIDS. Their exposures had been chiefly in the center of the continent, in Chad, Zaire, Uganda and Ghana. A female Danish surgeon had lived and worked in the region for over a decade before she returned to Denmark, in 1976, with an unexplained immunodeficiency that in retrospect clearly fulfills the CDC case definition for AIDS. In France and Belgium, other cases from the middle and late 1970's have also been recognized as exemplifying the disease, chiefly in African immigrants from Zaire and Chad.

The parallels with Haitians in the U.S. are too obvious to ignore. Many of the African immigrants with AIDS in Europe are non-drug abusers and deny homosexuality. Some had been living in Europe for fairly long periods—more than 5 years—before they became ill, while others apparently came already ill to France or Belgium. Like the Haitians, most of the cases of AIDS in Africans diagnosed in Europe have been characterized by opportunistic infections rather than by Kaposi's sarcoma. Finally, most of the women who have been diagnosed in Europe are linked to Africa.

The clear implication is that AIDS involves central Africa as well as Haiti, the U.S. and Europe. Judging from the dates of onset of some of the cases seen in Europe, AIDS was recognizable in African-associated patients even before it appeared in American homosexuals or Haitians.

AIDS in Health Workers

Because of the apparent analogy with the transmission of hepatitis B, it was long assumed that AIDS would eventually appear among those persons exposed, through their occupations, to the disease. Physicians, dentists, nurses, hospital aides and orderlies, operating room technicians, laundry and waste-disposal personnel, and laboratory technical staff dealing with blood and other secretions and excretions of AIDS patients, would be expected to be at immediate risk if the disease were highly contagious. The fact that few if any such individuals have been stricken, despite almost four years of contact while caring for AIDS patients in urban hospitals and other medical facilities, tells us that exposure to their breath, urine, stool, or even blood is not highly risky. Even accidental injury with needles from the patients hasn't yet been established as producing a case, although perhaps 50 individuals are known to have had such potentially hazardous exposure. It is conceivable that the Danish surgeon mentioned above could be a rare example of occupationally transmitted AIDS.

Recently, four cases of AIDS in hospital workers were reported by the CDC. This report, unfortunately, raised the already inflamed anxieties of this group still further. One of the cases, in a hospital housekeeping employee, seems reasonably well documented as having had no risk factors other than being stuck with a needle of some kind 11 months before he became ill. But the Baltimore hospital where he worked did not have a record of treating AIDS patients before the needlestick incident occurred. The other three cases are even less well defined as occupationally acquired. They had no clearcut exposure to blood or needles. One was an admitted user of mescaline, cocaine and marijuana, though she denied taking them intravenously. (A few of the early patients with AIDS, not hospital workers, similarly claimed they had used street drugs without injection.) Another of this group was from the island of Jamaica. (Some other cases associated with Caribbean background have been Jamaican.) The third, who admitted to homosexual contact as an adolescent, had antibodies to both hepatitis B and syphilis (both markers found frequently, though not exclusively, among sexually active gay men.) None of these three hospital workers was known to have had any direct contact with recognized AIDS patients.

While these cases can't be ignored in considering the prevention of AIDS among medical personnel, they need to be put in perspective. The health care system employs a significant proportion of all urban workers. On a purely random basis, some cases could be expected to appear among these individuals. Indeed, among our earliest cases of AIDS were medical personnel (male nurses and doctors) who also were homosexual. Because of reluctance to jeopardize job security in a hospital, it is not surprising that a history of drug abuse or homosexuality should be especially difficult to elicit from a worker in the health professions. Pretty clearly, a proportion of the cases classified as having "no known risk factor" include some who have lied or not given all the relevant facts about their background. And, statistically, some of these cases would probably be persons employed in a hospital or in a variety of medical clinics found in any large city where AIDS occurs.

Cases Without Obvious Risk Factors

Throughout the AIDS epidemic, the CDC has recorded a steady 5-7% of cases among people they felt did not fit into any of the known high risk groups. A disproportionate number of them are women: of the 109 female AIDS victims recorded by the CDC by June of 1983, 39% were unexplained. Out of the approximately 100 men and women considered to have no known risk factors, about half died before providing adequate information that might have better classified them. The rest include some who have been adequately interviewed but (though they may not be telling the truth) admit to no known exposure history. Also included in this group by CDC are cases that seem to us to have consistent risk factors. They are sexual partners of AIDS cases or of members of high risk groups, or recipients of blood transfusions. Also listed are patients having Kaposi's sarcoma without immunologic abnormalities, who may be unrelated to the epidemic.

Patients who truly fit into the unexplained category are of special interest to the epidemiologist, since they may provide critical lessons about the transmission of the disease. Certain negative information, while never absolutely definitive, has been helpful in delineating the modes of spread of AIDS. For instance, the fact that cases in this category don't seem to cluster geographically in areas favored by gays, such as the central wards of San Francisco or Greenwich Village in New York City, supports the notion that airborne spread of the disease doesn't occur. Lack of documented cases resulting from eating food in restaurants that employ gay men as waiters or cooks in these same areas suggests that foodborne transmission also isn't very likely. In short, it doesn't seem easy to "catch" AIDS. All but about 2% of the cases have a reasonable connection with the risk groups in which transmission occurs through intimate contact of one sort or another. The conclusion we can draw from epidemiologic analysis is that ways of transmitting disease are quite restricted, so that AIDS, while clearly communicable, is not highly contagious and should lend itself to containment through relatively simple public health measures.

What is a High Risk Group ?

The term "high risk group" is a statistical concept, indicating that persons in a particular, identifiable population have been found to be at greater risk of developing a particular disease than those in other groups. It does not condemn any individual to AIDS. Concern over the social reverberations associated with identifying Haitians as a high risk group has led to pressures on health officials, who appropriately use these statistical categorizations. Some Haitian immigrants and residents in the U.S. have objected strongly to being labelled as a high risk group for AIDS and have demanded that they be eliminated from such classification in public health reports. As a result, a distinction has been drawn between persons having risk factors (activities or situations that place individuals in jeopardy of acquiring AIDS) and risk groups (those who have these risk factors). Hemophiliacs, homosexuals and drug abusers all have recognizable risk factors, whereas Haitians don't. They are a risk group, based on their very high frequency of disease, but epidemiologists haven't been able to define a risk factor. The Health Department of the City of New York now formally classifies Haitians with AIDS as belonging to the "no known risk factor" category rather than as a high risk group.

CHAPTER 5

Hypotheses,

Speculations and

Predictions

Theories on the Cause(s) of AIDS

When posing a scientific question, one usually begins by constructing a hypothesis, a theoretical framework of ideas that can be tested experimentally. Several reasonable hypotheses concerning the pathogenesis of AIDS have been proposed. They actually don't differ very much from one another. Perhaps elements from several of these can be incorporated into a coherent theory of how AIDS comes about.

The most widely accepted idea, and the one we clearly favor, is that an infectious microorganism, transmitted from another area of the world, was introduced somehow into the groups that have been affected. Such a microorganism, communicable only by intimate physical contact, damages the immune system in some way that is not yet understood. This hypothesis can explain most of the known facts about AIDS, taking into account the modes of spread, the groups involved, and answering the question: "Why now?" The infectious agent hypothesis makes certain research goals imperative: understand its epidemiology, prevent its transmission; find the agent, prepare a vaccine, prevent the disease.

Infectious agent theories can be further broken down. The simplest idea is that a virus infects and directly damages some component of the immune system—a T cell or a large granular lymphocyte—and causes it to stop functioning. A logical implication of this would be that as the cells that the agent infects and destroys disappear, so would the agent itself. Such an idea would explain why it has been difficult to isolate a causal microbe. Or, the agent could infect a cell type but not kill it directly. Instead, infection could be accompanied by the expression on the cell surface of new virally-coded antigens that become a target for the patient's own immune system to attack. One step further leads into the autoimmune hypothesis, which holds that the immune system becomes confused: it no longer responds to just the viral antigens but mistakenly destroys all similar cells even though they are not necessarily infected. This concept would point to a primary causative role for the anti-T cell antibodies described in some patients with AIDS. As an alternative, the etiologic agent could persistently infect stem cells of a particular type, preventing them from maturing and producing clones of effector lymphocytes.

Several alternatives to the infectious agent hypothesis have been proposed, but as the epidemic has progressed, some of these have been discarded. When the disease was thought to involve only gay men, everyone wondered what was new in the gay community that could explain its development. Were there life-style changes that could be the cause? Early interest centered on the use of volatile nitrites. These chemicals (used to achieve a "high" and to relax the anal sphincter) were suspected of acting as carcinogens and immune suppressants. Their widespread use was seen as a way to explain the development of Kaposi's sarcoma and unusual infections. However, as the root cause of AIDS, nitrites had to be abandoned along with other gay life-style issues when the disease was found to affect many gay and straight non-users, men, women and children not sharing the suspicious life-styles. Nitrites are still being considered as possible cofactors in the pathogenesis of Kaposi's sarcoma.

Another hypothesis, suggesting that anal contact with

semen might itself be immunosuppressive, was based on experimental evidence that both sperm and white blood cells given anally or by vein led to the development of suppressor cells inhibiting aspects of immunity. This was later joined by additional reports indicating that inoculation of rabbit semen into rabbits incited the development of anti-T cell antibodies and particularly antibodies against a component of the surfaces of both sperm and T cells. Transplantation immunologists have observed that kidney graft recipients who have been transfused tolerate their replacement organs better than those who haven't been given blood. Rejection does not occur as frequently. This finding supports the hypothesis that repeated exposure to foreign cells can induce a kind of tolerance, which, if sufficiently generalized, might allow dangerous organisms to take hold. The idea that exposure to other peoples' white cells might be immunosuppressive could be applied to explain not only AIDS in gay men but also in those receiving blood transfusions and, by stretching things a bit, AIDS in drug addicts. It couldn't, however, account for the new occurrence of the syndrome, since homosexuality, transfusion and drug abuse have been around for a long time without producing AIDS. Nor could it explain the disease in infants, Haitians, hemophiliacs (whose clotting factor doesn't contain any cells) or female contacts of AIDS patients.

The "immunological overload" theory attempts to incorporate all these groups, arguing that AIDS is simply the result of overwhelming exposure of the immune system to far too many immune stimuli at once. Haitians exposed to poor sanitation, homosexuals with multiple partners, hemophiliacs who have seen too many vials of Factor VIII concentrate and drug addicts stuck with too many needles would all fill this particular bill. Those who proposed this hypothesis seem to have forgotten the vast panoply of antigenic stimuli to which all people have been exposed for eons in the form of normal microbial flora, foods and infections of various sorts. Overload doesn't make much sense when put into this perspective, even if we forget, again, that this theory also doesn't explain why AIDS suddenly appeared.

As a variant of the overload idea, it has also been argued

that if not antigens, then repeated exposure to commonly prevalent viruses such as CMV could more or less permanently turn off the immune system. Viral infections of all sorts, from measles to smallpox vaccination, can suppress immune functions. Once lowered beyond a certain point, abetted by semen-induced anti-T cell antibodies, the process sets up a vicious cycle of infection and immunosuppression, leading to AIDS. While this construct might have made some sense if AIDS had appeared sporadically as isolated cases of immunodeficiency among gay men over a period of many years, it simply doesn't fit with the reality of the epidemic, involving as it does such diverse population groups within the observed time frame. The main proponents of this viewpoint have actually conjectured that AIDS in homosexual males is a different disease from that which appears in the other risk groups.

A Working Hypothesis

Taking into account the data currently available permits us to form an overall picture of the pathogenesis of the disease, from which we can derive a working hypothesis. The supposed etiologic agent of the disease apparently doesn't affect all who encounter it in the same way. Our hypothesis assumes that AIDS resembles virtually all other infectious diseases in that its development depends on several factors. An agent is required, but perhaps not sufficient, to cause the disease. Something else, a genetic or environmental factor, comes into play.

Susceptibility or resistance to infection in the first place probably depends upon natural host factors that either permit or completely prevent entry of the agent into the body. The integrity of the mucous membranes of the anus could be such a resistance factor, as could the presence of appropriate natural antibodies in the secretions or of properly working natural killer cells. Once the infection is established, a person's genetically programmed immune apparatus will probably determine whether or not the body can clear the infection before it can do damage. If the process succeeds in doing so, a state of immunity is achieved. It is possible that some of the factors invoked in the other hypotheses, such as exposure to sperm, white cells, viruses or drugs, can suppress the ability of the adaptive immune system to respond. So might the immaturity of the immune systems of very young children and perhaps even exposure to Factor VIII. How much of an influence such external forces exert isn't known, but they may well play a part in opening the door for the entry of the crucial AIDS pathogen. The lymphadenopathy syndrome may represent the process of immunization: the swollen lymph nodes may be the outward manifestation of the internal struggle between the agent and its cellular targets.

Another possible result of exposure to a new infectious agent could be that an individual would become an asymptomatic carrier, as frequently happens with hepatitis B. In this type of situation, the immune system doesn't completely clear the infection but limits it so that the person isn't overtly ill. This state may be transitory, if the immune system eventually prevails, or, theoretically, it may become a permanent condition. The final possibility is that the person fails entirely to resist the AIDS agent, either because of a a specific, genetic defect or a non-specific, external factor; this would lead to the development of the broadbased immunodeficiency disease that eventuates in the full-blown case of AIDS.

Can this hypothesis embrace the pathogenesis of Kaposi's sarcoma, the other cancers, the development of autoimmune platelet, erythrocyte and leukocyte disorders, the appearance of immune complexes in the blood and the massive elevations of immunoglobulin levels seen in AIDS?

It is reasonable to consider the malignant tumors seen in AIDS as being intertwined with the basic immunodeficiency. These cancers can exist without AIDS, but are probably facilitated by its severe cellular immune defects. Herpesviruses are strongly implicated in the tumors associated with AIDS. These viruses are all capable of a dormant stage that is thought to be held in check by cellular immunity. The varying degrees to which they are endemic in the several AIDS high risk groups is reflected in the differing incidence rates for Kaposi's sarcoma in each of the groups.

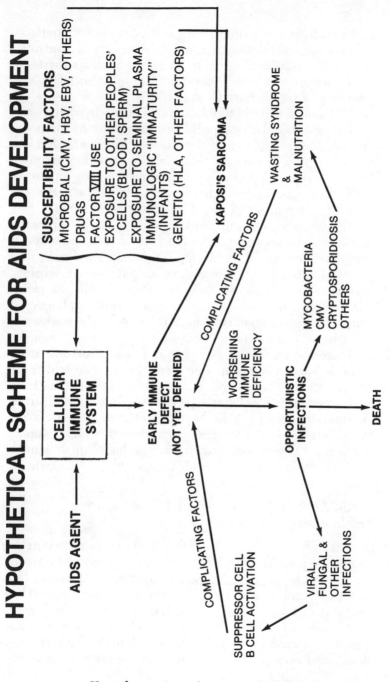

HYPOTHETICAL SCHEME FOR AIDS DEVELOPMENT

SUSCEPTIBILITY FACTORS
MICROBIAL (CMV, HBV, EBV, OTHERS)
DRUGS
FACTOR VIII USE
EXPOSURE TO OTHER PEOPLES'
 CELLS (BLOOD, SPERM)
EXPOSURE TO SEMINAL PLASMA
IMMUNOLOGIC "IMMATURITY"
 (INFANTS)
GENETIC (HLA, OTHER FACTORS)

AIDS AGENT

CELLULAR
IMMUNE
SYSTEM

EARLY IMMUNE
DEFECT
(NOT YET DEFINED)

KAPOSI'S SARCOMA

COMPLICATING FACTORS

WORSENING
IMMUNE
DEFICIENCY

WASTING SYNDROME
&
MALNUTRITION

OPPORTUNISTIC
INFECTIONS

MYCOBACTERIA
CMV
CRYPTOSPORIDIOSIS
OTHERS

DEATH

COMPLICATING FACTORS

SUPPRESSOR CELL
B CELL ACTIVATION

VIRAL,
FUNGAL &
OTHER
INFECTIONS

In individuals harboring these viruses, a failure of crucial cellular immune defenses could lead to loss of control of cell proliferation and result in a cancer. Such a situation is thought to play a role in the instigation of Burkitt's lymphoma by Epstein-Barr virus (EBV).

The uncontrolled stimulation of B cells by reactivated EBV is probably also responsible for several serum antibody-mediated abnormalities of the disease. Even in infectious mononucleosis, a common and usually benign disease caused by EBV, destruction of platelets and red cells by one's own antibodies sometimes occurs, so it should not be surprising if they happen in AIDS too. Also as in mononucleosis, production of immune complexes is found in AIDS. Depending on the laboratory where the tests are done, immune complexes are found in varying frequencies and are interpreted differently. Such complexes might bind to red cells, granulocytes, monocytes and even some T cells, in such a way that they become targets for destruction by phagocytic cells. The depletion of cells in AIDS may be the end result of such an "autoimmune" phenomenon.

Once the initial defect is established, opportunistic infections begin to appear, and with them come additional complications. Fungal and opportunistic viral agents stimulate suppressor T cells and suppressor monocytes, which continue the vicious cycle. Mycobacterial and enteric infections foster malnutrition and severe loss of weight, signalling further immunologic deterioration that ultimately leads to the downhill course now all too familiar.

Could Kaposi's Sarcoma and AIDS be Separate but Interacting Diseases?

An argument can be made that Kaposi's tumor occurring in certain patients who don't develop opportunistic infections is not a part of AIDS but an independent event. For one thing, the prognosis of Kaposi's sarcoma alone is far better than Kaposi's sarcoma with opportunistic infections, or with the infections in the absence of the tumor. According to a review of the NYU statistics, all of the patients who developed both Kaposi's sarcoma and opportunistic infections, but only about 15% of those with just Kaposi's sarcoma, died within three years. For another, we found a striking difference between these same two groups in the ability of cells from each type of patient to make alpha interferon. Those with the better prognosis usually make normal amounts of this immunologically active protein, while those with infections produce almost none.

There are several situations that were known to predispose a person to developing Kaposi's sarcoma long before we ever heard of AIDS. Excessive immunosuppression induced by drugs used in organ transplantation, in certain autoimmune diseases, or in the treatment of certain cancers, or the immunologic deficits consequent to certain neoplasms of the immune system (the lymphomas and leukemias) were capable of setting the stage for the disease. Perhaps the strongest evidence for the role of immunosuppression in its pathogenesis was the frequent regression of tumor if drug treatment was stopped.

There is strong evidence for a part played by CMV in the development of Kaposi's sarcoma, including its propensity to infect endothelial cells and its ability to suppress immunity. Repeated exposures to multiple CMV strains (one of which might be particularly likely to transform normal cells into those that proliferate without control) could lead not only to the development of the tumor, but also to an immunosuppressed state conducive to its persistence and growth. (Recently, gene fragments characteristic of EBV and of hepatitis B virus have also been found in Kaposi's sarcoma tissue, suggesting that CMV may not be uniquely related to this tumor.)

It seems possible that two independent events are required for the development of Kaposi's sarcoma: immunosuppression and infection with CMV, possibly only with certain strains having a relatively high tumor-causing potential. When infected with such transforming strains of CMV, some patients would develop Kaposi's sarcoma because they were mildly immunosuppressed by drugs, viral exposures (including CMV) or exposure to cells from unrelated donors, while others would develop KS after exposure to the AIDS agent. The presence of certain genes (for example, HLA-DR5) might cause a very specific form of immune deficiency which, in the presence of CMV, could lead also to the development of the tumor, or at least contribute to susceptibility.

Possible Causative Agents

Characteristics of an AIDS Agent Hinted by its Epidemiology

We can speculate further concerning the nature of an agent capable of causing AIDS, based on what we now know about its spread. Most investigators who accept that a specific agent causes AIDS (and there are still a few who don't) assume that it is a virus. Bacteria, protozoans and fungi seem too large and obvious not to have been detected through modern microscopy and other highly advanced technologies. However, we shouldn't forget that the same kind of thinking originally permeated investigations of the etiology of both Legionnaires' disease and Lyme arthritis, each subsequently found to be caused by bacteria.

Whatever its exact form, the agent initiating AIDS must be fairly fragile, not adapted to surviving a flight through the air, on water droplets propelled by a cough or on objects (such as an airmail letter, that could have transmitted the sturdy smallpox virus). It evidently can't tolerate being dried. It doesn't seem to be able to survive outside of a living cell except, perhaps, under the special conditions permitted by the production of Factor VIII concentrates. It must be fairly finicky in its nutritional requirements, since it doesn't want to grow in broths used to cultivate ordinary bacteria and fungi. Nor has it yet revealed its presence in the many cell types provided by virologists to entice it to grow in culture, suggesting that its favorite target cell may not have been detected yet. It's elusive, to say the least.

Known Microbes being Considered as the AIDS Agent

Certain known organisms, all viral agents, have been put forth as the primary cause of AIDS. To some extent, each fulfills the general predictions based on epidemiology. The major difficulty we face in identifying any agent as the cause lies in being sure it isn't just another opportunistic infection. This chicken-and-egg problem can only be resolved with difficulty, unless an experimental animal can be found to which AIDS can be transmitted at will. Since we do not at the moment have an animal model (some viruses that infect humans don't infect experimental animals), we will have to depend on circumstantial evidence such as was done to incriminate Epstein-Barr virus as the cause of infectious mononucleosis. If, for example, virtually all AIDS victims have antibodies against a particular microbe, while their serum taken several months or years before lack those antibodies, we could deduce that infection with the microbe is associated with the development of AIDS. If some persons we believe to be at high risk likewise have such antibodies, but less often than AIDS patients, and if people we do not expect to have exposure don't, the association strengthened. On the other hand failure to find antibodies among certain patients or groups of patients with AIDS, or finding antibodies too widely among persons not expected to have been exposed would tend to weaken the association between an agent and AIDS. Isolation of the agent repeatedly from all persons with the disease and not from those unexposed would further strengthen the case for the microbe. Development of a vaccine with a highly suspicious agent would provide additional clues. If vaccinees were protected specifically against AIDS, while unvaccinated persons continued to get the disease, the organism constituting the vaccine would be further implicated.

Cytomegaloviruses, as has been said before, are candidates because of their known immunosuppressive potential and their prevalence among the high-risk groups, particularly the gay men. Spread of a mutant strain or of a newly introduced one into a society that has not been exposed to it could explain the epidemic curve. Although apparently all gay men with AIDS who have been studied show evidence of having had exposure to these viruses, almost all of those without AIDS, from urban centers at least, also have antibodies. A main argument against the role of CMV rests in the observation that some non-homosexual patients with AIDS seem never to have been infected by it. Another comes from comparison of the genetic material, the DNA, from many isolates of CMV from AIDS patients, which does not indicate that a single, causal strain is common to all.

Other herpesviruses, because of their epidemiology, are not so likely to be causal in AIDS, though Epstein-Barr virus, Varicella-Zoster virus and Herpes simplex viruses have been implicated in several illnesses associated with the disease, and EBV may contribute to the eventual severity of the immune deficiency disorder.

Adenoviruses have been isolated from the stools and urines of patients with AIDS. About 35 types of adenovirus have been isolated from humans with various kinds of infection (mostly of the respiratory tract). These types are identifed by antisera that recognize differences in the proteins coating the viruses. Several of these "serotypes" have been represented among the adenoviruses found in patients with AIDS. However, when more sophisticated analysis (restriction endonuclease mapping) was done, it was found that almost all the adenoviruses from AIDS patients are identical in their DNA. The finding of a consistent type of adenovirus in the disease would be especially suggestive of its causal role, but for the fact that the same types of strains were originally isolated from patients who had drug-induced immunosuppression for kidney transplantation. This suggests they are opportunistic, rather than causal, in AIDS.

Viruses related to the human wart agents but originally isolated from monkeys infect simian lymphocytes. Antibodies against these lymphotropic papova viruses (LPV) have been said to be only rarely found in normal people; they are increasingly prevalent in well gay men, patients with the lymphadenopathy syndrome and those with fullblown AIDS. The propensity of these viruses to infect lymphoid cells and their epidemiologic features make LPV attractive to consider, but data supporting their involvement in AIDS are so far not very strong.

Hepatitis B virus, presumably because of its own epidemiology, affects the same groups of people who get AIDS. Since we know that this virus itself has been around for a long time, it isn't itself likely to be the cause of AIDS. However, one virus, known as the Delta agent, parasitizes the hepatitis B virus. By incorporating itself into the virus coat, the surface antigen, it becomes infective for humans. Delta agent is dependent on this help from another virus for its own replication and survival. It is an interesting relationship. What good, if any, the Delta agent does for the hepatitis virus isn't known. Delta itself causes a form of hepatitis. Serologic evidence seems to exclude the Delta agent as the cause of AIDS, but it might serve as a model for another causal agent, which would share the epidemiologic features of both hepatitis B and AIDS.

Parvoviruses are a group of incomplete viruses that, like Delta, need help from other microbes to become infectious. They share the epidemiologic features one would expect of an AIDS agent. Most have been isolated from domestic animals. A special virus, a mutant animal strain or one that ordinarily targets humans could be involved in the disease process. This group has evoked considerable interest. So far, the canine parvoviruses seem excluded from a causal role, but work in this area is in its infancy.

An epidemic of African Swine Fever (ASFV) occurred in Haiti in the 1970's. Previously the virus that causes this disease had been known since the turn of the century, when European-bred hogs imported into Africa by white settlers came into contact with indigenous wild boars. Because this zoonosis, originating in Africa, had spread to Haiti in the time-frame postulated for the AIDS epidemic, and could have affected humans, especially in a mutant form, ASFV has intriguing possibilities as a candidate for the AIDS agent. A search for antibodies to ASFV by Haitian scientists as well as by workers at the CDC was negative, but some epidemiologists have questioned whether the testing for ASFV has been extensive enough or has employed sufficiently sensitive methods.

A newly recognized group of human retroviruses, known as HTLV (Human T cell Leukemia Virus), has caused a flurry of interest in the search for the causative agent of

AIDS. Described by Dr. Robert Gallo and his coworkers at the NIH, this viral family has a propensity to infect and transform T cells into lymphomas and leukemias. These unusual cancers occur in clusters in Japan and the Caribbean basin. The NIH group reported finding antibodies to HTLV in the sera and found virus in cells cultured from some patients with AIDS. Their early studies apparently showed an increasing frequency of antibodies to viruses of this group as one goes from normal controls to lymphadenopathy patients to AIDS patients. At least three separate strains are said to have been identified, including two distinct ones from AIDS patients. One strain, corresponding closely to those isolated from Japanese and U.S. patients with leukemia, has been recovered from the T cells of two American AIDS victims out of about 100 so far studied. The virus could be found early but not late in the course of the disease, suggesting that the cells that carry the virus might have disappeared. Since HTLV is supposed to affect chiefly helper/inducer T cells, it could conveniently explain the loss of this subset of lymphocytes in AIDS. However, all the facts in this story are far from proven, and there remain a number of puzzling questions about the role of this agent in AIDS. The chief one that comes to mind is: if HTLV is so prevalent in Japanese leukemia patients as to be considered endemic to that area, why aren't there any cases of AIDS being reported from Japan?

Another, different strain of HTLV was isolated from cells of the previously mentioned non-homosexual French traveler in Haiti who had contracted AIDS after receiving blood transfusions there following an accident. Some antibodies to HTLV might be expected to react with all three known types of human retrovirus, and perhaps with another HTLV-related retrovirus that doesn't cause leukemia but possibly induces AIDS.

Central to the HTLV hypothesis is the knowedge that cats infected with an analogous C-type retrovirus, Feline Leukemia Virus (FeLV), go through a period of severe immunodeficiency and frequently die of opportunistic infections before they develop leukemia. HTLV appears to be extremely fragile, apparently requiring cell to cell contact for transmission. In this respect also, it exhibits a feature predicted for the AIDS agent. On the other hand, it would have to withstand separation with Factor VIII concentrates, perhaps unlikely for HTLV. While providing perhaps the most intriguing current candidates in the race to find an AIDS agent, HTLV-like viruses could easily turn out to be, like so many others, opportunistic microbes. The finding of more than one type of human retrovirus in AIDS patients suggests these too might be an effect rather than the cause of an underlying immune deficiency.

Speculations on the Origins of AIDS

An overview of the epidemiologic characteristics of AIDS can provide not only mechanisms for its control but also important clues to its origins. Is AIDS really a new disease, or was it imported into countries in the temperate zones from endemic areas, where certain of its manifestations would be obscured by local conditions? By now it should be obvious that a search for endemic areas must focus on equatorial Africa and Haiti, which are currently the prime suspects for locales of origin. It has been recognized for years that Kaposi's sarcoma and Burkitt's lymphoma, two diseases now closely associated with AIDS in the U.S., have been almost uniquely endemic to the very areas from which AIDS seems to have been imported into Europe by African immigrants. Neither disease has been observed in significant frequency elsewhere in the world. While apparently much more recent in its appearance, Kaposi's sarcoma was initially the sole manifestation of AIDS recognized in Haiti. This is perhaps due to the fact that the doctors making the early diagnoses were dermatologists rather than immunologists. Both Burkitt's lymphoma and Kaposi's sarcoma may really be manifestations of AIDS in these tropical countries. If so, many there who die of "malnutrition" and "tropical fevers" may actually be succumbing to AIDS.

The opportunistic infections we associate with AIDS in the U.S. wouldn't be recognized in remote tropical or subtropical environments with extremely poor sanitation and medical care. Severely immunodeficient persons in undeveloped regions would probably die untreated, without reaching the point at which they could be diagnosed. The spectrum of AIDS in the United States includes a small percentage of patients with minor immunodeficiency and Kaposi's sarcoma who do not seem prone to opportunistic infections. Perhaps in Haiti and Africa it is only those people with similarly minor immune defects who can survive long enough to be identified as having Kaposi's sarcoma. This would account for the fact that both in Africa and in Haiti (at least early on), Kaposi's sarcoma has been seen more frequently than opportunistic infections, whereas among Haitians in the United States and Africans in Belgium and France, opportunistic infections predominate in AIDS patients while Kaposi's sarcoma remains infrequent.

If the countries of Africa, Haiti (and perhaps others in the Caribbean basin) provide a focus for AIDS, how is it maintained there? Knowledge of its epidemiology in current industrialized societies requires that similar modes of transmission are involved in maintaining a reservoir of the disease. Recently, old world monkeys in primate centers in Massachusetts and California were reported to have suffered an epidemic of immunodeficiency resembling in some respects the outbreak of human AIDS. Although we don't know whether the disease in the monkeys is really related to AIDS, it seems possible that non-human primates in Africa could provide a reservoir for the organism of the disease. An insect vector, such as a mosquito, might carry the infection from the nonhuman primates to people. Judging from the evidence for a carrier state of AIDS in apparently unaffected individuals, the concept of a reservoir for the disease in humans is also not outlandish. If the disease is truly endemic to Africa, we would expect populations there to have built up some degree of immunologic resistance over long periods of time. Such resistance could facilitate the carrier state because the organism would be allowed to survive without killing its host.

Transmission from person to person may occur, as it does in the U.S., principally through intimate bodily contact. If the statistics from African Kaposi's sarcoma cases are analyzed, they provide some additional clues for the epidemiology of AIDS. Among adolescent and adult cases of Kaposi's sarcoma in Zaire and Chad, males greatly outnumber females; the male to female ratio approximates 15:1. In stark contrast, among children, Kaposi's sarcoma is found in perhaps equal numbers of boys and girls. While these discrepancies have usually been regarded as reflecting hormonal or genetic differences between the sexes, an alternative explanation could possibly involve homosexual practices or blood-brotherhood rituals among boys, starting in early adolescence. Hypothetically, AIDS in younger African children would be transmitted from carrier mothers during pregnancy or delivery, or from other persons via some different means (perhaps a mosquito vector) that equally affect males and females at random. Once social forces, such as secret male rites or homosexual activity, came into the picture at adolescence, sexual transmission might overtake the earlier pathways of spread.

Insect vectors, such as mosquitos and flies, play an important role in the spread of disease in Africa and other tropical regions. The vectors and the disease they carry almost always have a specifically adapted relationship to one another, in which part of the microorganism's life cycle takes place in the insect. Simple mechanical transfer of a disease from one human to another by sequential bites by the same mosquito isn't considered to be an effective means of transmission. The geographic distribution of Burkitt's lymphoma within equatorial Africa has always been related to hotspots of malaria, transmitted by Anopheles mosquitos. To a lesser extent, the map of Kaposi's sarcoma incidence also reflects this distribution, although higher altitudes apparently favor that disease over Burkitt's. Kaposi's sarcoma also has a somewhat wider spread, existing also along the east coast of the continent as far down as South Africa. A reasonable conclusion drawn from these demographic data is that strains of Anopheline mosquitos, which carry malaria, are somehow involved in the development of the lymphatic tumor. Perhaps the role of these insects is actually to transmit the AIDS agent in Africa. By altering immunity in persons already carrying Epstein-Barr virus or cytomegalovirus (both highly prevalent in Africa), such an agent could lead to the development of Burkitt's lymphoma or Kaposi's sarcoma in those individuals not promptly killed by opportunistic infections.

Haiti, like central Africa, harbors both malaria and its vectors. If an agent of AIDS were introduced there, the conditions of climate in Haiti would be compatible with survival and transmission. The U.S. has also had its share of Anopheline mosquitos, of which some species have, in the past, been capable of maintaining endemic malaria. Although there is so far no evidence for insect-borne AIDS in this country, the epidemiology of Burkitt's lymphoma and Kaposi's sarcoma in Africa points to the necessity of studying the possible role of insects here as well. Since our geography, climate and sanitation differ enormously from those of Africa, we don't necessarily have to expect similarities in transmission, but it is extremely important to rule out this nagging question.

If AIDS has existed for years in Africa, why wasn't it introduced into Europe sooner? Certainly missionaries and expeditions have gone repeatedly into that area of the world, neither reporting nor importing AIDS. Only in recent years, however, has western medicine been sophisticated enough to be able to distinguish an immunodeficiency disease from a non-specific tropical fever. Also recent is the heavy immigration of Africans to European countries, as a result of the breakdown of the European hold on Africa and the liberation of the African nations. As evidenced by the increasing flood of retrospective diagnoses of AIDS in Europe, the disease has been cropping up there apparently for years. These cases were undefined until the disease was identified in its epidemic form among American homosexuals. The epidemiologic data seem to indicate that Haiti also was only recently affected. Perhaps the disease was imported to Hispaniola (Haiti and the Dominican Republic) by immigrants or travellers from African nations. At an NIH-sponsored meeting on the epidemiology of AIDS in September, 1983, it was pointed out that about 500 Haitians were sent to Zaire in the 1960's to teach in that newly-independent nation. Presumably, many eventually found their way back to Haiti.

Information on what happened to these people may become important in unravelling the routes of transit of AIDS to the Western hemisphere. From there the odyssey of AIDS to the U.S. and Europe through immigrants and American gay men vacationing in Haiti (who may have passed the agent back to some Haitians) seems a simple itinerary.

How Many People Will be Affected?

At a Congressional hearing in August, 1983, one of the medical witnesses testified that by 1985 there might be as many as 20,000 cases of AIDS, and by 1988, 3.3 million people could be affected. He based these figures on a continued rise in the present epidemic curve, which has been doubling about every six months. These calculations don't even include the possibility that the doubling time might be speeded up as cases multiply. This is, of course, a "worst case scenario," which assumes that there is an infinite number of susceptible individuals available to infect, and that the process by which they become infected will continue without change.

This projection seems too pessimistic. The assumptions don't take into account that any chain letter eventually runs out of new people to continue it. Similarly, a disease that affects a circumscribed population, because of restricted modes of transmission, eventually runs out of victims. If AIDS is truly an infectious disease, it will behave like one. Even epidemics like the Black Plague and those caused by new influenza strains run their course. Those diseases are transmitted far more easily than is AIDS, so that essentially all people in their path may be exposed. Among those, many (how many depends on the strength of their "natural" immunity) will not become ill at all, although they may, as in the case of poliomyelitis, nevertheless transmit the disease to others. In the process, these persons, and those who recover from the illness, will mobilize their adaptive immune systems, their B and T cells. Perhaps no longer susceptible to the disease, they might become permanently immune. Thus, they wouldn't be able to transmit it to others. Eventually, the presence of many fully immune people within a group exposed to a disease greatly lessens the chances that those not yet immune will even be exposed, damping down the rate of the disease's spread and ultimately halting the epidemic. This phenomenon, known as "herd immunity," probably contributes to the endemic state of certain diseases.

We suspect that AIDS is endemic in Africa. When we know more about the agent and can see who in the population there has been exposed to it (by determining whose blood contains antibodies), we may find that most Africans are already immune. Some, the carriers, may serve as the reservoir for AIDS. Their immune systems, less protective than some, will permit persistence of the agent without evident disease. Or another species preserves the agent, occasionally transmitting it to still susceptible people in the vicinity. This is the usual nature of an endemic disease.

In the case of AIDS, if we suppose that it was imported by a sexually active gay man or men to New York City, for example, we would expect that promiscuous homosexual men there would be the first to be exposed and become ill. Initially, no other groups would be affected, because the agent had no means of spreading to them. The infection would spread rapidly among those who were promiscuous, but only rarely in those who were not. Among those exposed, some would become ill, others would become immune after a period of communicability, while still others might become chronic carriers (there is no current evidence for the existence of a chronic carrier state, but it occurs in hepatitis B, typhoid fever, giardiasis and many other diseases). During this process, because the number of symptomless people who are communicable increases, the chances of acquiring the disease from any single contact rise as well. We would therefore expect that less promiscuous gays would also begin to develop AIDS. Such a progression of likelihood of transmission to sexually less active men has already been observed. But the process can't go on forever. Eventually, all susceptible individuals in the gay population will be exposed and that population will be "saturated" with AIDS, with most persons who survive being fully immune. No new cases will then develop except among those who newly enter the risk group.

We might further expect that as the disease spread inland into new gay communities, the same process might repeat itself. Indeed, this too has been observed; in the cities of the Midwest, there has been a geometric spread of adenopathy and then fullblown AIDS. The question we must ask is whether reduction of promiscuity or other measures taken to lower the risk of exposure will have come too late to prevent the decimation of these gay communities. Given the apparently long incubation period, no one can really be sure.

Transmission to other groups requires intimate contact. Presumably, a gay drug abuser transmitted the disease to the New York City addicts, who then spread it among themselves by sharing unsterilized needles. Bisexual men might spread it to a few women. Up to now, there are no documented cases in which a man contracted AIDS exclusively through sexual contact with an affected woman.

The spread of AIDS beyond the original risk groups can be expected to be much slower than it has been within those populations. People who have neither sexual contact nor a blood connection with members of the high risk groups, which are quite circumscribed, stand only a remote chance of contracting the disease by a blood transfusion or possibly accidental injection. Therefore, the spread of AIDS to the vast majority of the general public is extremely unlikely.

CHAPTER **6**

Medical Care of

AIDS Patients

Patients with AIDS present a monumental challenge to the combined skills and ingenuity of several medical specialties. To the physician in infectious diseases, providing effective care involves determining the microorganism that is inflicting itself on the patient at the moment, the cause of the fever, weight loss, diarrhea or breathlessness, and then selecting the best antimicrobial drugs with which to treat.

For the oncologist, a physician who specializes in tumors, the task is to choose a protocol that will effectively palliate or cure the opportunistic malignancies (Kaposi's sarcoma, Burkitt's lymphoma, immunoblastic sarcoma and squamous cell carcinoma). In the course of treating AIDS patients, these specialized internists may have to orchestrate surgery, chemotherapy, radiotherapy and immunotherapy. They find themselves balancing between successful treatment and the side effects of drugs, which seem to be more common and more devastating among AIDS patients than among others.

Some of the adverse reactions to drugs, as well as the manifestations of AIDS itself, bring the hematologist onto the scene; this blood specialist must often investigate the paucity of granulocytes, anemias, and the bleeding tendency resulting from insufficient platelets. Many of the experimental treatments being tried require the use of sophisticated and expensive equipment, such as blood cell separators.

Specialists in lung disorders carry out diagnostic bronchoscopy and biopsy to define the variety of pneumonias and,
frequently charged with supervision of intensive care units,
all too often find themselves engaged in the final efforts
against death. With increasing successes in the management of the identifiable opportunistic infections has come a
series of ill-defined brain disorders that the neurologist and
neurosurgeon must try to deal with. Experts in diseases of
the bowel must help define and manage the abdominal pain,
intestinal bleeding and malnutrition that often supervene.
The immunologist has perhaps the most difficult role: to
attempt to find a way through only roughly charted waters
to the essential goal of immunologic reconstitution, without
which the patient's life cannot continue.

Treatment of Opportunistic Infections

Treatment of the infectious diseases associated with AIDS
has improved since the syndrome was first described, chiefly
because physicians now more or less know what organisms
to expect and how to detect them. We have learned to think
of Pneumocystis carinii pneumonia almost at the first sign
of breathlessness, and to start treatment even before the
bronchoscopy confirms its presence. We know to expect
Mycobacterium avium-intracellulare even when the biopsies fail to show granulomatous inflammation; we can make
the diagnosis much earlier than before and now have effective drugs that can cure it. Because physicians can now recognize ulcers caused by Herpes simplex, such lesions need
never reach the size they did in the early patients. We even
have, in acyclovir, a safe and effective drug that can inhibit
the virus causing the ulcers. By now most doctors know of
cryptosporidiosis, even though not much can be done about
it. However, as a result of earlier diagnosis, we can manage
many of the other microorganisms that complicate AIDS:
tuberculosis, salmonellosis, listeriosis, disseminated zoster,
candidiasis and sometimes even cryptococcal meningitis.
Once identified they can be treated conventionally, though
some special problems peculiar to AIDS patients must probably be confronted along the way.

Underlying the problem of medical management is the persisting and often progressive defect in immunity. We should remember that the effectiveness of many antibiotics depends upon an intact immune system, which destroys the organisms that the drugs have only slowed. Except for rifampin and its derivative ansamycin, used chiefly for treating mycobacterial infections, and acyclovir, which is activated by intracellular enzymes provided by the herpesviruses themselves, very few antimicrobial agents reliably enter the infected cells in which these organisms hide and proliferate. As a result, most antibiotics work slowly and only on those microbes that find themselves, having killed their protective host cell, in transit to infect another cell. Partly because of this inefficiency, antibiotics must be used for a long time—in some situations perhaps for the life of the patient —to suppress rather than cure certain infections. This is probably true of infections caused by Herpes simplex, for Toxoplasma gondii and for Candida albicans, each of which, unless managed by chronic or at least repeated intermittent drug administration, tends to recur. Oral acyclovir, not yet approved by FDA for general use, and ketoconazole, recently introduced for candidiasis, keep many AIDS patients out of hospitals.

Side effects of certain drugs are a special problem when the diseases they treat are life-threatening, and few, if any, adequate alternatives exist. In the treatment of pneumocystosis, the most pervasive difficulties stem from the use of trimethoprim-sulfamethoxazole (Bactrim, Septra, cotrimoxazole, TMP-SMZ). As many as 65% of AIDS patients develop either a severe drop in the granulocyte count or a skin eruption in response to this usually innocuous drug combination when administered in the high dosage required. The physician is confronted with a familiar dilemma—the low white cell count may lead to still more severe superinfections with second and third microbes, or the rash may itself become life-threatening. Yet, too brief a course of treatment (no data are yet available indicating how long is necessary) may permit the pneumocystis to recur. Changing to pentamidine, generally speaking a more toxic drug, has its own problems.

Therapy becomes a balancing act. We usually try to achieve at least three weeks of treatment for this lung disease with one or the other agent, depending on drug tolerance. Surprisingly, when some patients are bronchoscoped again at the end of their drug course they may have a persistence of organisms despite major clinical improvement. Another curious finding is that discontinuing the drugs doesn't always result in recurrent disease. Some patients have gone a year between episodes of Pneumocysitis carinii pneumonia without steadily taking drugs. They have almost certainly harbored the organism during their symptomless period.

The paradoxes associated with the management of this infection exemplify some of the problems physicians face in dealing with the opportunistic infections of AIDS. It is beyond the scope of this book to discuss them in detail. Medical textbooks don't provide much guidance to the treatment of AIDS. Specific information is first beginning to be published in journals. Considerable trial and error is still required as we learn to negotiate the intricacies of this difficult process.

Therapy of Malignancies in AIDS

No less a problem are the malignant tumors associated with AIDS. The most prominent, Kaposi's sarcoma, is disseminated and doesn't lend itself to surgery. It almost certainly must be regarded as a widespread, probably multicentric process, resulting from the neoplastic transformation of many separate cells at different sites, rather than spreading only by metastasis. Burkitt's lymphoma and immunoblastic sarcoma are also dispersed tumors, not amenable to surgery or radiotherapy alone. These cancers generally require systemically administered drugs that can reach the widely spread tumor cells. So far, chemotherapy or alpha interferon have been used with only modest successes in Kaposi's sarcoma and have been even less effective in the lymphomas.

Treatment of patients with Kaposi's sarcoma probably

should be individualized, since the disease seems to be so variable. Unfortunately, no controlled studies have been done to determine whether untreated patients with clinically indolent disease can survive or even undergo complete or partial spontaneous tumor regression; virtually all patients receive some form of therapy. From experience with Kaposi's sarcoma occurring in kidney transplant recipients it is known that the tumor can regress when the immunosuppressive drug treatments used to prevent graft rejection are stopped. Among those diagnosed as having AIDS are some patients, almost all young male homosexuals, who have Kaposi's sarcoma but who don't seem to be plagued, even in the long run, with opportunistic infections. The few long-term survivors in AIDS fall into this category. All such patients seem to have been treated for their Kaposi's sarcoma, but we obviously don't know if they really needed treatment. And some of these have relatively intact immunity, but we don't know whether their immune system was depressed earlier.

The other side of the coin, unfortunately the much more common one, is the patient who has clinically progressive Kaposi's sarcoma, generally together with opportunistic infections. For such patients, chemotherapy has major hazards, often dampening such essential remaining host defenses as granulocyte production and the integrity of the intestinal wall. Once breached, these permit entry of bacterial invaders that often prove fatal. Again, the physician must tread a narrow tightrope. The use of chemotherapy, often unavoidable in the face of rapidly progressive tumors, must be managed by experts backed up by first-rate diagnostic radiology and blood banking facilities. Many standard drugs are active, including actinomycin D, DTIC, vincristine and BCNU. In addition, there are several other experimental agents that have been used with apparent success in Africa.

Working at New York University Medical Center, where staging procedures and combination chemotherapy protocols for AIDS tumors were developed, Dr. Linda Laubenstein and her colleagues have perhaps the broadest experience with this sort of treatment. They have employed the triple drug regimen of adriamycin, bleomycin and velban for extensive and aggressive disease, and a single experimental drug, designated VP-16 (etoposide), for patients with less extensive disease. Although significant clinical responses were observed, many of the patients have died of opportunistic infections.

Partially in response to the difficulties associated with chemotherapy in these immunocompromised patients, clinical trials of interferon were begun. Interferons have been known to have anti-tumor effects, both by inhibiting the proliferation of certain malignant cells and by augmenting some of the natural defenses, such as natural killer cells and macrophages, thought to confront cancer's spread. The alpha interferons that were chiefly used in these trials were recently made available in almost limitless amounts by new recombinant DNA technology, which permits the production by bacteria of proteins normally made only by human cells.

It was hoped that the interferons, with their known effects on the immune system, might in part or completely reverse the immune defects of AIDS. While the regimens attempted so far haven't reversed the underlying immune deficiency, they seem active in controlling Kaposi's sarcoma in a proportion of AIDS patients. Twenty to thirty percent have been reported to achieve complete remission, and almost 50% have had at least some benefit, in preliminary though uncontrolled trials. More recent studies appear roughly to confirm these figures, indicating that this material may play an important role in the clinical management of Kaposi's sarcoma. Although a great deal of concern has been voiced over the side effects of interferon preparations, the recombinant material employed in these and other trials appears to be relatively benign. Considering the severity of the disease in some patients, a large-scale controlled trial, in which several medical centers across the country would collaborate, now seems necessary.

The Goal: Reconstitution
of the Immune System

Most observers of AIDS agree that unless the immune system failure is reversed, patients with the syndrome will keep dying. Their susceptibility to untreatable infectious diseases or to unexplained processes, such as those affecting the central nervous system, is so great that eventually one or another such process overtakes them. For as long as this immunodeficiency has been recognized, clinical immunologists, perceiving this fact, have been working to reverse it. The list of drugs and maneuvers that have been considered and tried is quite long.

Unfortunately, there has so far been no successful therapy, although the trials weren't sufficiently systematic or done early enough in the disease process to be regarded as definitely negative. The use of "immuno-modulatory" drugs, which have the potential for altering immune reactivity, is limited by lack of detailed knowledge of their mechanisms of action and even more so by their relative weakness and unpredictability even in the clinical situations for which they were originally employed. Their application to AIDS, a disease whose mechanism is far from being understood, is completely empirical. Making matters worse is that the disease is usually advanced by the time a definite diagnosis can be made. Reversal of the process, complicated as it is by multiple and often undefined infections, may by then be impossible. This situation may well be a chief impetus to the search for early diagnostic and prognostic criteria. If these were available, we could direct therapeutic trials at patients at the early, prodromal stage, well before the onset of opportunistic infections.

Drugs that Modify Immune Responses

Interferons

Of the biological response modifiers that have so far been tried, we have the most systematic experience with alpha interferon. A natural product of large, granular lymphocytes, interferon alpha has been given not only for the treatment of Kaposi's sarcoma but also to a group of patients who had opportunistic infections. A good therapeutic rationale exists for giving this substance since the cells of patients with opportunistic infections almost always produce less than normal amounts of it, at least in the test tube. Several crucial host defense functions that are defective in AIDS would be expected to improve by giving the patient alpha interferon. In a controlled clinical trial carried out at UCLA, twenty patients received, over a period of six months, a preparation of pure alpha interferon produced in bacteria. Unfortunately, like their counterparts in the Kaposi's sarcoma trials, the patients obtained no observable benefits, either in terms of fewer infections or changes in laboratory tests. Fortunately, serious adverse effects were not observed either, a point that probably justifies further trials using different dosage schedules.

Other types of interferon, notably gamma (derived from stimulated T lymphocytes), and perhaps other forms of alpha interferon have been or are in the process of being synthesized by the same recombinant DNA techniques employed in the manufacture of alpha-2, the type already tried. These will probably be tried under experimental protocols in AIDS patients.

Interleukin-2

Like interferons, interleukin-2 (IL-2) is another of the products of normal lymphoid cells that is theoretically useful in treating AIDS. Thought to be primarily a product of the helper T cells, IL-2 can influence other effector T cells (such as cytotoxic cells) to proliferate. If, as many investigators believe, deficits of helper T cells account for the susceptibility to infection in AIDS, the provision of this substance might circumvent the defect, stimulating remaining effector T cells and leading to clinical improvement. Preliminary data from the NIH suggest that, in vitro, some of the responses by AIDS patients' cytotoxic T cells to cytomegalovirus are stimulated when IL-2 is added. While this represents a promising lead, IL-2 is not yet available in large amounts from synthetic sources. It is now laboriously made from cultured human lymphocytes and is enormously expensive. Limited clinical trials a year ago at Memorial Sloan-Kettering Cancer Center demonstrated no significant benefits. The study, however, may have been inadequate because of the small quantities of the material that were available.

The role of IL-2 in the body under normal circumstances is probably to stimulate the T cells at a site of infection to enhance local immunologic defenses. IL-2 is a very short-lived substance; it's possible that this molecule's short term of activity functions as a fuse to limit the stimulation of cells elsewhere that might damage the body as a whole. The problem is that in order to provide as much to a patient as a healthy person's T cells would produce locally at sites of infection, enormous amounts of IL-2 would have to be given by continuous infusion. Such large doses could possibly have serious side effects. Only by carrying out a proper trial, which seems amply justified by the potential benefits, can the usefulness of this material be determined.

Transfer Factor

Transfer factor is yet another biologically active substance or complex of molecules obtained from lymphocytes. Described almost 30 years ago by Dr. Sherwood Lawrence, it provides a means of transfering delayed-type hypersensitivity from one person to another without the transfusion of whole cells. In preparing transfer factor, lymphocytes from persons having a strongly positive skintest to tuberculin, an antigen from M. tuberculosis, are broken up and filtered. The small molecules passing through the tiny pores of a dialysis bag include an active substance. When this material is given to a person who has a negative response in a tuberculin test, the skin test can become positive. Attempts to improve cellular immunity of AIDS patients with various transfer factor preparations have not been promising.

Thymic Humoral Factors and Modulatory Drugs

Thymic hormones that normally induce partial or complete maturation of T cells from their precursors have also been tried in a few patients with AIDS, but no reports of their usefulness have yet appeared. In the light of conflicting findings concerning the levels of the various hormones in the sera of patients with the disease, and of the lack of evidence suggesting thymic abnormalities as playing a primary part in the genesis of AIDS, there seems to be relatively little rationale for their use. Further trials of thymosin in patients considered to fall within the "AIDS prodrome" but who have not yet developed opportunistic infections are being planned.

Drugs

Several drugs that, in laboratory experiments, minimize the effects of suppressor cells are being tried or considered for clinical testing in AIDS. These include cimetidine (a special anti-histamine widely employed in treatment and prevention of peptic ulcer), indomethacin and other related anti-inflammatory agents (affecting the production of prostaglandins within the body, used in arthritis and other painful conditions), and lithium salts (known to increase the output of granulocytes by the bone marrow, but used chiefly in the treatment of manic-depressive psychosis). Also, levamisole and isoprinosine are pharmacologic agents that increase some functions of lymphocytes and other cells of the immune system.

Vitamin C has been advocated by some enthusiasts for use in AIDS, not only because of its health-giving reputation outside of established medical circles but also because of recent laboratory experiments showing that in very large amounts Vitamin C can inhibit the activity of a suppressor substance released by the white cells of some AIDS patients. Our impression is that because there are so many AIDS patients who have tried "megadoses" of this vitamin, without apparent benefit, their spontaneous efforts actually constitute a negative clinical trial.

Therapeutic Maneuvers

Bone Marrow Transplantation and Lymphocyte Infusion

Certainly the most dramatic approach to immunologic reconstitution in AIDS is marrow transplantation. It has the advantage of precedent in other cellular immune deficiency diseases and could, theoretically, circumvent most of the difficulties that are encountered in AIDS. By providing a source of new stem cells, a bone marrow graft could replenish a person's essential supply of lymphocytes as well as restore some of the non-specific host defense contributed normally by granulocytes.

We are aware of five attempts at marrow transplantation in adults with AIDS and of one in a child who probably had the disease. The first two were carried out by our team at the Mount Sinai Hospital, in New York City, in the Spring of 1982, using bone marrow from tissue-compatible relatives of the recipient. The child, also a patient from Mount Sinai, received his marrow at the Memorial Sloan-Kettering Cancer Center, in New York. Later that year, transplantation of identical twin marrow was attempted at UCLA and at the NIH. Because of the severe immune depression of each of the recipients, the chemotherapy that may have been necessary to permit engraftment wasn't tried. Most recently, marrow transplantation was attempted after such chemotherapy by a group of French physicians. With the possible exception of the French patient, about whom information hasn't yet become available, no significant clinical improvement was recognized in any of the patients. Fortunately, none of them suffered serious side effects as a result of the attempts.

The transfer of T cells and other leukocytes from normal donors, either compatible or deliberately incompatible, in order to, respectively, provide the missing cell or stimulate reactivity by the patient's own cells, has also been tried. Concurrent with transfer of cells from a normal identical twin to a twin with AIDS (who later received a marrow transplant) at NIH, conversion of delayed-type hypersensitivity skintests from negative to positive was observed. Presumably this phenomenon is attributable to the transitory presence of immunocompetent donor cells in the patient's blood and tissues. Despite this evident response, the patient wasn't benefited by any other apparent criterion, and continued to develop severe opportunistic infections. Another patient treated at the University of Colorado with his sister's lymphocytes responded similarly. Interestingly, both this man and the patients given marrow grafts at Mount Sinai Hospital had in their serum before cell infusion antibodies that reacted against T cells. These antibodies may have played a role in the disappearance of donor cells after they were infused into the patient.

Plasmapheresis

The removal of massive amounts of plasma, the liquid part of the blood, by a procedure known as plasmapheresis has gained some vogue in the treatment of AIDS. Patients with advanced disease often have extremely elevated levels of antibody molecules (immunoglobulins) in their blood, which include, in some but apparently not all, antibodies against T cells. They also have circulating clusters of these molecules, known as immune complexes, usually when opportunistic infections are present. The extent of damage to the functioning of the immune system, if any, contributed by these antibodies and complexes isn't determined, but several doctors have tried removing them.

The procedure of plasma exchange involves removing blood from an arm vein, then passing it through a continuously spinning cup, a kind of centrifuge, in a machine known as a cell separator. Fractions of the blood (red cells, white cells, platelets and plasma) can then be removed or returned to the patient. Several liters of the patient's own plasma may be taken and replaced by normal plasma or other forms of fluid. The net result is a depletion of immune complexes, possibly undesirable antibodies and a legion of other substances, for the most part unknown, that may be beneficial or detrimental to their former owner. Groups at several medical centers are using this procedure, alone or in combination with the administration of normal gamma globulins, and have claimed limited therapeutic successes.

Plasmapheresis is extremely expensive. It has been tried in a variety of other illnesses, including rheumatoid arthritis, systemic lupus erythematosis, myasthenia gravis and some lymphocyte disorders in which excessive amounts of single antibody proteins are made. As has often happened repeatedly when new treatments are introduced, results of plasmapheresis have been highly touted in all these disorders, only to be clouded by the stark reality of placebo-controlled clinical trials. Although cumbersome, controlled tests for plasmapheresis would be essential, since being connected to one of these impressive-looking machines carries with it significant psychological suggestibility for the patient. It would be best if such trials were organized soon, since it would be a shame to continue spending vast sums on such costly treatments if they turned out to be useless in AIDS. We used plasmapheresis in an attempt to permit marrow engraftment in one of our patients, but detected no change in his clinical condition; we also know of several other patients who seemed to have no clearcut benefit resulting from the process.

Administration of Intravenous Gamma Globulin

Patients with AIDS characteristically have elevated levels of immunoglobulins (antibody proteins) in their serum. Present information nevertheless indicates that they have a problem in their ability to produce specific antibodies in response to some antigenic challenges, as might be expected considering their severe paucity of helper T cells. The types of infections some patients have had suggest the presence of clinically significant antibody deficiency.

These findings may be sufficient to justify the use of passive immunization with immune (gamma) globulin. Such infusion is generally employed in the treatment of B cell deficiency diseases (hypogammaglobulinemia, agammaglobulinemia) in which the levels of circulating immunoglobulins (and thus also antibodies) are very depressed. A more controversial rationale might be drawn from the concept that gamma globulin exerts a negative feedback and can sometimes serve to lower excessively high immunoglobulin levels. By turning off overexuberant antibody production, one could perhaps stop the formation of immune complexes that are thought to cause problems.

Recent developments in the technology of immune globulin production have made it possible to administer safely and comfortably massive amounts of the material intravenously. Previously, only much smaller amounts could be given, which appear to be far less effective in controlling infections in individuals who are antibody deficient. Some investigators have begun to use this treatment in AIDS, hoping to find it useful against opportunistic infections. In a couple of medical centers, this approach is being combined with plasmapheresis, primarily the treatment of children thought to have AIDS.

General Measures to Alleviate Immunodeficiency

Is there anything the patient with AIDS can do himself to minimize the chances of developing an opportunistic infection, Kaposi's sarcoma or another complication? Do conscious alterations of diet, activity or stress affect the immune system? What about vitamins, macrobiotic diets, jogging, psychotherapy, celibacy?

It is probably fair to say at the outset that there is vanishingly little in the way of factual information, based on scientific investigation of any sort, with which to answer this kind of question. From our own information based on talking to patients, it's clear that all sorts of behavior modification and dietary manipulations have been tried by people with AIDS, none of which so far seems to have slowed the relentless progression of the disease. Some patients have on their own taken 10-15 grams of vitamin C daily. Without an objective, carefully designed study, the actual benefit or detriment resulting from this sort of informal treatment can't be assessed.

There are some actions that can contribute to a patient's well-being and, certainly, quality of life. The most important thing that people around the patients can do is to avoid inflicting on them physical and psychological isolation, a response to the panic that the mysterious and deadly nature of the disease has inspired. Even though at this point it may not be wise to express affection and warmth towards an AIDS patient with kissing or other intimacies, there is no cause to treat them as pariahs. The currently available epidemiology of AIDS indicates rather clearly the sorts of reasonable precautions that are warranted even if details are still not all in. Beyond fear of infection lies the perhaps greater fear of isolation, which often befalls people perceived as having a terminal illness, such as cancer. How do we talk to them? What can we possibly say? The continued support and counsel of friends and associates is vitally important, and particularly so in times of illness.

In an inherently stressful situation such as that of dealing with AIDS, it is, of course, a truism to advise that stress should be minimized as much as possible. There is experimental evidence from several studies showing that environmental, psychological pressures can reduce certain immunologic functions. It is not known whether these alterations are clinically important, but, until there's evidence to the contrary, we should assume they are.

Is it useful to the patient's own condition to avoid crowds, as some have recommended? Should the AIDS patient retire to the country, or move to a dry climate?Let's remember that the majority of microorganisms plaguing AIDS patients were already present in their bodies before they were ill. Sharing the air of restaurants or theaters with other people, therefore, probably carries little risk for the patient. The respiratory viruses such as those that cause the common cold, influenza or most adenoviruses (some of which are known to persist in patients with AIDS but have an unknown influence) could conceivably predispose to more serious forms of infection, perhaps pneumonia, but they aren't recognized to be specifically troublesome in AIDS. Prudence probably dictates that direct face-to-face contact with coughing or sneezing people should be avoided.

Although still unresolved, certain activities may, for a variety of reasons already discussed, be detrimental to immunologic function. Intimate contact with multiple partners, anal receptive intercourse, "recreational" drugs or intravenous heroin or cocaine use are all best eschewed to minimize potential pressures on the cellular immune system.

Patients with AIDS should be encouraged to live their lives as normally as is feasible within the constraints necessarily imposed by having a communicable disease. Reasonable amounts of work, travel, and recreation should probably be continued to the extent the patient feels comfortable in doing them. Management of ongoing drug or medical therapies should be as flexible as possible to meet the special needs of these individuals. Those providing care must be aware of the excruciating difficulties faced by AIDS patients, whose suffering on every level, including physical, psychological, social, economic and personal, is unprecedented.

CHAPTER 7

What Can Be Done

to Prevent AIDS?

AIDS can be prevented—the epidemiology of the disease tells us how to control it. Since the evident modes of transmission are limited, it should be possible to restrict the spread, even if we can't eliminate the cause. The obvious immediate solution would be avoidance of sexual activity or sharing of needles or blood with anyone who has possibly been exposed to the causative agent of AIDS. The chief questions are how to determine who has been exposed, and whether people are willing to change their practices.

Recommendations for Gay Men

There's no longer much doubt that AIDS is a sexually transmitted disease (STD) and that the surest way to prevent it would be abstinence from homosexual activity, at least for those men who have not maintained a truly monogamous relationship predating the AIDS epidemic. Short of that, there are some compromise measures that may reduce the risks but won't eliminate them entirely.

The spread of AIDS, primarily among male homosexuals, has probably been promoted by sociological factors favoring promiscuous behavior by some gay men. Sexual freedom has been facilitated by effective antibiotics that have kept most of the previously known STD in check. The increasing tolerance towards homosexuality as an alternative life-style, particularly in the larger cities, has attracted many gay people and has provided a high concentration of individuals available for homosexual contacts. Removal of homosexuality from the list of psychiatric disorders and from criminal codes in many states has enabled many gay men to come out of the closet. Whether impelled by an uncontrollable drive or by deliberate choice, some have opted for the role of sexual athlete, affirming or celebrating their sensuality through innumerable contacts, often with anonymous partners.

Sexual prowess as an end in itself by no means characterizes all homosexual men. Many have stable, restricted relationships and lead much less frenetic sex lives than those the CDC found to be typical of the early group of AIDS victims. But, as the pool of men exposed to the suspected causative agent within the gay communities widened, the chances for all sexually active men to come in contact with a carrier increased. The risks grew even for those who were not especially promiscuous. In the worst-case scenario, all actively gay men in an affected community, except those who have been restricted to longstanding monogamous unions, would eventually become exposed. How many of those will actually become sick depends on a susceptibility factor or factors that currently are a total mystery. In this extreme situation, anyone newly arriving in New York, San Francisco, Los Angeles or other city to seek sexual freedom in its gay society would run a significant risk of being exposed to AIDS and an as-yet incalculable chance of developing the disease within three years.

Considering this ominous possibility, it isn't really sufficient to recommend that gay men now seek monogamous relationships and stay with them. Such advice would perhaps have been adequate four years ago, before there were sizable numbers of exposed individuals. A couple of years ago there was already evidence of severe immunologic disturbance—T cell subset maldistribution—in a very high proportion (80%) of a sample of New York's sexually active gay population. We can't properly assess this statistic even now. It may only reflect the prevalence of sexually transmitted viral illnesses, but it could just as easily indicate that the AIDS agent was at that time already widely disseminated. Until a specific etiologic agent is identified and a diagnostic test developed, we can't make absolute recommendations. Clearly, some sensible measures must be tried now to stem the spread of the disease. Waiting for answers that may take a long time to emerge will result in needless deaths.

How any person accepts any recommendations depends on how much he values a particular life-style, including sexual freedom, and **how frightening the prospect of** an early death is, even if the odds of contracting AIDS were one in a thousand. The 1/1000 figure was an estimate based on the number of homosexual participants in the hepatitis B vaccine trials who have developed AIDS. Most likely, those individuals receiving the vaccine have been among the more sexually active, since they have in the past been at greater risk for hepatitis. But the actual risk now may be much higher, eventually perhaps as many as one in one hundred random homosexual men becoming ill. This figure is about half way (on a logarithmic scale) between the one per thousand estimate and a much higher incidence extrapolated from the occurrence of 4 cases of illness in a cluster of 19 men (about 21%) who variably shared both a house and intimacies at a gay beach community.

One reasonable approach to controlling the spread of AIDS might be to recommend a self-imposed division between those who have probably been exposed already and those who probably haven't. This would involve encouraging young men first entering the gay community to consort with one another, avoiding sexual contact with longstanding participants in the urban gay life. Although such a proposal might be controversial and undoubtedly difficult to put into practice, it may well be the only way to halt the spread of AIDS beyond its present boundaries while allowing for continued sexual activity. If leaders of the gay community endorsed such a plan, they might institute ways in which men new to the community could meet one another without engaging in sexual activity with the already exposed group. Frank disscussions about one's previous exposures should be encouraged.

For those who have been active but have had no direct contacts with AIDS patients, it would be advisable to establish monogamous relationships with other individuals whose sexual background is as similar to their own as possible. If and when specific tests distinguishing carriers from immune individuals become available, as they are for hepatitis B, the need for even this sort of Russian roulette will be eliminated. And, for those who know they have been exposed over a long period as lovers of men with the disease, there seems little reason to terminate the relationship, for the outcome will depend on individual resistance to the development of clinical illness.

Neither the specific mode of spread nor the length of the period of communicability is known exactly. Limited epidemiologic information suggests that people can transmit the disease before they themselves show clinical symptoms. If, as seems likely, few knowingly ill men continue to be sexually active, the relentless spread of AIDS must be attributable to individuals in such a symptomless carrier state. It is remotely possible that essentially all AIDS transmission occurs from those few sick men who continue (as some apparently do) to have sexual contact with others. If this is the case, the man who remains with his sick lover may be adding to his chances of coming down with AIDS. The truth is, we really don't yet have all the facts to make foolproof choices in this terrible dilemma.

Nor is it clear whether certain types of sexual intercourse aren't inherently more immunosuppressive than others. Some studies have suggested that the passive partner in anal intercourse is at greater risk of developing T cell imbalance. If this immune alteration results from a reaction to sperm or foreign white blood cells being introduced in the anus (rather than a response to viruses present in semen), it could possibly trigger immune suppression and contribute to making a person vulnerable to an AIDS agent.

Our preliminary data show that a substantial proportion of those men who have had truly monogamous relationships have normal T cell subset distributions. This seems to indicate that passive anal intercourse within such a relationship doesn't, by itself, compromise immunity, but that it requires the introduction of a virus or foreign microorganism to induce the immunologic state reflected by the subset imbalances. Until this question is settled by systematic study, anal intercourse, even with one partner, should not be practiced without a condom. By limiting, through the use of a condom, access of foreign cells as well as microorganisms to the rectal tissues, the potential for immunosuppression should be minimized.

The strongest argument for employing condoms is the presence of cytomegalovirus strains in the semen of an extremely high proportion of sexually active gay males. Cytomegaloviruses are known to suppress human immunity and are also implicated in the process of tumor induction in Kaposi's sarcoma, which is far more common among homosexual AIDS patients than among the other risk groups with AIDS.

How should gay men who already have the disease protect others? Are there any safe sexual interactions? What are their legal responsibilities? Clearly the moral responsibility of anybody having a communicable disease is to avoid giving it to another person. Although we don't know for a fact that people already ill are capable of transmitting AIDS, caution demands the presumption that they are. Until proven otherwise, the implication is that any intimate contact by an AIDS patient with another person (who has not already been exposed) carries with it the risk of inflicting death. This statement is not at all fanciful, and should be considered seriously. Under New York State Public Health Law (and there may be similar statutes in other states) a person with a communicable disease or even a "carrier" who behaves as a menace to others can be investigated by public health officers, following a complaint by a doctor. If such a person is judged to be dangerous, officials can initiate proceedings to have the individual confined to an appropriate hospital or institution for treatment.

In summary, homosexual men who have AIDS, and even those suspected—because of chronic lymphadenopathy or other "prodromal" symptoms—of having it, should for the time being refrain from sexual activity except with their longstanding partners or perhaps with others who are similarly afflicted. Well homosexual men who want to remain sexually active should restrict their intercourse according to the extent of their likely past exposure, and in any case limit the number of different contacts. The lack of scientific data as yet confirming that condoms prevent AIDS should not discourage their use. They carry no risk and possibly confer protection from some organisms. Newly active homosexual males should be encouraged to seek out one another and to avoid intimate sexual contacts with those gay men who have been active for a long time. This moderately restrictive approach could help preserve a limited degree of sexual freedom while cutting down on further spread. And, until such time as questions involving the carrier state are resolved, gay men should voluntarily refrain from giving blood, even if they consider themselves safe donors.

Controversy About Gay Bars and Bathhouses

Health officials have been urged by various individuals and groups to ban the distribution of nitrites and other "recreational" drugs that until now have been readily available, and, even more emphatically, to close commercial establishments, such as gay bars and bathhouses, that encourage the open practice of homosexual promiscuity. Attempts to outlaw substances that are widely used have never been very successful. Furthermore, extensive experience in venereal disease control over the years has shown that restrictive measures are impractical and sometimes even self-defeating, separating those needing assistance from those capable of providing it. Similarly, laws against homosexuality have generally not succeeded in eliminating it but only in driving it underground for most of history. To outlaw the gathering places of gay men and their use of poppers could lead to greater difficulties in obtaining medical information and perhaps discourage cooperation with public health officers at a time when such communication is increasingly important.

We have to keep in mind, however, that the gay baths in particular are actively promoting and commercially exploiting anonymous promiscuity, a practice now clearly linked with the transmission of a lethal disease. Anonymous sex is highly risky because unfamiliar sexual partners may be unknowingly or knowingly ill or may have been exposed to others with AIDS, and intercourse with a large number of contacts just multiplies all the risks. The response of many gay men to the obvious message of the AIDS epidemic has apparently already had the effect of altering some sexual patterns. It would be best if the gay community itself could achieve the elimination of such places by educating their patrons and putting pressure on their operators. If that doesn't happen soon, health departments may have little choice but to condemn them. It could be fairly argued that allowing such hazardous activity to continue betrays official indifference to the lives of gay men, who should be protected by public health agencies. Closing the baths, though possibly an impractical action, may be the best of a number of imperfect alternatives.

Prevention of AIDS in Drug Abusers

Transmission of AIDS among the users of illicit intravenous drugs will be much more difficult to contain than among homosexuals. Drug abusers often behave as if they had a deathwish, and don't respond appropriately to warnings concerning health. Severe, life-threatening infections of the heart valves have long been a problem for those injecting unsterile solutions or suspensions of heroin and other substances intravenously. Yet, many drug addicts, having already been close to death by undergoing open heart surgery for valve replacement (which makes them especially susceptible to reinfection), continue to inject themselves, returning to the same hospitals with the same problem until they die. In many cases, knowledge of the hazards and fear of death don't seem to be enough to overcome their addiction.

One factor contributing to the spread of the disease in this population seems to be, as it is among homosexuals, the proliferation of commercial operations exploiting compelling drives. These "shooting galleries," which rent out unsterile needles by the injection, favor multiple needle sharing, a practice that may not be prevalent among individual drug addicts on the street. Despite the fact that such shops are already illegal, their continued operation only confirms that legislating controls is not an adequate solution to the problem. Some workers have pointed out that many patrons of these shooting galleries are not true addicts but abusers who take advantage of them for the occasional "high." Educational campaigns directed at the more casual patrons of these shops might be helpful in reducing the spread of AIDS, even if they didn't affect true addicts.

Most cases of AIDS among heterosexuals so far involve drug abuse by the man, the woman or both partners. Women with the disease are likely to have husbands or sexual contacts who are addicts, if they aren't drug abusers themselves. Should significant spread to heterosexuals actually occur, it is likely that the drug culture will have played a major role in its passage. The interesting paucity of cases of AIDS among drug abusers outside the metropolitan area of New York City may reflect a greater sociologic separation elsewhere between risk groups. This should provide an impetus towards intensified efforts to educate young people to shun these lethal practices and establishments. There may still be time to prevent the spread of AIDS to drug addicts in areas of the country in which they have not already been overtly affected.

One definite recommendation we can make is that paid blood collection in areas frequented by drug users should be immediately and effectively halted. Monetary incentives for giving blood, to be used for manufacture of components, can attract donors motivated to conceal their drug use or, for that matter, other AIDS risk factors. Voluntary blood donation is not a high priority of those devoted to illicit drugs, and thus the elimination of payment will tend to weed out potentially infected donors.

Safety Measures for Recipients of Blood Products and Transfusions

Assuring the safety of blood products during this period of uncertainty required making assumptions that may, in the end, be seen as overly cautious. The costs of policies that minimize the chances of transmission are unavoidably high. There has already been some stigmatization of those perceived as risky donors, with accompanying concerns about civil rights issues and confidentiality. Blood supplies have suffered to some extent as a result of loss from the donor pool not only of those who are excluded but also, because of misinformation and misinterpretation, some who need not be. Panic concerning blood-borne transmission, furthered by sensationalist reports in the news media, has led to the formation of blood donor cooperatives and demands from those about to receive blood transfusions that only their own specified donors be used. These pressures have already caused problems in blood banking and have led hospitals in various communities to arrive at an assortment of quite different solutions to the quandary of blood transfusions.

Fortunately, an apparently rational and effective approach to blood donation has been developed that answers many of the questions while avoiding many of the pitfalls: confidential, voluntary self-exclusion. Coupled with the cooperative response of most people to publicity surrounding the blood donor issue, the new guidelines should greatly advance the desired goal of a safe blood supply.

Blood components were first suspected as a possible vehicle for transmission of AIDS in the summer of 1982, when the initial reports came out of hemophiliacs having the disease, and, somewhat later, with the appearance of transfusion-related cases. The reports were greeted with disbelief by some blood bankers, but the problem could not be ignored, and within a few months action was taken. The Office of Biologics of the Food and Drug Administration, after meeting with concerned groups, including representatives of the affected communities, developed recommendations in March, 1983, to mitigate the problem. These were immediately implemented in all registered blood collection centers within the United States.

New Guidelines for Blood Donations

The intent of the guidelines was to remove from the donor pool all who might be identified either as having AIDS or otherwise being at an increased risk of transmitting it. The approach is to inform persons at high risk as well as those workers responsible for exclusion of donors on the basis of medical history. The list of questions regularly asked of prospective donors was expanded to call to attention symptoms suggestive of AIDS. Blood taken inadvertently from individuals suspected of having the disease was to be considered highly contagious and to be disposed of according to standard procedures.

Individual blood collecting agencies developed local methods for implementation of these guidelines. The Greater New York Blood Program, for instance, was aware that many regular donors to blood drives in corporations and other work settings might be compromised if it became known that they suddenly were excluded from donating blood. A mechanism was developed through which those considering themselves at risk could continue to donate. A questionnaire was designed whereby a donor could select, in private, whether the blood should be used for transfusion or for research purposes only. Units from non-responders, as well as from those indicating use for research, would be excluded from the pool used for transfusions or for processing further into blood products.

Starting in January, 1983, the blood units designated for research were studied to determine whether any blood test, or combination of blood tests, could be used to identify special characteristics of those persons who excluded themselves. The object was to find a "surrogate marker," a test that could be routinely employed to objectively predict and remove blood likely to carry AIDS, even in the absence of a specific test for the disease. The search for such an index was motivated in part by pressures from leaders of the risk groups, who found it distasteful for all their members to be stigmatized by exclusion from the donor pool. The marker thought most likely to succeed was a test for antibodies to "core antigen," a component of the hepatitis B virus, since most patients with AIDS would be expected to have such antibodies in their blood. Other surrogate markers considered included such nonspecific abnormalities frequently found in AIDS as cytomegalovirus antibodies, T cell subset imbalance, and low lymphocyte counts.

Though it did not yield any useful surrogate marker, the study (with follow-up) did show a gradual decline in those men donating blood who had hepatitis B core antibodies and had indicated their blood should be used only for research. In the early phase of the study, there was a significant proportion of male donors opting "for research only," who had the characteristics expected of the high-risk gay population; eventually such donors dropped out of the donor pool. These findings suggested that the potential AIDS carriers who had a homosexual profile had stopped donating voluntarily in response to the publicized possible dangers.

Voluntary versus Paid Blood Donation

Over 98% of the nation's blood transfusions come from volunteer donors. Undoubtedly, this contributes significantly to the safety of the blood supply, which, as mentioned before, annually provides more than 10 million units of blood components to over 3 million recipients. Spokesmen for the agencies responsible point out that since the start of the

AIDS outbreak three years ago, perhaps 10 million persons have received blood components (not including hemophiliacs receiving pooled clotting factors), but only about 20 cases of AIDS have been tentatively linked to blood transfusions during this period. Only in one of these cases has the source of the recipient's disease been clearly traced to a donor with AIDS. According to retrospective analysis, the risks of coming down with the disease from a blood transfusion are one in a million (0.0001%). By comparison, around 6% of blood transfusions result in transmission of hepatitis (usually now not very serious because of the elimination of most hepatitis B), and about one in every 500,000 transfusions (0.005%) results in death because the wrong unit of blood was given. The chance of death from routine surgery for appendectomy is about one in 5,000, for D & C (dilation and curettage, for abortion or for other reasons) about one in 600. In short, transfusion is not very dangerous with respect to contracting AIDS. Nevertheless, blood transfusions should always be administered with caution and only for clear-cut indications.

While the potential for transmitting AIDS from volunteer blood donors now seems extremely limited, both because of the guidelines that have been instituted and its very low frequency to begin with, the problem of pooled plasma derivatives, and the related issue of paid blood donors, are more difficult to assess and to control. "Source plasma," the raw material from which Factor VIII, Factor IX (another clotting protein), albumin and various types of gamma globulins are made, is largely derived from commercial blood banks. These institutions either belong to or supply the major pharmaceutical companies engaged in the preparation of biologicals for human use. In contrast to the altruistic motivations of volunteer blood donors, those of the paid donor are more suspect, particularly since the commercial donor centers tend to draw an indigent, often addicted or alcoholic clientele in need of cash. These donors are far less likely to exclude themselves voluntarily even if they are aware they are carrying a communicable disease. Indeed, one of the recent transfusion-associated cases of AIDS in an elderly woman who had had heart surgery may have derived from a donation from such a commercial blood bank. Attempts by public health officials to trace the donor were frustrated when they found that the facility had gone out of business and its records had been burned.

Some collection centers operating for various specialized reasons, such as the accumulation of rare blood types, have not earned the unfavorable reputation associated with the more routine commercial blood banks. However, the dangers inherent in the paid donor system are great enough that a law has been enacted requiring units of blood from paid donors to be clearly labelled as such in large letters, so that recipients can see what they are getting and can presumably complain (if they are aware enough to do so). This rule seems to us to be placing the burden of choice on the wrong people, but it may eventually have the desirable effect of severely curtailing the use of purchased donor units.

In contrast to the rare transmission of AIDS by single unit blood transfusions, the frequency of AIDS in severe hemophiliacs is very high, both because their treatment depends on clotting factor concentrates derived from a plasma pool, and because the factor itself may be immunosuppressive. The unfortunate reality is that AIDS is now second only to bleeding as a cause of death among Factor VIII-deficient males in the U.S.; among severe hemophiliacs, one out of 500 has already developed the disease. Because of this high incidence of AIDS in its constituents, the National Hemophilia Foundation has called for restriction of blood and plasma donation by persons in the recognized high risk groups, and was understandably in the forefront of the movement that led to the FDA recommendations.

Commercial collection agencies for source plasma were actually among the first to respond to this outcry, so there is reasonable hope that donors contributing even to these organizations will be restricted sufficiently to limit the contribution of clotting factor concentrates capable of transmitting AIDS.

Perhaps more important is the recent development of a new process (for briefly heating Factor VIII concentrates) capable of inactivating viruses of certain types. Until now, the purification procedures that allowed preservation of the clotting factors' activity also preserved the infectivity of viral agents such as hepatitis B. It is hoped that the new treatment, cleared for use by the the Food and Drug administration, will also inactivate the presumed agent of AIDS.

Hepatitis B Vaccine

Another biological product of plasma collection, hepatitis B vaccine (Heptavax B), has also provoked anxiety concerning transmission of AIDS. Only recently approved by the FDA, this vaccine has been shown through extensive clinical trials to be highly protective against a potentially deadly form of hepatitis. It consists of purified hepatitis B surface antigen, the immunogenic coat of the virus deprived of its infectious DNA. Because the original source of the material was plasma from homosexual men, which contained hepatitis viruses, the vaccine has understandably met with some hesitancy. On the basis of a retrospective analysis comparing incidence of AIDS among recipients of the vaccine with non-recipient homosexuals, and the demonstrated efficacy of the chemical inactivation procedures employed in its manufacture, Heptavax B has been regarded as safe. It continues to be licensed by the FDA and recommended by the agencies responsible for overseeing immunization practices for those at risk of contracting hepatitis B.

Several thousand male homosexuals participated in the clinical trials defining the value and safety of Heptavax B. Recipients of early batches of the vaccine, prepared for the most part before the AIDS outbreak, and a similar control group have been followed for evidence of AIDS. Because the vaccine was evidently so effective, the men in the control group were also inoculated, with later batches, so that they could also receive its benefits. The data from these groups do not suggest that the vaccine transmits AIDS: there was approximately equal incidence of the disease in the original vaccinees and the gay men who had been controls. While seemingly reassuring, these data fail to take into account the fact that the material used in the original trials was collected before AIDS appeared in this country and would therefore not be expected to contain an agent of that disease. Probably more relevant is information on the purification and inactivation procedures used in the manufacture of the vaccine. The surface antigen is isolated by two separate ultracentrifugation steps that render the material pure, as far as can be detected by the electron microscope. Next, the vaccine is treated by three separate procedures, with high concentrations of urea, with pepsin and formalin. Each step is known to inactivate overlapping groups of viruses; when subjected to a combination of these three, all known types of viral agents become noninfectious, including, of course, those currently proposed as possible causes of AIDS.

Protection of Medical Personnel

Because health care providers now widely accept the idea that AIDS is probably transmitted like hepatitis B, many are worried about contracting AIDS in the course of their work. It may be helpful to keep in mind, however, that while the routes of transmission may be similar, the ease of spread may be considerably less for AIDS, so that precise similarities may not really exist. In the four years since the start of the outbreak, none among those who have worked regularly in close proximity to AIDS patients—examining them, passing tubes into their lungs and intestines, conducting dialysis to replace their failed kidneys, drawing and performing tests on their blood, changing and laundering their linen and clearing away their food utensils and bodily wastes—have been clearly shown to have contracted the disease as a consequence.

Many hospital employees are concerned about their own safety in the face of a devastating, mysterious disease. Despite the perceived danger, most health professionals and ancillary staff of those hospitals that routinely care for an increasing number of AIDS patients have continued to carry out their work conscientiously. There have been isolated instances of health workers refusing to deal with the patients, and nurses and house staff have admitted to varying degrees of reluctance in handling AIDS victims. In some cases, fear has led to the physical and psychological isolation of patients, but, for the most part, the record has been good.

Understandably, there has been a great deal of concern for the protection of those in the health field. In November, 1982, in response to requests from AIDS investigators and hospital administrators in New York and elsewhere, the CDC and the Division of Safety of the NIH published — in *MMWR*—guidelines for clinical and laboratory workers involved with AIDS patients and their specimens. Another set of recommendations, for dentists and morticians, appeared in September, 1983. These guidelines are reprinted in their entirety in the Appendix.

The gist of the CDC recommendations is to urge medical and laboratory personnel to avoid "direct contact of skin and mucous membranes with blood, blood products, excretions, secretions and tissues of persons judged likely to have AIDS." The strongest directives are aimed at preventing the contamination of broken skin with potentially infectious patient material, especially through needle punctures. Containment of bloody articles, proper disposal of needles, and frequent handwashing are recommended, as is the use of gloves and gowns under certain, but not all, circumstances. Wearing of masks by hospital personnel and the quarantine of patients are not advised, unless specifically warranted for other reasons (such as fecal incontinence, bleeding or demented behavior).

Those working with AIDS patients' specimens in the laboratory are additionally cautioned to avoid vaporizing (aerosolizing) blood and tissues, to wear gloves when handling the material, and to employ biological safety cabinets that keep samples isolated from their handlers—as much as possible. Mouth pipetting, smoking in the laboratories, and any other activities tending to bring hands to mouths are to be avoided. Decontamination procedures and routine handwashing are urged. Additional specific recommendations are outlined for persons inoculating experimental animals with materials from AIDS patients.

The guidelines were not intended to be restrictive, merely to provide the minimum necessary precautions for safety based upon available epidemiologic information. They are considered adaptable to specific local situations and to the special problems of various professional groups, such as dentists and their assistants, surgeons, pathologists or undertakers.

Various medical institutions around the country and even in the same city have had different responses to the guidelines and have adopted some regulations of their own. Some hospitals have developed extremely restrictive procedures, while others have accepted the CDC guidelines. To some extent, these actions have been influenced by the anxieties of hospital staff members. In some hospitals, the flood of AIDS patients has made even the Federal recommendations difficult to carry out fully.

Experience with the patterns of AIDS transmission so far has been reassuring that the CDC recommendations are adequate. There is still no convincing case in which a health worker became ill from direct contact with an AIDS patient. As we have said, it is difficult to accept as occupationally acquired the four cases of hospital employees described in *MMWR*, of which at least three seem unrelated to AIDS patient care. Even so, health workers can't expect to escape entirely from this disease, no matter how careful they are. Accidents and breaks in technique occur inevitably even among the most experienced and conscientious personnel. By now, probably well over 100 people have injured themselves with sharp objects previously in contact with AIDS patients' blood; and the number of inadvertently contaminated cuts and other seemingly innocuous events associated with the daily care of patients and laboratory specimens is uncounted and uncountable. So, we must await their outcomes with some trepidation while hoping for the breakthrough that will identify the agent and pave the way for the production of a preventive vaccine. If success comes, much of it will be due to the efforts of many health providers who have worked hard and with an uncertain degree of personal risk to contain this devastating epidemic.

Safeguarding Contacts and Children
of AIDS Patients

Prevention of the spread of AIDS to heterosexual contacts at present needs to follow generally the recommendations made for homosexual men. There is no currently available information indicating the relative safety of vaginal, as opposed to anal, intercourse. Nor, for that matter, are there any solid data concerning the danger or safety of any specific sexual practice, including intimate kissing. Until more is known about this, extreme caution must be used to avoid intimate physical contact with any person suspected of having AIDS. This advice is unpleasant to give and understandably hard to follow.

Women who have had sexual contacts with bisexual men in affected communities, such as in New York City and San Francisco, are theoretically at some risk and should be conscious of the AIDS warning signals. Like their male counterparts, women who have been potentially exposed should avoid intimacy with new partners and shun promiscuity.

Female sex partners of AIDS victims are of special importance to studies of how the disease is transmitted; they can be extremely helpful to the understanding of AIDS and are urged to make themselves known to public health officers or clinical investigators for examination and close follow-up. They may be asked to give a frank and detailed account of their sexual exposures. Only through such interviews will specific sexual practices, such as vaginal, oral or anal intercourse, be implicated or exonerated as modes of AIDS transmission. It's interesting that only one female prostitute (who denied being a drug abuser) is known to have had AIDS; this low incidence might be explained on the basis that there is probably little intimate contact between such women and the major groups likely to transmit the disease.

The female AIDS victim or the wife of an AIDS patient should avoid becoming pregnant because of her potential for transmitting the disease to the child. For such a woman who is already pregnant, abortion may be a choice to consider. It must be pointed out that there is woefully little information at present on the frequency, or even the actuality, of transplacental transmission of the disease, especially by mothers who are not overtly ill. Any decision on this issue is fraught with uncertainty and worry. Pregnant wives of newly discovered AIDS patients have asked for recommendations in this situation; in the absence of significant statistics, they have been advised that any woman who decides to carry the baby to term must be willing to accept the possibility that the child might be affected. As is the case with most other grey areas surrounding AIDS, this one will be clarified only when specific antibody or other tests can determine with certainty who has been exposed and who hasn't.

Long-Range Prevention

Effective preventive measures beyond those restricting sexual and needle-borne transmission will depend on better clarification of the cause or causes of AIDS. To those of us who think there is inescapable evidence that a newly introduced infectious agent has caused the AIDS epidemic, the most important goal is the development of a vaccine which would be capable of preventing the entire process in most people and of providing "herd immunity" protective of the rest. The identification, isolation and inactivation of the specific causative agent will be necessary.

A shortcut might be obtained by the production of a crude empirical vaccine even before the isolation of the etiologic organism. Such a provisional vaccine could perhaps be prepared from the sera of AIDS victims, inactivated by the approaches used in making the hepatitis B vaccine. Because we are dealing with a deadly agent, clinical trials of such a vaccine would represent a risky proposition. More than likely, rapidly developing recombinant DNA technology will provide a synthetic vaccine and also a method for identifying the suspected microbe of AIDS. Availability of an animal model on which to test any vaccine would be useful but not essential.

If it takes as long to find the AIDS agent as it did to

uncover the hepatitis B virus, we may have to resort to half way measures for years. Just because we desperately want a speedy solution, we shouldn't lose sight of the realities of medical progress. Quite a few "old" diseases—rheumatoid arthritis, systemic lupus erythematosus, sarcoidosis, Hodgkin's disease, "non-A, non-B" hepatitis—have behaved convincingly like infections and have led scientists to many dead ends during their quest for causative agents. Good luck combined with the involvement of many good minds led to the discovery of the causes of Lyme arthritis and Legionnaires' disease; both were for a time perplexing to researchers. With these experiences in mind, we ought to get on with the serious business of preventing AIDS, employing the means we already have at our disposal. Otherwise, things may get a great deal worse before they start getting better.

CHAPTER 8

Solving the Riddle of AIDS: Research and Planning

When an epidemic that kills nearly all its victims continues to expand unabated for four years, people justifiably ask: "Why haven't they found a cure yet?" As anxieties rise among persons who consider themselves at high risk for AIDS and among others who are deeply concerned with the problem, pressures mount on those responsible for the public health to provide rapid solutions. Unfortunately, the process of scientific discovery and medical progress is not as fast as we would like. Years of frustrating trial and error often go by; research hardly ever follows a predicted path. Dr. Lewis Thomas, a prominent biologist and physician, puts it aptly in his book *The Youngest Science:*

> Making guesses at what might lie ahead, when the new facts have arrived, is the workaday business of science, but it is never the precise, surefooted enterprise that it sometimes claims credit for being. . . . In real life, research is dependent on the human capacity for making predictions that are wrong, and on the even more human gift for bouncing back to try again. This is the way the work goes. The predictions, especially the really important ones

that turn out, from time to time to be correct, are pure guesses. Error is the mode.

Several of the witnesses invited to testify before a Congressional subcommittee in August, 1983 charged that the Federal government had done very little about the problem of AIDS, even after the Secretary of Health and Human Services had proclaimed it to be the "number one priority" of her department. The criticisms were directed most vociferously at the apparent delay between the recognition of AIDS as an epidemic disease in June, 1981 and the first funding of specifically earmarked research grants in May, 1983. Representatives of the gay community denounced the response of health officials to the AIDS problem, calling it agonizingly, unconscionably slow, "bordering on the negligent."

Some of those testifying called for an independent blue-ribbon panel outside the governmental scientific bureaucracy to develop a master plan for AIDS research and to guide its execution. Among their suggestions was that the National Academy of Sciences, a prestigious body of scientists from many fields, be enlisted to plan and oversee AIDS research and funding. Experts from the medical community, however, cautioned that the concept of guided research according to a master plan is unrealistic and not the way the process works best. Most of those testifying, however, agreed on the urgent need to intensify governmental efforts in epidemiology, basic research, surveillance, and education, as well as the necessity to increase funding for a host of support services to AIDS patients.

Public Funding for AIDS Research and Health Care

It has become a cliché to point out that the health care and research systems of the world's richest and most advanced country have so far proved inadequate to handle a national medical disaster like AIDS. Leaders of homosexual groups have accused the U.S. government of dragging its feet on allocating funds for work on AIDS. The director of the National Gay Task Force, Virginia Apuzzo, charged at a Congressional hearing that "the government's slow response on AIDS is directly related to *who* is affected—gay men, Haitians, IV drug users... " and that these groups are "traditionally victims of discrimination, often officially sanctioned." She contrasted the government's "sluggish" response with the vigorous efforts of volunteer groups from the gay and lesbian communities, which have budgeted more than $2.5 million for AIDS projects in 1983, and another $6.8 million for 1984, exclusive of local and state governmental grants.

Some public officials, of course, see it differently. Dr. Edward N. Brandt, Jr., Assistant Secretary for Health of the U.S. Department of Health and Human Services (HHS), denied that the Federal response has been anything but prompt, and asserted that since AIDS was first reported by the CDC in June, 1981, the combined Federal agencies of the CDC, the NIH, and the FDA had spent $5.5 million for AIDS-related work in fiscal year 1982. He estimated that expenditures for 1983 would rise to $14.5 million, and in 1984 they would total around $17.7 million.

Early Responses to the Epidemic

Few people realize that medical researchers began to respond to AIDS almost from the appearance of the earliest patients, even before they were consciously perceived as being part of any epidemic. This happened because there was a biomedical research community in the major medical centers, developed over forty years of Federal support for basic, nondirected research. The problems pursued by these scientists certainly did not anticipate a yet-to-be-described disease, but many of the techniques they developed and insights they gained from their previous work became relevant when AIDS appeared on the scene. The funding provided was, in some instances, sufficiently flexible that it could be diverted to the investigation of AIDS.

The education of the coterie of clinical investigators who provided the cutting edge of AIDS research was also chiefly attributable to a supportive national effort, from the 1950's to the early 1970's, to train and encourage some doctors to pursue a research career. The U.S. Armed Forces and the Public Health Service taught many of these young physicians practical public health and preventive medicine, and Federal grants made possible the functioning of the immunology, microbiology, hematology and cancer research labs, at NIH itself and at independent medical schools and research institutes, in which others carried out advanced investigations. No one could have predicted that such specialized and diverse backgrounds and training would be called upon 15 to 20 years later to deal with a major, international health problem.

At several centers in New York City, as well as in Los Angeles, San Francisco, Atlanta and Miami, physicians were trying to figure out obscure immunodeficiency syndromes in children and adults. The work in these rare disorders was mainly academic; some of it was expected eventually to help such patients. But the main idea was that through improved information about such "experiments of nature," much could be learned about normal and abnormal immunity against infection. These clinician-investigators happened to be in the path of AIDS when it appeared, and were prepared to jump into the fray. Without realizing it, they had begun a prospective study of AIDS with the earliest patients, in labs that were in effect extramural arms of the NIH.

The CDC committed itself vigorously to the epidemic as soon as it was recognized in 1981, establishing a task force on AIDS and placing at its head Dr. James Curran, an epidemiologist and specialist in sexually transmitted diseases. In order to carry out its mission in AIDS, the CDC had to divert its already tight funds from other important work. Symptomatic of its budget crunch was the end of free distribution of *MMWR*, the CDC's weekly publication that had been sent gratis to any health professional requesting it. Many viewed the new annual subscription fee as a setback to the efficient dissemination of information on epidemic diseases and a disservice to public health in general. A cutback in CDC funding seemed particularly shortsighted when the nation was being threatened with a new, potentially epidemic disease.

In March, 1982, Dr. David Sencer, Commissioner of Health of the City of New York, convened a series of monthly meetings for professionals involved with AIDS in the N.Y. Metropolitan area. Although some investigators had research funds, they were usually geared to in-depth study of a few patients and clearly insufficient to deal with a citywide, not to mention a national, public health emergency. There was even then no existing mechanism to quickly obtain support for the major effort needed to work out the epidemiology, etiology, immunology and therapy of AIDS. In May, 1982, Dr. Sencer wrote to Dr. James Wyngaarden, the Director of NIH, requesting Federal help.

Three months elapsed before the first request for research applications (RFA) to deal specifically with AIDS was released by the NIH. Those responding applications that had obtained sufficiently high approval ratings from NIH scientific reviewers began actually to receive monies on May 1, 1983, almost a year after Dr. Sencer's letter, and almost two years after the outbreak had been officially reported by the CDC. Administrators of the NIH indicated that this RFA had a shorter turnaround time than most such applications because of efforts to speed up peer review. The long delays in providing Federal funding for AIDS prompted concern over the nation's ability to respond to new epidemic diseases in general.

In May, arguing against the necessity for a bill designed to authorize a contingency fund for public health emergencies such as AIDS, Dr. Brandt of HHS stated that there were already existing funding mechanisms that could be mobilized for such purposes. Disregarding his assurances, Congress, in June, 1983 enacted legislation setting up a $30 million annual revolving fund available for public health emergencies, and in August voted an additional $12 million for the first year to supplement already budgeted funds for research in AIDS. State and local governments have also begun allocating funds. In New York State, the legislature appropriated $4.5 million for AIDS investigation, which, after some political haggling, was eventually approved by Governor Mario Cuomo. Another $1.5 million was allotted for health care and support services to AIDS patients.

Despite a severe lack of earmarked funds, things were not standing still in AIDS research between 1981 and early 1983. Many independent investigators turned their attention and research support from other projects to this new one. The National Institutes of Health (NIH) also became involved, admitting cases for study to the Clinical Center, holding meetings in Bethesda and funding others elsewhere. The Food and Drug Administration (FDA) began to do basic investigation and to provide guidance for the improved safety of blood products.

Current Research by National Health Agencies

The United States Public Health Service (USPHS) oversees and coordinates research aimed at understanding the etiology and epidemiology of AIDS, through the National Institutes of Health (NIH). The National Cancer Institute (NCI) and the National Institute of Allergy and Infectious Diseases (NIAID) at the NIH have promoted projects to identify the immunologic, genetic, and possibly viral risk factors for AIDS. They are also interested in developing improved methods of diagnosis and treatment, and in clarifying the relationship of Kaposi's sarcoma to AIDS.

At the government's agency for epidemiology, the Centers for Disease Control (CDC), Dr. James Curran and his team of medical detectives that comprise the AIDS Activity task force are engaged in the surveillance and tallying of all cases reported nationwide. They investigate in depth unusual cases without known risk factors. Such cases comprise about 7% of the approximately 150 AIDS patients being reported each month. Their work includes case-control studies of homosexuals and Haitians (to define differences between those who get AIDS and those who don't), surveillance of childhood cases of AIDS and investigation of blood-borne or blood-product transfusion cases. In addition, they are conducting a prospective study of health care workers who have had occupational accidents with needles or other materials from AIDS patients.

Within NIAID, Dr. Kenneth Sell heads a research group that is strongly oriented towards the study of viruses, including papovaviruses, adenoviruses, CMV, EBV and even the so-called slow viruses, with the aim of isolating the yet-undefined agent of AIDS. This team is also conducting epidemiologic surveys in Haiti, as well as in Baltimore, where new cases of AIDS have recently surfaced. The clinical aspect of NIAID's work involves trial therapies with interferons, interleukin-2, acyclovir and lymphocyte transfusions from healthy close relatives of AIDS patients. Recently, interest has focused on a fungus—"cy-AIDS"—that may be immunosuppressive.

Another intramural group from NCI, directed by Drs. Robert Biggar, Prem Sarin, and Jack Killen, is pursuing a number of projects. One of the chief resources of this group is a tissue bank, in which cells and sera from 250 gay men in various stages of disease have been stored so they can be compared with samples collected from the same men in the future. In another of their prospective studies, Danish homosexuals who have had contact with American gay men are being followed via their stored specimens. Another project is the analysis of the role of HTLV in AIDS (discussed above). Clinical researchers are also attempting to treat Kaposi's sarcoma with total skin electron beam therapy and with a type of chemotherapy that does not interact with the radiation. Like many other groups, some at the NCI are trying out various interferons and interleukin-2.

To inform the public about the disease, the Department of Health and Human Services has established a toll-free AIDS information hotline, staffed by employees of the PHS and available for calls from 8:30 to 5:30 (Eastern Daylight Time). The number in the continental U.S. is: *800-342-*

AIDS. People from Hawaii and Alaska can call collect on 202-245-6867. Since it was set up in July, 1983, the hotline has answered many thousands of calls per week.

Funded Research Projects at Major Medical Centers

Grants totalling $2 million for the first year of research were awarded by the NCI and by NIAID in May, 1983 to a number of investigators at independent medical research institutions. In New York City, Los Angeles, San Francisco, Boston, Houston and other cities, medical schools and hospitals are actively involved in research projects on AIDS, supported in large part by these recently allocated Federal funds. The following summaries are only brief indications of the type of work going on in some representative labs; they are not intended to be comprehensive discussions of all projects nor a detailed account of any particular group's work.

At Cornell University Medical Center, Drs. Gregory Siskind and Warren Johnson head up teams interested in laboratory studies of lymphocyte and macrophage function. Some among their groups are studying a suppressor factor, derived from blood cells of patients, that is apparently able to inhibit the function of T cells from normal people. Other experiments have centered on anti-sperm antibodies and immune complexes in AIDS patients, which don't seem to be present in normal subjects. An important contribution of the Cornell group has been their epidemiologic study of AIDS in Haiti. Their initial data suggest that the disease in Haiti is much the same as in the U.S., except that Kaposi's sarcoma is less common among Haitians than among American homosexuals.

At Memorial Sloan-Kettering Cancer Center, a group led by Dr. Bijan Safai has played an active role in studies to clarify the association between the histocompatibility antigens DR2/DR5 and the development of Kaposi's sarcoma. They have also been interested in exploring the relationship of the immune defect to natural killer cell activity and supressor/cytotoxic T cells. His group is continuing trials of high-dose alpha interferon therapy in KS, achieving a degree of clinical success in about half the patients; modest improvements in laboratory tests of immune function in the patients were also observed. In those responding to interferon therapy, opportunistic infections have not yet developed. The group also plans to use interleukin-2 in a clinical trial.

At Mount Sinai Medical Center, we (Dr. Frederick P. Siegal, principal investigator) have studied a very large series of patients with AIDS and associated syndromes, in collaboration with Dr. Carlos Lopez at Sloan-Kettering Institute and Dr. Sheldon Landesman at SUNY/Downstate Medical Center. Our laboratories have studied hundreds of samples from gay men, drug addicts, Haitians, sexual contacts of AIDS patients, children and hemophiliacs, in various stages of disease, with a special interest in functional studies of suppressor lymphocytes, monocytes, natural killer cells, large granular lymphocytes and suppressor factors. Our most important observation has been that the cells of patients with opportunistic infections fail to produce alpha interferon, in contrast to those of most patients with KS alone or those of normal subjects. The funded research is directed at defining the significance of this impaired interferon production and the role of other defects of cellular immunity. Attempts have been made to correct the underlying immunodeficiency of two AIDS patients via bone marrow transplants from relatives. Evidence of only transient engraftment was obtained.

At New York University, Dr. Frederick Valentine's lab has been primarily interested in studying individual cells to determine how they fail to perform their normal helper or suppressor functions. Cultures of cells from patients with AIDS have been successfully grown, and their characteristics are being closely studied. At Yeshiva University in the Bronx, Dr. Arye Rubenstein and his colleagues have been studying drug addicts and their heterosexual partners, and also following about 25 children considered to have the syndrome. He has found evidence for transmission of AIDS to such babies from infected mothers before or during birth. At still another New York Hospital, St. Vincent's, Dr. Pearl Ma has concentrated on cryptosporidiosis, in AIDS patients as well as in normal subjects who acquire this organism.

In California, two teaching hospitals of the University of California are heavily involved in AIDS research. Drs. John Fahey and Michael Gottlieb lead a team of doctors at UCLA who have followed a large number of patients, mostly gay men, at their clinics. They have performed a randomized trial of alpha interferon in AIDS patients without Kaposi's sarcoma, to define whether it decreases the propensity to infection, without much apparent success so far. Other biological response modifiers and antiviral drugs are also being tried. The laboratory part of their effort involves quantitation of suppressor and helper T cells. At UC-San Francisco, Dr. Paul Volberding is conducting surveillance of AIDS cases and contacts, and performing serial immunologic profiles of their cells. His group too is interested in studying viral infections in gay men, particularly the course of CMV, and is trying to isolate the organisms, using cell lines and experimental animals. In addition, standard chemotherapeutic agents as well as interferons are being tried, in collaboration with the group at UCLA.

The Boston area has several groups doing AIDS research. At the Harvard School of Public Health, a team led by Dr. James Mullins is pursuing the possible role of HTLV and other retroviruses, studying antibodies to these organisms in the sera of AIDS and lymphadenopathy patients. Sophisticated recombinant-DNA techniques are being employed to identify the viruses by their genetic material. At Massachusetts General Hospital, Dr. Martin Hirsch is the principal investigator of another lab directed at defining the role of viruses such as EBV, CMV and HTLV in a spectrum ranging from healthy homosexuals to cases with advanced AIDS. They are also studying the ability of CMV to transform particular cell lines into malignant ones.

At the M.D. Anderson Hospital in Houston, Texas, research efforts led by Dr. Evan Hersh have emphasized prodrome patients, studying their immunological and clinical status in relation to their life-styles and attempting to prevent the progression to full-blown AIDS by trial therapies with such drugs as cimetidine, lithium and azemexon. Gamma interferon is being explored for the treatment of Kaposi's sarcoma.

Another investigator, Dr. Walter T. Hughes, at St. Jude's in Memphis, Tenn., is trying to develop new treatments for Pneumocystis carinii pneumonia by using rats immunosuppressed with steroids. Federally funded projects at several other institutions are being carried out with laboratory animals. Some experiments employ rats, mice or guinea pigs for the testing of potentially useful drugs, and others include the injection of human serum or tissues to determine whether they are infectious. As far as is known, no laboratory has yet succeeded in transferring AIDS to an animal. Primates, such as monkeys and marmosets, most closely related to the human species but extremely expensive and cumbersome to work with, have yielded no better experimental results. A natually occurring disease in monkeys, which has been called by analogy Simian Acquired Immune Deficiency Syndrome (SAIDS), has generated hopes of an animal model for AIDS, but efforts to transmit an infectious agent to small monkeys have not yet worked. Considering the presumed lengthy incubation period of such an AIDS agent, if SAIDS is really a similar disease, there may still be a chance of useful answers from such experiments.

In assessing how much the medical-research community has so far accomplished with AIDS, we need to take into account the accumulation of facts contained in books and articles on AIDS that are now proliferating. This information didn't just come out of thin air but was derived from a good deal of painstaking, potentially dangerous investigation by hundreds or perhaps even thousands of health workers. The early gains in the disease, such as its initial identification and characterization, can be attributed partly to the longterm public investment in academic medical centers. This in turn depended on the past governmental commitment to basic research and to the training of young people for biomedical investigation. Although the need for immediate expenditures for directly applicable AIDS research are obvious and urgent, it is to be hoped that our country's government will not shortchange the health of future generations by failing to set aside funds for basic science.

Goals and Hopes of Research in AIDS

The quest for an etiologic agent and a comprehension of how it demolishes the immune system are the central issues in AIDS research. Answers to these basic questions will be the wellspring of effective prevention and treatment. Identification of an agent will permit detailed mapping of its modes of spread. We will learn which specific sexual practices are or aren't safe. We will determine whether Africa and Haiti are really endemic areas, and what public health measures can be undertaken to eradicate AIDS in the tropics or in the U.S. We will be able to survey communities to define who, if anyone, is immune and who still susceptible, who is a carrier in danger of spreading the disease and who is safe. And we will be able to test blood products to define their safety, and learn how to sterilize them they if they become contaminated. We may be able to develop a specific animal model with which to test therapeutic agents. We may figure out the relationship of T cell subset deviations and the lymphadenopathy syndrome to AIDS as we now define it; this understanding may change the case definition itself. Better insight into the immune defect should lead to rational treatment protocols and clinically useful tests, even if there is a long delay or failure to find a causative agent. Most important, we will have expanded our knowledge of the ways in which cellular immunity contains infectious diseases and certain kinds of cancers. Information of this kind will be of immense importance to the growth of the science of immunobiology, which was virtually undeveloped forty years ago.

Many practical inquiries also urgently need responses; some will await answers to the central questions but others may be solved by especially incisive experiments or by thorough epidemiologic investigation. How risky is it to work with patients with AIDS? How should accidental exposures be taken care of? Are blood banking measures effective; if not, how can they be improved? Can any currently available drug, treatment or their combinations affect the course of AIDS? Are promising leads being rapidly brought to collaborative clinical trials carried out among several medical institutions? Can we advance the timing of therapy through early diagnosis so that those who are still in the early, prodromal stage can be helped? These and many other questions are being addressed by researchers throughout the United States and, now, in other countries as well.

Protecting Confidentiality in AIDS Surveillance

Any research on human subjects, whether it involves the gathering of crucial epidemiologic data or the testing of experimental drugs or therapies, must be conducted with an awareness of the basic rights of all persons to medical confidentiality. Because the people that have been affected by AIDS have often been from groups associated with unconventional or illegal activities, they have generally been reluctant to give personal information to health workers, who are frequently government officials. In half of the states in the U.S. homosexual acts are still a crime, and non-medical intravenous drug use and most immigration from Haiti are illicit. It is not suprising, therefore, that the issue of confidentiality should be a particularly sensitive one among people in the AIDS risk groups. Aside from incurring the stigma that AIDS can inspire, victims may feel threatened with the loss of their jobs, arrest or deportation if their names end up in the wrong government computer file. Those who represent gay rights groups have stated that they don't trust employees of the government, even epidemiologists, to protect individual privacy, and have asked for strictures on questioning by health officers.

The dilemma is that restrictive rules that would tend to impede the flow of information about an infectious disease don't protect the broader interest of the public's health. And, for the sake of AIDS victims themselves, the need is desperately urgent to gather as much information as possible, as efficiently as possible. Medical investigators must now walk a vanishingly thin line between the need to elicit accurate facts about a person's origins, drug habits, sexual activities and contacts, and to avoid violating a person's right to privacy. In an effort to comply with requests for procedures that would strengthen confidentiality, the CDC has announced that it will no longer accept names on reports of AIDS patients from doctors or hospitals, but will require an exact date of birth, presumably as a way of distinguishing each case. Some epidemiologists, fearing that this is an overreaction to pressure by groups with relatively narrow interests, favor a less restrictive policy. Other systems, therefore, are being explored to facilitate the surveillance process.

Making Provisions for AIDS Patients

The cost of medical care for current and future AIDS patients is staggering. Rough estimates of an average AIDS patient's hospital, doctor, drug and other treatment costs range from $50,000 to $100,000. Many AIDS patients spend several months in the hospital, some of that time in intensive care units. Since most patients quickly deplete their financial resources and insurance companies have been reluctant to assume the costs, the bill is obviously paid largely by society. The Social Security Administration has recently accepted AIDS as a qualification for disability payments. As there already have been well over 2,000 people identified with the disease in some form, the cost of caring for just these patients will amount to between $100-$200 million. If the cases continue to increase at an exponential rate, as some authorities expect, the total cost of such care by the end of 1985 will be an unimaginable $4-$8 billion.

Aside from the financial burden, another potentially overwhelming problem is finding adequate facilities for treating AIDS patients. Current hospitals, clinics, nursing homes, and hospices are not sufficiently equipped to handle additional large loads of very ill people, many of whom require isolation. Some people have suggested that special centers should be set up for the care of AIDS patients. While it can be argued that such facilities, with staffs specially trained to handle infectious diseases, would benefit the patients and expedite clinical research in AIDS, it's easy to foresee difficulties in recruiting personnel for such centers. Creation of such separate institutions would imply acceptance of AIDS as being highly contagious; this idea, fortunately, doesn't seem borne out by what we already know after four years of experience with the disease. Planning for the care of AIDS victims presents almost as great a challenge as finding its cause. How well we manage to solve these great problems will be a measure of our civilization.

APPENDIX I:

New York State AIDS Bill

AN ACT to amend the public health law, in relation to the acquired immune deficiency syndrome (AIDS), providing for the creation of a research council, an information program and community action programs and creating a temporary state commission on the acquired immune deficiency epidemic and making appropriations therefor

The People of the State of New York, represented in Senate and Assembly, do enact as follows:

Section 1. Legislative findings. The legislature finds that the acquired immune deficiency symdrome (AIDS) has been termed potentially the twentieth century's most virulent epidemic. One of the two major locations of the outbreak is centered within the state of New York. In the period since nineteen hundred seventy-nine when the syndrome was first detected one thousand three hundred thirty-nine persons have been diagnosed and in this group five hundred five individuals have died, a mortality rate approaching a staggering forty percent. The great smallpox epidemic earlier in this century killed twenty-five percent of its victims. The incidence of AIDS has nearly tripled in the past year alone.

The medical resources of governments at the federal, state and local level have not yet been effectively marshalled to fight this epidemic.

The federal government must shoulder the largest burden of costs in the research and eventual elimination of this dread condition. However, the state of New York within resources that realistically can be made available can make an important contribution. The state of New York has a strong

175

record of accomplishment in the general fields of public health and important contributions have been made in specific areas like cancer, kidney disease, burns and birth defects.

State and local health agencies are called upon for an immediate reallocation of any discretionary resources from any lower priority areas to wage a war on AIDS.

It is imperative that steps be taken towards establishing a comprehensive program to combat acquired immune deficiency syndrome (AIDS) to be implemented through the combined correlated efforts of state and local governments, medicine, universities, non-profit organizations and individuals.

A program of state assisted basic and applied research in acquired immunosuppressive diseases is clearly indicated.

*S2. The creation of an acquired immune deficiency research council of a reasonable but indeterminate number of members is hereby authorized and provided for as specified herein. Such entity as may qualify shall have the status of a contract agency of the state for the public purpose of the promotion of the scientific investigations of acquired immunosuppressive diseases. The members shall be representative of recognized centers engaged in the scientific investigation of acquired immunosuppressive diseases. Such council shall administer a program of financial support, under contracts with the director of the division of the budget, of (a) scientific investigations into the cause, prevention, methods of treatment, and cure of the acquired diseases of immunosuppression; (b) professional education and training and improvements in instrumentation, necessary adjuncts to such scientific investigations; and (c) the conduct of programs of support and counseling services for persons afflicted with acquired immunosuppressive diseases and participating in such investigations. Personal data in such investigations and all reports and information relating thereto shall be kept confidential and be afforded all of the protections provided by the provisions of paragraph (j) of subdivision one of section two hundred six of the public health law. The council may, however, from time to time publish analyses of such scientific investigations in such a manner as to assure that the identities of the individuals concerned cannot be ascertained.

*S3. Subdivision one of section two hundred six of the public health law is amended by adding a new paragraph (p) to read as follows:

(p) direct and montior a comprehensive effort for the treatment and prevention of acquired immune deficiency syndrome (AIDS) including but not limited to scientific studies and research into its causes, treatment and prevention and the allocation of available public health services at the state and local level for the care, treatment and containment of the epidemic for which funds are or shall hereafter be made available.

*S4. A temporary state commission on the acquired immune deficiency syndrome epidemic is hereby created to examine and assess the public health requirements for a comprehensive program to adequately provide for the research, treatment and prevention of acquired immune deficiency syndrome (AIDS) and make recommendations relating thereto.

*S5. The commission shall consist of nine members, each to serve for a term of two years, to be appointed as follows: one shall be appointed by the temporary president of the senate and one by the minority leader of the senate; one shall be appointed by the speaker of the assembly and one by the minority leader of the assembly; five shall be appointed by the governor. The appointees shall include representatives experienced in the field of public health and of the public at large. The governor shall designate the chairman and vice chairman from among his appointees. Vacancies in the membership of the commission and among its officers shall be filled in the manner provided for original appointments.

*S6. The commission may employ and at pleasure remove such personnel as it may deem necessary for the performance of its functions and fix their compensation within the amounts made available therefor.

*S7. The commission may meet within and without the

state, shall hold public hearings, and shall have all the powers of a legislative committee pursuant to the legislative law.

*S8. The members of the commission shall receive no compensation for their services but shall be allowed their actual and necessary expenses incurred in the performance of their duties hereunder.

*S9. To the maximum extent feasible, the commission shall be entitled to request and receive and shall utilize and be provided with such facilities, resources and data of any court, department, division, board, bureau, commission or agency of the state or any political subdivision thereof as it may reasonably request to carry out properly its powers and duties hereunder.

*S10. The commission shall make a first preliminary report to the governor and the legislature of its findings, conclusions, and recommendations not later than December first, nineteen hundred eighty-three, a second preliminary report of its findings, conclusions and recommendations not later than March first, nineteen hundred eighty-four and a final report of its findings, conclusions and recommendations not later than March first, nineteen hundred eighty-five, and shall submit with its reports such legislative proposals as it deems necessary to implement its recommendations.

*S11. The sum of two hundred fifty thousand dollars ($250,000), or so much thereof as may be necessary, is hereby appropriated to pay the expenses including personal service, in carrying out the provisions of sections four through ten of this act. Such moneys shall be payable out of the state treasury after audit by and on the warrant of the comptroller upon vouchers certified or approved by the chairman or vice chairman of the commission as prescribed by law.

*S12. The sum of one hundred fifty thousand dollars ($150,000), or so much thereof as may be necessary, is hereby appropriated to the department of health from any moneys in the state treasury in the general fund to the credit of the state purposes account not otherwise appropriated to establish, promote and maintain a public information program regarding the acquired immune deficiency syndrome

178

(AIDS) for the purpose of providing educational, outreach, health and counseling services for the general public, health professionals and targeted high risk populations. No moneys shall be available for expenditure from this appropriation until a certificate of approval has been issued by the director of the budget and a copy of such certificate or any amendment thereto has been filed with the state comptroller, the chairman of the senate finance committee and the chairman of the assembly ways and means committee.

*S13. The sum of four million five hundred thousand dollars ($4,500,000), or so much thereof as may be necessary, is hereby appropriated from any moneys in the state treasury in the general fund to the credit of the state purposes account not otherwise appropriated for the purpose of carrying out the provisions of section two of this act. No moneys shall be available for expenditure from this appropriation until a certificate of approval has been issued by the director of the budget and a copy of such certificate or any amendment thereto has been filed with the state comptroller, the chairman of the senate finance committee and the chairman of the assembly ways and means committee.

*S14. The sum of three hundred fifty thousand dollars ($350,000), or so much thereof as may be necessary, is hereby appropriated to the department of health out of any moneys in the state treasury in the general fund to the credit of the state purposes account and not otherwise appropriated, for contracts with nonprofit community organizations for programs designed to alert and educate the populations at risk and the general public about the nature of the acquired immune deficiency syndrome (AIDS) crisis; providing patient support services including, but not limited to, the operation of a hot line, maintenance of crisis intervention units, home attendant teams, legal aid units and, amelliorative and supportive therapies.

*S15. This act shall take effect immediately.

APPENDIX II:

Selected Testimony to

New York State Senate

and U.S. Congress

Remarks of Michael Callen
to the New York Congressional Delegation
May 10, 1983

I am a gay man with AIDS and I have been asked to speak to you this morning to *personalize* the tragedy of AIDS. I will attempt to do this, but since what brings us together is the fact that you are politicians, I will also try to explain how the political context surrounding AIDS inevitably becomes part of the experience of each AIDS patient.

Each person's experience with AIDS is different. I can only tell you my story.

I was diagnosed with AIDS in December, 1981, although I believe I was immune depressed for over a year before.

I have been hospitalized twice since then and continue to have my health monitored by my physician and by a number of privately funded research projects.

Although I believe I will beat this disease, I am continually confronted by media reports telling me that no one has recovered from this syndrome, and that my chances of living past 1984 are poor. Figures provided by the Centers for

Disease Control indicate that 80% of those diagnosed when I was are now dead.

My life has become totally controlled by AIDS and my fight to recover. I begin each day by checking my body for Kaposi's sarcoma lesions and other signs of serious health complications. I am subject to fevers and night sweats and an almost unendurable fatigue. I live with the fear that every cold or sore throat or skin rash may be a sign of something more serious.

At age 28, I wake up every morning to face the very real possibility of my own death.

I am a member of a support group for AIDS patients which meets once a week in the cramped offices of the National Gay Task Force. In addition, in August of 1982, I formed a support group of gay men who have been diagnosed with AIDS. Because we have no community service center or other space in which to meet, the support group I formed meets in my living room.

Whenever I am asked by members of the media or by curious healthy people what we talk about in our groups, I am struck by the intractible gulf that exists between the sick and the well: What we talk about is *survival*.

We talk about how we're going to buy food and pay rent when our savings run out.

We talk about how we are going to earn enough money to live when some of us are too sick to work.

We talk about how it feels to get fired from our jobs because of unjustified fears of raging and lethal contagion —fears based on ignorance and unfounded speculation —fears which are being fanned by the Centers for Disease Control's endorsement of the view that we may be carrying and spreading a lethal, cancer-causing virus—fears that AIDS may be spread by casual, non-sexual contact which are being spread by men like Dr. Anthony Fauci of the National Institutes of Health.

We talk about the pain we feel when our lovers leave us out of fear of AIDS.

We talk about the friends who have stopped calling.

We talk about what it feels like when our families refuse

to visit us in the hospital because they are afraid of catching that—quote—"gay cancer"—unquote.

We talk about what it feels like to be kept away from our nieces and nephews and the children of our friends because our own brothers and sisters and friends are afraid we'll infect their children with some mysterious, new, killer virus.

We compare doctors and treatments and hospitals.

We share our sense of isolation—how it feels to watch doctors and nurses come and go wearing gowns, gloves and masks.

We share our anger that there are doctors and health care workers who refuse to treat AIDS patients.

We share our tremendous sense of frustration and desperation at being denied treatments such as plasmapheresis because many hospitals fear that our blood may "contaminate" the machines.

We share our fears about quarantine—the rumors that separate wards are being created to isolate us from other patients–rumors that certain hospital workers' unions have threatened to strike if forced to treat AIDS patients or wash their laundry—rumors that closed hospitals are being readied for the quarantine of AIDS patients and maybe even healthy members of at-risk groups.

We talk about our fears that the personal data we have volunteered to the CDC to help solve the mystery of AIDS may be used against us in the future. We are asked if we have had sex with animals. We are asked to detail sexual practices which are illegal in a number of states. We are asked to admit to the use of illegal drugs. The answers to these questions are stored in government computers. We are asked to trust that the confidentiality of this information is being safeguarded—only to find out that the CDC has already made available its list of AIDS patients to The New York Blood Center. We wonder who else has seen this information.

Mostly we talk about what it feels like to be treated like lepers who are treated as if we are morally, if not literally, contagious.

We try to share what hope there is and to help each other live our lives one day at a time.

What we talk about is survival.

AIDS patients suffer in two basic ways: We suffer from a life-threatening illness; and we suffer the stigma attached to being diagnosed with AIDS.

The end to both aspects of this suffering depends on finding the cause(s) and cure(s) for AIDS. And that can only happen if research money is released in amounts proportional to the seriousness of this health emergency. In order to confront and challenge the ignorance and insensitivity which we, as AIDS patients, must face on a daily basis, we need answers to the pressing questions of cause, cure and contagion.

The political context in which AIDS is occurring cannot be ignored. AIDS is affecting groups which remain disenfranchised segments of American society: homosexual men, heroin abusers, Haitian entrants and hemophiliacs. This so-called 4-H club has been joined by prisoners (most of whom are either Hispanic, IV drug abusers or both); female prostitutes; and the children of high risk groups who are also victims of poverty.

Despite the fact that in the four years since AIDS was first recognized, AIDS has killed more people than swine flu, toxic shock syndrome, Legionnaires disease and the Tylenol incident *combined*, the response of the federal government to AIDS—the worst epidemic since polio—has been to ignore it and hope it just goes away. If such a deadly disease were affecting more privileged members of American society, there can be no doubt that the government's response would have been immediate and matched to the severity of the emergency.

As a gay man, I could never decide whether I should be pleased with how far the gay rights movement has come since 1969 or whether I should be disgusted and angry at how far we have to go.

The government's non-response to the AIDS crisis has answered this question for me.

I was raised as a small-town boy from Ohio: white, male and middle class. As a gay man, the pain I suffered from prejudice was largely emtional—not for the most part economic. So my political response was modified by patience. On the whole, I *believed* in democracy. I *believed* in America.

I felt that it would only be a matter of time before education and the destigmatization of gayness would bring me my civil rights.

But now I am fighting for my life. I am facing a life and death crisis that only the resources of the federal government can end, and I am shocked to find how naive I've been.

Not only is my government unwilling to grant my right to love whom I choose—my right to be free from job discrimination—my right to the housing public accommodation of my choosing. This same government—my government—does not appear to care whether I live or die.

Prejudice and oppression are words often bandied about too freely. But the tragedy of AIDS has made many gay men take a new look at the situation of America's other disenfranchised groups. We are beginning to see that homophobia and racism are not, as some of us thought, totally unrelated. We are beginning to see that America's fear and ignorance of homosexuals and its hatred and bigotry toward black and brown people are not just co-incidental. We are beginning to see that a Haitian infant dying in poverty in the South Bronx and the death of a white, middle class gay man in Manhattan are sadly, but undeniably, interconnected.

These are the politics of AIDS. When the history of this country's response to this health crisis is written, it will stand as yet another appalling example of American apathy, indifference and inaction.

History teaches that such prejudice and bigotry ultimately poisons the *whole* society—not just those at whom it is directed. If the personal suffering of human beings is not enough to motivate you to fight for increased AIDS-related funding, let me offer you another way to justify to your constituents the release of federal research funds.

Newsweek recently called AIDS "the medical mystery of the century." Solving this mystery will surely benefit *all* Americans—indeed all humankind. Finding the cause of AIDS may well hold the key to cancer—maybe to all disease.

Do not allow the shortsightedness of prejudice to delay

184

us any longer from discovering how the immune system defends us all from disease.

Whatever you and your colleagues do or don't do, whatever sums are or are not allocated, whatever the future holds in store for me and the hundreds of other men, women and children whose lives will be irrevocably changed—perhaps tragically ended—by this epidemic, the fact that the Congress of the United States did so little for so long will remain a sad and telling commentary on this country and this time.

I do not envy you your role in this matter any more than you must envy mine. 1983 is a very bad year to be an elected official, just as it is a very bad year to be a gay man, a Haitian entrant or a child living in poverty. And surely when you first dreamed of holding public office you did not, in the furthest reaches of your imagination, foresee that your duties would include having breakfast on a Monday morning with a homosexual facing a life-threatening illness. You can be sure that 10—5—or even one year ago, I could not have imagined the possibility that I, too, would be up here begging my elected representatives to help me save my life. But there you are. Here I am. And that is exactly what I am doing.

Thank you.

Michael Callen
c/o Gay Men With AIDS
P.O. Box 106
70 Greenwich Avenue
New York, NY 10011

Remarks of Marcus A. Conant, M.D.
To Committee on Government Operations,
House of Representatives,
Testimony on August 1, 1983

My name is Marcus A. Conant. I am a physician at the University of California at San Francisco and the co-director of its Kaposi Sarcoma Clinic. I wish to thank Representative Weiss for calling this hearing.

Some time three or four years ago, in a manner that will probably forever remain unknown, a new and terrifying illness was introduced into the human population. At first, we did not even know that it had arrived. Instead, it was thought that for some bizarre reason there was an epidemic of a rare skin cancer called Kaposi Sarcoma among homosexual men in a few large cities. At about the same time, it was also noted that others in the same population group were coming down with a lethal form of pneumonia in unusually large numbers. It was not until several months later that public health officials realized that the illnesses they were seeing were actually only the symptoms of a much more fearsome disease, the phenomenon we have come to call Acquired Immune Deficiency Syndrome. AIDS has since become America's most feared acronym. The statistics on its proliferation have become numbing, but they bear repeating here. Last year, there were a few hundred persons with AIDS. Now there are 1,800. The number of AIDS victims currently doubles every six months, and by the end of the year, more than 3,000 people will have it. As the number of persons with AIDS grows, the growth rate of the disease itself also increases, with the AIDS population expected to be doubling—first every four months, and then every two. The number of people with AIDS could easily reach tens of thousands in the very near future. Because the incubation period for AIDS is so long—we believe it to be 18 months—even if a vaccine were found today, the number of victims would continue to grow until at least 1985. The final statistic in this grim litany is that nearly 60 percent of the people who contract AIDS die from it. The disease, quite simply, is the most lethal infectious killer known to modern medicine, and it is on a rampage in this country.

In the face of this appalling specter, one would expect the government of the United States, the world's most affluent and technically advanced nation, to be sparing no resource in its fight to stop AIDS. But as a physician and researcher who has worked with this problem from the beginning, I have to characterize the federal response to AIDS as bordering on the negligent. I see in my office every day young men who should be in the prime of life but who instead are wasting away towards an early, pointless but once-preventable death. They regularly ask me why their own government does not seem to care if they live or die. The question is not a rhetorical one. I have no answer for it.

I would like in my testimony to explain briefly how the federal response has been inadequate, and then to propose what I think we as a nation should be doing.

Recently, the administration announced that conquering AIDS is, in the words of the Secretary of Health and Welfare, the nation's number one health priority. We welcome this verbal support, especially after such a long period of official silence. However, I wish it was being backed up with financial support as well. The record clearly shows that it is not.

We often hear from the National Institute of Health that it has all of the money it needs to deal with AIDS. However, my every experience with AIDS contradicts that. I can, with no effort at all, think of two dozen research projects that could be crucial to the fight against AIDS that aren't being carried out for the simple lack of grant money. I know of any number of colleagues who, instead of staying in their laboratories doing vital research, have to spend their time chasing funds. Compared to the enormity of the problem, the federal funding response has been, relatively speaking, a pittance. The failure of the federal government and the NIH to respond promptly and forcefully to this crisis is a national disgrace. It has helped the spread of two epidemics, one of a deadly disease, the other of public hysteria. I cannot help but conclude that federal officials who say that enough money is being spent on AIDS are simply mouthing some required political line that has nothing to do with reality. I wish they could be with me in my office every day as I have to face yet another patient who will likely die because a major federal commitment to fighting AIDS was not made sooner.

I would also question whether the federal government has actually committed as much money to this fight as it says it has. I believe that the NIH has been less than candid in describing the amount it is spending on AIDS. For example, the NIH includes in its figures monies it was spending on projects that have nothing directly to do with AIDS; projects that were underway before the AIDS epidemic even began. I also know that the National Cancer Institute has not released some of the monies for research projects that it has already approved through its laborious peer review process. It is almost as though dubious accounting methods are being used to inflate the federal government's purported AIDS budget in order to create the appearance of a major effort being undertaken, when in fact that is not the case.

The United States can be proud that its research establishment is the ablest in the world. It stands ready to be unleashed against AIDS: all that is needed is the backing of the federal government. The tremendous intellectual resources of the public sector, including private industries and the universities of America, must be utilized in solving this problem. This can only be accomplished if Congress appropriates enough money to stimulate research outside of the NIH and the Centers for Disease Control. I am sure we all have different opinions about how active the federal government should be in matters of social welfare. But no matter what your notion of the proper federal role is, it has to include taking the lead in a fight against a disease that has struck citizens in every state of the union; a fight that *only* the federal government has the resources to undertake.

There is one point I would like to address here briefly before moving on. Most of my patients with AIDS are gay, and almost to a man, they tell me that they believe the federal government would have acted against AIDS with a vengeance had it only struck a segment of the population that was in better standing at the moment in the nation's capitol. While gay men are by no means the only persons afflicted by AIDS, it is clear they have suffered from it more than any other group. I personally find it hard to believe that any member of Congress would deny funds for research into a disease because they did not approve of certain aspects of the lifestyles of most of the people contracting it. AIDS is a medical problem, and questions of the legitimacy or illegitimacy of the modern gay movement must be left to some other forum. But if anyone is reluctant to fund the fight against AIDS because most of its victims happen to be gay, let me lead them to the crib of a newborn child who has AIDS, so they can watch as the infant screams with pain. There alone they will find reason enough to want to halt this killer.

One misconception frequently heard from funding agencies is that AIDS is such a complex, enigmatic pathological phenomenon that providing funds for research would be like throwing money down a bottomless hole. The analogy is sometimes drawn to cancer, where a final cure is probably still many years away. This is a grievously mistaken assumption, which if not corrected, could spell the deaths of tens of thousands of Americans.

AIDS is a baffling medical mystery. But it is a *solveable* medical mystery. AIDS is a new infectious disease agent, and all available evidence indicates that it is some form of virus. Fortunately, at this point in the twentieth century (thanks in no small part to the support for scientific research provided in the past by the Congress), we have the knowledge and tools at our disposal to isolate a virus. We can then proceed to sequence the genetic information in the virus; to produce a vaccine that will protect people from acquiring the virus without incurring the disease; to clone that genetic material; and to then produce large amounts of the vaccine for public distribution. We are hopeful that, given the proper support, we can accomplish all of this reasonably quickly, and thus break the chain of transmission of this desease.

But even with that achieved, there would remain another enormous medical and social problem connected with AIDS. By the time a vaccine is developed, there will likely be tens or hundreds of thousands of persons already afflicted with AIDS. In those cases, a vaccine would be useless, since the virus is already present in their bodies and wreaking havoc with their immune systems. We therefore need to continue, at fever pitch, research into the exact mechanism by which AIDS does its work. This is so we can save the lives of those already with the disease, and the many more we know will be contracting it before the vaccine is available.

These, then, are the two ultimate goals of AIDS research —creating a vaccine for the well and finding a course of treatment for the ill. How do we accomplish all of this?

I would like to put forward the proposal that AIDS is such an unparalleled threat to the American people that an emergency task force be created at the very highest level of government. The task force would be headed by an emergency coordinator whose job it would be to act as steward while we, as a nation, join together to fight this threat. The group would report directly to the President or to the Secretary of Health and Welfare.

There are dedicated men and women throughout the country making heroic efforts every day to solve the AIDS mystery. I have nothing but respect for my research colleagues at the NIH and the CDC. Without them, we would be crippled in this effort. But the work of those scientists, along with those at research centers throughout the country, is not being coordinated; it is as though they are along the rim of a wheel that has no center. A task force would be that center of the wheel. This is not some symbolic action or hollow public relations gesture, but a desperate need. Today, with no one group overseeing the entire AIDS effort, it is easy for research to be duplicated; for vital scientific findings not be be passed along to those needing them; for researchers in one part of the country to pursue leads already discredited somewhere else. As you can well guess, any of those scenarios can be deadly in such a time of crisis. Equally deadly is the business-as-usual attitude of federal health officials in the timetables they use to approve funds for research studies. We desperately need to expedite the funding of worthy projects. If the Jonas Salk of AIDS were to come to Washington today with a research proposal, he would probably be told to come back in two years after his papers had been reviewed.

The National Conference of Mayors, at its recent annual conference, passed a resolution asking the Congress to appropriate $50 million a year to combat the AIDS threat. I think that is an acceptable minimum amount. In considering the question of funding, the Congress must understand that AIDS is a new disease being visited on the population, and therefore new monies must be made available to deal with it. Some have suggested that AIDS research be funded by diverting money from other public health projects. But it makes no more sense to do that than it does to find the money for Social Security payments for a new retiree by cutting off payments to someone already in the system. The public health concerns towards which those earlier funds were appropriated are still with us even with AIDS, and they deserve continued federal support. As a researcher, I would also wish to point out that it would be extremely shortsighted to fund AIDS by cutting money that was earmarked for other, more basic, research. We would be helpless in the fight against AIDS—or in any other battle in medicine—had it not been for the basic research done in years past. Continuing that research is part of our commitment to the future.

I would like to make one additional observation about money. I think it demeans this body to suggest that it would only make a judgement on matters of life and death because of economics. The main reason we must vanquish AIDS is because it is the only moral choice presented to us. But should anyone need further persuading, consider the simple dollars and cents of the matter. It now costs about $70,000 to provide care for a patient with AIDS. Thousands have, or will get, the disease. Simple multiplication makes it clear that it is cheaper for us to cure AIDS than to treat it.

I have already spelled out the ultimate goals of AIDS research and asked you to commit federal resources to help us achieve those goals. But there are a number of other steps we must take in the interim.

• While everything possible must be done to disseminate information about AIDS to all interested researchers, this must be done in such a way that patient confidentiality is preserved at the same time. Growing millions of Americans are completely comfortable with their homosexuality and do not regard it as any source of embarrasment. But there are, of course, many others who are unwilling to be publicly identified as being gay. As a result, a firm federal policy on patient confidentiality would be a boon to research, since it would make closeted homosexuals much more willing to fully and candidly discuss their AIDS problems and related issues with their doctors. Such a policy would also respect the right to privacy that every American cherishes.

• We need to greatly expand the extramural research being done into the epidemiology of AIDS. The disease baffles us on a number of fronts, not the least of which is the networks by which it is transmitted. Some examples of the questions we would like answered—San Francisco has a very large Asian population, yet there are only four Asian-Americans there with AIDS, while most other ethnic groups have the illness in proportion to their percentage of population. Why is this so? In the first sets of studies on AIDS patients, they were revealed frequently to be highly promiscuous gay men. This is not at all the case today. Why the change? Among the Haitian males who have AIDS, nearly 100 have described themselves as heterosexuals. How did the disease spread to them? The questions go on and on.

• Fundings for research proposals are generally reviewed through the peer review process of the National Institute of Health. This is a time-honored procedure, and one that all scientists, including myself, regard as the very cornerstone of our work. Truth flourishes and science advances only in an atmosphere of skepticism, questioning and caution. I think we must also remember, though, that we are in the middle of a public health emergency unlike any other of our generation, and that, as I indicated earlier, the slow, deliberative evaluations that in less critical times are the lifeblood of research could, in this instance, quite literally spell the death of untold thousands of Americans. In the average case, the time that elapses between a proposal being put before the NIH and the funds for the project being released is 18 months to two years. As I think you can appreciate, that is close to an eternity when it comes to the current AIDS crisis. The NIH needs to very quickly establish an ad hoc review committee made up of able, dedicated experts who can review proposals for AIDS research on an emergency basis. These scientists would bring with them both their expertise as researchers as well as their recognition that a grave public health crisis exists that demands prompt action.

• I also think it is important for the NIH to issue a general call for research proposals dealing with AIDS. This would send a signal from the federal government to the scientific community that it is genuinely serious about AIDS. I know of a number of able scientists who currently will not even bother spending the time putting together an AIDS-related proposal because they feel it will not be seriously considered by the authorities in Washington.

• Every American has an interest in seeing to it that the nation's blood supply is protected. Efforts must be made to develop a reliable, scientific method of screening that supply for infectious agents such as AIDS. In recent months, as it has become suspected that AIDS may be transmitted through blood tranfusions, the vast majority of gay men have taken themselves out of the pool of blood donors for the duration of this health emergency. Most blood banks have also cut back on blood drives in gay neighborhoods. But a policy of protecting the blood supply by screening donors, rather than blood, is ultimately shortsighted and ineffective. It is easy to imagine, for example, an office blood bank drive where a closeted gay man, and a potential AIDS carrier, wishes to "prove" his heterosexuality to his co-workers by going along with the others and donating blood. No amount of pre-donation screening or questioning can prevent a person like that from donating blood. And a massive screening effort to determine who is, and who is not, a homosexual (or, for that matter, an intravenous drug user or a Haitian or a hemophiliac) is a social policy that is, at very best, of questionable wisdom, and at worst Orwellian. As far as the nation's blood supply is concerned, the emphasis must therefore shift from the donor to the blood.

193

• There needs to be increased federal support for persons actually afflicted with AIDS. The cost of AIDS treatment is staggering, and is simply beyond the financial resources of Americans. In the case of kidney dialysis, the federal government long ago realized that it was not befitting a civilized nation for its citizens to die because they could not afford the cost of medical care. The situation is much the same way today with AIDS, and I believe the federal response should be the same.

• Six months ago, those of us doing research into AIDS were frightened by two things—the disease itself, and the complete lack of awareness of it outside of the gay community. Now, we have the opposite problem. There are, in fact, now two AIDS epidemics; one involving immunology, the other involving fear. There are any number of horror stories in this regard; one of the most appalling has to do with a San Francisco bus driver who, out of a fear of contracting AIDS from a tattered slip of paper, refused to take a bus transfer from a man he presumed to be a homosexual. I also hear too-frequent reports of hospital workers refusing to care for AIDS patients. It is a sad time indeed when members of the healing professions no longer wish to care for the sick.

I don't wish to belittle the fear of AIDS; no one knows more than myself what a truly fearsome medical phenomenon it is. But I think there is a considerable public education project ahead of us to tell the public who is, and who is not, at risk. It cannot be repeated too often that there is no evidence that AIDS is transmitted through causal social contact. Common sense alone would lead one to that conclusion. If AIDS were easily transmitted, then by now millions of Americans would have it, not 1,800, most of whom are gay men.

In several ways, this fear of AIDS is a public health problem in its own right. The health and welfare department's new toll-free phone line is a small step in the right direction. (I would point out, though, that the phone lines are receiving up to 10,000 calls a day—testimony indeed to the concerns Americans have about AIDS.) There are also grave questions of social justice in this regard. I have heard too many stories of persons with AIDS being fired from their jobs or evicted from their homes once their condition became known. There are also economic aspects to the AIDS hysteria. My businessmen friends back in San Francisco have started to worry about the effect of the fear of AIDS on tourism in that city. They also say that friends in other big cities have started to echo the same concern. There is even the worry that foreign tourism to the U.S. could begin to suffer because of the world-wide attention given to AIDS. All of these AIDS-related fears are, of course, groundless. A high-level task force could do much towards re-assuring the public of that fact.

• The definition of AIDS must be broadened by the Social Security Administration for the purposes of providing benefits. Currently, the Social Security use the definition provided by the Centers for Disease Control, which defines an AIDS patient as a person under 60 with either Karposi sarcoma or pneumocystis pneumonia, and a few other diseases. However, we have recently seen a number of new infectious agents take hold in AIDS patients. These people are just as disabled, just as in need of Social Security help, as a person with KS. Yet they are currently denied help because of an outdated definition of the problem.

• Due to the publicity AIDS has received in large cities with substantial gay populations, most physicians and other health care workers are now familiar with the clinical manifestations of AIDS, as well as the appropriate treatment protocols. But this awareness of AIDS must be spread to doctors all over the country, so that persons suffering from the disease are diagnosed correctly, and from the very start receive appropriate medical care. This will help save the lives of these patients; it will also help curb the spread of the disease.

In closing, I would like to point out that last week alone, my home city of San Francisco buried four of its sons; young men who only months ago were in the prime of their lives. At a time such as this, one can't help but recall that it is the right to life that is the first of the three unalienable rights set forth in our Declaration of Independence; and that, as Jefferson wrote 207 years ago, it is to secure those rights that governments are instituted among man. Any government has no higher purpose than to protect the lives of its citizens, and the citizens of the United States today face no greater public health threat than they do from AIDS. We have the profound moral obligation to take every step necessary to conquer it as rapidly as is humanly possible.

Thank you.

Statement of Mr. Mel Rosen
Gay Men's Health Crisis, New York City
to the Subcommittee On Intergovernmental
Relations and Human Resources
on Government Operations
August 1, 1983

In January 1982 about 80 people who had lost friends and loved ones to a new and mysterious disease gathered at author Larry Kramer's apartment in New York City. There they learned from Dr. Alvin Friedman-Kien of New York University Medical Center that what appeared to be a new disease was spreading among a number of divergent populations. Dr. Friedman-Kien warned that if the numbers continued to rise in the following months as they had in the previous months we would shortly be in the middle of a new epidemic. One member of the group which was predominantly gay commented that this could turn out to be a terrible health crisis for gay men, hence the name Gay Men's Health Crisis. The group decided that they would raise funds for research into this new disease and organized a fundraiser that April which netted $50,000. At this point they applied for tax exempt not-for-profit status. The money raised went to research and the establishment of an AIDS hotline.

Two months later I read about this new organization giving away its money to research and was so impressed that I sent them a letter offering help, explaining that I was Vice President of a large social service agency. Within 24 hours, (the mail service worked that day) I was having lunch with the President of the Board who asked me to put an organization together. While I did not say I would do so, I promised to look into the matter. Over the next two weeks I spoke with doctors, researchers and patients. I did an unscientific needs assessment survey which made me come to the shocking conclusion that the automatic safeguards that I thought the government had in place to warn and protect people from epidemics did not exist in this case. In

197

a conversation with the CDC at that time I remember asking for month-by-month statistics on cases and mortality. I remember telling the CDC that either they were crazy or I was crazy but their numbers reflected an epidemic. I remember visiting Dr. Roger Enlow at Beth Israel Hospital who introduced me to a dying patient. Imagine my horror when that patient turned out to be an acquaintance of mine. The patient did not die during that bout with that opportunistic infection but became my client (I am a social worker) whom I followed through a progression of terrible and painful infections until his death three weeks ago. This was a man who made $40,000 per year but died destitute. By carrying him as a client I was able to help build an agency which would respond to the special needs of people with AIDS. Most of these services would have been automatic for any terminally ill patient. In the cases of the AIDS patients those services were not forthcoming. Fear of the diseases, fear of death, fear of disenfranchised minorities all added to the lack of services by private and government agencies. What we did to compensate is the following.

When a person is told he or she has AIDS it is not like hearing that they have cancer, for example. When you have cancer you are told what the diagnosis, prognosis and treatments are. When you are told that you have AIDS you are hearing that you have a time bomb inside of you. That any day you will get an opportunistic infection and one of these infections would kill you, usually within three years. The person goes into a crisis. In many cases the person with AIDS does not have a nuclear family for support. We therefore created a Crisis Intervention Unit of trained lay counselors who get to the person with AIDS within 12 hours of their initial phone call to us. This counselor actively works with the person with AIDS and helps them cope during this initial period. We started with fifteen counselors last October; today we have 175.

Hopefully the person realizes after a while that they may not die tomorrow, next month or next year. At this point we introduce them to one of our support groups. People who have learned to cope from each other's experiences. In October we started one group. Today we have 12 groups not only for people with AIDS but groups for husbands, wives, lovers, friends, mothers, fathers, and significant others. Although our name starts with the word gay, our services are offered to and used by all affected people and those around them.

We found that there were many people sent home from hospitals who were too sick to take care of themselves. We therefore created a Buddy System or Home Attendant Service made up of people who cook, clean and generally care for the person at home with AIDS who is too sick to take care of themselves. In one case a person with AIDS was being thrown out of their house so the buddies found him a new apartment and moved him in one weekend. We started with 7 buddies; we now have 75.

The disease does not discriminate for or against people who are rich or poor. We found that people making forty thousand dollars a year like my client were losing everything they had. Even people who were well-insured were wiped out after numerous stays in the hospitals. Each opportunistic infection could mean a month or more in the hospitals. We set up a financial aid committee that assisted people with AIDS to apply for public assistance benefits they were entitled to. We also assisted numerous legislators to put pressure on the Social Security Administration to create a definition for AIDS so people could get Disability Insurance. Even when the definition was added it was inadequate. Only people with the CDC definition of AIDS are eligible today. This forces people with prodromal symptoms to continue to work when it is possible that working could hasten a case of full blown AIDS. Our Financial Aid Committee is stretched to its limits at this point.

Our Hotline, which I mentioned earlier, started receiving about 20 calls a week last summer. It now handles over 1,000 calls a week. Callers range from those in search of a medical doctor familiar with AIDS to people calling in a complete panic over what they perceive as a symptom. Thirty volunteers and one full time staff member operate this line.

While misinformation or sensationalistic reporting has created the perception that the general public can contract AIDS through casual contact, the reality is that people with

AIDS can contract opportunistic infections through casual contact with the general population. People with AIDS sometimes become shut-ins. We have tried to combat this by creating recreational groups that get people out of their homes and into social and recreational situations.

People with AIDS have an average age of 35. In addition they often are in non-traditional conjugal relationships. These two factors create a multitude of legal problems in terms of will and power of attorney. Hospitals in many cases do not recognize what should be considered a common-law relationship between two people. We have attempted to deal with these legal problems by coordinating a network of legal services which advise the person with AIDS of their legal rights and responsibilities.

We have networked with the American Red Cross to establish a transportation service providing the means for people with AIDS to get back and forth from hospital treatments. In addition the Red Cross trains our buddies in modern home attendant care practice.

The non-response by the public health agencies at all levels of government forced us to create and furnish educational and informational services. Two newsletters which were really booklets containing everything we know to date have been distributed across the country to anyone who asks for them at no charge. This includes not only people who request them but hospitals, clinics, mental health facilities and public health facilities. In addition, we created a health recommendation brochure which has been distributed to half a million people. This brochure contains information ranging from the symptoms of this new disease to a recommendation by a number of physicians for people to limit their number of multiple sexual contacts.

We have an AIDS information van which travels to different neighborhoods and distributes educational materials. Trained counselors are available to speak with people who feel the need to talk with someone.

We have traveled across the United States to give technical assistance to any group who wish to start an AIDS self-help organization.

We have rented auditoriums and presented seminars to

the community presenting doctors, social workers, psychologists, psychiatrists, legal experts, and insurance experts. 2,500 people showed up at our last open forum seminar. No one can understand what problems develop when young people in the community are thrust into the mind set of elderly people who are adjusted to death as a fact of life.

We present seminars in hospitals to doctors, nurses and social workers. These seminars focus in on the psychosocial affects of AIDS. The Health and Hospital Corporation has contracted with us to present these seminars to every one of the hospitals within their system. We are currently providing seminars to at least one voluntary hospital each week. So many health groups have asked for seminars that we had to procure an auditorium and present a seminar to all of them at once.

In the area of research we have granted $60,000 to research projects which would have had to stop for lack of funding.

In the past three months a new problem has developed: housing. People with AIDS are being discharged from hospitals penniless and homeless. The most that can be done through the city at this time is placement in a SRO building. These buildings are dirty, dangerous and certainly not a place where a very sick person should live. The distorted image that the press has given this disease has caused many people with AIDS to be thrown out of their homes. Although we would rather not get into the housing buisines we are being pushed to buy a house in order to shelter these sick people. I don't think this is our job.

Over the past year we have gone from an organization of 40 volunteers to 1,000 volunteers. We now have a full time core staff of 7, everyone elsc volunteering their time. As a not-for-profit agency we of course want to provide medical insurance to our staff. However, every major carrier we have contacted has turned us down. If this is a sign of the future then we must act swiftly so that people in high risk groups are not discriminated against when applying for insurance.

I sit before you a very changed man from a year ago when I called the CDC. I have discovered that medicine, research and the so-called safeguards we have in place to warn us about pending disasters are political and do not work when disenfranchised minorities are involved. When toxic shock and Legionaire's disease first came on the scene there was an immediate response by government and press. Why did hundreds of poeple have to die before anyone moved in this case? Single people pay a very high percentage of their salaries to the federal tax structure. Since most of the affected individuals are single they expect something back from the government they trust. It is the American way for us to respect and care for the individual person who is in trouble in our country. I have become disillusioned about this in the past year in relation to our government. However, I take heart in the response of the community itself. People from all walks of life have come forward. The President of our board is a Fortune 500 corporate executive who was a Green Beret in Vietnam. Our Crisis Intervention Coordinator was a marine in Vietnam. We have policemen, firemen, doctors, nurses, social workers, priests, rabbis; people from all walks of life volunteer with us.

The federal government has not done its share. You must appropriate massive sums of money for research into this disease. You must appropriate money to the States so they can distribute monies to local self-help organizations or set up their own programs. If you are not motivated to help disenfranchised groups let me tell you something as a professional social worker. Although it is not much talked about, sexuality is not static. People have different sexual preferences throughout their lives. This is part of the human condition. Talk by people who would turn a medical problem into a political one is disgraceful and belongs in the dark ages. For those who would consider legislating morality, this has been tried before without success. The human condition is continuously in flux. Since most researchers and health officials have determined that this disease is sexually transmitted, it is probably the long incubation period that has kept the disease for the most part confined to certain groups. This will change shortly. There is a steaming locomotive roaring down the tracks at the general population. The people of this country depend on your God-given wisdom to ascertain the eventuality of certain events and to protect them.

I call upon you to not only appropriate the necessary funds but to create an office inside the Department of Health and Human Services that does two things: 1) to establish a national effort that coordinates services to affected individuals and a national educational effort to the public at large and 2) gives resources and technical assistance to states and self-help organizations in locations where the disease is spreading or likely to spread.

Thank you for the opportunity to speak with you.

Appendix III

Health Resources:

Clinics, Hot Lines,

and Referral Centers

National Resources

Lesbian and Gay People in Medicine—AMSA
1910 Association Drive
Restin, Virginia 22091
(703) 620-6600

The National Coalition of Gay Sexually Transmitted Disease Services (NCGSTDS)
P.O. Box 239
Milwaukee, Wisconsin 53201
Issues *Guidelines and Recommendations for Healthful Gay Sexual Activity* and the NCGSTDS newsletter.

The National Gay Health Education Foundation
P.O. Box 834
Linden Hill, New York 11354
Issues a *National Gay Health Directory*.

National Gay Task Force
80 Fifth Avenue, Suite 1601
New York, New York 10011
(800) 221-7044 (hot line)
(212) 807-6016

Homosexual Health Report
Mary Ann Liebert, Inc., Publishers
157 East 85th Street
New York, New York 10028
(212) 289-2300

National VD Hot Line.
Telephone (800) 227-8922.
Provides phone referrals to local STD treatment centers.

Centers for Disease Control
Center for Prevention Services
Technical Information Services
1600 Clifton Road
Atlanta, Georgia 30333
Issue several books on STDs.

American Association of Physicians for Human Rights
152 Hedge Road
Menlo Park, California 94025
(415) 327-6642

American Foundation for the Prevention of VD, Inc.
527 Madison Avenue, Suite 1415
New York, New York 10022
Issues a booklet about prevention.

Herpes Resource Center
P. O. Box 100
Palo Alto, California 94302
Publishes a quarterly booklet about herpes.

Local Services (by state and city)

Alaska

   Anchorage:
      STD Clinic of Anchorage
      825 L Street, 99501
      (907) 264-4611

Arizona

Tucson:
Gay Health Project
P. O. Box 2807, 85702
(602) 748-7339

California

Berkeley:
Berkeley Gay Men's Health Collective
2339 Durant Avenue, 94702
(415) 548-2570

Gay Switchboard and Counseling
(415) 841-6224

Davis:
Davis Gay Task Force
433 Russell Boulevard, 95617
(916) 753-2090

Garden Grove:
Gay Community Center of Orange County
12832 Garden Grove Boulevard, Suite H, 92643
(714) 534-3261

Los Angeles:
AIDS Project
937 North Cole #3, 90038
(213) 650-4123

Gay Community Services Center
1213 North Highland Avenue, 90038
(213) 464-7400

L.A. Sex Information Hot Line
8405 Beverly Boulevard, 90048
(213) 653-2118

Sacramento:
  Sacramento Hepatitis B Project
  P. O. Box 160486, 95816
  (916) 453-8995

San Diego:
  Beach Area Community Clinic
  3705 Mission Boulevard, 92109
  (619) 488-0644

  Gay Center for Social Services
  (619) 692-4297

  San Diego Physicians for Human Rights
  P. O. Box 16242, 92116

San Francisco:
  Bay Area Physicians for Human Rights
  P. O. Box 14546, 94114
  (415) 673-3189

  Haight Ashbury Free Medical Clinic
  558 Clayton Street, 94117
  (415) 431-1714

  The Resource Foundation
  130 Church Street, 94114
  (415) 864-0550

  KS Research and Education Foundation
  470 Castro Street #207
  Box 3360, 94114
  (415) 864-4376

  The KS Clinic—U.C.S.F.
  Medical Center, A-312, 94143
  (415) 666-1407

Colorado

Denver:
Gay Community Center of Colorado, Inc.
1436 Lafayette Street, 80218
(303) 831-6268 or 837-1598

Gay and Lesbian Health Alliance
P.O. Box 6101, 80206
(303) 831-6268

Connecticut

New Haven:
Yale Self-Care Network
17 Hillhouse Avenue, 06520

District of Columbia

Washington:
Whitman-Walker Gay Men's VD Clinic
2335 18th Street NW, 20009
(202) 332-5295

Florida

Key West:
Monroe County Health Department
Public Service Building
Jr. College Road, 33040
(305) 294-1021

Georgia

Atlanta:
Atlanta Gay Center
848 Peachtree Street, NE 30308
(404) 876-5372

AIDS-Atlanta
P.O. Box 52785, 30305
(404) 872-0600

Illinois

Chicago:
Howard Brown Memorial Clinic
2676 North Halsted Street, 60614
(312) 871-5778

Maryland

Baltimore:
Gay Community Center Clinic
241 West Chase Street, 21201
(301) 837-2050

Massachusetts

Amherst:
People's Gay Alliance
413 Student Union
University of Massachusetts 01003
(413) 545-0154

Boston:
Fenway Community Health Center
AIDS Action Committee
16 Haviland Street, 02115
(617) 267-7573

Mayor's Task Force on AIDS
c/o Brian McNaught
Mayor's Gay Liaison
1 City Hall Square, 02201

Michigan

Ann Arbor:
Gay and Lesbian STD Clinic
207 Fletcher Avenue
University Health Services, 48109
(313) 763-4186

Lambda Health Project
530 South State Street
(313) 763-4186

Detroit:
Palmer Clinic
22750 Woodward Avenue, Suite 309
Ferndale, Michigan 48220
(313) 823-5653

Ypsilanti:
Washtenaw County VD Clinic
555 Towner, 48197
(313) 485-2181

Minnesota

Minneapolis:
Lesbian and Gay Community Service Center, Inc.
124 West Lake Street, Suite E, 55408
(612) 827-5614

New Hampshire

Portsmouth:
New Hampshire Feminist Health Center
232 Court Street, 03801
(603) 436-6171

New York

Albany:
Capitol District Gay Community Center
332 Hudson Avenue, 12210
(518) 462-6136

Buffalo:
Mattachine Gay Hot Line
P.O. Box 155
Ellicott Station, 14205
(716) 881-5335

New York:
  Chelsea Health Center
  303 Ninth Avenue (at 28th Street), 10001
  (212) 239-1700

  Gay Men's Health Project
  74 Grove Street, Room 2J, 10014
  (212) 691-6969

  Gay Men's Health Crisis
  Box 274
  132 West 24th Street, 10011
  (212) 685-4952 (hotline)

  New York Blood Center Hepatitis Program
  310 East 67 Street, 10021
  (212) 570-3312

  New York City Department of Public Health
  Office of Gay and Lesbian Health Concerns
  93 Worth Street, #806, 10013
  (212) 566-7103

  St. Mark's Clinic
  88 University Place, 10003
  (212) 691-8282

  Stuyvesant Polyclinic
  137 Second Avenue, 10003
  (212) 674-0220

Ohio

  Cleveland:
    Free Medical Clinic of Greater Cleveland
    12201 Euclid Avenue, 44106
    (216) 721-4010

Oklahoma

  Tulsa:
    Oklahomans for Human Rights
    1932 C South Cheyenne, 74119
    (918) 583-7323

Oregon

Portland:
NW Fountain
125 NW 20th Place, 97209
(503) 248-1990

Pennsylvania

Philadelphia:
Gay Switchboard
(215) 546-7100

Rittenhouse Medical Association
2031 Locust Street, 19103
(215) 567-2031

Philadelphia Community Health Alternative
Philadelphia AIDS Task Force
P.O. Box 7529, 19101
(215) 232-8055

Pittsburgh:
Pittsburgh Free Clinic
121 South Highland Avenue, 15206
(412) 661-6604

Texas

Houston:
Montrose Clinic
104 Westheimer, 77006
(713) 528-5535

Kaposi Sarcoma Committee of Houston
P.O. Box 1155
3317 Montrose, 77006
(713) 666-8251

Virginia

Richmond:
Fan Free Clinic
1721 Hanover Avenue, 23220
(804) 358-8538

Washington

Seattle:
Seattle Gay Clinic
P. O. Box 20066, 98102
(206) 329-8390

Wisconsin

Madison:
Blue Bus Clinic
1552 University Avenue, 53706
(608) 262-7440

Milwaukee:
Brady East STD Clinic
1240 East Brady Street, 53202
(414) 272-2144

Health Department, Social Hygiene Clinic
841 North Broadway, Room 110, 53202
(414) 278-3631

Canada

Quebec

Montreal:
Montreal Health Press
P. O. Box 1000
Station G, H2W2N1
(514) 272-5441

APPENDIX IV:

Selected Extracts from **MMWR**

Mortality and Morbidity Weekly

Pneumocystis Pneumonia — Los Angeles

In the period October 1980-May 1981, 5 young men, all active homosexuals, were treated for biopsy-confirmed *Pneumocystis carinii* pneumonia at 3 different hospitals in Los Angeles, California. Two of the patients died. All 5 patients had laboratory-confirmed previous or current cytomegalovirus (CMV) infection and candidal mucosal infection. Case reports of these patients follow.

Patient 1: A previously healthy 33-year-old man developed *P. carinii* pneumonia and oral mucosal candidiasis in March 1981 after a 2-month history of fever associated with elevated liver enzymes, leukopenia, and CMV viruria. The serum complement-fixation CMV titer in October 1980 was 256; in May 1981 it was 32.* The patient's condition deteriorated despite courses of treatment with trimethoprim-sulfamethoxazole (TMP/SMX), pentamidine, and acyclovir. He died May 3, and postmortem examination showed residual *P. carinii* and CMV pneumonia, but no evidence of neoplasia.

Patient 2: A previously healthy 30-year-old man developed *P. carinii* pneumonia in April 1981 after a 5-month history of fever each day and of elevated liver-function tests, CMV viruria, and documented seroconversion to CMV, i.e., an acute-phase titer of 16 and a convalescent-phase titer of 28* in anticomplement immunofluorescence tests. Other features of his illness included leukopenia and mucosal candidiasis. His pneumonia responded to a course of intravenous TMP/SMX, but, as of the latest reports, he continues to have a fever each day.

Patient 3: A 30-year-old man was well until January 1981 when he developed esophageal and oral candidiasis that responded to Amphotericin B treatment. He was hospitalized in February 1981 for *P. carinii* pneumonia that responded to oral TMP/SMX. His esophageal candidiasis recurred after the pneumonia was diagnosed, and he was again given Amphotericin B. The CMV complement-fixation titer in March 1981 was 8. Material from an esophageal biopsy was positive for CMV.

Patient 4: A 29-year-old man developed *P. carinii* pneumonia in February 1981. He had had Hodgkins disease 3 years earlier, but had been successfully treated with radiation therapy alone. He did not improve after being given intravenous TMP/SMX and corticosteroids and died in March. Postmortem examination showed no evidence of Hodgkins disease, but *P. carinii* and CMV were found in lung tissue.

Patient 5: A previously healthy 36-year-old man with a clinically diagnosed CMV infection in September 1980 was seen in April 1981 because of a 4-month history of fever, dyspnea, and cough. On admission he was found to have *P. carinii* pneumonia, oral candidiasis, and CMV retinitis. A complement-fixation CMV titer in April 1981 was 128. The patient has been treated with 2 short courses of TMP/SMX that have been limited because

*Paired specimens not run in parallel.

f a sulfa-induced neutropenia. He is being treated for candidiasis with topical nystatin.

The diagnosis of *Pneumocystis* pneumonia was confirmed for all 5 patients ante-mortem by closed or open lung biopsy. The patients did not know each other and had no known common contacts or knowledge of sexual partners who had had similar illnesses. The 5 did not have comparable histories of sexually transmitted disease. Four had sero-logic evidence of past hepatitis B infection but had no evidence of current hepatitis B surface antigen. Two of the 5 reported having frequent homosexual contacts with various partners. All 5 reported using inhalant drugs, and 1 reported parenteral drug abuse. Three patients had profoundly depressed numbers of thymus-dependent lymphocyte cells and profoundly depressed *in vitro* proliferative responses to mitogens and antigens. Lymphocyte studies were not performed on the other 2 patients.

Reported by MS Gottlieb, MD, HM Schanker, MD, PT Fan, MD, A Saxon, MD, JD Weisman, DO, Div of Clinical Immunology-Allergy, Dept of Medicine, UCLA School of Medicine; I Pozalski, MD, Cedars-Mt. Sinai Hospital, Los Angeles; Field Services Div, Epidemiology Program Office, CDC.

Editorial Note: *Pneumocystis* pneumonia in the United States is almost exclusively limited to severely immunosuppressed patients (*1*). The occurrence of pneumocystosis in these 5 previously healthy individuals without a clinically apparent underlying immu-nodeficiency is unusual. The fact that these patients were all homosexuals suggests an association between some aspect of a homosexual lifestyle or disease acquired through sexual contact and *Pneumocystis* pneumonia in this population. All 5 patients described in this report had laboratory-confirmed CMV disease or virus shedding within 5 months of the diagnosis of *Pneumocystis* pneumonia. CMV infection has been shown to induce transient abnormalities of *in vitro* cellular-immune function in otherwise healthy human hosts (*2,3*). Although all 3 patients tested had abnormal cellular-immune function, no definitive conclusion regarding the role of CMV infection in these 5 cases can be reached because of the lack of published data on cellular-immune function in healthy homo-sexual males with and without CMV antibody. In 1 report, 7 (3.6%) of 194 patients with pneumocystosis also had CMV infection; 40 (21%) of the same group had at least 1 other major concurrent infection (*1*). A high prevalence of CMV infections among homosexual males was recently reported: 179 (94%) of 190 males reported to be exclusively homo-sexual had serum antibody to CMV, and 14 (7.4%) had CMV viruria; rates for 101 con-trols of similar age who were reported to be exclusively heterosexual were 54% for sero-positivity and zero for viruria (*4*). In another study of 64 males, 4 (6.3%) had positive tests for CMV in semen, but none had CMV recovered from urine. Two of the 4 reported recent homosexual contacts. These findings suggest not only that virus shedding may be more readily detected in seminal fluid than in urine, but also that seminal fluid may be an important vehicle of CMV transmission (*5*).

All the above observations suggest the possibility of a cellular-immune dysfunction related to a common exposure that predisposes individuals to opportunistic infections such as pneumocystosis and candidiasis. Although the role of CMV infection in the pathogenesis of pneumocystosis remains unknown, the possibility of *P. carinii* infection must be carefully considered in a differential diagnosis for previously healthy homosexual males with dyspnea and pneumonia.

July 3, 1981

Kaposi's Sarcoma and *Pneumocystis* Pneumonia Among Homosexual Men — New York City and California

During the past 30 months, Kaposi's sarcoma (KS), an uncommonly reported malig-nancy in the United States, has been diagnosed in 26 homosexual men (20 in New York City [NYC]; 6 in California). The 26 patients range in age from 26-51 years (mean 39 years). Eight of these patients died (7 in NYC, 1 in California)—all 8 within 24 months after KS was diagnosed. The diagnoses in all 26 cases were based on histopathological examination of skin lesions, lymph nodes, or tumor in other organs. Twenty-five of the 26 patients were white, 1 was black. Presenting complaints from 20 of these patients are shown in Table 1.

Skin or mucous membrane lesions, often dark blue to violaceous plaques or nodules, were present in most of the patients on their initial physician visit. However, these lesions were not always present and often were considered benign by the patient and his physician.

A review of the New York University Coordinated Cancer Registry for KS in men under age 50 revealed no cases from 1970-1979 at Bellevue Hospital and 3 cases in this age group at the New York University Hospital from 1961-1979.

Seven KS patients had serious infections diagnosed after their initial physician visit. Six patients had pneumonia (4 biopsy confirmed as due to *Pneumocystis carinii* [PC]) and one had necrotizing toxoplasmosis of the central nervous system. One of the patients with *Pneumocystis* pneumonia also experienced severe, recurrent, herpes simplex infection; extensive candidiasis; and cryptococcal meningitis. The results of tests for cytomegalovirus (CMV) infection were available for 12 patients. All 12 had serological evidence of past or present CMV infection. In 3 patients for whom culture results were available, CMV was isolated from blood, urine and/or lung of all 3. Past infections with amebiasis and hepatitis were commonly reported.

Since the previous report of 5 cases of *Pneumocystis* pneumonia in homosexual men from Los Angeles (1), 10 additional cases (4 in Los Angeles and 6 in the San Francisco Bay area) of biopsy-confirmed PC pneumonia have been identified in homosexual men in the state. Two of the 10 patients also have KS. This brings the total number of *Pneumocystis* cases among homosexual men in California to 15 since September 1979. Patients range in age from 25 to 46 years.

Reported by A Friedman-Kien, MD, L Laubenstein, MD, M Marmor, PhD, K Hymes, MD, J Green, MD, A Ragaz, MD, J Gottleib, MD, F Muggia, MD, R Demopoulos, MD, M Weintraub, MD, D Williams, MD, New York University Medical Center, NYC; R Oliveri, MD, J Marmer, MD, NYC; J Wallace, MD, I Halperin, MD, JF Gillooley, MD, St. Vincent's Hospital and Medical Center, NYC; N Prose, MD, Downstate Medical Center, NYC; E Klein, MD, Roosevelt Hospital, NYC; J Vogel, MD, B Safai, MD, P Myskowski, MD, C Urmacher, MD, B Koziner, MD, L Nisce, MD, M Kris, MD, D Armstrong, MD, J Gold, MD, Sloan-Kettering Memorial Institute, NYC; D Mildran, MD, Beth Israel Hospital, NYC; M Tapper, MD, Lenox Hill Hospital, NYC; JB Weissman, MD, Columbia Presbyterian Hospital, NYC; R Rothenberg, MD, State Epidemiologist, New York State Dept of Health; SM Friedman, MD, Acting Director, Bur of Preventable Diseases, New York City Dept of Health; FP Siegal, MD, Dept of Medicine, Mount Sinai School of Medicine, City College of New York, NYC; J Groundwater, MD, J Gilmore, MD, San Francisco; D Coleman, MD, S Follansbee, MD, J Gullett, MD, SJ Stegman, MD, University of California at San Francisco; C Wofsy, MD, San Francisco General Hospital, San Francisco; D Bush, MD, Franklin Hospital, San Francisco; L Drew, MD, PhD, Mt. Zion Hospital, B Braff, MD, S Dritz, MD, City/County Health Dept, San Francisco; M Klein, MD, Valley Memorial Hospital, Salinas; JK Preiksaitis, MD, Stanford University Medical Center, Palo Alto; MS Gottlieb, MD, University of California at Los Angeles; R Jung, MD, University of Southern California Medical Center, Los Angeles; J Chin, MD, State Epidemiologist, California Dept of Health Services; J Goedert, MD, National Cancer Institute, National Institute of Health; Parasitic Diseases Div, Center for Infectious Diseases, VD Control Division, Center for Prevention Services, Chronic Diseases Div, Center for Environmental Health, CDC.

TABLE 1. Presenting complaints in 20 patients with Kaposi's sarcoma

Presenting complaint	Number (percentage) of patients
Skin lesion(s) only	10 (50%)
Skin lesions plus lymphadenopathy	4 (20%)
Oral mucosal lesion only	1 (5%)
Inguinal adenopathy plus perirectal abscess	1 (5%)
Weight loss and fever	2 (10%)
Weight loss, fever, and pneumonia (one due to *Pneumocystis carinii*)	2 (10%)

Editorial Note: KS is a malignant neoplasm manifested primarily by multiple vascular nodules in the skin and other organs. The disease is multifocal, with a course ranging from indolent, with only skin manifestations, to fulminant, with extensive visceral involvement (2).

Accurate incidence and mortality rates for KS are not available for the United States, but the annual incidence has been estimated between 0.02-0.06 per 100,000; it affects primarily elderly males (3,4). In a series of 92 patients treated between 1949 and 1975 at the Memorial Sloan-Kettering Cancer Institute in NYC, 76% were male, and the mean age was 63 years (range 23-90 years) at the time of diagnosis (5).

The disease in elderly men is usually manifested by skin lesions and a chronic clinical course (mean survival time is 8-13 years) (2). Two exceptions to this epidemiologic pattern have been noted previously. The first occurs in an endemic belt across equatorial Africa, where KS commonly affects children and young adults and accounts for up to 9% of all cancers (3). Secondly, the disease appears to have a higher incidence in renal transplant recipients (6-9) and in others receiving immunosuppressive therapy (10-12).

The occurrence of this number of KS cases during a 30-month period among young, homosexual men is considered highly unusual. No previous association between KS and sexual preference has been reported. The fulminant clinical course reported in many of these patients also differs from that classically described for elderly persons.

The histopathologic diagnosis of KS may be difficult for 2 reasons. Changes in some lesions may be interpreted as nonspecific, and other cutaneous and soft tissue sarcomas, such as angiosarcoma of the skin, may be confused with KS (13,14).

That 10 new cases of *Pneumocystis* pneumonia have been identified in homosexual men suggests that the 5 previously reported cases were not an isolated phenomenon (1). In addition, CDC has a report of 4 homosexual men in NYC who developed severe, progressive, perianal herpes simplex infections and had evidence of cellular immunodeficiencies. Three died, 1 with systemic CMV infection. The fourth patient is currently undergoing therapy. It is not clear if or how the clustering of KS, pneumocystis, and other serious diseases in homosexual men is related. What is known is that the patients with *Pneumocystis* pneumonia described in the previous report showed evidence of impaired cellular immunity and previous or current CMV infection (1). Furthermore, serologic evidence of past CMV infection and active shedding of CMV have been shown to be much more common among homosexual men than heterosexual men attending sexually transmitted disease clinic (15). A specific serologic association with CMV infection has been demonstrated among American and European patients with KS (16, 7) and herpes-type virus particles have been demonstrated in tissue culture cell lines from African cases of KS (18). It has been hypothesized that activation of oncogenic virus during periods of immunosuppression may result in the development of KS (19). Although immunosuppression often results in CMV infection, it is not yet clear whether CMV infection precedes or follows the above-mentioned disorders.

Although it is not certain that the increase in KS and PC pneumonia is restricted to homosexual men, the vast majority of recent cases have been reported from this group. Physicians should be alert for Kaposi's sarcoma, PC pneumonia, and other opportunistic infections associated with immunosuppression in homosexual men.

August 28, 1981

Follow-Up on Kaposi's Sarcoma and *Pneumocystis* Pneumonia

Twenty-six cases of Kaposi's sarcoma (KS) and 15 cases of *Pneumocystis carinii* pneumonia (PCP) among previously healthy homosexual men were recently reported (1,2). Since July 3, 1981, CDC has received reports of an additional 70 cases of these 2 conditions in persons without known underlying disease. The sex, race, sexual preference, and

mortality data known for 108 persons with either or both conditions are summarize
in Table 1.

The majority of the reported cases of KS and/or PCP have occurred in white me
Patients ranged in age from 15-52 years; over 95% were men 25-49 years of age. Ninet
four percent (95/101) of the men for whom sexual preference was known were hom
sexual or bisexual. Forty percent of the reported cases were fatal. Of the 82 cases fr
which the month of diagnosis is known, 75 (91%) have occurred since January 1980, wit
55 (67%) diagnosed from January through July 1981. Although physicians from sever
states have reported cases of KS and PCP among previously healthy homosexual me
the majority of cases have been reported from New York and California.

*Reported by SM Friedman, MD, YM Felman, MD, New York City Dept of Health; R Rothenber
MD, State Epidemiologist, New York State Dept of Health; S Dritz, MD, E Braff, MD, City/Coun
Health Dept, San Francisco; S Fannin, MD, Los Angeles County Dept of Health Svcs; I Heindl, M
California Dept of Health Svcs; RK Sikes, DVM, State Epidemiologist, Georgia Dept of Human R
sources; RA Gunn, MD, State Epidemiologist, Florida State Dept of Health and Rehabilitative Svc
MA Roberts, PhD, State Epidemiologist, Oklahoma State Dept of Health; Task Force on Kaposi
Sarcoma and Opportunistic Infections, Center for Prevention Svcs, Center for Infectious Disease
Center for Environmental Health, Field Svcs Div, Consolidated Surveillance and Communicatio
Activities, Epidemiology Program Office, CDC.*

Editorial Note: KS is a rare, malignant neoplasm seen predominantly in elderly me
in this country. In elderly men the disease is manifested by skin lesions and a chron
clinical course; it is rarely fatal (3). In contrast, the persons currently reported to ha
KS are young to middle-aged men, and 20% of the cases have been fatal. Although son
of the patients have presented with the violaceous skin or mucous membrane lesior
typical of KS, many such lesions have been initially overlooked. Other patients ha
been diagnosed by lymph-node biopsy after a prodrome consisting of fever, weight los
and lymphadenopathy. Seven (13%) of fifty-four KS patients also had PCP. In mar
cases the histopathologic diagnosis from skin, lymph node, or visceral-lesion tissue h
been difficult even in specialized hands.

The occurrence of *Pneumocystis carinii* pneumonia in patients who are not immun
suppressed due to known underlying disease or therapy is also highly unusual (4). A
though 7 (11%) of the 61 patients with PCP also had KS, in many instances pneumon
preceded the tumor. Although most of the patients with PCP reported recent respirato
symptoms, some gave a history of weeks to months of systemic symptoms includir
weight loss and general malaise, similar to the prodrome described by patients who deve
oped lymphadenopathic KS. Several of the patients with PCP had other serious infe
tions, including gastrointestinal candidiasis, cryptococcal meningitis, and disseminate
infections with Mycobacteriaceae and herpes simplex. Many of the PCP and KS patien
have had positive cultures or serologic evidence of infection with cytomegalovirus.

The apparent clustering of both *Pneumocystis carinii* pneumonia and KS among hom
sexual men suggests a common underlying factor. Both diseases have been associated wi
host immunosuppression (4-6), and studies in progress are showing immunosuppression
some of these cases. The extent or cause of immune suppression is not known. Physicia
should be aware of the possible occurrence of these diseases and other opportunist

**TABLE 1. Cases of Kaposi's sarcoma (KS) and *Pneumocystis carinii* pneumonia (PC
reported to CDC with dates of onset between January 1976 and July 1981**

Diagnosis (number of patients)	Sex		Race of men				Sexual preference of men			Fatality (percentage)
	Male	Female	White	Black	Hispanic	Unknown	Homosexual or bisexual	Heterosexual	Unknown	
KS and PCP (N=7)	7	0	5	0	1	1	7	0	0	3/7 (43
KS only (N=47)	47	0	41	3	3	0	44	1	2	8/47 (17
PCP only (N=54)	53	1	33	9	7	4	44	5	4	32/54 (59
Total (N=108)	107	1	79	12	11	5	95	6	6	43/108 (40

218

infections, particularly among men with symptoms suggestive of these disorders or their prodromes, since therapy is specific and verification of the diagnosis requires biopsy.

Several state and local health departments and CDC are conducting active surveillance for KS, PCP, and opportunistic infections in persons without known predisposing underlying disease. A national case-control study will be implemented shortly.

May 21, 1982

Persistent, Generalized Lymphadenopathy among Homosexual Males

Since October 1981, cases of persistent, generalized lymphadenopathy—not attributable to previously identified causes—among homosexual males have been reported to CDC by physicians in several major metropolitan areas in the United States. These reports were prompted by an awareness generated by ongoing CDC and state investigations of other emerging health problems among homosexual males (1).

In February and March 1982, records were reviewed for 57 homosexual men with lymphadenopathy seen at medical centers in Atlanta, New York City, and San Francisco. The cases reviewed met the following criteria: 1) lymphadenopathy of at least 3 months' duration, involving 2 or more extra-inguinal sites, and confirmed on physical examination by the patient's physician; 2) absence of any current illness or drug use known to cause lymphadenopathy; and 3) presence of reactive hyperplasia in a lymph node, if a biopsy was performed.

The 57 patients had a mean age of 33 years and the following characteristics: all were male; 81% were white, 15% black, and 4% Hispanic; 83% were single, 6% married, and 11% divorced; 86% were homosexual, 14% bisexual. The median duration of lymphadenopathy was 11 months. Ninety-five percent of patients had at least 3 node chains involved (usually cervical, axillary, and inguinal). Forty-three patients had had lymph node biopsies showing reactive hyperplasia. Approximately 70% of the patients had some constitutional symptoms including fatigue, 70%; fever, 49%; night sweats, 44%; and weight loss of ≥5 pounds, 28%. Hepatomegaly and/or splenomegaly was noted among 26% of patients.

Recorded medical histories for the 57 patients suggested that the use of drugs such as nitrite inhalants, marijuana, hallucinogens, and cocaine was common. Many of these patients have a history of sexually transmitted infections (gonorrhea 58%, syphilis 47%, and amebiasis 42%). Of 30 patients skin-tested for delayed hypersensitivity response, 8 were found to be anergic on the basis of at least 2 antigens other than purified protein derivative (PPD).

Immunologic evaluation performed at CDC for 8 of the above patients demonstrated abnormal T-lymphocyte helper-to-suppressor ratios (<0.9) for 2 patients. Since this review, immunologic evaluations at CDC of 13 additional homosexual males with lymphadenopathy from Atlanta and San Francisco revealed 6 with ratios of <0.9. The normal range of T-lymphocyte helper-to-suppressor ratios established in the CDC laboratory for healthy heterosexual patients is 0.9-3.5 (mean of 2.3). The normal range is being established for apparently healthy homosexual males.

Since the initiation of this study, 1 patient with lymphadenopathy has developed Kaposi's sarcoma.

Reported by D Mildvan, MD, U Mathur, MD, Div of Infectious Diseases, Beth Israel Medical Center, R Enlow, MD, Rheumatology Dept, Hospital for Joint Diseases, D Armstrong, MD, J Gold, MD, C Sears, MD, B Wong, MD, AE Brown, MD, S Henry, MD, Div of Infectious Disease, B Safai, MD, Dermatology Svc, Dept of Medicine, Z Arlin, MD, Div of Hematology, Memorial Sloan-Kettering Medical Center, A Moore, MD, C Metroka, MD, Div of Hematology-Oncology, L Drusin, MD, MPH, Dept of Medicine, The New York Hospital-Cornell Medical Center, I Spigland, MD, Div of Virology, Montefiore Hospital and Medical Center, DC William, MD, St. Luke's-Roosevelt Hospital Center, F Siegal, MD, Dept of Medicine, J Brown, MD, Dept of Neoplastic Diseases, Mt. Sinai Medical Center, J Wallace, MD, Dept of Medicine, St. Vincent's Hospital and Medical Center, D Sencer, MD, SM Friedman, MD, YM Felman, MD, New York City Dept of Health, R Rothenberg, MD, State Epidemiologist, New York State Dept of Health; RK Sikes, DVM, State Epidemiologist, Georgia Dept of Human Resources; W Owen, MD, Bay Area Physicians for Human Rights, S Dritz, MD, C Rendon, Bureau of Communicable Disease Control, San Francisco Dept of Public Health, J

Chin, MD, State Epidemiologist, California Dept of Health Svcs; J Sonnabend, MD, Uniformed Svcs University of Health Sciences, Bethesda, E Israel, MD, State Epidemiologist, Maryland State Dept of Health and Mental Hygiene; Special Studies Br, Center for Environmental Health, Div of Viral Diseases, Div of Host Factors, Center for Infectious Diseases, Field Svcs Div, Epidemiology Program Office, Task Force on Kaposi's Sarcoma and Opportunistic Infections, Office of the Centers Director, CDC.

Editorial Note: The report above documents the occurrence of cases of unexplained, persistent, generalized lymphadenopathy among homosexual males. There are many known causes of generalized lymphadenopathy including viral infections (e.g., hepatitis B, infectious mononucleosis, cytomegalovirus infection, rubella), tuberculosis, disseminated *Mycobacterium avium-intracellulare*, syphilis, other bacterial and fungal infections, toxoplasmosis, connective tissue disorders, hypersensitivity drug reactions, heroin use, and neoplastic diseases (including leukemia and lymphoma) (*2*). Causes for the persistent lymphadenopathy among patients discussed above were sought but could not be identified.

This unexplained syndrome is of concern because of current reports of Kaposi's sarcoma (KS) and opportunistic infections (OI) that primarily involve homosexual males (*1,3*). Epidemiologic characteristics (age, racial composition, city of residence) of the homosexual patients with lymphadenopathy discussed here are similar to those of the homosexual KS/OI patients. Thirty-two (44%) of 73 Kaposi's sarcoma patients and 14 (23%) of 61 *Pneumocystis carinii* pneumonia patients reported to CDC in the period mid-June 1981-January 1982 had a history of lymphadenopathy before diagnosis (*3*). *Mycobacterium avium-intracellulare* (an opportunistic agent) has been isolated from the lymph nodes of a homosexual patient (*4*). Moreover, the findings of anergy and depressed T-lymphocyte helper-to-suppressor ratios in some of the patients with lymphadenopathy suggest cellular immune dysfunction. Patients with KS/OI have had severe abnormalities of cellular immunity (*5,6*). The relationship between immunologic findings for patients with lymphadenopathy and patients with KS/OI remains to be determined.

Although these cases have been identified and defined on the basis of the presence of lymphadenopathy, this finding may be merely a manifestation of an underlying immunologic or other disorder that needs to be characterized further. Virologic and immunologic studies on many of these patients are currently under way. An analysis of trends in incidence for lymphadenopathy over the past several years is being conducted to determine whether this syndrome is new and whether homosexual males are particularly affected. Results of these studies and follow-up of these patients are necessary before the clinical and epidemiologic significance of persistent, generalized lymphadenopathy among homosexual males can be determined. Homosexual male patients with unexplained, persistent, generalized lymphadenopathy should be followed for periodic review.

June 18, 198

A Cluster of Kaposi's Sarcoma and *Pneumocystis carinii* Pneumonia among Homosexual Male Residents of Los Angeles and Orange Counties, California

In the period June 1, 1981-April 12, 1982, CDC received reports of 19 cases of biopsy-confirmed Kaposi's sarcoma (KS) and/or *Pneumocystis carinii* pneumonia (PCP) among previously healthy homosexual male residents of Los Angeles and Orange counties, California. Following an unconfirmed report of possible associations among cases in southern California, interviews were conducted with all 8 of the patients still living and with the close friends of 7 of the other 11 patients who had died.

Data on sexual partners were obtained for 13 patients, 8 with KS and 5 with PCP. For any patient to be considered as a sexual contact of another person, the reported exposures of that patient had to be either substantiated or not denied by the other person involved in the relationship (or by a close friend of that person).

Within 5 years of the onset of symptoms, 9 patients (6 with KS and 3 with PCP) had had sexual contact with other patients with KS or PCP. Seven patients from Los Angeles County had had sexual contact with other patients from Los Angeles County, and 2 from Orange County had had sexual contact with 1 patient who was not a resident of California. Four of the 9 patients had been exposed to more than 1 patient who had KS or PCP. Three of the 6 patients with KS developed their symptoms after sexual contact with persons who already had symptoms of KS. One of these 3 patients developed symptoms of KS 9 months after sexual contact, another patient developed symptoms 13 months after contact, and a third patient developed symptoms 22 months after contact.

The other 4 patients in the group of 13 had no known sexual contact with reported cases. However, 1 patient with KS had an apparently healthy sexual partner in common with 2 persons with PCP; 1 patient with KS reported having had sexual contact with 2 friends of the non-Californian with KS; and 2 patients with PCP had most of their anonymous contacts (≥80%) with persons in bathhouses attended frequently by other persons in Los Angeles with KS or PCP.

The 9 patients from Los Angeles and Orange counties directly linked to other patients are part of an interconnected series of cases that may include 15 additional patients (11 with KS and 4 with PCP) from 8 other cities. The non-Californian with KS mentioned earlier is part of this series. In addition to having had sexual contact with 2 patients with KS from Orange County, this patient said he had sexual contact with 1 patient with KS and 1 patient with PCP from New York City and 2 of the 3 patients with PCP from Los Angeles County.

Reported by S Fannin, MD, County of Los Angeles Dept of Health Svcs, MS Gottlieb, MD, UCLA School of Medicine, JD Weisman, DO, E Rogolsky, MD, Los Angeles, T Prendergast, MD, County of Orange Dept of Public Health and Medical Svcs, J Chin, MD, State Epidemiologist, California Dept of Health Svcs; AE Friedman-Kien, MD, L Laubenstein, MD, New York University Medical Center, S Friedman, MD, New York City Dept of Health, R Rothenberg, MD, State Epidemiologist, New York Health Dept; Task Force on Kaposi's Sarcoma and Opportunistic Infections, CDC.

Editorial Note: An estimated 185,000-415,000 homosexual males live in Los Angeles County.[*] Assuming that they had a median of 13.5 to 50 different sexual partners per year over the past 5 years,[†] the probability that 7 of 11 patients with KS or PCP would have sexual contact with any one of the other 16 reported patients in Los Angeles County would seem to be remote. The probability that 2 patients

---

[*]Estimates of the homosexual male population are derived from Kinsey *et al.*(*1*) who reported that 8% of adult males are exclusively homosexual and that 18% have at least as much homosexual as heterosexual experience for at least 3 years between the ages of 16 and 55 years; and the U. S. Bureau of the Census, which reported that approximately 2,304,000 males between the ages of 18 and 64 years lived in Los Angeles County in 1980.

[†]Estimates of sexual activity are derived from data collected by Jay and Young (*2*), indicating that 130 homosexual male respondents in Los Angeles had a median of 13.5 different sexual partners in 1976, and from CDC data showing that 13 patients with KS and/or PCP in the Los Angeles area tended to report having more sexual partners in the year before onset of symptoms (median=50) than did homosexual males surveyed by Jay and Young.

with KS living in different parts of Orange County would have sexual contact with the same non-Californian with KS would appear to be even lower. Thus, observations in Los Angeles and Orange counties imply the existence of an unexpected cluster of cases.

The cluster in Los Angeles and Orange counties was identified on the basis of sexual contact. One hypothesis consistent with the observations reported here is that infectious agents are being sexually transmitted among homosexually active males. Infectious agents not yet identified may cause the acquired cellular immunodeficiency that appears to underlie KS and/or PCP among homosexual males (3-6). If infectious agents cause these illnesses, sexual partners of patients may be at increased risk of developing KS and/or PCP.

Another hypothesis to be considered is that sexual contact with patients with KS or PCP does not lead directly to acquired cellular immunodeficiency, but simply indicates a certain style of life. The number of homosexually active males who share this lifestyle may be much smaller than the number of homosexual males in the general population.

Exposure to some substance (rather than an infectious agent) may eventually lead to immunodeficiency among a subset of the homosexual male population that shares a particular style of life. For example, Marmor et al. recently reported that exposure to amyl nitrite was associated with an increased risk of KS in New York City (7). Exposure to inhalant sexual stimulants, central-nervous-system stimulants, and a variety of other "street" drugs was common among males belonging to the cluster of cases of KS and PCP in Los Angeles and Orange counties.

June 4, 1982

Diffuse, Undifferentiated Non-Hodgkins Lymphoma among Homosexual Males — United States

A recent outbreak of Kaposi's sarcoma, *Pneumocystis carinii* pneumonia, and other opportunistic infections (KSOI) involving homosexual males and associated with an acquired cellular immunodeficiency syndrome has been described (1,2). While the pathogenesis of these disorders among homosexual males in San Francisco was being studied, 4 cases of diffuse, undifferentiated non-Hodgkins lymphoma (DUNHL) were diagnosed between March 1981 and January 1982. Because of the rarity of this malignancy and the potential relationship of these cases to the KSOI syndrome, they are reported here.

Patient 1: A 28-year-old hospital clerk complained of back and shoulder pain starting in early March 1981. Within a few days he had swelling of the right eye and an unsteady gait and he was hospitalized on March 21. "Shotty" peripheral lymphadenopathy was present. A biopsy of an orbital mass and an enlarged cervical lymph node disclosed DUNHL. A myelogram revealed a T4-T6 block by an extradural mass. Radiation and chemotherapy led to complete remission. In September 1981, another tumor in the spinal cord was treated with radiation. The ensuing remission was temporary, and the patient died with disseminated DUNHL on January 15, 1982.

Patient 2: A 33-year-old nurse developed a tumor in his left lower jaw in October 1981. Penicillin was given for a suspected abscess, but the mass enlarged. A biopsy on November 24 disclosed DUNHL. Tumor cells contained surface IgM, kappa type, indicating a B-cell tumor. The tumor involved a left axillary lymph node, the retroperitoneum, the bone marrow, and the meninges. Generalized "reactive" lymphadenopathy and mild splenomegaly were present. Systemic and intrathecal chemotherapy led to temporary tumor regression; the patient relapsed and died in March 1982.

Patient 3: A 35-year-old janitor developed an enlarged cervical lymph node in October 1981. A dental extraction was performed for a suspected abscess, but lymphadenopathy persisted. A biopsy on December 12 revealed DUNHL. Tumor cells contained surface IgM, kappa type. Tumor was detected in the mediastinum, retroperitoneum, both kidneys, bone marrow, and meninges. Moderate generalized lymphadenopathy and splenomegaly were present. Systemic and intrathecal chemotherapy led to rapid tumor regression; however, this patient has recently relapsed.

Patient 4: A 24-year-old clerk developed backache and fatigue in November 1981. On January 21, 1982, an exploratory laparotomy showed DUNHL with extensive retroperitoneal involvement. Tumor cells contained surface IgM, kappa type. Combination chemotherapy has led to complete remission.

All these patients were homosexual males living in San Francisco. They had no known contact with each other, had no known sexual partners in common, and had no known contact with patients with Kaposi's sarcoma (KS). Each gave a history of a life style that included use of such drugs as nitrite inhalants, amphetamines, and marijuana. Medical histories indicated that all 4 patients had had 1 or more of such infections as hepatitis B, anal warts, gonorrhea, and syphilis. All patients had generalized lymphadenopathy, and 3 had splenomegaly of uncertain duration. Detailed virology and immunology studies are in progress.

Reported by JL Ziegler, MD, G Wagner, MD, VA Medical Center, San Francisco, JS Greenspan, BDS, PhD, MRC Path, EJ Shillitoe, BDS, PhD, D Greenspan, BDS, J Beckstead, MD, C Cassavant, PhD, D Abrams, MD, W Chan, DDS, S Silverman, DDS, F Lozada, DDS, University of California San Francisco, School of Medicine and Dentistry, L Drew, MD, E Rosenbaum, MD, R Miner, BS, L Mintz, MD, J Gershow, MD, R Weiss, MD, Mt. Zion Hospital, San Francisco, K Yamamoto, MD, K Chick, MD, St Mary's Hospital, San Francisco, S Dritz, MD, MPH, Dept of Public Health, San Francisco, D Austin, MD, MPH, Dept of Health Svcs, Berkeley, J Chin, MD, State Epidemiologist, California Dept of Health Svcs; W McGuire, MD, University of Illinois Hospital, I Iossifides, MD, Abraham Lincoln School of Medicine, Chicago, BJ Francis, MD, State Epidemiologist, Illinois State Dept of Public Health; J Costa, MD, National Cancer Institute, National Institutes of Health; Chronic Disease Div, Center for Environmental Health, Center for Infectious Diseases, the Task Force on Kaposi's Sarcoma and Opportunistic Infections, CDC.

Editorial Note: Since July 1981, CDC has received reports of 162 cases of Kaposi's sarcoma among young homosexual males; the above report documents the possible appearance of a second unusual malignancy among this group of young males—i.e., DUNHL, a B-cell lymphoma (3).

The difficulty in distinguishing DUNHL histologically from Burkitt's lymphoma (BL) (3), a tumor often associated with Epstein-Barr virus, and the lack of consensus on the classification of non-Hodgkin's lymphoma (NHL) (4) make the precise determination of incidence difficult. About 0.7%-2.4% of all cases of NHL are DUNHL (4,5)—for a crude incidence rate of 0.06-0.21/100,000 population/year. No cases of DUNHL and only 1 case of BL were reported in 1977-1980 among 20-39 year olds to the Surveillance Epidemiology and End Results Cancer Registry in the San Francisco-Oakland-Standard Metropolitan Statistical Area, emphasizing the unusual occurrence of 4 cases within 10 months in the San Francisco homosexual male population. CDC has also recently received a report from Chicago of another case of DUNHL affecting a young homosexual male.

Underlying immune deficiency appears to be the common denominator for the development of the opportunistic infections and tumors associated with the KSOI syndrome (6-8). A similar syndrome, with an increased risk for NHL but a different time course and spectrum of opportunistic diseases, appears among renal allograft recipients (4,9). Lymphoreticular tumors also occur much more frequently among patients with primary immunodeficiency disorders (4). The cause of the acquired cellular immunodeficiency among homosexual males is being studied.

This report of DUNHL suggests that more than one kind of tumor may occur in association with the KSOI syndrome; assessment of these patients' immunologic findings will help to document the relationship between such tumors and the KSOI syndrome. The full range of potential outcomes (i.e., opportunistic tumors and infections) is probably only now being elucidated. There have also been recent case reports of other malignancies affecting the homosexual population, including carcinoma of the anal rectum (*10*) and squamous cell carcinoma of the oral cavity (*11,12*). The excess of carcinoma of the anus and anal rectum appears to antedate the onset of KSOI syndrome (*13*). The relationship between these malignancies and the KSOI syndrome is uncertain.

Many homosexual males with persistent, unexplained, generalized lymphadenopathy and biopsies reportedly demonstrating only reactive hyperplasia have also been reported to CDC and are under active investigation (*14*). Homosexual males with clinical findings similar to DUNHL or lymphadenopathic KS (*15*) should be carefully evaluated and followed.

June 11, 1982

Update on Kaposi's Sarcoma and Opportunistic Infections in Previously Healthy Persons — United States

Between June 1, 1981, and May 28, 1982, CDC received reports of 355 cases* of Kaposi's sarcoma (KS) and/or serious opportunistic infections (OI), especially *Pneumocystis carinii* pneumonia (PCP), occurring in previously healthy persons between 15 and 60 years of age. Of the 355, 281 (79%) were homosexual (or bisexual) men, 41 (12%) were heterosexual men, 20 (6%) were men of unknown sexual orientation, and 13 (4%) were heterosexual women. This proportion of heterosexuals (16%) is higher than previously described (*1*).

Five states—California, Florida, New Jersey, New York, and Texas—accounted for 86% of the reported cases. The rest were reported by 15 other states. New York was reported as the state of residence for 51% of homosexual male patients, 49% of the heterosexual males, and 46% of the females. The median age at onset of symptoms was 36.0 years for homosexual men, 31.5 years for heterosexual men, and 29.0 years for women. The distribution of homosexual and heterosexual KSOI cases by date of onset is shown in Figure 2. Overall, 69% of all reported cases have had onset after January 1, 1981.

PCP accounted for a significantly higher proportion of the diagnoses for both male (63%) and female (73%) heterosexual patients than for homosexual patients (42%) (p<0.05). The ratio of homosexual to heterosexual males with PCP only, by year of onset of symptoms, was 5:1 in 1980, 3:1 in 1981 and 4:1 thus far in 1982. Reported case-fatality ratios for PCP cases with onset in 1980 and 1981 were 85% and 47%, respectively, for homosexual men and 67% and 41% for heterosexual men. The distribution of PCP cases by diagnosis, sexual orientation, race, and overall case-fatality ratio is shown in Table 1.

TABLE 1. Reported cases of *Pneumocystis carinii* pneumonia in previously healthy persons, June 1, 1981-May 28, 1982, United States

	Race					
	Total	White	Black	Hispanic	Case-fatality ratio	IV-Drug Use†
Homosexual men*	118	80	22	15	51%	11/80 (14%)
Heterosexual men*	26	8	11	6	35%	17/26 (65%)
Heterosexual women*	8	1	4	2	50%	4/7 (57%)

*Race data lacking for 1 case
†Data not available on all cases

*A case is defined as illness in a person who 1) has either biopsy-proven KS or biopsy- or culture-proven, life-threatening opportunistic infection, 2) is under age 60, and 3) has no history of either immunosuppressive underlying illness or immunosuppressive therapy.

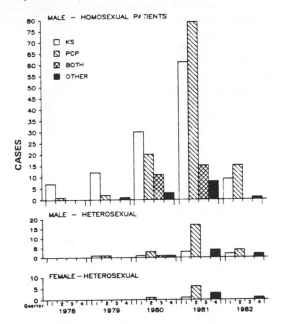

Both male and female heterosexual PCP patients were more likely than homosexual patients to be black or Hispanic (p=0.0001). Of patients with PCP for whom drug-use information was known, 14% of homosexual men had used intravenous drugs at some time compared with 63% of heterosexual men (p=0.001) and 57% of heterosexual women (p=0.001)(Table 1).

Editorial Note: Sexual orientation information was obtained from patients by their physicians, and the accuracy of reporting cannot be determined; therefore, comparisons between KSOI cases made on the basis of sexual orientation must be interpreted cautiously. Similarities between homosexual and heterosexual cases in diagnoses and geographic and temporal distribution suggest that all are part of the same epidemic. Masur et al (2) also reported that lymphocyte dysfunction and lymphopenia were similar in heterosexual and homosexual cases of PCP. However, differences in race, proportion of PCP cases, and intravenous drug use suggest that risk factors may be different for these groups. A laboratory and interview study of heterosexual patients with diagnosed KS, PCP, or other OI is in progress to determine whether their cellular immune function, results of virologic studies, medical history, sexual practices, drug use, and life-style are similar to those of homosexual patients.

References

1. CDC. Follow-up on Kaposi's sarcoma and *Pneumocystis* pneumonia. MMWR 1981;30:409-10.
2. Masur H, Michelis M, Greene JB, et al. An outbreak of community-acquired *Pneumocystis carinii* pneumonia: initial manifestations of cellular immune dysfunction. N Engl J Med 1981;305:1431-8

June 25, 1982

Inactivated Hepatitis B Virus Vaccine

Introduction

Worldwide, recommendations for using hepatitis B virus (HBV) vaccine will vary in accordance with local patterns of HBV transmission. In the United States, an area of low HBV prevalence, certain groups are at substantially greater risk than the general population of acquiring infection. It is for these higher-risk groups that the vaccine is currently recommended. To date, 12,000 individuals have been given this vaccine, and no untoward effects have been observed over periods of time extending up to 3 years. The recommendations that follow are intended as initial guides for immunization practice, and will be modified as additional data and experience are accumulated. Because the cost of this vaccine is high, a discussion of the cost effectiveness of prevaccination susceptibility testing is included.

Hepatitis B Virus Infection in the United States

The estimated lifetime risk of HBV infection in the United States varies from almost 100% for the highest-risk groups to approximately 5% for the population as a whole. An estimated 200,000 persons, primarily young adults, are infected each year. One-quarter of them become ill with jaundice. More than 10,000 patients are hospitalized with hepatitis B each year, and an average of 250 die of fulminant disease. Between 6% and 10% of young adults with HBV infection become carriers. The United States currently contains an estimated pool of 400,000-800,000 infectious carriers. Chronic active hepatitis develops in over 25% of carriers (100,000-200,000), and often progresses to cirrhosis. Furthermore, recent studies have demonstrated an association between the HBV carrier state and the occurrence of liver cancer. It is estimated that 4,000 persons die from hepatitis B-related cirrhosis each year in this country, and that more than 800 die from hepatitis B-related liver cancer.

The role of the HBV carrier is basic to the epidemiology of HBV transmission. A carrier is defined as a person who is HBsAg positive on at least 2 occasions, at least 6 months apart. Although the degree of infectivity is best correlated with HBeAg positivity, any person with a positive test for HBsAg is potentially infectious. The likelihood of developing the carrier state varies inversely with the age at which infection occurs. During the perinatal period, HBV transmitted from HBeAg-positive mothers results in HBV carriage in up to 90% of infected infants whereas 6%-10% of acutely infected adults become carriers.

Carriers and persons with acute cases have highest concentrations of HBV in the blood and serous fluids; less is present in other body fluids, such as saliva and semen. Transmission is via percutaneous or permucosal routes. Infective blood or body fluids can be introduced by means of contaminated needles or through sexual contact. Close personal contacts such as those that occur among household contacts of HBV carriers or among children in institution for the mentally retarded can also spread infection. Transmission of infection by transfusion of contaminated blood or blood products has been greatly reduced since the advent of routine screening with highly sensitive tests for HBsAg.

Although subtypes of HBV exist, infection or immunization with 1 subtype confers immunity to all subtypes.

Serologic surveys demonstrate that although HBV infection is uncommon among adults in the general population, it is highly prevalent in certain groups. Those at risk, based on the presence of serologic markers of infection, are described in Table 1. Immigrants/refugees and their descendants from areas of high HBV endemicity are at high risk of HBV infection. Homosexually active males and users of illicit injectable drugs are among the highest-risk groups acquiring infection soon (10%-20%/year) after adopting these lifestyles. Inmates of prisons also appear to be at high risk, possibly as a consequence of drug abuse or homosexual practices. Patients and staff in custodial institutions for the mentally retarded are also at increased risk of having HBV infection. Classroom contacts of some deinstitutionalized carriers may also be at higher risk than the general population. Intimate household and sexual contact with HBV carriers increases risk, as does receiving certain pooled plasma products and undergoing hemodialysis.

There is increased risk for certain medical and dental workers, and related laboratory and support personnel, who have frequent contact with blood from infective patients. Employ-

TABLE 1. Expected hepatitis B virus prevalence in various population groups

	Prevalence of serologic markers of HBV infection	
	HBsAG (%)	All markers (%)
High risk		
Immigrants/refugees from areas of high HBV endemicity	13	70-85
Clients in institutions for the mentally retarded	10-20	35-80
Users of illicit parenteral drugs	7	60-80
Homosexually active males	6	35-80
Household contacts of HBV carriers	3-6	30-60
Patients of hemodialysis units	3-10	20-80
Intermediate risk		
Prisoners (male)	1-8	10-80
Staff of institutions for the mentally retarded	1	10-25
Health-care workers Frequent blood contact	1-2	15-30
Low risk		
Health-care workers No or infrequent blood contact	0.3	3-10
Healthy Adults (first-time volunteer blood donors)	0.3	3-5

ment in a hospital without exposure to blood carries no greater risk than that for the general population.

Vaccine

Hepatitis B virus vaccine is a suspension of inactivated, alum-adsorbed 22-nm surface antigen particles that have been purified from human plasma by a combination of biophysical (ultracentrifugation) and biochemical procedures. Inactivation is a 3-fold process using 8-M urea, pepsin at pH 2, and 1:4,000 formalin. Each of these processes has been shown to inactivate HBV and representative viruses from all known groups, and thus should inactivate any viruses potentially contaminating the vaccine. HBV vaccine contains 20 μg/ml of HBsAg protein.

After a series of 3 intramuscular doses of HBV vaccine, an average of over 90% of healthy adults developed protective antibody (1,2). A course of 3 10-μg doses induces antibody in virtually all infants and children 3 months through 9 years of age tested to date. Protective antibody titers have persisted during 3 years of observation, although a gradually declining titer has been observed.

Field trials of the United States-manufactured vaccine have shown 80%-95% efficacy in preventing infection or hepatitis among susceptible persons (3,4). Protection against illness was complete for persons who developed antibodies after vaccination but before exposure. The duration of protection and the consequent need for booster doses are not yet known.

Studies are planned or are under way in various settings to assess the value of vaccination after HBV exposure. For post-exposure prophylaxis, see the ACIP recommendations for the use of immune globulin (5); see below for recommendations regarding infants born to moth ers who are HBV carriers and for sexual contacts of patients with acute hepatitis B.

Vaccine Usage

Primary adult vaccination consists of 3 intramuscular doses of 1.0 ml of vaccine (2 μg/1.0 ml) each. The second and third doses should be given 1 and 6 months, respectivel after the first. For patients undergoing hemodialysis, and for other immunosuppressed pa tients, 3 2-ml doses (40 μg) should be used. For children under 10 years of age, 3 similar spaced doses of 0.5 ml (10 μg) are sufficient. Vaccine doses administered at longer interva than those stipulated provide equally satisfactory protection, but optimal protection is n conferred until after the third dose. Since HBV vaccine is an inactivated (non-infective) prod uct, it is presumed that there will be no interference with other simultaneously administere vaccine(s). The duration of protection and the need for booster doses have not yet bee determined.

Vaccine Storage

Vaccine should be stored at 2C-8C but not frozen. *Freezing destroys the potency of th vaccine.*

Side Effects and Adverse Reactions

Side effects among 12,000 recipients of HBV vaccine observed to date have been limite to soreness and redness at the injection site (3,4).

Data are not available on the safety of the vaccine for the developing fetus, but because contains only non-infectious HBsAg particles, the risk to the fetus from the vaccine should b negligible. In contrast, HBV infection in a pregnant woman may result in severe disease for th mother and chronic infection for the newborn. Pregnancy should not be considered a contrain dication to the use of this vaccine for persons who are otherwise eligible.

Effect of Vaccination on Carriers

The vaccine produces neither therapeutic nor adverse effects in HBV carriers (6).

Vaccination of Immune Persons

Vaccination of individuals who possess antibodies against HBV from a previous infectio is not necessary but will not cause adverse effects. Such individuals will have a pos vaccination increase in their anti-HBs levels. Passively acquired antibody, whether from hepatitis B immune globulin (HBIG) administration or from the transplacental route, will not in terfere with active immunization (7).

Prevaccination Serologic Screening for Susceptibility

HBV carriers and those having antibody from previous infection need not be vaccinate but serologic screening to detect such individuals before vaccination may or may not be co effective. The decision to screen potential vaccine recipients is an economic one that depend on 3 variables: 1) the cost of vaccination, 2) the cost of testing for susceptibility, and 3) th prevalence of immune individuals in the group. All are important in estimating whether routin selective, or no screening will be most economical in an HBV vaccination program.

Figure 1 shows the relative cost effectiveness of screening, given different costs of scree ing tests and the expected prevalence of immunity. In constructing the figure, the assumptic was made that the cost of 3 doses of vaccine is $100 and that there are additional costs f administration. For any combination of screening costs and immunity to hepatitis, the cost e fectiveness can be estimated. For example, if the expected prevalence of serologic marke for HBV is over 20%, screening is cost effective if costs of screening are no greater tha $30/person. If the expected prevalence of markers is less than 8%, and if the costs of scree ing are greater than $10 per person, vaccination without screening is cost effective.

Screening in groups with the highest risk of HBV infection (e.g., users of illicit injectab

rugs, homosexually active males, and institutionalized mentally retarded persons) will be
ost effective unless testing costs are extremely high. For groups at intermediate risk (e.g.,
ealth-care workers with an expected prevalence of 8%-20%), cost effectiveness of screening
nay be marginal, and vaccination programs may or may not utilize screening. For groups with
  low expected prevalence of HBV serologic markers (e.g., entering health professionals)
creening will not be cost effective.

   For routine screening, only 1 antibody test, either anti-HBc or anti-HBs, need be used. Anti-
HBc will identify all previously infected persons, both carriers and those who are not carriers,
ut will not discriminate between members of the 2 groups. Anti-HBs will identify those previously infected except for carriers. For groups expected to have carrier rates of <2%, such
s health-care workers, neither test has a particular advantage. For groups with higher carrier
ates, anti-HBc may be preferred to avoid unnecessary vaccination of carriers. If a radioimmu-
noassay (RIA) anti-HBs test is used for screening, a minimum of 10 RIA sample ratio units
should be used to designate immunity (2.1 is the usual designation of a positive test) (4).

Serologic Confirmation of Post-Vaccination Immunity

   HBV vaccine produces protective antibody (anti-HBs) in more than 90% of healthy persons
(1-2). Revaccination of those persons who did not respond to the primary series has produced antibody in only one-third. Thus, there seems little need to test for immunity following
vaccination except for dialysis patients, whose subsequent management depends on knowing
their immune status.

Pre-Exposure Vaccination

   Persons at substantial risk of HBV infection who are demonstrated or judged likely to be
susceptible should be vaccinated. They include:

FIGURE 1. Cost effectiveness of pre-vaccination screening of hepatitis B virus vaccine
candidates*

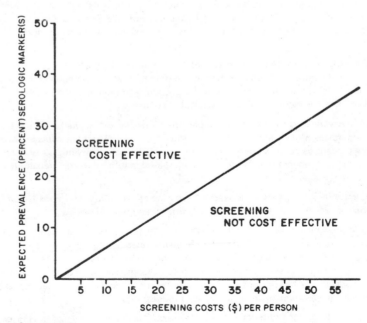

See text for assumptions.

Health-Care Workers — Health-care workers (medical, dental, laboratory, and support groups) have varied risks of exposure to HBV depending on their jobs. Those workers for whom vaccine is recommended should be vaccinated as soon as possible after beginning work in a high-risk environment, ideally during their period of training.

Hospital Staff — Hospital staff are at increased risk of HBV infection because of contact with blood and blood products. The risk for hospital personnel can vary both among hospitals and within hospitals. In developing specific immunization strategies, hospitals should use available published data about the risk of infection (8-10) and, in addition, may wish to evaluate their own clinical and institutional experience with hepatitis B.

Studies in urban centers have indicated that occupational groups with frequent exposure to blood and/or needles have a substantial risk of acquiring HBV infection. The highest risk is for individuals with frequent blood exposure, including the following groups: medical technologists, operating room staff, phlebotomists and intravenous therapy nurses, surgeons and pathologists, and oncology and dialysis unit staff. Other groups that have been shown to be at increased risk in some hospitals include: emergency room staff, nursing personnel, and physicians. To quantitate HBV risks among workers, groups can be ranked according to their frequency of blood/needle exposure. Additional information can be obtained from employee health records, serologic prevalence surveys, and estimates of HBsAg prevalence among patients.

Other Health-Care Workers — Other health workers, based outside of hospitals, who have frequent contact with blood or blood products are at increased risk of acquiring HBV infection. These include dental professionals (dentists, oral surgeons, dental hygienists), laboratory and blood bank technicians, dialysis center staff, morticians, and similar professionals.

Clients and Staff of Institutions for the Mentally Retarded — Susceptible clients and selected staff of institutions for the mentally retarded should be vaccinated. Risks for staff are comparable to those for health-care personnel in other high-risk environments. However, the risk in institutional environments is associated not only with blood exposure, but is also consequent to bites and contact with skin lesions, saliva, and other infective secretions.

Hemodialysis Patients — Numerous studies have established the high risk of HBV virus transmission in hemodialysis units. While recent data have shown a decrease in the rate of HBV infection in hemodialysis units following introduction of environmental control measures, vaccination is recommended for susceptible patients.

Homosexually Active Males — Susceptible homosexually active males should be vaccinated regardless of their age or duration of their homosexual practices. It is important to vaccinate persons as soon as possible after their homosexual activity begins. Homosexually active females do not appear to be at increased risk of sexually transmitted HBV infection.

Illicit Injectable Drug Users — All users of illicit injectable drugs who are susceptible to HBV should be vaccinated as early as possible after their drug use begins.

Recipients of Certain Blood Products — Although screening of all blood donors for HBsAg has decreased the incidence of transfusion-related HBV infection, patients with clotting disorders who receive factor VIII or IX concentrates have an elevated risk of HBV infection. Vaccination is recommended for these persons, and should be initiated at the time their specific clotting disorder is identified. Screening is recommended for patients who have already received multiple infusions of these products.

Household and Sexual Contacts of HBV Carriers — Household contacts of HBV carriers are at high risk of HBV infection. Sexual contacts appear to be at greatest risk. Vaccination of susceptible household contacts of carriers is recommended. At present, most carriers are identified through routine screening of donated blood, diagnostic testing in hospitals, or through other screening programs among high-risk groups. As part of expanded HBV control programs, additional screening to identify HBV carriers may be warranted.

Other Contacts of HBV Carriers — Persons in contact with carriers at schools, offices, etc., are at minimal risk of contracting HBV, and vaccine is not routinely recommended for them. However, classroom contacts of deinstitutionalized mentally retarded HBV carriers who behave aggressively or have special medical problems that increase the risk of exposure to their blood or serous secretions may be at risk. In such situations, vaccine may be offered to classroom contacts.

Special High-Risk Populations — Some American populations, such as Alaskan Eskimos, and immigrants and refugees from areas with highly endemic disease (particularly eastern Asia and sub-Saharan Africa) have high HBV infection rates and deserve special attention. Depending on specific epidemiologic and public health considerations, more extensive vaccination programs may be warranted.

Inmates of Long-Term Correctional Facilities — The prison environment may provide a favorable setting for the transmission of HBV because of the frequent use of illicit injectable drugs and homosexual practices. In such institutions, prison officials may elect to undertake screening and vaccination programs.

Post-Exposure Vaccination

Infants Born to HBsAg-Positive Mothers — Pregnant women who are HBsAg positive should be informed about the risk of transmission to their infants. Infants born to these women should receive HBIG (5,11). Infants whose mothers are chronic carriers will be continuously exposed to HBV throughout their childhood; therefore these infants should receive vaccine. The optimum timing for vaccination in conjunction with HBIG administration has not been established. Pending additional information, it is recommended that vaccination begin at 3 months of age or shortly thereafter. Studies to determine the immunogenicity and efficacy of vaccine at birth, with or without HBIG, are currently under way.

Sexual and Household Contacts of Acute Hepatitis B Cases and Health Workers Who Receive Needle Sticks from HBsAg-Positive Patients — Possible alternatives for post-exposure prophylaxis include HBIG, immunoglobulin (IG), HBV vaccine, or a combination of vaccine and an immune globulin. Recommendations for immune globulin use have already been published (5). Studies are currently under way to evaluate the use of vaccine in some of these settings. No recommendations can be made at this time for post-exposure use of HBV vaccine.

July 9, 1982

Opportunistic Infections and Kaposi's Sarcoma among Haitians in the United States

Reports of opportunistic infections and Kaposi's sarcoma among Haitians residing in the United States have recently been received at CDC. A total of 34 cases in 5 states have been reported to date.

Florida: From April 1, 1980, through June 20, 1982, 19 Haitian patients admitted to Jackson Memorial Hospital, Miami, had culture, biopsy, or autopsy evidence of opportunistic infections, and 1 other patient had biopsy- and autopsy-confirmed Kaposi's sarcoma. The infections identified included *Pneumocystis carinii* pneumonia (6 patients), cryptococcal meningitis or fungemia (4), toxoplasmosis of the central nervous system (CNS) (7), *Candida albicans* esophagitis (7) and thrush (5), esophageal or disseminated cytomegalovirus infection (3), progressive herpes simplex virus infection (1), disseminated tuberculosis (8), and chronic enteric *Isospora belli* infection (2). Fourteen patients had multiple opportunistic infections. Three patients had recurring infection. The clinical course has been severe; 10 patients have died. The type of infection was initially recognized at autopsy for 6 patients.

The 20 patients ranged in age from 22 to 43 years (mean 28.4 years); 17 were males. All the patients had been born in Haiti and had resided in the Miami-Dade County area for periods ranging from 1 month to 7 years (median 20.5 months).

When initially seen, 18 of the 20 patients had peripheral lymphopenia ($<$ 1,000 lymphocytes/mm^3). Skin tests performed on 17 patients with various combinations of tuberculin, mumps, streptokinase/streptodornase, *Candida*, and *Trichophyton* antigens were all negative. Immunologic studies at CDC on specimens from the 11 patients tested showed severe T-cell dysfunction. Monoclonal antibody analysis of peripheral-blood T-cell subsets revealed a marked decrease of the T-helper cell subset with inversion of the normal ratio of T-helper to T-suppressor cells.

Of the 7 patients with histologically confirmed toxoplasmosis of the CNS, 5 have died. Because there was no history of underlying conditions or drugs associated with immunosuppression, CNS toxoplasmosis was not considered in the premortem diagnosis of the first 4 cases. Pathology findings for all these patients were confirmed with an immuno-peroxidase method for toxoplasmosis and, in one instance, with electron microscopy as well. Tachyzoites were the predominant form of the parasite observed; encysted forms were rare or absent in many tissue blocks.

In addition to the 20 cases reported from Miami, a Haitian female from Naples, Florida, was reported to have *P. carinii* pneumonia.

New York: From July 1, 1981, through May 31, 1982, 10 Haitian residents of Brooklyn were diagnosed as having the following opportunistic infections: *P. carinii* pneumonia (5 patients), CNS toxoplasmosis (2), disseminated cryptococcosis (1), esophageal candidiasis (1), and disseminated tuberculosis (2). None had any underlying disease or history of therapy known to cause immunosuppression. Five died of their infections.

All 10 patients were males and ranged in age from 22 to 37 years. Eight stated they were heterosexual; the sexual orientation of the other 2 was not known. One patient gave a history of intravenous (IV) drug abuse; 8 denied drug abuse, and for 1, no information was available on drug use. The 10 had resided in the United States for periods ranging from 3 months to 8 years (the majority, for 2 years or less). At least 1 patient had onset of illness before arriving in the United States. Immunologic studies performed at CDC on specimens from 2 patients showed results comparable to those for the 11 patients from Miami.

Other States: Opportunistic infections or Kaposi's sarcoma were also reported for 3 other Haitians located in California, Georgia, and New Jersey. All 3 were heterosexual males who denied IV drug abuse. One patient had *P. carinii* pneumonia, another had Kaposi's sarcoma, and the third had esophageal candidiasis.

Reported by GT Hensley, MD, LB Moskowitz, MD, AE Pitchenik, MD, MA Fischl, MD, SZ Tabei MD, Kory, MD, MJ Post, MD, FK Conley, MD (Stanford University School of Medicine), G Dickinson, MD, Becker, MD, A Fournier, MD, M O'Connell, MD, G Scott, MD, University of Miami School of Medicine, R Morgan, MD, JQ Cleveland, MD, Dade County Health Dept, H Tennis, Metropolitan Dade County, H Janowski, MPH, RA Gunn, MD, MPH, State Epidemiologist, Florida Dept of Health and Rehabilitative Svcs; J Viera, MD, S Landesman, MD, E Frank, MD, J Nadler, MD, Kings County Hospital, SUNY Downstate Medical Center, Brooklyn, C Metroka, MD, T Nash, MD, New York Hospital, SM Friedman, MD, D Sencer, MD, New York City Dept of Health, R Rothenberg, MD, State Epidemiolgist, New York State Dept of Health; T Howard, MD, Cedars-Sinai Medical Center, M Gottlieb, MD, UCLA Medical Center, S Fannin, MD, Los Angeles County Dept of Health Svcs, J Chin, MD, State Epidemiologist, California Dept of Health Svcs; R Kapila, MD, New Jersey College of Medicine and Dentistry, IC Guerrero, WE Parkin, DVM, State Epidemiologist, New Jersey Dept of Health; J Hawkins, MD, Medical College of Georgia, RK Sikes, DVM, State Epidemiologist, Georgia Dept of Human Resources; Div of Parasitic Diseases, Div of Host Factors, Center for Infectious Diseases, Field Svcs Div, Epidemiology Program Office, Task Force on Kaposi's Sarcoma and Opportunistic Infections, CDC.

Editorial Note: The occurrence of severe opportunistic infections among 32 Haitians recently entering the United States is a new phenomenon. The in vitro immunologic findings and the high mortality rate (nearly 50%) for these patients are similar to the pattern recently described among homosexual males and IV drug abusers (1-4). None of the 23 Haitian males questioned reported homosexual activity, and only 1 of 26 gave a history of IV drug abuse—substantially lower than the prevalence reported for heterosexual patients of other racial/ethnic groups who had Kaposi's sarcoma or opportunistic infections. Of the 34 patients discussed above with opportunistic infections or Kaposi's sarcoma, 30 (88%) were males. All patients were between 20 and 45 years of age. Data from medical screening of 10,780 Haitians entering the United States between March and November 1980 indicated that 73% were adult males. Only 2% of those screened were <12 years old, and over 90% were <45 years old (5).

The occurrence of opportunistic infections among adult Haitians with no history of underlying immunosuppressive therapy or disease has not been reported previously. However, 11 cases of disseminated Kaposi's sarcoma have been diagnosed by dermatologists in Port au Prince, Haiti, over a period of 2 1/2 years (6). The reason for the high prevalence of disseminated tuberculosis among the group of patients discussed above is not known; but a high prevalence of tuberculosis has been documented among recent Haitian entrants (7), and the disease has been reported to disseminate more frequently among persons who are immunocompromised (8,9).

To date, it has not been established whether the cases of toxoplasmosis represent reactivation of old lesions acquired in Haiti or whether they are progressive primary infections acquired in the United States. However, serum specimens obtained from 2 patients in Miami and tested at CDC by indirect immuno-fluorescence (IIF) were negative for IgM antibody to Toxoplasma. This suggests that the infections of these 2 patients were not recently acquired. Serologic tests such as the IIF may be helpful in establishing or excluding a diagnosis of toxoplasmosis for patients with CNS symptoms. Tachyzoites in tissue specimens can be visualized more effectively using Giemsa stain or a recently developed immuno-peroxidase method (10) than with the standard hemotoxylin and eosin staining.

plasmosis for patients seen with CNS symptoms. Tachyzoites in tissue specimens can be visualized more effectively using Giemsa stain or a recently developed immuno-peroxidase method (10) than with the standard hemotoxylin and eosin staining.

It is not clear whether this outbreak is related to similar outbreaks among homosexual males, IV drug abusers, and others, but the clinical and immunologic pictures appear quite similar. CDC is currently collaborating with local investigators to define this problem and identify risk factors.

Physicians who care for Haitian patients should be aware that opportunistic infections may occur in this population. Health-care providers who diagnose opportunistic infections or Kaposi's sarcoma among persons who do not have underlying disease and are not on immunosuppressive therapy are requested to report such cases to CDC through their appropriate state and local health departments.

July 16, 1982

Pneumocystis carinii Pneumonia among Persons with Hemophilia A

CDC recently received reports of three cases of *Pneumocystis carinii* pneumonia among patients with hemophilia A and without other underlying disease. Two have died; one remains critically ill. All three were heterosexual males; none had a history of intravenous (IV) drug abuse. All had lymphopenia, and the two patients who were specifically tested have had *in vitro* laboratory evidence of cellular immune deficiency. The case reports follow.

Patient 1: A 62-year-old resident of Westchester County, New York, with a history of chronic hepatitis had received frequent injections of Factor VIII concentrate for severe hemophilia for many years. In February 1981, he began to experience weight loss and vague right upper quadrant abdominal discomfort associated with laboratory evidence of increasing hepatic dysfunction. In December 1981, while hospitalized in Miami, Florida, for elective knee surgery, he complained of cough and fever. He was lymphopenic, and chest X-ray revealed interstitial infiltrates compatible with viral pneumonia. He was discharged in late December after a brief course of corticosteroids associated with overall clinical improvement. He returned in severe respiratory distress a few days later. Open lung biopsy on January 5 revealed *P. carinii*, for which he received sulfamethoxazole/trimethoprim (SMZ/TMP) during the 2 weeks before death. *P. carinii* pneumonia and micronodular cirrhosis were documented at post-mortem examination.

Patient 2: A 59-year-old lifelong resident of Denver, Colorado, noted the onset of gradual weight loss, dysphagia associated with pharyngitis, aphthous-like ulcers, and anterior cervical adenopathy beginning in October 1980. As a patient with severe hemophilia, he had received frequent injections of Factor VIII concentrate for several years. Weight loss continued over a period of months. Oropharyngeal candidiasis was diagnosed in February 1982. He was hospitalized in May 1982 with symptoms including nausea, vomiting, and recurrent fever. Pneumonia was diagnosed, and *P. carinii* and cytomegalovirus (CMV) were repeatedly identified from lung tissue or bronchial secretions using histopathologic and culture techniques. Therapy with SMZ/TMP and pentamidine isethionate continued until death on July 5, 1982. Laboratory evidence for cellular immune dysfunction included absent mitogen responses and depletion of the T-helper lymphocyte cell population, relative increase in T-suppressor cells, and resultant inverted T-helper/T-suppressor ratio.

Patient 3: A previously healthy 27-year-old lifelong resident of northeastern Ohio developed fever, urinary frequency and urgency, and extreme lassitude in July 1981. He had frequently received parenteral Factor VIII concentrate for severe hemophilia. Bilateral pneumonia was diagnosed in October 1981, and open lung biopsy revealed *P. carinii*. He responded successfully to a 3-week course of SMZ/TMP. In February 1982, he received ketoconazole to suppress repeated episodes of oral candidiasis. He was hospitalized again in April with fever, splenomegaly, anemia, and lymphopenia. An extensive tumor work-up (including laparotomy) did not uncover an underlying malignancy. Cultures of bone marrow, liver, mesenteric lymph nodes, and blood grew *Mycobacterium avium*. *In vitro* immunological testing in March indicated a reduction in absolute number of circulating T-cells. Subsequent, more extensive testing documented the lack of lymphocyte responsiveness to mitogens, absolute and relative decrease in T-helper cells, relative increase in T-suppressor cells, and resultant inverted T-helper/T-suppressor ratio.

For each patient, records of the administration of Factor VIII concentrate were reviewed to determine manufacturer and lot numbers. No two of the patients are known to have received concentrate from the same lots.

Reported by: NJ Ehrenkranz, MD, South Florida Hospital Consortium for Infection Control, J Rubini, MD, Cedars of Lebanon Hospital, Miami, R Gunn, MD, State Epidemiologist, Florida Dept of Health and Rehabilitative Svcs; CR Horsburgh, MD, T Collins, MD, U Hasiba, MD, W Hathaway, MD, University of Colorado School of Medicine, W. Doig, MD, R Hopkins, MD, State Epidemiologist, Colorado Dept of Health; Elliott, MD, W Hoppes, MD, I Patel, MD, Aultman Hospital, Canton, CE Krill, MD, Children's Hospital Akron, T Halpin, MD, State Epidemiologist, Ohio Dept of Health; Field Services Div, Epidemiology Program Office, Div of Host Factors, Center for Infectious Diseases, Task Force on Kaposi's Sarcoma and Opportunistic Infections, CDC.

Editorial Note: *Pneumocystis carinii* pneumonia has not been previously reported among hemophilia patients who have had no other underlying diseases and have not had therapy commonly associated with immunosuppression. A review of the Parasitic Disease Drug Service's records of requests for pentamidine isethionate for 1980-1982 failed to identify hemophilia among the underlying disorders of patients for whom pentamidine was requested for *Pneumocystis carinii* therapy.

The clinical and immunologic features these three patients share are strikingly similar to those recently observed among certain individuals from the following groups: homosexual males, heterosexuals who abuse IV drugs, and Haitians who recently entered the United States.(*1-3*) Although the cause of the severe immune dysfunction is unknown, the occur-nce among the three hemophiliac cases suggests the possible transmission of an agent rough blood products.

Hemophilia A is a sex-linked, inherited disorder characterized by a deficiency in Factor VIII ctivity. There are an estimated 20,000 patients with hemophilia A in the United States (4). everity of disease is classified according to percentage of endogenous Factor VIII activity. pproximately 60% of the 20,000 are classified as severe, and 40% are classified as moder-te (4). Factor VIII deficiency can be treated with intravenous administration of exogenous actor VIII as either cryoprecipitate made from individual units of fresh frozen plasma or ophilized Factor VIII concentrate manufactured from plasma pools collected from as many s a thousand or more donors.

CDC has notified directors of hemophilia centers about these cases and, with the National emophilia Foundation, has initiated collaborative surveillance. A Public Health Service ad-sory committee is being formed to consider the implication of these findings. Physicians di-gnosing opportunistic infections in hemophilia patients who have not received antecedent mmunosuppressive therapy are encouraged to report them to the CDC through local and ate health departments.

September 3, 1982

Hepatitis B Virus Vaccine Safety: Report of an Inter-Agency Group

On June 25, 1982, the Immunization Practices Advisory Committee (ACIP) recom-ended using inactivated hepatitis B virus (HBV) vaccine for individuals who are at gh risk for HBV infection because of their geographic origins, life styles, or expo-res to HBV at home or work (1). The recommendations included statements on vac-ne efficacy and safety. However, requests for additional information on safety con-ue to be received, primarily because of the plasma origins of the antigen used to epare the vaccine. In response to these requests, the Inter-Agency Group to Monitor ccine Development, Production, and Usage, with representatives from the Centers r Disease Control (CDC), Food and Drug Administration (FDA), and National Insti-tes of Health (NIH), has further reviewed the available data. Its conclusions on vac-ne production and safety evaluation follow.

HBV vaccine licensed in the United States is prepared from human plasma contain-g hepatitis surface antigen (HBsAg) (2). Hypothetical side effects from the vaccine clude reactions to blood substances or to infectious agents present in donor plasma. trials involving approximately 1900 persons, reactions among vaccine recipients ere compared with reactions among placebo recipients, and only minor immediate mplaints, primarily of soreness at the injection site, were observed (3,4). Infectious ents that might be present in donor plasma are most likely to be viruses. Virus trans-ssion by blood or blood products requires the virus to circulate in plasma or in cellu- elements such as leukocytes. The chance of virus transmission increases with the ration of the viremic state. HBV is the only well-characterized extra-cellular human us with a prolonged carrier state. Other agents, presumably viruses, which remain identified despite their common association with post-transfusion hepatitis, are re-onsible for non-A/non-B hepatitis.

Beginning in 1978, a disease or group of diseases was recognized, manifested by posi's sarcoma and opportunistic infections, associated with a specific defect in ll-mediated immunity. This group of clinical entities, along with its specific immune ficiency, is now called acquired immune deficiency syndrome (AIDS). The epide-ology of AIDS suggests an unidentified and uncharacterized blood-borne agent as a possible cause of the underlying immunologic defect (5-7). Because AIDS occur among populations that are sources of HBV-positive plasma, this syndrome should b considered in regard to the inherent safety of HBV vaccine.

Vaccine plasma donors are screened, and only healthy individuals (HBsAg positive are selected. The plasmapheresis centers are licensed and inspected by the FDA. A physician gives each donor a complete physical examination, which includes a histor and suitable laboratory tests. At the time of each donation, the donor's hemoglobin hematocrit, and serum protein levels must be within normal limits. HBsAg-positiv donors' levels of serum aminotransferase activity are permitted to exceed those limit set for otherwise healthy donors, but they must be stable.

The process for producing each lot of licensed HBV vaccine is designed to remov or inactivate infectious HBV and other viruses from the desired immunogen, the 2 nm HBsAg particle. The process relies on both biophysical elimination of infectiou particles and treatments which inactivate viruses (pepsin at pH 2, 8M urea, an formalin). The elimination of infectious virus by biophysical purification depends o the density and flotational property of HBsAg in contrast with those of infectious viru particles. The double ultracentrifugation process (isopyknic and rate zonal) has bee proven effective in removing 10^4 infectious doses of HBV/ml, as measured by chim panzee inoculation (8). Pepsin treatment alone (1 μg/ml, pH 2.0, 37 C for 18 hour inactivates 10^5 or more infectious doses of HBV/ml, as measured by chimpanze inoculation, and has been shown to inactivate viruses in the rhabdovirus, poxviru togavirus, reovirus, herpesvirus and coronavirus groups (9, 10). Urea treatment alon (8M, 37 C for four hours) inactivates 10^5 or more infectious doses of HBV/ml and ha been shown to inactivate viruses in the rhabdovirus, myxovirus, poxvirus, togaviru reovirus, picornavirus, herpesvirus, and coronavirus groups (9). Slow viruses, cha acterized by the viruses of kuru and Creutzfeld-Jakob disease, are inactivated by 6 urea, a lesser concentration than that routinely applied to the HBV vaccine (11 Formalin alone inactivates HBV (9), as well as many other virus groups, including pa voviruses (12), retroviruses (13, 14) and the delta agent (15).

Each lot of HBV vaccine is tested for sterility, innocuousness in animals, and pyr genicity and is free of detectable viruses, as shown by inoculation into both huma and monkey cell-culture systems. Additionally, 22 doses of each vaccine lot are in culated intravenously into four chimpanzees.

United States licensed vaccine (produced by Merck, Sharp, and Dohme) has bee given to over 19,000 persons, 6,000 of whom received vaccine between Octob 1975 and December 1981 and 13,000 of whom received it in 1982. The vaccine h been demonstrated to protect recipients from HBV infection (3,4), and no eviden of hepatitis has been observed as a result of HBV vaccination. Also, studies by CD FDA, and others of aminotransferase levels in chimpanzees and humans confirm th HBV vaccine does not transmit the non-A/non-B agent(s).

In three vaccine-placebo trials (two among homosexual men between 1978 a 1980 [3,4] and one among hospital employees in 1981), 549, 714, and 6 persons, respectively, received vaccine, and equal numbers received placebo. Follo up surveillance of participants in these studies was 24, 15, and 18 mont respectively, after the first dose of vaccine with no cases of AIDS being reported. addition to the vaccine/placebo trials, 17,602 persons (including 8,941 health-ca workers and 5,985 healthy adults, children, and infants from non-high-risk gro settings) have received Merck HBV vaccine in various study settings. Periods

llow-up of these vaccine recipients have ranged from a few months to over 7 years.
wever, lots used in early studies may have been produced before the occurrence of
DS. Some of the groups from which HBV vaccine is prepared or for which it is
commended are also at high risk for AIDS; therefore reports of AIDS among donors
d vaccinees at some future time may be expected on the basis of chance alone.

To summarize, these findings support the ACIP statement on hepatitis vaccine: 1)
mediate side effects are minimal after receipt of HBV vaccine; 2) no long-term reac-
ns have been reported; 3) the purification and inactivation process is known to
activate representatives of all known groups of animal viruses; 4) each lot is safety
sted in primates; 5) no known cases of hepatitis B or non-A/non-B hepatitis have
en transmitted by the vaccine and no known occurrence of AIDS has been associat-
d with the vaccine.

ported by the Inter-Agency Group to Monitor Vaccine Development, Production, and Usage,
presented by the Centers for Disease Control, Food and Drug Administration, and National In-
titutes of Health.

September 24, 1982

Update on Acquired Immune Deficiency Syndrome (AIDS) — United States

Between June 1, 1981, and September 15, 1982, CDC received reports of 593 cases of ac-
ired immune deficiency syndrome (AIDS).* Death occurred in 243 cases (41%).

Analysis of reported AIDS cases shows that 51% had *Pneumocystis carinii* pneumonia
CP) without Kaposi's sarcoma (KS) (with or without other "opportunistic" infections [OOI]
edictive of cellular immunodeficiency); 30% had KS without PCP (with or without OOI); 7%
d both PCP and KS (with or without OOI); and 12% had OOI with neither PCP nor KS. The
erall mortality rate for cases of PCP without KS (47%) was more than twice that for cases of
 without PCP (21%), while the rate for cases of both PCP and KS (68%) was more than three
es as great. The mortality rate for OOI with neither KS nor PCP was 48%.

The incidence of AIDS by date of diagnosis (assuming an almost constant population at risk)
s roughly doubled every half-year since the second half of 1979 (Table 1). An average of one
two cases are now diagnosed every day. Although the overall case-mortality rate for the cur-
t total of 593 is 41%, the rate exceeds 60% for cases diagnosed over a year ago.

Almost 80% of reported AIDS cases in the United States were concentrated in six metropoli-
 areas, predominantly on the east and west coasts of the country (Table 2). This distribution
s not simply a reflection of population size in those areas; for example, the number of cases
 million population reported from June 1, 1981, to September 15, 1982, in New York City
d San Francisco was roughly 10 times greater than that of the entire country. The 593 cases
re reported among residents of 27 states and the District of Columbia, and CDC has received
ditional reports of 41 cases from 10 foreign countries.

Approximately 75% of AIDS cases occured among homosexual or bisexual males (Table 3),
ong whom the reported prevalence of intravenous drug abuse was 12%. Among the 20% of
wn heterosexual cases (males and females), the prevalence of intravenous drug abuse was
out 60%. Haitians residing in the United States constituted 6.1% of all cases (*2*), and 50% of
 cases in which both homosexual activity and intravenous drug abuse were denied. Among
 14 AIDS cases involving males under 60 years old who were not homosexuals, intravenous
g abusers, or Haitians, two (14%) had hemophilia A.[†] (*3*)

Reported AIDS cases may be separated into groups based on these risk factors: homosexual
 bisexual males—75%, intravenous drug abusers with no history of male homosexual

___
rmerly referred to as Kaposi's sarcoma and opportunistic infections in previously healthy persons. (*1*)
third hemophiliac with pneumocystosis exceeded the 60-year age limit of the AIDS case definition.

237

TABLE 1. Reported cases and case-mortality rates of AIDS, by half-year of diagnosis, 1979-1982, (as of September 15, 1982) — United States

Half-year of diagnosis		Cases	Deaths	Case-mortality rate (%)
1979	1st half	1	1	100
	2nd half	6	5	83
1980	1st half	17	13	76
	2nd half	26	22	85
1981	1st half	66	46	70
	2nd half	141	79	56
1982	1st half	249	67	27

*Excluding 4 cases with unknown dates of diagnosis

activity — 13%, Haitians with neither a history of homosexuality nor a history of intraveno… drug abuse — 6%, persons with hemophilia A who were not Haitians, homosexuals, or intrav… nous drug abusers — 0.3%, and persons in none of the other groups — 5%.

Reported by the Task Force on Acquired Immune Deficiency Syndrome, CDC

Editorial Note: CDC defines a case of AIDS as a disease, at least moderately predictive of defect in cell-mediated immunity, occurring in a person with no known cause for diminish… resistance to that disease. Such diseases include KS, PCP, and serious OOI.[§] Diagnoses a… considered to fit the case definition only if based on sufficiently reliable methods (genera… histology or culture). However, this case definition may not include the full spectrum of AI… manifestations, which may range from absence of symptoms (despite laboratory evidence … immune deficiency) to non-specific symptoms (e.g., fever, weight loss, generalized, persiste… lymphadenopathy) (*4*) to specific diseases that are insufficiently predictive of cellular immun… deficiency to be included in incidence monitoring (e.g., tuberculosis, oral candidiasis, herp… zoster) to malignant neoplasms that cause, as well as result from, immunodeficiency[¶] (a…

[§]These infections include pneumonia, meningitis, or encephalitis due to one or more of the followi… aspergillosis, candidiasis, cryptococcosis, cytomegalovirus, nocardiosis, strongyloidosis, toxoplasmos… zygomycosis, or atypical mycobacteriosis (species other than tuberculosis or lepra); esophagitis due… candidiasis, cytomegalovirus, or herpes simplex virus; progressive multifocal leukoencephalopath… chronic enterocolitis (more than 4 weeks) due to cryptosporidiosis; or unusually extensive mucocutaneo… herpes simplex of more than 5 weeks duration.

[¶]CDC encourages reports of any cancer among persons with AIDS and of selected rare lymphom… (Burkitt's or diffuse, undifferentiated non-Hodgkins lymphoma) among persons with a risk factor for AID… This differs from the request for reports of AIDS cases regardless of the absence of risk factors.

TABLE 2. AIDS cases per million population,* by standard metropolitan statistical ar… (SMSA) of residence, reported from June 1, 1981 to September 15, 1982 — United Stat…

SMSA of residence	Cases	Percentage of total	Cases per million population
New York, N.Y.	288	48.6	31.6
San Francisco, Calif.	78	13.2	24.0
Miami, Fla.	31	5.2	19.1
Newark, N.J.	15	2.5	7.6
Houston, Texas	15	2.5	5.2
Los Angeles, Calif.	37	6.2	4.9
Elsewhere (irrespective of SMSA)	129	21.8	0.6
Total	593	100.0	2.6

*From the 1980 Census

ABLE 3. Cases of AIDS, by sexual orientation and intravenous drug abuse, reported **m** June 1, 1981, to September 15, 1982 — United States

x	Sexual orientation	Cases	Percentage distribution by sexual orientation	Intravenous drug abuse*			Percentage using IV drugs[†]
				Yes	No	Unknown	
le	Homosexual or bisexual	445	75.0	42	300	103	12.3
	Heterosexual	84	14.2	49	33	2	59.8
	Unknown	30	5.1	11	11	8	50.0
ale	Heterosexual	34	5.7	20	12	2	62.5
al		593	100.0	122	356	115	25.5

gardless of when the last such activity occurred.

cluding cases with unknown history of IV drug abuse.

nversely, some patients who are considered AIDS cases on the basis of diseases only moder-
ly predictive of cellular immunodeficiency may not actually be immunodeficient and may not
part of the current epidemic. Absence of a reliable, inexpensive, widely available test for
OS, however, may make the working case definition the best currently available for incidence
nitoring.

Two points in this update deserve emphasis. First, the eventual case-mortality rate of AIDS,
ew years after diagnosis, may be far greater than the 41% overall case-mortality rate noted
ove. Second, the reported incidence of AIDS has continued to increase rapidly. Only a small
centage of cases have none of the identified risk factors (male homosexuality, intravenous
g abuse, Haitian origin, and perhaps hemophilia A). To avoid a reporting bias, physicians
uld report cases regardless of the absence of these factors.

Physicians aware of patients fitting the case definition for AIDS are requested to report such
es to CDC through their local or state health departments.

November 5, 1982

Acquired Immune Deficiency Syndrome (AIDS): Precautions for Clinical and Laboratory Staffs

The etiology of the underlying immune deficiencies seen in AIDS cases is unknown. One
othesis consistent with current observations is that a transmissible agent may be
olved. If so, transmission of the agent would appear most commonly to require intimate,
ct contact involving mucosal surfaces, such as sexual contact among homosexual males,
through parenteral spread, such as occurs among intravenous drug abusers and possibly
ophilia patients using Factor VIII products. Airborne spread and interpersonal spread
ugh casual contact do not seem likely. These patterns resemble the distribution of disease
modes of spread of hepatitis B virus, and hepatitis B virus infections occur very frequently
ng AIDS cases.

here is presently no evidence of AIDS transmission to hospital personnel from contact
affected patients or clinical specimens. Because of concern about a possible transmissi-
agent, however, interim suggestions are appropriate to guide patient-care and laboratory
onnel, including those whose work involves experimental animals. At present, it appears
ent for hospital personnel to use the same precautions when caring for patients with
S as those used for patients with hepatitis B virus infection, in which blood and body
s likely to have been contaminated with blood are considered infective. Specifically,

patient-care and laboratory personnel should take precautions to avoid direct contact of sk
and mucous membranes with blood, blood products, excretions, secretions, and tissues
persons judged likely to have AIDS. The following precautions do not specifically address ou
patient care, dental care, surgery, necropsy, or hemodialysis of AIDS patients. In genera
procedures appropriate for patients known to be infected with hepatitis B virus are advise
and blood and organs of AIDS patients should not be donated.

The precautions that follow are advised for persons and specimens from persons with: op
portunistic infections that are not associated with underlying immunosuppressive disease
therapy; Kaposi's sarcoma (patients under 60 years of age); chronic generalize
lymphadenopathy, unexplained weight loss and/or prolonged unexplained fever in person
who belong to groups with apparently increased risks of AIDS (homosexual males, intrav
nous drug abusers, Haitian entrants, hemophiliacs); and possible AIDS (hospitalized f
evaluation). Hospitals and laboratories should adapt the following suggested precautions
their individual circumstances; these recommendations are not meant to restrict hospita
from implementing additional precautions.

A. The following precautions are advised in providing care to AIDS patients:

1. Extraordinary care must be taken to avoid accidental wounds from sharp instrumer
   contaminated with potentially infectious material and to avoid contact of open skin l
   sions with material from AIDS patients.

2. Gloves should be worn when handling blood specimens, blood-soiled items, body fluic
   excretions, and secretions, as well as surfaces, materials, and objects exposed to them.

3. Gowns should be worn when clothing may be soiled with body fluids, blood, secretio
   or excretions.

4. Hands should be washed after removing gowns and gloves and before leaving the roor
   of known or suspected AIDS patients. Hands should also be washed thoroughly and ir
   mediately if they become contaminated with blood.

5. Blood and other specimens should be labeled prominently with a special warning, su
   as "Blood Precautions" or "AIDS Precautions." If the outside of the specimen containe
   visibly contaminated with blood, it should be cleaned with a disinfectant (such as a 1:
   dilution of 5.25% sodium hypochlorite [household bleach] with water). All blood spe
   mens should be placed in a second container, such as an impervious bag, for transpe
   The container or bag should be examined carefully for leaks or cracks.

6. Blood spills should be cleaned up promptly with a disinfectant solution, such as sodi
   hypochlorite (see above).

7. Articles soiled with blood should be placed in an impervious bag prominently labe
   "AIDS Precautions" or "Blood Precautions" before being sent for reprocessing
   disposal. Alternatively, such contaminated items may be placed in plastic bags of a p
   ticular color designated solely for disposal of infectious wastes by the hospital. Dispo
   ble items should be incinerated or disposed of in accord with the hospital's policies
   disposal of infectious wastes. Reusable items should be reprocessed in accord v
   hospital policies for hepatitis B virus-contaminated items. Lensed instruments should
   sterilized after use on AIDS patients.

8. Needles should not be bent after use, but should be promptly placed in a punctu
   resistant container used solely for such disposal. Needles should not be reinserted i
   their original sheaths before being discarded into the container, since this is a comr
   cause of needle injury.

9. Disposable syringes and needles are preferred. Only needle-locking syringes or one-pi
   needle-syringe units should be used to aspirate fluids from patients, so that collec
   fluid can be safely discharged through the needle, if desired. If reusable syringes
   employed, they should be decontaminated before reprocessing.

10. A private room is indicated for patients who are too ill to use good hygiene, sucl

240

those with profuse diarrhea, fecal incontinence, or altered behavior secondary to central nervous system infections.

Precautions appropriate for particular infections that concurrently occur in AIDS patients should be added to the above, if needed.

B. The following precautions are advised for persons performing laboratory tests or studies on clinical specimens or other potentially infectious materials (such as inoculated tissue cultures, embryonated eggs, animal tissues, etc.) from known or suspected AIDS cases:

1. Mechanical pipetting devices should be used for the manipulation of all liquids in the laboratory. Mouth pipetting should not be allowed.
2. Needles and syringes should be handled as stipulated in Section A (above).
3. Laboratory coats, gowns, or uniforms should be worn while working with potentially infectious materials and should be discarded appropriately before leaving the laboratory.
4. Gloves should be worn to avoid skin contact with blood, specimens containing blood, blood-soiled items, body fluids, excretions, and secretions, as well as surfaces, materials, and objects exposed to them.
5. All procedures and manipulations of potentially infectious material should be performed carefully to minimize the creation of droplets and aerosols.
6. Biological safety cabinets (Class I or II) and other primary containment devices (e.g., centrifuge safety cups) are advised whenever procedures are conducted that have a high potential for creating aerosols or infectious droplets. These include centrifuging, blending, sonicating, vigorous mixing, and harvesting infected tissues from animals or embryonated eggs. Fluorescent activated cell sorters generate droplets that could potentially result in infectious aerosols. Translucent plastic shielding between the droplet-collecting area and the equipment operator should be used to reduce the presently uncertain magnitude of this risk. Primary containment devices are also used in handling materials that might contain concentrated infectious agents or organisms in greater quantities than expected in clinical specimens.
7. Laboratory work surfaces should be decontaminated with a disinfectant, such as sodium hypochlorite solution (see A5 above), following any spill of potentially infectious material and at the completion of work activities.
8. All potentially contaminated materials used in laboratory tests should be decontaminated, preferably by autoclaving, before disposal or reprocessing.
9. All personnel should wash their hands following completion of laboratory activities, removal of protective clothing, and before leaving the laboratory.

C. The following additional precautions are advised for studies involving experimental animals inoculated with tissues or other potentially infectious materials from individuals with known or suspected AIDS.

1. Laboratory coats, gowns, or uniforms should be worn by personnel entering rooms housing inoculated animals. Certain nonhuman primates, such as chimpanzees, are prone to throw excreta and to spit at attendants; personnel attending inoculated animals should wear molded surgical masks and goggles or other equipment sufficient to prevent potentially infective droplets from reaching the mucosal surfaces of their mouths, nares, and eyes. In addition, when handled, other animals may disturb excreta in their bedding. Therefore, the above precautions should be taken when handling them.
2. Personnel should wear gloves for all activities involving direct contact with experimental animals and their bedding and cages. Such manipulations should be performed carefully to minimize the creation of aerosols and droplets.
3. Necropsy of experimental animals should be conducted by personnel wearing gowns and gloves. If procedures generating aerosols are performed, masks and goggles should be worn.

4. Extraordinary care must be taken to avoid accidental sticks or cuts with sharp instruments contaminated with body fluids or tissues of experimental animals inoculated with material from AIDS patients.

5. Animal cages should be decontaminated, preferably by autoclaving, before they are cleaned and washed.

6. Only needle-locking syringes or one-piece needle-syringe units should be used to inject potentially infectious fluids into experimental animals.

The above precautions are intended to apply to both clinical and research laboratories. Biological safety cabinets and other safety equipment may not be generally available in clinical laboratories. Assistance should be sought from a microbiology laboratory, as needed, to assure containment facilities are adequate to permit laboratory tests to be conducted safely.

November 12, 1982

Cryptosporidiosis: Assessment of Chemotherapy of Males with Acquired Immune Deficiency Syndrome (AIDS)

Since December 1979, 21 males with severe, protracted diarrhea caused by the parasite, *Cryptosporidium*, have been reported to CDC by physicians in Boston, Los Angeles, Newark, New York, Philadelphia, and San Fransisco. All 21 have acquired immune deficiency syndrome (AIDS); 20 are homosexual; and one is a heterosexual Haitian. Their ages range from 23 to 62 years with a mean of 35.7 years. Most had other opportunistic infections or Kaposi's sarcoma in addition to cryptosporidiosis. Eleven had *Pneumocystis carinii* pneumonia (PCP); nine had Candida esophagitis; two had a disseminated *Mycobacterium avium-intracellulare* infection; one had a disseminated cytomegalovirus infection; and two had Kaposi's sarcoma. T-lymphocyte helper-to-suppressor ratios were decreased (< 0.9) in all 18 patients on whom this test was performed. Fourteen patients have died.

The illness attributed to *Cryptosporidium* was characterized by chronic, profuse, watery diarrhea. The mean duration of diarrhea was 4 months, often continuing until the patient's death. Bowel movement frequency ranged from six to 25 per day. The estimated maximum volume of stool during illness ranged from 1 to 17 liters per day with a mean of 3.6 liters per day. Diagnosis of cryptosporidiosis was made by histologic examination of small bowel biopsies (13 patients) or large bowel biopsies (four patients), or by stool examination using a sucrose concentration technique (16 patients) (*1*). More than one type of diagnostic method was positive for several patients.

Table 1 shows the drugs given to the 21 patients while they had diarrhea attributed to *Cryptosporidium*. Only two patients (9.5%) have had sustained resolution of their diarrhea with negative follow-up stool examinations. The first was being treated with prednisone (60 mg daily) for chronic active hepatitis at the time his diarrhea began. When cryptosporidiosis was diagnosed, he was started on diloxanide furoate (500 mg three times daily for 10 days), and the prednisone was tapered over 2 weeks and then stopped. Two weeks later, his diarrhea was improving; in another 2 weeks, his diarrhea had completely resolved. He has had no diarrhea for 8 months. Follow-up stool examinations 2 weeks and 6 weeks after discontinuation of diloxanide furoate were negative for *Cryptosporidium*.

The second patient, who also had a clinical and parasitologic response, subsequently died of PCP. In early February 1982, 6 months before his death, he had onset of watery diarrhea, and a small bowel biopsy showed *Cryptosporidium*. Treatment with furazolidone (100 mg four times a day) was initiated on May 5, and within 6 days, the patient had gained 1.1 kilograms (2.4 pounds); parenteral nutrition was discontinued, although he continued to produce a liter of watery stool each day. Ten days after treatment was started, his stools became formed for the first time in 4 months, but *Cryptosporidium* oocysts were still present. Furazolidone was increased to 150 mg four times daily. Twenty days after therapy was started (10 days after the higher dose of furazolidone was begun), the patient had one bowel movement day, but his stool was still positive for *Cryptosporidium* and remained positive despite continued use of furazolidone at 150 mg four times daily for a total of 2 months. At that time, two stool examinations failed to detect oocysts, and the furazolidone was stopped. One week later, the patient developed PCP; despite treatment with trimethoprim-sulfamethoxazole, he died 2 weeks later on July 22. An autopsy was not permitted.

After various treatment regimens, seven patients have had partial or transitory decreases in their diarrhea. Two received no anti-parasitic drugs. A third patient temporarily improved after treatment with furazolidone (100 mg orally four times a day for 7 days), although 2 weeks elapsed between the end of treatment with furazolidone and the onset of clinical improvement. The patient's diarrhea abated, but follow-up stool examinations remained positive for *Cryptosporidium*. Three months after furazolidone therapy, he again developed diarrhea, and his stools were positive for *Cryptosporidium*. Two patients had less diarrhea when given tetracycline. The first received tetracycline 500 mg orally four times a day for 4 months. His diarrhea decreased from 12 watery stools to three loose stools per day, but stool examination after 4 months of therapy still showed *Cryptosporidium*. The second patient,

TABLE 1. Drugs used to treat males with cryptosporidiosis and AIDS

Drug*	Dose and route of administration†	Number of patients	Unchanged n	(%)	Improved§ n	(%)	Cured¶ n	(%)
No treatment	—	2	0	(0.0)	2	(100.0)	0	(0.0)
Trimethoprim/ sulfamethoxazole	25 mg/kg QID of sulfamethoxazole	7	7	(100.0)	0	(0.0)	0	(0.0)
Trimethoprim/ sulfamethoxazole	800 mg PO BID of sulfamethoxazole	4	4	(100.0)	0	(0.0)	0	(0.0)
Furazolidone	100 mg PO QID	6	4	(66.7)	1	(16.7)	1	(16.7)
Furazolidone	300 mg PO QID	1	1	(100.0)	0	(0.0)	0	(0.0)
Metronidazole	750 mg PO TID	5	4	(80.0)	1	(20.0)	0	(0.0)
Metronidazole	750 mg IV TID	1	0	(0.0)	1	(100.0)	0	(0.0)
Pyrimethamine/ sulfa	25 mg PO per day of pyrimethamine	4	4	(100.0)	0	(0.0)	0	(0.0)
Diloxanide furoate	500 mg PO TID	3	2	(66.7)	0	(0.0)	1**	(33.3)
Quinacrine	100 mg PO TID	3	3	(100.0)	0	(0.0)	0	(0.0)
Diiodohydroxyquin	650 mg PO TID	2	2	(100.0)	0	(0.0)	0	(0.0)
Tetracycline	500 mg PO QID	3	1	(33.3)	2	(66.6)	0	(0.0)
Doxycycline	100 mg PO per day	2	2	(100.0)	0	(0.0)	0	(0.0)
Pentamidine	4 mg/kg IM per day	2	2	(100.0)	0	(0.0)	0	(0.0)
Chloroquine/ primaquine	500 mg PO per day of chloroquine	1	1	(100.0)	0	(0.0)	0	(0.0)

* Some patients received more than one drug.
† BID = twice daily; TID = three times daily; QID = four times daily; PO = orally; IV = intravenously
§ Decrease in number of stools by at least 50%.
¶ Absence of diarrhea for more than 2 weeks and stool examination negative for *Cryptosporidium*.
** Improvement temporally related to stopping prednisone.

given the same treatment, also had a reduction in the number of stools. When the drug was discontinued, his diarrhea again increased.

Two patients' diarrhea stopped following treatment with opiates and metronidazole, given orally in one case and intravenously in the other. Neither patient had diarrhea after a few days of treatment, but both died within 1 week, and autopsies were not allowed. The first patient died from suspected peritonitis; the second died with disseminated Kaposi's sarcoma and pneumonia.

The remaining 12 patients have had continuous, severe diarrhea. In addition to the drugs listed in Table 1, bovine-transfer factor has been given to one patient and intravenous gamma globulin to two patients; neither was effective. At present, 14 (66.7%) of the 21 individuals have died, and six are alive with persistent diarrhea. In no instance was cryptosporidiosis thought to be the direct cause of death, but the associated severe malnutrition was often considered a contributing factor.

Shortly before cryptosporidiosis was recognized in AIDS patients, investigators at the U.S. Department of Agriculture National Animal Disease Center (NADC) began testing drugs for efficacy against *Cryptosporidium* in animals; results of these initial studies were published in February, 1982 (2). More recently, five additional drugs have been evaluated at the NADC. Calves or pigs up to 14 days old without infection were given the drugs orally twice daily. One day after the drugs were started, each animal received a single oral inoculation of *Cryptosporidium*. The following drugs (with doses in mg/kg/day) were tested: amprolium (10.7), difluoromethylornithine (1250) plus bleomycin (6 IM), diloxanide furoate (125.0), dimetridazole (19.0), ipronidazole (23.8), lasalocid (0.7), metronidazole (23.8), monensin (4.8), oxytetracycline (50.0), pentamidine (10.0), quinacrine (11.9), salinomycin (6.0), sulfaquinoxaline (200.0), sulfadimidine (119.0), and trimethoprim (4.8) plus sulfadiazine (23.8). Although small numbers of animals were tested in each treatment group, no drugs prevented fecal shedding of oocysts or reduced the number of *Cryptosporidium* seen on intestinal biopsies.

Reported by J Goldfarb, MD, H Tanowitz, MD, Albert Einstein College of Medicine, Bronx, R Grossman, MD, Medical Arts Center Hospital, C Bonanno, MD, D Kaufman, MD, P Ma, PhD, St. Vincent's Medical Center, R Soave, MD, New York Hospital-Cornell Medical Center, D Armstrong, MD, J Gold, MD, Memorial Sloan-Kettering Cancer Center, S Dikman, MD, M Finkel, MD, H Sacks, MD, Mt. Sinai Medical Center, R Press, MD, New York University Medical Center, D William, MD, St. Luke's-Roosevelt Hospital, Friedman, MD, New York City Dept of Health, R Rothenberg, MD, State Epidemiolgist, New York State Dept of Health; S Brown, MD, United Hospitals, Newark, WE Parkin, DVM, State Epidemiologist, New Jersey State Dept of Health; EJ Bergquist, MD, Thomas Jefferson University Hospital, Philadelphia, C Hays, MD, State Epidemiologist, Pennsylvania State Dept of Health; P Forgacs, MD, Lahey Clinic Medical Center, Burlington, L Weinstein, MD, Brigham and Women's Hospital, Boston, NJ Fiumara, MD, State Epidemiologist, Massachusetts State Dept of Public Health; D Busch, MD, San Francisco, M Derezin, MD, M Gottlieb, MD, J Matthew, MD, W Weinstein, MD, UCLA Center for Health Sciences, J Chin, MD, State Epidemiologist, California Dept of Health Svcs; H Moon, PhD, National Animal Disease Center, Ames, Iowa; AIDS Activity, Div of Parasitic Diseases, Center for Infectious Diseases, CDC.

Editorial Note: *Cryptosporidium* is a protozoan parasite; it is a well recognized cause of diarrhea in animals, especially calves, but has only rarely been associated with diarrhea in humans (3). Individuals with normal immune function who have developed cryptosporidiosis have self-limited diarrhea lasting 1-2 weeks, but immunosuppressed individuals have developed chronic diarrhea. An effective drug to treat cryptosporidiosis has not been identified, and the above reports are equally discouraging. Of seven patients who are still living, only one has no diarrhea at present. His recovery coincided with treatment with diloxanide furoate and discontinuation of prednisone. It seems unlikely that diloxanide furoate was responsible for his recovery, since three other patients who received the drug did not respond, and the drug was ineffective in experimentally infected pigs given nearly six times the recommended human dose. It is similarly difficult to be certain that improvement reported in other patients was due to the drugs they received because only a few patients receiving a drug responded, responses were brief, and the same or similar drugs were ineffective in preventing infection in experimental animals. The difficulty in interpreting isolated responses is underscored by the two patients who improved before any specific therapy began.

Since none of the drugs reported above appears clearly efficacious, additional tests of other anti-parasitic drugs in animals are needed. Until an effective drug for cryptosporidiosis is identified or the underlying immune deficiency in patients with AIDS becomes correctable, management of diarrhea due to cryptosporidiosis will continue to focus on supportive care.

December 10, 1982

Update on Acquired Immune Deficiency Syndrome (AIDS) among Patients with Hemophilia A

In July 1982, three heterosexual hemophilia A patients, who had developed *Pneumocystis carinii* pneumonia and other opportunistic infections, were reported (*1*). Each had in vitro evidence of lymphopenia and two patients who were specifically tested had evidence of T-lymphocyte abnormalities. All three have since died. In the intervening 4 months, four additional heterosexual hemophilia A patients have developed one or more opportunistic infections accompanied by in-vitro evidence of cellular immune deficiency; these four AIDS cases and one highly suspect case are presented below. Data from inquiries about the patients' sexual activities, drug usage, travel, and residence provide no suggestion that disease could have been acquired through contact with each other, with homosexuals, with illicit drug abusers, or with Haitian immigrants—groups at increased risk for AIDS compared with the general U.S. population. All these patients have received Factor VIII concentrates, and all but one have also received other blood components.

Case 1: A 55-year-old severe hemophiliac from Alabama developed anorexia and progressive weight loss beginning in September 1981. He had developed adult-onset diabetes mellitus in 1973, which had required insulin therapy since 1978. He had had acute hepatitis (type unknown) in 1975. In March 1982, he was hospitalized for herpes zoster and a 17-kg weight loss. Hepatosplenomegaly was noted. The absolute lymphocyte count was 450/mm^3. Liver enzymes were elevated; antibodies to hepatitis B core and surface antigens were present. A liver biopsy showed changes consistent with persistent hepatitis. Evaluation for an occult malignancy was negative. The zoster resolved following 5 days of adenosine arabinoside therapy.

In early June, he was readmitted with fever and respiratory symptoms. Chest x-ray showed bibasilar infiltrates. No causative organism was identified, but clinical improvement occurred coincident with administration of broad spectrum antibiotics. Laboratory studies as an outpatient documented transient thrombocytopenia (63,000/mm^3) and persistent inversion of his T-helper/T-suppressor ratio (T_H/T_S =0.2). He was readmitted for the third time in early September with fever, chills and nonproductive cough. His cumulative weight loss was now 47 kg. Chest x-ray demonstrated bilateral pneumonia, and open lung biopsy showed infection with *P. carinii.* He responded to sulfamethoxazole/trimethoprim (SMZ/TMP). His T-cell defects persist.

Case 2: A 10-year-old severe hemophiliac from Pennsylvania had been treated with Factor VIII concentrate on a home care program. He had never required blood transfusion. He had been remarkably healthy until September 1982 when he experienced intermittent episodes of fever and vomiting. Approximately 2 weeks later, he also developed persistent anorexia, fatigue, sore throat and nonproductive cough. On October 20, he was admitted to a hospital with a temperature of 38.4 C (101.2 F) and a respiratory rate of 60/min. Physical examination revealed cervical adenopathy but no splenomegaly. The absolute number of circulating lymphocytes was low (580/mm^3) and the T-helper/T-suppressor ratio was markedly reduced (T_H/T_S = 0.1). His platelet count was 171,000/mm^3. Serum levels of IgG, IgA, and IgM were markedly elevated. Chest x-rays showed bilateral pnuemonia and an open lung biopsy revealed massive infiltration with *P. carinii* and *Cryptococcus neoformans*. Intravenous SMZ/TMP and amphotericin B have led to marked clinical improvement, but the T-cell abnormalities persist.

Case 3: A 49-year-old patient from Ohio with mild hemophilia had been treated relatively infrequently with Factor VIII concentrate. During the summer of 1982, he noted dysphagia and a weight loss of approximately 7 kg. In October, he was treated for cellulitis of the right hand. Two weeks later, he was observed by a close relative to be dyspneic. He was admitted in November with progressive dyspnea and diaphoresis. Chest x-rays suggested diffuse pneumonitis. His WBC count was 11,000/mm^3 with 9% lymphocytes (absolute lymphocyte number 990/mm^3). The T_H/T_S ratio was 0.25. Open lung biopsy revealed *P. carinii*. The patient was treated with SMZ/TMP for 6 days with no improvement, and pentamidine isethionate was added. Virus cultures of sputum and chest tube drainage revealed herpes simplex virus. He died on November 22.

Case 4: A 52-year-old severe hemophiliac from Missouri was admitted to a hospital in April 1982 with fever, lymphadenopathy, and abdominal pain. Persistently low numbers of circulating lymphocytes were noted (480/mm^3). Granulomata were seen on histopathologic examination of a bone marrow aspirate. Cultures were positive for *Histoplasma capsulatum*. The patient improved after therapy with amphotericin B. During the following summer and early fall, he developed fever, increased weight loss, and difficulty thinking. On readmission in early November, he had esophageal candidiasis. Laboratory tests showed profound leukopenia and lymphopenia. A brain scan showed a left frontal mass, which was found to be an organizing hematoma at the time of craniotomy. A chest x-ray showed "fluffy" pulmonary infiltrates. Therapy with SMZ/TMP was begun. Exploratory laparotomy revealed no malignancy. A splenectomy was performed. Biopsies of liver, spleen, and lymph node tissue were negative for *H capsulatum* granulomata. The lymphoid tissue including the spleen showed an absence of lymphocytes. His total WBC declined to 400/mm^3 and the T_H/T_S cell ratio was 0.1. He died shortly thereafter.

Suspect Case: Described below is an additional highly suspect case that does not meet the strict criteria defining AIDS. A 7-year-old severe hemophiliac from Los Angeles had mild mediastinal adenopathy on chest x-ray in September 1981. In March 1982, he developed a spontaneous subdural hematoma requiring surgical evacuation. In July, he developed parotitis. In August, he developed pharyngitis and an associated anterior and posterior cervical adenopathy, which has not resolved. In late September, he developed herpes zoster over the right thigh and buttock, and oral candidiasis. Chest x-rays revealed an increase of the mediastinal adenopathy and the appearance of new perihilar infiltrates. In late October, enlargement of the cervical nodes led to a lymph node biopsy. Architectural features of the node were grossly altered, with depletion of lymphocytes. Heterophile tests were negative. IgG, IgA, and IgM levels were all elevated. He has a marked reduction in T-helper cells and a T_H/T_S ratio equal to 0.4. Recent progressive adenoid enlargement has caused significant upper airway obstruction and resultant sleep apnea.

Reported by M-C Poon, MD, A Landay, PhD, University of Alabama Medical Center; J Alexander, MD, Jefferson County Health Dept, W Birch, MD, State Epidemiologist, Alabama Dept of Health; ME Eyster, MD, H Al-Mondhiry, MD, JO Ballard, MD, Hershey Medical Center, E Witte, VMD, Div of Epidemiology, Hayes, MD, State Epidemiologist, Pennsylvania State Dept of Health; LO Pass, MD, JP Myers, MD, Politis, MD, R Goldberg MD, M Bhatti, MD, M Arnold, MD, J York, MD, Youngstown Hospital Association T Halpin, MD, State Epidemiologist, Ohio Dept of Health; L Herwaldt, MD, Washington University Medical Center, A Spivack, MD, Jewish Hospital, St. Louis, HD Donnell MD, State Epidemiologist, Missouri Dept of Health; D Powars, MD, Los Angeles County-University of Southern California Medical Center, S Fannin, MD, Los Angeles County Dept of Health Svcs, J Chin, MD, State Epidemiologist, California State Dept of Health; AIDS Activity, Div of Host Factors, Div of Viral Diseases, Center for Infectious Diseases, Field Svcs Div, Epidemiology Program Office, CDC.

Editorial Note: These additional cases of AIDS among hemophilia A patients share several features with the three previously reported cases. All but one are severe hemophiliacs, requiring large amounts of Factor VIII concentrate. None had experienced prior opportunistic fections. All have been profoundly lymphopenic (< 1000 lymphocytes/mm^3) and have had reversible deficiencies in T-lymphocytes. Clinical improvement of opportunistic infections with medical therapy has been short lived. Two of the five have died.

In most instances, these patients have been the first AIDS cases in their cities, states, or regions. They have had no known common medications, occupations, habits, types of pets, or any uniform antecedent history of personal or family illnesses with immunological relevance.

Although complete information is not available on brands and lot numbers for the Factor VIII concentrate used by these additional five patients during the past few years, efforts to collect and compare these data with information obtained from the earlier three cases are under way. No common lot number has been found among the lots of Factor VIII given to the five patients from whom such information is currently available.

These additional cases provide important perspectives on AIDS in U.S. hemophiliacs. Two of the patients described here are 10 years of age or less, and children with hemophilia must now be considered at risk for the disease. In addition, the number of cases continues to increase, and the illness may pose a significant risk for patients with hemophilia.

The National Hemophilia Foundation and CDC are now conducting a national survey of hemophilia treatment centers to estimate the prevalence of AIDS-associated diseases during the past 5 years and to provide active surveillance of AIDS among patients with hemophilia.

Physicians are encouraged to continue to report AIDS-suspect diseases among hemophilia patients to the CDC through local and state health departments.

December 17, 1982

Unexplained Immunodeficiency and Opportunistic Infections in Infants — New York, New Jersey, California

CDC has received reports of four infants (under 2 years of age) with unexplained cellular immunodeficiency and opportunistic infections.

Case 1: The infant, a black/hispanic male weighing 5 lb 14 oz, was born in December 1980 following a 36-38-week pregnancy. Pregnancy had been complicated by bleeding in the fourth month and by preeclampsia in the ninth month. The infant was well until 3 months of age, when oral candidiasis was noted. At 4 months, hepatosplenomegaly was observed, and at 7 months, he had staphylococcal impetigo. Growth, which had been slow, stopped at 4 months. Head circumference, which had been below the third percentile, also stopped increasing. At 9 months, serum levels of IgG and IgA were normal; IgM was high-normal. T-cell studies were normal, except for impaired in-vitro responses to *Candida* antigen and alloantigen.

At 17 months of age, the infant had progressive pulmonary infiltrates, as well as continuing oral candidiasis, and was hospitalized. *Mycobacterium avium-intracellulare* was cultured from sputum and bone marrow samples. A CAT scan of the head revealed bilateral calcifications of the basal ganglia and subcortical regions of the frontal lobes. Repeat immunologic studies done at age 20 months showed lymphopenia, decreased numbers of T-lymphocytes, and severely impaired T-cell function in vitro; immunoglobulin determinations are pending. The infant remains alive and is receiving therapy for his mycobacterial infection.

The infant's mother, a 29-year-old resident of New York City, gave a history of intravenous drug abuse. Although she was in apparently good health at the time of the infant's birth, she developed fever, dyspnea, and oral candidiasis in October 1981. One month later, she was hospitalized and died of biopsy-proven *Pneumocystis carinii* pneumonia (PCP). She had been lymphopenic during the hospitalization; further immunologic studies were not done. At autopsy, no underlying cause for immune deficiency was found.

Case 2: The infant, a Haitian male weighing 6 lb 11 oz, was born in January 1981 following full-term pregnancy. The immediate postpartum period was complicated by respiratory distress. Diarrhea developed at 2 weeks of age and persisted. His physical development was retarded. At 5 months, he was hospitalized because of fever and diarrhea. On examination, he had hepatosplenomegaly, lymphadenopathy, and otitis media. While on antibiotics, he developed pulmonary infiltrates. An open lung biopsy revealed *Pneumocystis carinii, Cryptococcus neoformans,* and cytomegalovirus. Serum IgG, IgA, and IgM concentrations were elevated. The percentage of T-lymphocytes was decreased, but T-cell response to mitogens was normal. The infant died of respiratory insufficiency at 7½ months of age. At autopsy, the thymus, spleen, and lymph nodes showed lymphocyte depletion. His parents were residents of Brooklyn, New York; their health status is unknown.

Case 3: The infant, a Haitian male weighing 8 lb, was born in November 1981 following a normal, full-term pregnancy. He was apparently healthy until 5 months of age, when he was hospitalized with fever and respiratory distress. On examination, he had hepatosplenomegaly. A chest x-ray showed bilateral pulmonary infiltrates. Despite antibiotic therapy, the infant's condition deteriorated, and an open lung biopsy revealed PCP. Immunologic studies showed elevated serum concentrations of IgG, IgA and IgM, decreased percentage of T-lymphocytes, and impaired T-cell function in vitro. The infant died in May 1982. At autopsy, no cardiovascular anomalies were seen; the thymus was hypoplastic, but all lobes were present. His parents were residents of Newark, New Jersey; their health status is unknown.

Case 4: The infant, a white female weighing 5 lb, was born in April 1982 following a normal 35-week pregnancy. She was well until 2 months of age, when oral and vaginal *Candida* infections were noted. She responded to antifungal therapy, but at 5 months, candidiasis recurred, and she had hepatosplenomegaly. Immunologic evaluation showed that serum IgG, IgA, and IgM levels, normal at 2 months, were now elevated. The percentage of T lymphocytes was decreased, and lymphocyte response to alloantigen was impaired. At 6 months of age, the infant was hospitalized because of fever and cough. Open lung biopsy revealed PCP. Despite appropriate antibiotic therapy, she died in November 1982.

The infant's mother, a 29-year-old resident of San Francisco, is a prostitute and intravenous drug abuser with a history of oral candidiasis and mild lymphopenia. She has had two other female children by different fathers. These half-sisters also have unexplained cellular immunodeficiency; one died of PCP. The children had not lived together.

None of the four infants described in the case reports was known to have received blood or blood products before onset of illness.

Other cases with opportunistic infections: Six additional young children with opportunistic infections (five with PCP, one with *M. avium-intracellulare*) and unusual cellular immunodeficiencies are under investigation. Three are male. All six children have died. One was half-sister of the infant in Case 4.

Other cases without opportunistic infections: Physicians from New York City, New Jersey, and California have reported another 12 young children with immunodeficiencies similar to those seen in cases 1-4 but without life-threatening opportunistic infections. One is the other half-sister of the infant in Case 4. All the children are living; their ages range from to 4 years. Eight are male. Clinical features seen in these 12 infants include: failure to thrive (83%), oral candidiasis (50%), hepatosplenomegaly (92%), generalized lymphadenopathy (92%), and chronic pneumonitis without a demonstrable infection (83%). Of the nine mothers for whom information is available, seven are reported to be intravenous drug abusers. None Haitian.

Reported by R O'Reilly, MD, D Kirkpatrick, MD, Memorial Sloan-Kettering Cancer Center, C Butkus Small, MD, R Klein, MD, H Keltz, MD, G Friedland, MD, Montefiore Hospital and Medical Center, K Bromberg, MD, S Fikrig, MD, H Mendez, MD, State University of New York, Downstate Medical Center, Rubinstein, MD, Albert Einstein College of Medicine, M Hollander, MD, Misericordia Hospital Medical Center, F Siegal, MD, Mt Sinai School of Medicine, J Greenspan, MD, Northshore University Hospital, Lange, MD, St Lukes-Roosevelt Hospital Center, S Friedman, MD, New York City Dept of Health, Rothenberg, MD, State Epidemiologist, New York State Dept of Health; J Oleske, MD, C Thomas MD, Cooper, MD, A de la Cruz, MD, St Michaels Medical Center, A Minefore, MD, St Josephs Medical Center.

Guerrero, MD, B Mojica, MD, W Parkin, DVM, State Epidemiologist, New Jersey State Dept of Health; M
Cowan, MD, A Ammann, MD, D Wara, MD, University of California at San Francisco, S Dritz, MD,
City/County Health Dept, San Francisco, J Chin, MD, State Epidemiologist, California State Dept of
Health Svcs, Field Svcs Div, Epidemiology Program Office, AIDS Activity, Div of Host Factors, Center for
Infectious Diseases, CDC.

Editorial Note: The nature of the immune dysfunction described in the four case reports is
unclear. The infants lacked the congenital anomalies associated with Di George's syndrome.
The immunologic features of high-normal or elevated immunoglobulin levels and T-
lymphocyte depletion are not typical of any of the well-defined congenital immunodeficiency
syndromes. They have, however, been described in a few children with variants of Nezelof's
syndrome, a rare, poorly characterized illness of unknown etiology (1,2). The occurrence of
immune deficiency in the infant in case 4 and in her half-sisters raises the possibility of an inherited disorder. However, inheritance would have to have occurred in a dominant manner, an
inheritance pattern not previously described for immunodeficiency resembling that seen in
these half-sisters.

It is possible that these infants had the acquired immune deficiency syndrome (AIDS). Although the mother of the infant in case 1 was not studied immunologically, her death from
PCP was probably secondary to AIDS. The mothers of the other three infants were Haitian or
intravenous drug abusers, groups at increased risk for AIDS (3). The immunologic features
described in the case reports resemble those seen both in adults with AIDS (4) and in a child
reported to have developed immunodeficiency following receipt of blood products from a patient with AIDS (5). Case 2 had essentially normal T-cell responses to mitogens in vitro. This
finding is atypical for AIDS, but it has been seen in a few adult AIDS cases (6).

Although the etiology of AIDS remains unknown, a series of epidemiologic observations
suggests it is caused by an infectious agent (3,5,7-9). If the infants described in the four case
reports had AIDS, exposure to the putative "AIDS agent" must have occurred very early.
Cases 2-4 were less than 6 months old when they had serious opportunistic infections. Case
1 had oral candidiasis beginning at 3 months of age, although M. avium-intracellulare infection was not documented until 17 months. Transmission of an "AIDS agent" from mother to
child, either in utero or shortly after birth, could account for the early onset of immunodeficiency in these infants.

The relationship between the illnesses seen in the reported cases with severe opportunistic
infection and the 12 infants without such infections is unclear at present. The immune dysfunction seen in the children and the sociodemographic profiles of the mothers appear similar in
both groups. Prospective study of the 12 children is necessary to define the natural history of
their illnesses and the possible relationship of their illnesses to AIDS.

January 7, 1983

Immunodeficiency among Female Sexual Partners of Males
with Acquired Immune Deficiency Syndrome (AIDS) — New York

CDC has received reports of two females with cellular immunodeficiency who have been
steady sexual partners of males with the acquired immune deficiency syndrome (AIDS).

Case 1: A 37-year-old black female began losing weight and developed malaise in June
1982. In July, she had oral candidiasis and generalized lymphadenopathy and then developed
fever, non-productive cough, and diffuse intestitial pulmonary infiltrates. A transbronchial
biopsy revealed Pneumocystis carinii pneumonia (PCP). Immunologic studies showed elevated immunoglobulin levels, lymphopenia, and an undetectable number of T-helper cells. She responded to antimicrobial therapy, but 3 months after hospital discharge had lymphadenop-
thy, oral candidiasis, and persistent depletion of T-helper cells.

The patient had no previous illnesses or therapy associated with immunosuppression. She
admitted to moderate alcohol consumption, but denied intravenous (IV) drug abuse. Since

1976, she had lived with and had been the steady sexual partner of a male with a history of IV drug abuse. He developed oral candidiasis in March 1982 and in June had PCP. He had laboratory evidence of immune dysfunction typical of AIDS and died in November 1982.

Case 2: A 23-year-old Hispanic female was well until February 1982 when she developed generalized lymphadenopathy. Immunologic studies showed elevated immunoglobulin levels, lymphopenia, decreased T-helper cell numbers, and a depressed T-helper/T-suppressor cell ratio (0.82). Common infectious causes of lymphadenopathy were excluded by serologic testing. A lymph node biopsy showed lymphoid hyperplasia. The lymphadenopathy has persisted for almost a year; no etiology for it has been found.

The patient had no previous illnesses or therapy associated with immunosuppression and denied IV drug abuse. Since the summer of 1981, her only sexual partner has been a bisexual male who denied IV drug abuse. He developed malaise, weight loss and lymphadenopathy in June 1981 and oral candidiasis and PCP in June 1982. Skin lesions, present for 6 months, were biopsied in June 1982 and diagnosed as Kaposi's sarcoma. He has laboratory evidence of immune dysfunction typical of AIDS and remains alive.

Reported by C Harris, MD, C Butkus Small, MD, G Friedland, MD, R Klein, MD, B Moll, PhD, E Emeson, MD, I Spigland, MD, N Steigbigel, MD, Depts of Medicine and Pathology, Montefiore Medical Center, North Central Bronx Hospital, and Albert Einstein College of Medicine, R Reiss, S Friedman, MD, New York City Dept of Health, R Rothenberg, MD, State Epidemiologist, New York State Dept of Health; AIDS Activity, Center for Infectious Diseases, CDC.

Editorial Note: Each reported female patient developed immunodeficiency during a close relationship, including repeated sexual contact, with a male who had AIDS. Patient 1 fits the CDC case definition of AIDS used for epidemiologic surveillance (1). Patient 2 does not meet this definition, but her persistent, generalized lymphadenopathy and cellular immunodeficiency suggest a syndrome described among homosexual men (2). The epidemiologic and immunologic features of this "lymphadenopathy syndrome" and the progression of some patients with this syndrome to Kaposi's sarcoma and opportunistic infections suggest it is part of the AIDS spectrum (3,4). Other than their relationships with their male sexual partners, neither patient had any apparent risk factor for AIDS. Both females specifically denied IV drug abuse.

Epidemiologic observations increasingly suggest that AIDS is caused by an infectious agent. The description of a cluster of sexually related AIDS patients among homosexual males in southern California suggested that such an agent could be transmitted sexually through other intimate contact (5). AIDS has also been reported in both members of a male homosexual couple in Denmark (6). The present report supports the infectious-agent hypothesis and the possibility that transmission of the putative "AIDS agent" may occur among both heterosexual and male homosexual couples.

Since June 1981, CDC has received reports of 43 previously healthy females who had developed PCP or other opportunistic infections typical of AIDS. Of these 43 patients, were reported as neither Haitians nor IV drug abusers. One of these 13 females is described case 1; another four, including two wives, are reported to be steady sexual partners of male IV drug abusers. Although none of the four male partners has had an overt illness suggesting AIDS, immunologic studies of blood specimens from one of these males have shown abnormalities of lymphoproliferative response (7). Conceivably, these male drug abusers are carriers of an infectious agent that has not made them ill but caused AIDS in their infected female sexual partners.

January 7, 1983

Acquired Immune Deficiency Syndrome (AIDS) in Prison Inmates — New York, New Jersey

CDC has received reports from New York and New Jersey of 16 prison inmates with the acquired immune deficiency syndrome (AIDS).

New York: Between November 1981 and October 1982, ten AIDS cases (nine with *Pneu-*

mocystis carinii pneumonia [PCP] and one with Kaposi's sarcoma [KS]) were reported among nmates of New York State correctional facilities. The patients had been imprisoned from 3 to 36 months (mean 18.5 months) before developing symptoms of these two diseases.

All ten patients were males ranging in age from 23 to 38 years (mean 29.7 years). Four were black, and of the six who were white, two were Hispanic. Four of the nine patients with PCP died; the patient with KS is alive. All nine patients with PCP also developed oral candidiasis. None of the patients was known to have an underlying illness associated with immunosuppression, and no such illness was found at postmortem examination of the four patients who died. PCP was diagnosed in all nine cases by means of transbronchial or open-lung biopsy, while KS was diagnosed by biopsy of a lesion on the leg.

Evidence of cellular immune dysfunction was present in the nine patients with PCP: eight were lymphopenic, and all nine were anergic to multiple cutaneous recall antigens. An abnormally low ratio of T-helper to T-suppressor cells was present in six of seven patients tested, and in vitro lymphocyte proliferative responses to a variety of mitogens and antigens were significantly depressed or negative in the six patients tested. The one patient with KS had cutaneous anergy and a decreased proportion of T-cells in his peripheral blood. The ratio of T-helper to T-suppressor cells was normal; studies of lymphoproliferative response were not done.

All ten patients reported that they were heterosexual before imprisonment; one is known to have had homosexual contacts since confinement. However, the nine patients with PCP were regular users of intravenous (IV) drugs (principally heroin and cocaine) in New York City before imprisonment. The seven patients who were extensively interviewed denied regular IV drug use since confinement, although two reported occasional use of IV drugs while in prison. The ten patients were housed in seven different prisons when they first developed PCP or KS. Three patients who developed symptoms of PCP within 1 month of each other were confined in the same facility. However, they were housed in separate buildings, and each denied any social interaction (including homosexual contact and drug use) with the other patients.

All inmates of the New York State correctional system receive a medical evaluation when transferred from local or county jails; this usually includes a leukocyte count. Of the nine AIDS patients who initially had leukocyte counts, seven did not then have symptoms of AIDS. Four of these seven asymptomatic males had leukocyte counts below 4000/mm³. For these four, the time between leukocyte counts and development of clinical PCP symptoms ranged from 4 to 19 months (mean 11.5 months).

New Jersey: Of the 48 AIDS cases reported from New Jersey since June 1981, six have involved inmates of New Jersey State correctional facilities. All six had PCP. They were imprisoned from 1 to 36 months (mean 17.5 months) before onset of symptoms.

All six patients were males ranging in age from 26 to 41 years (mean 32 years). Three were black; three, white. Four of the six died within 1-8 months of onset of their illnesses. None of the six was known to have underlying illness associated with immune deficiency. Immunologic studies of the two survivors have shown cutaneous anergy, leukopenia, lymphopenia, and increased circulating immune complexes. T-cell studies were not done.

All six patients have histories of chronic IV drug abuse. Of the five for whom sexual orientation was reported, four were heterosexual, and one was homosexual. The two living patients have denied both IV drug use and homosexual activity since imprisonment. No two of the six patients had been confined in the same facility at the same time.

Reported by: G Wormser, MD, F Duncanson, MD, L Krupp, MD, Dept of Medicine, Westchester County Medical Center, R Tomar, MD, Dept of Pathology, Upstate Medical Center, DM Shah, MD, Horton Memorial Hospital, B Maguire, G Gavis, MD, New York State Dept of Corrections, W Gaunay, J Lawrence, J Wasser, Medical Review Board, New York State Commission of Corrections, D Morse, MD, New York State Bureau of Communicable Disease Control, R Rothenberg, MD, State Epidemiologist, New York State Dept of Health; P Vieux, MD, K Vacarro, RN, St. Francis Hospital, R Reed, MD, A Koenigfest, New Jersey State Dept of Corrections, I Guerrero, MD, W Parkin, DVM, State Epidemiologist, New Jersey State Dept of Health; Field Svcs Div, Epidemiology Program Office, Div of Host Factors and AIDS Activity, Center for Infectious Diseases, CDC.

Editorial Note: Since male homosexuals and IV drug abusers are known to be at increased risk for AIDS (*1*), the occurrence of AIDS among imprisoned members of these groups might have been anticipated. Increasingly, epidemiologic observations suggest that AIDS is caused by an infectious agent transmitted sexually or through exposure to blood or blood products. Because of the difficulties inherent in interviewing prisoners, data elicited in such interviews must be viewed cautiously. Given this caution, the histories obtained from the inmates indicate that all or most of their drug use, and, by inference, their exposure to a blood-borne agent, occurred before confinement.

The presence of leukopenia in some of the prisoners tested on admission to the prison system may imply that laboratory evidence of immune dysfunction may precede clinical illness by months.

Health care personnel for correctional facilities should be aware of the occurrence of AIDS in prisoners, particularly prisoners with histories of IV drug abuse. AIDS cases identified in prisoners should be reported to local and state correctional and health departments and to CDC.

March 4, 1983

Prevention of Acquired Immune Deficiency Syndrome (AIDS): Report of Inter-Agency Recommendations

Since June 1981, over 1,200 cases of acquired immune deficiency syndrome (AIDS) have been reported to CDC from 34 states, the District of Columbia, and 15 countries. Reported cases of AIDS include persons with Kaposi's sarcoma who are under age 60 years and/or persons with life-threatening opportunistic infections with no known underlying cause for immune deficiency. Over 450 persons have died from AIDS, and the case-fatality rate exceeds 60% for cases first diagnosed over 1 year previously (*1,2*). Reports have gradually increased in number. An average of one case per day was reported during 1981, compared with three to four daily in late 1982 and early 1983. Current epidemiologic evidence identifies several groups in the United States at increased risk for developing AIDS (*3-7*). Most cases have been reported among homosexual men with multiple sexual partners, abusers of intravenous (IV) drugs, and Haitians, especially those who have entered the country within the past few years. However, each group contains many persons who probably have little risk of acquiring AIDS. Recently, 11 cases of unexplained, life-threatening opportunistic infections and cellular immune deficiency have been diagnosed in patients with hemophilia. Available data suggest that the severe disorder of immune regulation underlying AIDS is caused by a transmissible agent.

A national case-control study and an investigation of a cluster of cases among homosexual men in California indicate that AIDS may be sexually transmitted among homosexual or bisexual men (*8,9*). AIDS cases were recently reported among women who were steady sexual partners of men with AIDS or of men in high-risk groups, suggesting the possibility of heterosexual transmission (*10*). Recent reports of unexplained cellular immunodeficiencies and opportunistic infections in infants born to mothers from groups at high risk for AIDS have raised concerns about in utero or perinatal transmission of AIDS (*11*). Very little is known about risk factors for Haitians with AIDS.

The distribution of AIDS cases parallels that of hepatitis B virus infection, which is transmitted sexually and parenterally. Blood products or blood appear responsible for AIDS among hemophilia patients who require clotting factor replacement. The likelihood of blood transmission is supported by the occurrence of AIDS among IV drug abusers. Many drug abusers share contaminated needles, exposing themselves to blood-borne agents, such as hepatitis B virus. Recently, an infant developed severe immune deficiency and an opportunistic infection several months after receiving a transfusion of platelets derived from the blood of a man subsequently found to have AIDS (*12*). The possibility of acquiring AIDS through blood compoents or blood is further suggested by several cases in persons with no known risk factors who have received blood products or blood within 3 years of AIDS diagnosis (2). These cases are currently under investigation.

No AIDS cases have been documented among health care or laboratory personnel caring for AIDS patients or processing laboratory specimens. To date, no person-to-person transmission has been identified other than through intimate contact or blood transfusion.

Several factors indicate that individuals at risk for transmitting AIDS may be difficult to identify. A New York City study showed that a significant proportion of homosexual men who were asymptomatic or who had nonspecific symptoms or signs (such as generalized lymphadenopathy) had altered immune functions demonstrated by in vitro tests (2,13,14). Similar findings have been reported among patients with hemophilia (2,15,16). Although the significance of these immunologic alterations is not yet clear, their occurrence in at least two groups at high risk for AIDS suggests that the pool of persons potentially capable of transmitting an AIDS agent may be considerably larger than the presently known number of AIDS cases. Furthermore, the California cluster investigation and other epidemiologic findings suggest a "latent period" of several months to 2 years between exposure and recognizable clinical illness and imply that transmissibility may precede recognizable illness. Thus, careful histories and physical examinations alone will not identify all persons capable of transmitting AIDS but should be useful in identifying persons with definite AIDS diagnoses or related symptoms, such as generalized lymphadenopathy, unexplained weight loss, and thrush. Since only a small percentage of members of high-risk groups actually has AIDS, a laboratory test is clearly needed to identify those with AIDS or those at highest risk of acquiring AIDS. For the above reasons, persons who may be considered at increased risk of AIDS include those with symptoms and signs suggestive of AIDS; sexual partners of AIDS patients; sexually active homosexual or bisexual men with multiple partners; Haitian entrants to the United States; present or past abusers of IV drugs; patients with hemophilia; and sexual partners of individuals at increased risk for AIDS.

Statements on prevention and control of AIDS have been issued by the National Gay Task Force, the National Hemophilia Foundation, the American Red Cross, the American Association of Blood Banks, the Council of Community Blood Centers, the American Association of Physicians for Human Rights, and others. These groups agree that steps should be implemented to reduce the potential risk of transmitting AIDS through blood products, but differ in the methods proposed to accomplish this goal. Public health agencies, community organizations, and medical organizations and groups share the responsibility to rapidly disseminate information on AIDS and recommended precautions.

Although the cause of AIDS remains unknown, the Public Health Service recommends the following actions:

1. Sexual contact should be avoided with persons known or suspected to have AIDS. Members of high risk groups should be aware that multiple sexual partners increase the probability of developing AIDS.

2. As a temporary measure, members of groups at increased risk for AIDS should refrain from donating plasma and/or blood. This recommendation includes all individuals belonging to such groups, even though many individuals are at little risk of AIDS. Centers collecting plasma and/or blood should inform potential donors of this recommendation. The Food and Drug Administration (FDA) is preparing new recommendations for manufacturers of plasma derivatives and for establishments collecting plasma or blood. This is an interim measure to protect recipients of blood products and blood until specific laboratory tests are available.

3. Studies should be conducted to evaluate screening procedures for their effectiveness in identifying and excluding plasma and blood with a high probability of transmitting AIDS. These procedures should include specific laboratory tests as well as careful histories and physical examinations.

4. Physicians should adhere strictly to medical indications for transfusions, and autolo gous blood transfusions are encouraged.

5. Work should continue toward development of safer blood products for use b hemophilia patients.

The National Hemophilia Foundation has made specific recommendations for managemen of patients with hemophilia (*17*).

The interim recommendation requesting that high-risk persons refrain from donating plasma and/or blood is especially important for donors whose plasma is recovered from plas mapheresis centers or other sources and pooled to make products that are not inactivate and may transmit infections, such as hepatitis B. The clear intent of this recommendation is t eliminate plasma and blood potentially containing the putative AIDS agent from the supply Since no specific test is known to detect AIDS at an early stage in a potential donor, th recommendation to discourage donation must encompass all members of groups at increase risk for AIDS, even though it includes many individuals who may be at little risk of transmittin AIDS.

As long as the cause remains unknown, the ability to understand the natural history o AIDS and to undertake preventive measures is somewhat compromised. However, the abov recommendations are prudent measures that should reduce the risk of acquiring and transmit ting AIDS.

Reported by the Centers for Disease Control, the Food and Drug Administration, and the National Insti tutes of Health.

May 13, 198:

Human T-Cell Leukemia Virus Infection in Patients with Acquired Immune Deficiency Syndrome: Preliminary Observations

Recent evidence suggests that human T-cell leukemia virus (HTLV) infection occurs in pa tients with acquired immune deficiency syndrome (AIDS). HTLV has been isolated from peripheral blood T-lymphocytes from several patients with AIDS (*1, 2*), and a retrovirus, relat ed to but clearly distinct from HTLV, has been isolated from cells from a lymph node of a pa tient with lymphadenopathy syndrome (LAS) (*3*), a syndrome that may precede AIDS itself Also, HTLV nucleic acid sequences have been detected by nucleic acid hybridization in lym phocytes from two (6%) of 33 AIDS patients (*4*). In addition, antibodies to antigens expresse on the cell surface of HTLV-infected lymphocytes have been detected by an indirect immuno fluorescent technique in sera from 19 (25%) of 75 AIDS patients (*5*), including patients with Kaposi's sarcoma alone (10/34), *Pneumocystis carinii* pneumonia alone (7/30), or patients with both diseases '2/11). Similar antibodies were detected in six (26%) of 23 patients with LAS. Such antibodies were rarely found in sera collected from homosexual men in New York City who served as controls during a case-control study in the fall of 1981 (1/81), homosexu al men from whom sera were collected in 1978 during visits to a Chicago venereal disease clinic (0/118), and blood donors from a mid-Atlantic state who gave blood in 1977 but were unselected for sexual preference (1/137).

Reported by Laboratory of Tumor Cell Biology, National Cancer Institute, National Institutes of Health Dept of Cancer Biology, Harvard School of Public Health; Department of Virology, Institut Pasteur, Paris Div of Host Factors, Div of Viral Diseases, Div of Hepatitis and Viral Enteritis, AIDS Activity, Center for In fectious Diseases, CDC.

Editorial Note: HTLV agents are retroviruses that have recently been associated with certain types of adult T-cell lymphoreticular neoplasms of man (*6*). HTLV-1 has been associated with acute T-cell leukemia and a related, but clearly different, viral agent, HTLV-2, with "hairy-cell" T-cell leukemia.

Retroviruses are ribonucleic acid (RNA) viruses containing the enzyme, reverse transcriptase, which allows production of a deoxyribonucleic acid (DNA) copy of their RNA genome. The DNA copy can then be integrated into the genome of the cell. Infections with ret roviruses other than HTLV have been associated with a variety of neoplastic diseases in animals including chickens, cats, cattle and gibbons. The feline retrovirus also causes immune suppression.

HTLV agents are the only presently known retroviruses associated with human diseases. Clinically, however, the diseases previously associated with HTLV in endemic areas do not resemble AIDS. Infections are thought rarely to result in malignancies. HTLV may spread from some infected persons to their very close contacts, and concern has been expressed that it may be transmissible by blood or blood derivatives (7). HTLV infects and immortalizes* T-helper lymphocytes, and the virus can be isolated from infected patients by co-cultivation of their lymphocytes with uninfected human T-lymphocytes.

In the above studies, the reported low frequency of detecting HTLV sequences may reflect depletion of infected T-helper lymphocytes, since patients initially positive for such sequences have had negative tests several months later (4).

HTLV-infected cells express specific virus structural and virus-induced cellular proteins. Antibodies reactive with these virus-specific proteins are moderately prevalent (12% of blood donors) in residents of southwest Japan, an area with a relatively high prevalence of adult T-cell leukemia, and in residents of some Caribbean Islands (4% of St. Vincent blood donors); they have rarely been found in healthy Americans or western Europeans, although these population groups have not been studied extensively.

While the above serologic findings associate AIDS with antibody to HTLV-specific cell surface-associated antigens, such antibodies were identified in only about one quarter of the AIDS patients tested. This relatively low frequency of antibody in AIDS patients might represent a lack of test sensitivity, too stringent criteria for positive tests, infection of AIDS patients with an agent related to but not identical with HTLV, nonspecific polyclonal B-cell responses, inability of many AIDS patients to mount antibody responses to these antigens, collection of sera from patients at improper times during disease evolution, or combinations of these and other yet-to-be identified factors. Alternatively, HTLV or an HTLV-like agent might simply represent yet another opportunistic agent in these multiply infected AIDS patients.

Further study is required to determine if any etiologic relationship exists between HTLV and AIDS.

June 24, 1983

Acquired Immunodeficiency Syndrome (AIDS) Update — United States

As of June 20, 1983, physicians and health departments in the United States and Puerto Rico had reported a total of 1,641 cases of acquired immunodeficiency syndrome (AIDS). These cases were diagnosed in patients who had Kaposi's sarcoma (KS) or an opportunistic infection suggestive of an underlying cellular immunodeficiency. Of these patients, 644 (39%) are known to have died; the proportion of patients with KS alone who have died (22%) is less than half that of patients with opportunistic infections who have died (46%). Fifty-five (3%) cases were diagnosed before 1981; 225 (14%), in 1981; 832 (51%), in 1982; and 529 (32%), to date in 1983. *Pneumocystis carinii* pneumonia (PCP) is the most common life-threatening opportunistic infection in AIDS patients, accounting for 51% of primary diagnoses; 26% of patients have KS without PCP, and 8% have both PCP and KS. Many of these patients may also have other opportunistic infections, and 15% of AIDS patients have such infections without KS or PCP. Over 90% of AIDS patients are 20-49 years old; almost 48% are 30-39 years old. Cases have occurred in all primary racial groups in the United States. Only 109 (7%) cases have been reported in women.

Groups at highest risk of acquiring AIDS continue to be homosexual and bisexual men (71% of cases), intravenous drug users (17%), persons born in Haiti and now living in the United States (5%), and patients with hemophilia (1%)*. Six percent of the cases cannot be

_____

*The risk groups listed are hierarchically ordered; cases with multiple risk factors are tabulated only in the risk group listed first.

placed in one of the above risk groups; approximately half of these are patients for whom information regarding risk factors is either absent or incomplete. The remainder includes, in order of decreasing frequency, patients with no identifiable risk factors, heterosexual partners of AIDS patients or persons in risk groups, recipients of blood transfusions, and KS patients with normal immunologic studies. Of the 109 cases among females, 52% occurred among drug users and 9% among Haitians; for 39%, the risk group is unknown.

In addition to the 1,641 reported AIDS cases, 21 infants with opportunistic infections and unexplained cellular immunodeficiencies have been reported to CDC. Infant cases are recorded separately because of the uncertainty in distinguishing their illnesses from previously described congenital immunodeficiency syndromes.

Most cases continue to be reported among residents of large cities. New York City has reported 45% of all cases meeting the surveillance definition[†]; San Francisco, 10% of cases; and Los Angeles, 6% of cases. Cases have been reported from 38 states, the District of Columbia, and Puerto Rico (Figure 1).

Reported by State and Territorial Epidemiologists, AIDS Activity, Center for Infectious Diseases, CDC.

Editorial Note: During 1982 and early 1983, city and state health departments throughout the United States began assuming an increasingly active role in the surveillance and investigation of AIDS. At the annual Conference of State and Territorial Epidemiologists in May 1983, the group affirmed the urgency of AIDS as a public health problem and passed, as one part of a resolution on AIDS, the recommendation that AIDS be added to the list of notifiable diseases in all states. The method of making a disease notifiable varies markedly in different states, ranging from a change in state law to regulatory action by the Board of Health or executive de-

---

[†]For the limited purposes of epidemiologic surveillance, CDC defines a case of AIDS as a reliably diagnosed disease that is at least moderately indicative of an underlying cellular immunodeficiency in a person who has had no known underlying cause of cellular immunodeficiency nor any other cause of reduced resistance reported to be associated with that disease.

FIGURE 1. Acquired immunodeficiency syndrome (AIDS) cases meeting the surveillance definition reported to CDC, by state — United States

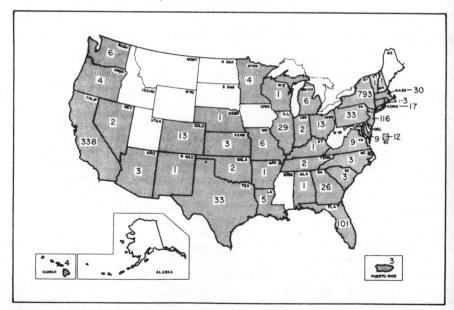

sion by the health officer. Several states have already made AIDS notifiable; other states
re taking similar action.

Case counts of patients with AIDS listed by cities or states may differ from those listed by
DC. The standard surveillance definition of AIDS does not apply to suspected subclinical or
ild cases of AIDS—to the extent they occur—or to cases involving persistent generalized
mphadenopathy or other conditions in persons from high-risk groups. Some AIDS patients
ay seek treatment in cities other than those in which they reside and may be reported
rough health departments in cities where they are treated. CDC eliminates duplicate reports
nd assigns each patient to the city and state of residence at the time of reported onset of
ness. In addition, the processing of case reports may result in a delay between diagnosis,
eporting, and entry of a case into the registry at the different health departments or CDC.

Physicians aware of patients fitting the case definition for AIDS are requested to report
uch cases to CDC through their local or state health departments. AIDS patients who do not
elong to any of the recognized risk groups or who are recipients of blood or blood products
ncluding anti-hemophiliac factors) should be reported immediately.

The vast majority of cases continue to occur among persons in the major identified risk
ategories. The cause of AIDS is unknown, but it seems most likely to be caused by an agent
ansmitted by intimate sexual contact, through contaminated needles, or, less commonly, by
ercutaneous inoculation of infectious blood or blood products. No evidence suggests trans-
ission of AIDS by airborne spread (1). The failure to identify cases among friends relatives,
nd co-workers of AIDS patients provides further evidence that casual contact offers little or
 risk. Most of the 21 infants with unexplained immunodeficiency have been born to mothers
elonging to high-risk groups for AIDS (2). If this syndrome is, indeed, AIDS, the occurrence
 young infants suggests transmission from an affected mother to a susceptible infant
efore, during, or shortly after birth. Previously published guidelines to prevent the transmis-
on of AIDS and precautions for health care and laboratory workers are still applicable (1,3).

August 5, 1983

Update: Acquired Immunodeficiency Syndrome (AIDS) —
United States

Between June 1981 and August 1, 1983, physicians and health departments in the United
tates and Puerto Rico reported 1,972 cases of acquired immunodeficiency syndrome (AIDS)
eeting the surveillance definition*. These cases were diagnosed in patients who have Kapo-
's sarcoma (KS) or an opportunistic infection suggestive of an underlying cellular
mmunodeficiency. Three hundred thirty-one cases (17% of the total) were reported to CDC
ver the last 6 weeks; the average of 53 cases reported per week during July 1983 compares
ith an average of 11 per week in July 1982 and 24 per week in January 1983 (Figure 1) Of
ll patients, 759 (38%) are known to have died; the mortality rate for patients with oppor-
unistic infections continues to be over twice that of patients with KS alone. *Pneumocystis
arinii* pneumonia (PCP) is the most common life-threatening opportunistic infection in AIDS
atients; many of the patients may have multiple opportunistic infections. either sequentially
r simultaneously Of the reported cases, 71% have homosexual or bisexual orientation; 95%
f the patients with KS are in this group.

Over 90% of AIDS patients are 20-49 years old; almost 47% are 30-39 years old. Cases
ave occurred in all primary racial groups in the United States. One hundred twenty-nine (7%)
ases have been reported in women; the ratio of male to female patients (14:1) has been
lmost constant over the last year Most cases are reported among residents of large cities

---

*For the limited purposes of epidemiologic surveillance, CDC defines a case of AIDS as a reliably diag-
osed disease that is at least moderately indicative of an underlying cellular immunodeficiency in a
erson who has had no known cause of underlying cellular immunodeficiency or any other underlying re-
uced resistance reported to be associated with that disease.

257

FIGURE 1. Cases of acquired immunodeficiency syndrome (AIDS), by quarter of report
United States, second quarter 1981 — second quarter 1983

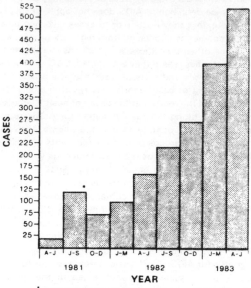

New York City has reported 44 of all cases meeting the surveillance definition; S
Francisco, 10 of cases, and Los Angeles, 6 of cases. Cases have been reported from 3
states, the District of Columbia, and Puerto Rico (Figure 2).

FIGURE 2. Acquired immunodeficiency syndrome (AIDS) cases reported to CDC, b
state — United States, as of August 1, 1983

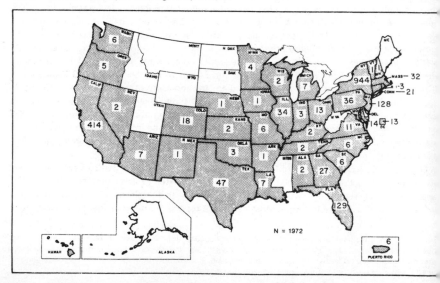

258

Reported by city, state, and territorial epidemiologists. AIDS Activity. Center for Infectious Diseases, CDC.

Editorial Note: To date, CDC has been notified that at least 18 states and territories have made AIDS reportable, and approximately 26 have introduced or are considering measures to make it reportable. Some states that have not taken specific action have cancer registries or already require many opportunistic infections to be reported. Physicians aware of patients fitting the case definition for AIDS are requested to report such cases through their local or state health departments. AIDS patients who do not belong to any of the recognized risk groups or who are recipients of blood or blood products (including anti-hemophiliac factors) should be reported immediately. CDC will soon make available a reporting format by which patients' names need not be sent to CDC.

Concern has been expressed about potential transmission of AIDS from hospitalized patients to health-care personnel (1). Although no instance of direct transmission has been reported (2), accidental needlestick injuries or similar types of accidents occasionally occur. To evaluate the possible risk of AIDS transmission after such accidents, the Hospital Infections Program, CDC, in cooperation with several state health departments, has initiated a study at selected hospitals of health-care personnel who have had documented parenteral or mucous membrane exposure to blood of definite or suspected AIDS patients. This study is being expanded to include additional hospitals. Hospital infection control staff who have been notified of these types of personnel exposures in their hospitals and wish to obtain additional information about participation in the study should contact the Hospital Infections Program, (404) 329-3406.

Acquired Immunodeficiency Syndrome (AIDS): Precautions for Health-Care Workers and Allied Professionals

Acquired immunodeficiency syndrome (AIDS) was first recognized in 1981. The epidemiology of AIDS is consistent with the hypothesis that it is caused by a transmissible infectious agent (1-3). AIDS appears to be transmitted by intimate sexual contact or by percutaneous inoculation of blood or blood products. There has been no evidence of transmission by casual contact or airborne spread, nor have there been cases of AIDS in health-care or laboratory personnel that can be definitely ascribed to specific occupational exposures (4).

CDC has published recommended precautions for clinical and laboratory personnel who work with AIDS patients (5). Precautions for these and allied professionals are designed to minimize the risk of mucosal or parenteral exposure to potentially infective materials. Such exposure can occur during direct patient care or while working with clinical or laboratory specimens and from inadvertent or unknowing exposure to equipment, such as needles, contaminated with potentially infective materials. Caution should be exercised in handling secretions or excretions, particularly blood and body fluids, from the following: (1) patients who meet the existing surveillance definition of AIDS (1); (2) patients with chronic, generalized lymphadenopathy, unexplained weight loss, and/or prolonged unexplained fever when the patient's history suggests an epidemiologic risk for AIDS (1,2); and (3) all hospitalized patients with possible AIDS.

These principles for preventing AIDS transmission also need to be adopted by allied professionals not specifically addressed in the previous publications but whose work may bring them into contact with potentially infective material from patients with the illnesses described in the above three groups.

The following precautions are recommended for those who provide dental care, perform postmortem examinations, and perform work as morticians when working with persons with histories of illnesses described in the above three groups:

DENTAL-CARE PERSONNEL

1. Personnel should wear gloves, masks, and protective eyewear when performing dental or oral surgical procedures.
2. Instruments used in the mouths of patients should be sterilized after use (5-9).

PERSONS PERFORMING NECROPSIES OR PROVIDING MORTICIANS' SERVICES

1. As part of immediate postmortem care, deceased persons should be identified as belonging to one of the above three groups, and that identification should remain with the body.
2. The procedures followed before, during, and after the postmortem examination are similar to those for hepatitis B. All personnel involved in performing an autopsy should wear double gloves, masks, protective eyewear, gowns, waterproof aprons, and waterproof shoe coverings. Instruments and surfaces contaminated during the postmortem examination should be handled as potentially infective items (5-7).
3. Morticians should evaluate specific procedures used in providing mortuary care and take appropriate precautions to prevent the parenteral or mucous-membrane exposure of personnel to body fluids.

These and earlier recommendations outline good infection control and laboratory practices and are similar to the recommendations for prevention of hepatitis B. As new information becomes available on the cause and transmission of AIDS, these precautions will be revised as necessary.

September 9, 1983

Update: Acquired Immunodeficiency Syndrome (AIDS) — United States

As of September 2, 1983, physicians and health departments in the United States and Puerto Rico had reported 2,259 persons with acquired immunodeficiency syndrome (AIDS) who met the surveillance case definition.* Of these, 917 (41%) are known to have died. Fifty-eight (3%) cases were diagnosed before 1981; 231 (10%) in 1981; 883 (39%) in 1982; and 1,087 (48%) to date in 1983. *Pneumocystis carinii* pneumonia (PCP) is the most common life-threatening opportunistic infection in AIDS patients, accounting for 52% of primary diagnoses; 26% of patients have Kaposi's sarcoma (KS) without PCP, and 7% have both PCP and KS. Many of these patients may also have other opportunistic infections, and 15% of AIDS patients have such infections without KS or PCP. The proportion of patients with each of these primary diagnoses has remained relatively constant during the last 12 months, although the proportion with KS has decreased slightly, and the proportion with opportunistic infections other than PCP has increased from approximately 10% of all cases a year ago. Cases have occurred in all primary racial/ethnic groups in the United States: 57% of those reported have been white, 26% black, 14% Hispanic, and 3% other or unknown. One hundred forty-seven (7%) cases have been reported in women.

Eighty-nine percent of patients with AIDS can be placed in groups[†] that suggest a possible means of disease acquisition: 71% are men with homosexual or bisexual orientations; 17% (including 51% of the women) have used intravenous (IV) drugs; and 1% are hemophiliacs. Of the other 11% of cases, means of disease acquisition is less clear, but in none of these cases does casual contact appear to be involved. This group of 11% includes cases for whom information about risk factors is either absent or incomplete (3% of total), and others whose risk

*For the limited purposes of epidemiologic surveillance, CDC defines a case of AIDS as a reliably diagnosed disease that is at least moderately indicative of an underlying cellular immunodeficiency in a person who has had no known underlying cause of cellular immunodeficiency and no other cause of reduced resistance reported to be associated with that disease.

[†]The groups listed are hierarchically ordered; cases with characteristics of more than one group are tabulated only in the group listed first.

nd exposure factors are under investigation. The latter includes patients who were born in Haiti but are now living in the United States (5% of total). Also under investigation are heterosexual partners of persons with AIDS or persons at increased risk of AIDS (1% of total), and those exposed to blood transfusions (1% of total). Finally, some thoroughly investigated cases belong to none of the above groups (1% of total).

Almost 47% of AIDS patients are 30-39 years old at diagnosis; an additional 22% are 20-29 and 40-49 years old respectively. The age of drug-abuse patients clusters more tightly, with 81% being 20-39 years old. Compared with the average for all AIDS patients, Haitian entrants with AIDS tend to be younger (47% are 20-29 years old); the patients who received blood transfusions before developing AIDS tend to be older (median age more than 50 years old); and those with hemophilia tend to have a broader age range without clustering.

Most cases continue to be reported among residents of large cities. The New York City standard metropolitan statistical area (SMSA) has reported 42% of all cases meeting the surveillance definition; the San Francisco SMSA, 11% of cases; the Los Angeles SMSA, 7% of cases; and the Miami SMSA, 5% of cases. Cases have been reported from 41 states, the District of Columbia, and Puerto Rico (Figure 4).

Reported by City, State, and Territorial Epidemiologists; AIDS Activity, Center for Infectious Diseases, CDC.

Editorial Note: AIDS cases have been classified into groups at greatest risk of acquiring the disease. Classification is an essential element of any epidemiologic investigation and serves such purposes as formulating prevention recommendations, providing direction for research, and identifying medical needs. However, the classification of certain groups as being more closely associated with the disease has been misconstrued by some to mean these groups are likely to transmit the disease through non-intimate interactions. This view is not justified by available data. Nonetheless, it has been used unfairly as a basis for social and economic discrimination.

FIGURE 4. Acquired immunodeficiency syndrome (AIDS) cases meeting the surveillance definition reported to CDC, by state — United States, as of September 2, 1983

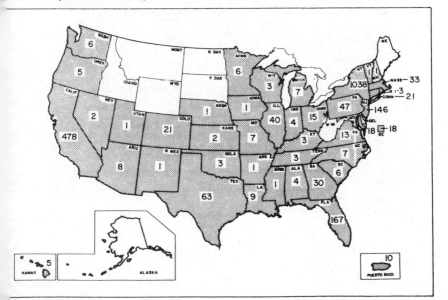

The occurrence of AIDS cases among homosexual men, IV drug abusers, persons with hemophilia, sexual partners of members of these groups, and recipients of blood transfusions is consistent with the hypothesis that AIDS is caused by an agent that is transmitted sexually or, less commonly, through contaminated needles or blood. About 91% percent of reported cases have occurred in these patient groups. Among the remaining cases, there has been no evidence that the disease was acquired through casual contact with AIDS patients or with persons in population groups with an increased incidence of AIDS. AIDS is not known to be transmitted through food, water, air, or environmental surfaces.

The great majority of persons in population groups with increased incidences of AIDS have not been affected by the disease. Until epidemiologic studies identify the subgroups within these populations that are truly at increased risk for acquiring AIDS, the classification system will lack precision. However, such classifications should not be construed to imply that usual social contact with such groups is involved in the transmission of AIDS.

BIBLIOGRAPHY

Ammann, A.J., Wara, D.W., Dritz, S., Cowan, M.J., Weintrub, P., et al. *Lancet*, 1983, 1(8331), 956-958. Acquired immunodeficiency in an infant: possible transmission by means of blood products.

Andreani, T., Le Charpentier, Y., Brouet, J.-C., Lachance, J.-R., Modigliani, R., et al. *Lancet*, 1983, 1(8335), 1187-1191. Acquired immunodeficiency with intestinal cryptosporidiosis: possible transmission by Haitian whole blood.

Barré-Sinoussi, F., Chermann, J.C., Rey, F., Nugeyre, M.T., Chamaret, S., et al. *Science*, 1983, 220(4599), 868-871. Isolation of a T-lymphotropic retrovirus from a patient at risk for acquired immune deficiency syndrome (AIDS).

Barry, M., Stansfield, S.K. and Bia, F.J. *Annals of Internal Medicine*, 1983, 98(6), 1018-1020. Haiti and the Hopital Albert Schweitzer.

Boncy, M., Laroche, A.C., Liautaud, B., Mathurin, J.-R., Pape, J.W., et al. *New England Journal of Medicine*, 1983, 308(23), 1419-1420. Acquired immunodeficiency in Haitains.

Brunet, J.B., Bouvet, E., Chaperon, J., Gluckman, J.C., Kernbaum, S., et al. *Lancet*, 1983, 1(8326), 700-701. Acquired immunodeficiency syndrome in France.

Bygbjerg, I.C. *Lancet*, 1983, 1(8330), 925. AIDS in a Danish surgeon (Zaire, 1976).

CDC Task Force on Kaposi's Sarcoma and Opportunistic Infections. *New England Journal of Medicine*, 1982, 306(4), 248-252. Epidemiologic aspects of the current outbreak of Kaposi's sarcoma and opportunistic infections.

Centers for Disease Control *Journal of the American Medical Association*, 1983, 249(14), 1812. Trends: Safety of hepatitis B virus vaccine.

Ciobanu, N., Andreeff, M., Safai, B., Koziner, B. and Mertelsmann, R. *Annals of Internal Medicine*, 1983, 98(2), 151-155. Lymphoblastic neoplasia in a homosexual patient with Kaposi's sarcoma.

Clumeck, N., Mascart-Lemone, F., de Maubeuge, J., Brenez, D. and Marcelis, L. *Lancet*, 1983, 1(8325), 642. Acquired immune deficiency syndrome in black Africans.

Colaert, J. *Lancet*, 1983, 1(8333), 1098. African swine fever virus antibody not found in AIDS patients.

Coppola, V., West, R. and Huck, J. *Newsweek*, 1983, April 18, 80. The AIDS epidemic: The change in gay life-style.

Conte, J.E., Hadley, W. K., Sande, M., and the UCSF Task Force on AIDS: Infection Control Guidelines for Patients with the Acquired Immunodeficiency Syndrome (AIDS), *New England Journal of Medicine*, Vol. 309, No. 12, P. 740 (1983), (Special Report).

Curran, J.W., Evatt, B.L. and Lawrence, D.N. *Annals of Internal Medicine*, 1983, 98(3), 401-403. Acquired immune deficiency syndrome: The past as prologue.

Current, W.L., Reese, N.C., Ernst, J.V., Bailey, W.S., Heyman, M.B., et al. *New England Journal of Medicine*, 1983, 308(21), 1252-1257. Human cryptosporidiosis in immunocompetent and immunodeficient persons.

Davis, K.C., Horsburgh, C.R., Jr., Hasiba, U., Schocket, A.L. and Kirkpatrick, C.H. *Annals of Internal Medicine*, 1983, 98(3), 284-286. Acquired immunodeficiency syndrome in a patient with hemophilia.

Desforges, J.F. *New England Journal of Medicine*, 1983, 308(2), 94-95. AIDS and preventive treatment in hemophilia.

Detels, R., Fahey, J.L., Schwartz, K. Greene, R.S., Visscher, B. R. and Gottlieb, M.S. *Lancet*, 1983, 1(8325), 609-611. Relation between sexual practices and T-cell subsets in homosexually active men.

Destefano, E., Friedman, R. M., Friedman-Kien, A.E., Goedert, J.J., Henriksen, D., et al. *Journal of Infectious Diseases*, 1982, 146(4), 451-455. Acid-labile human leukocyte interferon in homosexual men with Kaposi's sarcoma and lymphadenopathy.

Doll, D.C. and List, A. I. *Lancet*, 1982, 1(8279), 1026-1027. Burkitt's lymphoma in a homosexual.

Dournon, E., Penalba, C., Wolff, M., Coulaud, J.P., Saimot, A.G., et al. *Lancet*, 1983, 1(8332), 1040-1041. AIDS in a Haitian couple in Paris.

Drew, W. L., Conant, M. A., Miner, R. C., Huang, E. S., Ziegler, J. L., et al. *Lancet*, 1982, 2(8290), 125-127. Cytomegalovirus and Kaposi's sarcoma in young homosexual men.

Essex, M., McLane, M.F., Lee, T.H., Falk, L., Howe, C.S., et al. *Science*, 1983, 220(4599), 859-862. Antibodies to cell membrane antigens associated with human T-cell leukemia virus in patients with AIDS.

Fahey, J.L., Detels, R., and Gottlieb, M. *New England Journal of Medicine*, 1983, 308(14), 842-843. Immune-cell augmentation (with altered T-subset ratio) is common in healthy homosexual men.

264

Friedman-Kien, A.E. *Journal of the American Academy of Dermatology*, 1981, 5(4), 468-471. Disseminated Kaposi's sarcoma syndrome in young homosexual men.

Friedman-Kien, A. E., Laubenstein, L. J., Rubinstein, P., Buimovici-Klein, E., Marmor, M., et al. *Annals of Internal Medicine*, 1982, 96(6 pt. 1), 693-700. Disseminated Kaposi's sarcoma in homosexual men.

Friedman-Kien, A.E. and Stevens, C. E. *Annals of Internal Medicine*, 1982, 97(5), 787. Kaposi's sarcoma and hepatitis B vaccine.

Gallo, R.C., Sarin, P.S., Gelmann, E.P., Robert-Guroff, M., Richardson, E., et al. *Science*, 1983, 220(4599), 865-868. Isolation of human T-cell leukemia virus in acquired immune deficiency syndrome (AIDS).

Gerstoft, J., Malchow-Moller, A., Bygbjerg, I., Dickmeiss, E., Enk, C., Halberg, P., et al. Br. Med. J. (*Clinical Research*), 1982, 285(6334), 17-19. Severe acquired immunodeficiency in European homosexual men.

Giraldo, G., Beth, E. and Huang, E.S. *International Journal of Cancer*, 1980, 26(1), 23-29. Kaposi's sarcoma and its relationship to cytomegalovirus (CMV). III. CMV, DNA, and CMV early antigens in Kaposi's sarcoma.

Goedert, J. J., Neuland, C.Y., Wallen, W. C., Greene, M. H., Mann, D. L., Murray, C., et al. *Lancet*, 1982, 1(8269), 412-416. Amyl nitrite may alter T-lymphocytes in homosexual men.

Gold, K.D., Thomas, L. and Garrett, T. J. *New England Journal of Medicine*, 1982, 307(8), 498. Aggressive Kaposi's sarcoma in a heterosexual drug addict.

Golden, J.A. *New England Journal of Medicine*, 1983, 308(19), 1163. No increased incidence of AIDS in recipients of hepatitis B vaccine.

Gorin, I., Picard, O., Laroche, L., Escande, J.-P. and Hewitt, J. *Lancet*, 1982, 1(8277), 908. Kaposi's sarcoma without the U.S. or "popper" connection.

Gottlieb, M.S., Schroff, R., Schanker, H.M., Weisman, D.O., Fan, P.T., Wolf, R.A. and Saxon, A. *New England Journal of Medicine*, 1981, 305(24), 1425-1431. *Pneumocystis carinii* pneumonia and mucosal candidiasis in previously healthy homosexual men: evidence of a new acquired cellular immunodeficiency.

Grady, D. *Discover*, 1983, July, 74-77. AIDS: A plague of fear.

Groopman, J.E. and Gottlieb, M.S. *Nature*, 1983, 303, 575-576. AIDS: the widening gyre.

Harris, C., Small, C.B., Klein, R.S., Friedland, G.H., Moll, B., et al. *New England Journal of Medicine*, 1983, 308(20), 1181-1184. Immunodeficiency in female sexual partners of men with the acquired immunodeficiency syndrome.

265

Hassett, J.M., Zaroulis, C.G., Greenberg, M.L., and Siegal, F. P. Bone Marrow Transplantation in AIDS. *New England Journal of Medicine*, 1983, 309, No. 11m, p.665.

Hassett, J., Zaroulis, C.G., Greenberg, M.L., Fotino, M. and Siegal;, F. P. *Clinical Research*, 1983, 31(2), 344A. Allogeneic marrow transplantation in endstage acquired immunodeficiency syndrome.

Haverkos, H. W. and Curran, J. W. *CA*, 1982, 32(6), 330-339. The current outbreak of Kaposi's sarcoma and opportunistic infections.

Henig, R.M. *New York Times*, 1983, Feb. 6, Sect. 6, 28-44. AIDS: a new disease's deadly odyssey.

Hymes, K.B., Cheung, T., Greene, J.B., Prose, N.S., Marcus, A., et al. *Lancet*, 1981, 2(8247), 598-600. Kaposi's sarcoma in homosexual men: a report of eight cases.

Joncas, J.H., Delage, G., Chad, Z. and Lapointe, N. *New England Journal of Medicine*, 1983, 308(14), 842. Acquired (or congenital) immunodeficiency syndrome in infants born of Haitian mothers.

Kornfeld, H., Vande Stouwe, R. A., Lange, M., Reddy, M. M. and Grieco, M. H. *New England Journal of Medicine*, 1982, 307(12), 729-731. T-lymphocyte subpopulations in homosexual men.

Krown, S.E., Real, F.X., Cunningham-Rundles, S., Myskowski, P., Koziner, B., et al. *New England Journal of Medicine*, 1983, 308(18), 1071-1076. Preliminary observations on the effect of recombinant leukocyte A interferon in homosexual men with Kaposi's sarcoma. *Lancet*, 1983, 1(8335), 1200. HTLV and AIDS.

Lederman, M.M., Ratnoff, O.D., Scillian, J.J., Jones, P. K. and Schacter, B. *New England Journal of Medicine*, 1983, 308(2), 79-83. Impaired cell-mediated immunity in patients with classic hemophilia.

Levine, A. S. *Cancer Treatment Report*, 1982, 66(6), 1391-1395. The epidemic of acquired immune dysfunction in homosexual men and its sequelae - opportunistic infections, Kaposi's sarcoma, and other malignancies: an update and interpretation.

Lopez, C., Fitzgerald, P.A. and Siegal, F. P. *Journal of Infectious Diseases*, 1983, in press. Severe acquired immunodeficiency syndrome in male homosexuals: Diminished capacity to make interferon-alpha *in vitro* is associated with severe opportunistic infections.

Leo, J. *Time*, 1983, July 4, 56-58. The real epidemic: fear and despair.

Leonidas, J.-R. and Hyppolite, N. *Annals of Internal Medicine*, 1983, 98(6), 1020-1021. Haiti and the acquired immunodeficiency syndrome.

Marmor, M., Friedman-Kien, A. E., Laubenstein, L., Byrum, R. D., William, D. C., et al. *Lancet*, 1982, 1(8281), 1083-1086. Risk factors for Kaposi's sarcoma in homosexual men.

Marx, J.L. *Science*, 1983, 219(4580), 42-43. Spread of AIDS sparks new health concern.

Marx, J.L. *Science*, 1983 219(4582), 271-272. Health officials seek ways to halt AIDS.

Marx, J.L. *Science*, 1983, 220(4599), 806-809. Human T-cell leukemia virus linked to AIDS.

Masur, H., Michelis, M.A., Greene, J.B., Onorato, I., Vande Stouwe, R., A., Holzman, R.S., et al. *New England Journal of Medicine*, 1981, 305(24), 1431-1438. An outbreak of community-acquired *Pneumocystis carinii* pneumonia: initial manifestation of cellular immune dysfunction.

Masur, H., Michelis, M. A., Wormer, G. P., Lewin, S. and Gold, J. *Annals of Internal Medicine*, 1982, 97(4), 533-538. Opportunistic infection in previously healthy women: initial manifestations of a community-acquired cellular immunodeficiency.

Miller, J. R., Barrett, R. E., Britton, C. B., Tapper, M. L., Bahr, G. S. *New England Journal of Medicine*, 1982, 307(23), 1436-1438. Progressive multifocal leukoencephalopathy in a male homosexual with T-cell immune deficiency.

Moss, A.R., Bacchetti, P., Gorman, M., Dritz, S., Conant, M., et al. *Lancet*, 1983, 1(8330), 923-924. Aids in the "gay" areas of San Francisco.

Pitchenik, A.E., Fischl, M.A., Dickinson, G.M., Becker, D.M., Fournier, A.M., et al. *Annals of Internal Medicine*, 1983, 98(3), 277-284. Opportunistic infections and Kaposi's sarcoma among Haitians: Evidence of a new acquired immunodeficiency state.

Poon M.-C., Landay, A., Prasthofer, E. F. and Stagno, S. *Annals of Internal Medicine*, 1983, 98(3), 287-290 Acquired immunodeficiency syndrome with *Pneumocystis carinii* pneumonia and *Mycobacterium avium-intracellulare* infection in a previously healthy patient with classic hemophilia.

Post, M.J., Chan, J.C., Hensley, G.T., Hoffman, T.A., Moskowitz, L.B., et al. *American Journal of Respiratory Diseases*, 1983, 140, 861-868. Toxoplasma encephalitis in Haitian adults with acquired immunodeficiency syndrome: a clinical-pathologic-CT correlation.

Ratnoff, O.D., Menitove, J. E., Aster. R.J. and Lederman, M.M. *New England Journal of Medicine*, 1983, 308(8), 439-442. Coincident classic hemophilia and "idiopathic" thrombocytopenic purpura in patients under treatment with concentrates of antihemophilic factor (Factor VIII).

Seligmann, J., Gosnell, M., Coppola, V. and Hager, M. *Newsweek*, 1983, April 18, 74-79. The AIDS epidemic: The search for a cure.

Shearer, G.M. *New England Journal of Medicine*, 1983, 308(4), 223-224.

Allogeneic leukocytes as a possible factor in induction of AIDS in homosexual men.

Siegal, F. P. *New England Journal of Medicine*, 1982, 307(3), 184. Normal delayed-type skin reactions in early stages of acquired cellular immunodeficiency.

Siegal, F.P., Lopez, C., Hammer, G.S., Brown, A.E., Kornfeld, S.J., et al. *New England Journal of Medicine*, 1981, 305(24), 1439-1444. Severe acquired immunodeficiency in homosexual males, manifested by chronic perianal ulcerative herpes simplex lesions.

Small, C. B., Klein, R. S., Friedland, G.H., Moll, B., Emeson, E.E., et al. *American Journal of Medicine*, 1983, 74, 433-441. Community-acquired opportunistic infections and defective cellular immunity in heterosexual drug abusers and homosexual men.

Stahl, R.E., Friedman-Kien, A., Dubin, R., Marmor, M. and Zolla-Pazner, S. *American Journal of Medicine*, 1982, 73(2), 171-178. Immunologic abnormalities in homosexual men. Relationship to Kaposi's sarcoma.

Stevens, C.E. *New England Journal of Medicine*, 1983, 308(19), 1163-1164. No increased incidence of AIDS in recipients of hepatitis B vaccine.

Sullivan, R. *New York Times*, 1983, May 17, B1. Experts testify AIDS epidemic strikes the city.

Teas, J. *Lancet*, 1983, 1(8330), 923. Could AIDS agent be a new variant of African swine fever virus?

Templeton, A.C. *Pathology Annual*, 1981, 16(2), 315-336. Kaposi's sarcoma.

Urmacher, C., Myskowski, P., Ochoa, M., Jr., Kris, M. and Safai B. *American Journal of Medicine*, 1982, 72(4), 569-575. Outbreak of Kaposi's sarcoma with cytomegalovirus infection in young homosexual men.

Vandepitte, J., Verwilghen, R. and Zachee, P. *Lancet* 1983, 1(8330), 925-926. AIDS and cryptococcosis (Zaire, 1977).

Vieira, J., Frank, E. and Landesman, S. *New England Journal of Medicine*, 1983, 308(23), 1420. Acquired immunodeficiency in Haitians.

Vieira, J., Frank, E., Spira, T.J. and Landesman, S.H. *New England Journal of Medicine*, 1983, 308(3), 125-129. Acquired immune deficiency in Haitians: opportunistic infections in previously healthy Haitian immigrants.

Volberding, P., Conant, M.A., Stricker, R.B. and Lewis, B.J. *American Journal of Medicine*, 1983, 74, 652-656. Chemotherapy in advanced Kaposi's sarcoma. Implications for current cases in homosexual men.

Wallace, J.I. et al. *Lancet*, 1983, 1(8314/5), 58-59. T-cell ratios in New York City prostitutes.

Wormser, G.P., Krupp, L.B., Hanrahan, J.P., Gavis, G., Spira, T.J., et al. *Annals of Internal Medicine*, 1983, 98(3), 297-303. Acquired immunodeficiency syndrome in male prisoners.

Ziegler, J.L., Drew, W.L., Miner, R.C., Mintz, L., Rosenbaum, G., et al. *Lancet*, 1982, 2(8299), 631-633. Outbreak of Burkitt's-like lymphoma in homosexual men.

About the Authors

Frederick P. Siegal, M.D. is a central figure in the AIDS field. Currently Chief of Immunology at Mt. Sinai Medical Center, Dr. Siegal previously conducted immunology research at Rockefeller University and Memorial Sloan-Kettering Cancer Center. **Marta Siegal, M.A.** has worked for the last ten years at Sloan-Kettering Institute and Mount Sinai Hospital as a researcher and laboratory supervisor.